THE CURSE OF MUZIRIS

Hamish Morjaria was born and brought up in North London. After spending three decades in the business world, working for leading brands and retailers, he finally indulged his passion for ancient history and thrillers to create The Harveen Gill Mysteries, with *The Curse of Muziris* as the first book in the series. When not writing, Hamish can be found watching cricket or walking his dog Simba during the day, and sitting in front of the fire with a cup of tea and a good book in the evening. He lives in Buckinghamshire with his wife Kalpa and two children.

THE CURSE OF MUZIRIS

HAMISH MORJARIA

PAN

First published 2024 by Pan
an imprint of Pan Macmillan Publishing India Private Limited
707 Kailash Building
26 K. G. Marg, New Delhi 110001
www.panmacmillan.co.in

Pan Macmillan, The Smithson, 6 Briset Street, Farringdon, London EC1M 5NR
Associated companies throughout the world
www.panmacmillan.com

ISBN 978-93-6113-442-5

Illustrated map 'Trade Routes of the Erythraean Sea' by Bhavana

3 5 7 9 8 6 4 2

Typeset in Minion Pro by R. Ajith Kumar, New Delhi
Printed and bound in India by Replika Press Pvt. Ltd.

FSC
www.fsc.org
MIX
Paper | Supporting responsible forestry
FSC™ C016779

For Kalpa, who has shown me
what true courage is

'A small body of determined spirits fired by an unquenchable faith in their mission can alter the course of history'

MAHATMA GANDHI

Roman Empire
Rome
Ostia
Laodicea
Alexandria
Jerusalem
Apologou
Petra
Myos Hormos
Lefki komi
LIBYA
ARABIA
Trade Routes of the Erythraean Sea
1st century AD
Ptolemais of the Hunt
Adulis
Muza
Aden
Avalites
BERBERS
Mundus
Oponi
Sarapion
BEYOND THESE PLACES THE UNEXPLORED OCEAN CURVES AROUND TOWARDS THE WEST AND MINGLES WITH THE WESTERN SEA
KEY
SEA ROUTE
LAND ROUTE
Roman Empire
Indo-Parthian Empire

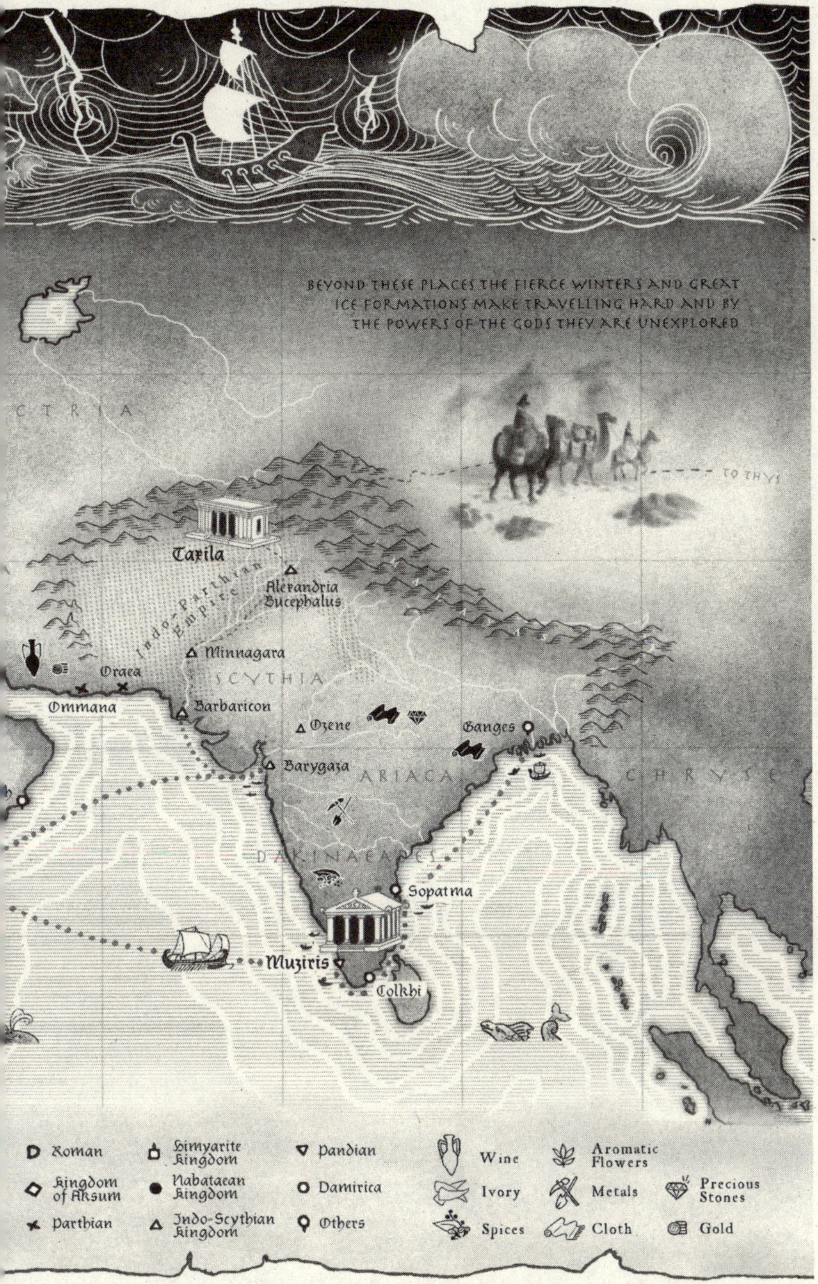
BEYOND THESE PLACES THE FIERCE WINTERS AND GREAT ICE FORMATIONS MAKE TRAVELLING HARD AND BY THE POWERS OF THE GODS THEY ARE UNEXPLORED
TO THYS
Taxila
Alexandria Bucephalus
Indo-Parthian Empire
Minnagara
SCYTHIA
Oraea
Ommana
Barbaricon
Ozene
Ganges
Barygaza
ARIACA
CHRYSE
Sopatma
Muziris
Colkhi
Roman
Kingdom of Aksum
Parthian
Himyarite Kingdom
Nabataean Kingdom
Indo-Scythian Kingdom
Pandian
Damirica
Others
Wine
Ivory
Spices
Aromatic Flowers
Metals
Cloth
Precious Stones
Gold

Preface

Muziris, Southern India
AD 72

The ardent heat of the morning sun and the persistent rains of the past few days had made the underground chamber quite oppressive. The old man stood there alone, wondering if his precautions would be enough to protect his people from what he was burying.

Although the walls of the chamber were made of stone, the distinct smell of wet earth permeated the air, somehow making the chamber feel claustrophobic. He imagined this was what the spirits of the buried dead had to eternally endure. Jayesh felt unable to move as he contemplated his own actions which had led to the terrible events culminating in this moment: his final chance to bury the curse and save his people. The tortured screams of his friends that always lingered in the back of his mind now grew as loud and clear as the day he had heard them. The chamber seemed to amplify the aches in his body, and he wanted nothing more than to lie down and for the pain to end.

As the flames on the torches mounted on the wall began to wane, the walls threatened to close in on him. Somehow, Jayesh summoned the strength to keep going. It was up to him to do everything in his power to protect the deadly secret.

He had carefully prepared a warning note and placed it inside a wooden box, which he now pushed into a small cavity in the wall, hoping for it to act as a final deterrent to anyone who may come looking to unearth it again. His words could scarcely convey the horror of what lay beyond the wall. He sealed the cavity with a small stone marked with his family crest before silently offering a final desperate prayer that his warning be heeded.

Jayesh needed help climbing through the narrow aperture back to the surface. He stared into the murky chamber one last time, watching the flames of the torches finally die out before instructing his men to seal it forever.

His venerated friend and advisor, Nannan, was waiting for him. The two men shared a nervous look just as they had shared so much over the years, and began walking together in silence. The profound sense of loss they both felt was unspoken but hung heavy between them.

'The legends were true – its power is too great for any man,' Jayesh said.

Nannan nodded in agreement. They had discussed this many times over the past few days. As they walked a little further, Jayesh thought the scene laid out before him looked so benign and innocent. The recent rainfall had infused a vibrance into the grass. The sunlight and the rich scent of the flowers almost made him forget the stench of the chamber below. Several men busily sealed its entrance as Jayesh had instructed.

'They may come looking,' Nannan said quietly. The thought seemed to be troubling him. They continued walking, each lost in considering the implications of what devastation might ensue if the curse was unleashed again.

'If they do, we must make sure at any cost they cannot find what we have hidden.'

1

Rome, Italy
16 July 2016

'Kill him. Bring the scroll directly to me.' Dino Rossi, the Head of the Santa Alleanza, delivered his message clearly and precisely with no hint of emotion. Don hesitated for a moment. They had determined how to deal with the archaeologist when he had first been assigned the task and Rossi's tone made it evident that there was no room for further discussion.

'Don?' Rossi pushed.

'Understood,' he replied and terminated the call. The scroll had been safely retrieved and was in a secure case by his feet. Another case contained the necessary materials to set fire to the archaeologist's office, which would kill him and destroy all evidence of the scroll. He glanced at his silver Rolex; it was a minute past 4 a.m. There was plenty of time to plant the small explosive device in the right place and remove any trace of his presence before the target arrived between 8 and 8:15 a.m.

As Don worked, he thought carefully about the first few months of his service in the Vatican Secret Police and how he was now about to kill an elderly archaeologist, who had unfortunately made a discovery that would unveil an uncomfortable early secret of the Church.

The Head of the Santa Alleanza had called Don into his elaborate office in the secret underground complex underneath the Vatican some weeks ago.

'Ah, Donatello,' he had begun, 'as you must know, we have agents all around the world monitoring archaeological digs and sending us word of new and fascinating historical findings. You would also know that our network is particularly robust here in Italy. I've been informed that confirmed intelligence has been received that a local dig in Rome has uncovered some documents dating back to the eleventh century.' Rossi often spoke like a professor, his supercilious manner both irritating and condescending.

'Okay,' said Don. 'And what seems to be the issue, signor?'

'The finds are mostly unremarkable and incomplete. Except for one particular scroll, which is troubling me. The document alleges that the statue believed by pilgrims to have been built in the image of St Peter and housed for centuries now in his eponymous basilica in Rome was originally that of the pagan god Jupiter.'

Don was very familiar with this statue and had visited it to pay obeisance many times. It was a bronze sculpture which held a prime position in the St Peter's Basilica, depicting a seated figure with a distinctive sun-like wheel over its head. Don knew that the disc was a key feature of the many representations of Jupiter. 'Does it have to do with the wheel? That story has been around for as long as the statue itself,' he said.

'No, Don. The scroll is a firsthand account describing how the statue was forcibly removed from the Pantheon and re-designated as St Peter, since there were no statues of the saint available at the time to decorate the new church. It could cause the Church considerable embarrassment if word gets out.'

'I can go and ask the archaeologist to hand it over—'

'The lead archaeologist is, unfortunately, not very cooperative. He's reluctant to give the document to the Vatican for our authentication and is currently making his own independent enquiries into dating and validating its contents. We cannot let him get to the bottom of it all. It is one of the most important icons of the church.'

'What would you like me to do, signor?' Don was keen to impress his powerful new boss.

'Retrieve the document, of course, but also destroy any evidence of its existence, especially any photos. Make sure that archaeologist is no longer an issue to us. Ever.' Rossi's meaning was clear.

'What about the enquiries he has already made?'

'The Santa Alleanza already has experts from around the world working to discredit the source and its accusations. As long as the original document is never found again, the findings will be dismissed as an anti-Christian conspiracy theory. Everything has been arranged. It's just you who needs to do your part now. Are you ready to prove your allegiance to the Alleanza?'

'Certainly, signor,' Don had said. What else could he do? Don knew that he had been specifically recruited from the Gruppo di Intervento Speciale for his skill as an assassin.

Since then, he had spent days inspecting the classified records held in the Vatican Secret Archives, just so he wouldn't lose sight of the truth in this gruesome quest to do the Church's bidding. He had been shocked to find that the scroll was right – the statue had indeed been that of Jupiter;

that it was only one of numerous historically important artefacts around the Vatican masquerading as Christian, when in truth they had simply been stolen and hurriedly repurposed to provide legitimacy to the new church.

As Don got closer to carrying out his mission, his misgivings about the very nature of the job deepened. His missions for the Italian military had typically involved targets that held strategic value; going after terrorists and foreign agents was one thing. This felt altogether different.

Don was seated outside the coffee shop directly across from the offices at 7:40 a.m. – everything was ready. The plot was underway. He understood the risks of being so close to the scene; his broad, six-foot-three frame was impossible to disguise, and his deep voice was far more memorable than he liked. The narrow scar snaking down from his left eye to his jaw had faded over the years, but up close, it was still visible enough to identify him. It was of the essence that he ensured the plan worked. He had been made to fully understand the importance of what was at stake.

Don reflected on the elegance of his plan. The archaeologist was always the first to come into the office. Don knew from days of observation that he went into the small kitchen to start his coffee machine as soon as he arrived. The old fuse box on the wall was already a hazard and the accelerants that Don had put in strategic places would ensure that all evidence would be burnt long before any fire services could arrive at the scene. The fire would kill the man right there too, if he got the timing right.

Don spotted the archaeologist. Small and wiry with bird-like features, he was neat and presentable in his tweed jacket. Only his shock of wispy white hair was unkempt. He walked leisurely, like a man without a care in the world. He waltzed into a small shop to collect his daily newspaper on the way to his office – just as he did every day. Don knew that he would reappear in less than two minutes with the paper tucked under his right arm.

Don fidgeted. Although the archaeologist's wife had passed away three years ago, he had four children and six grandchildren, the youngest of whom was a three-year-old girl called Helena. Could he really sit here and watch this innocent man die?

Before Don had a chance to resolve his dilemma, the archaeologist, Señor Varane, emerged from the shop. Don knew that using his name would humanize him and make him feel like less of a target. The mobile phone he would use to trigger the explosion felt heavier in his hand. He considered all the targets he had killed during his career. They would all have had families too. This was not so different. He only had seconds to decide what to do.

Varane stopped a few feet from his door. There was an old lady sitting on the pavement with a handmade sign. Don had rushed past her earlier without a thought. A beggar – Eastern European, he would have guessed. There were more and more on the streets of Rome lately. Varane crouched next to her with a smile on his face and they exchanged a few words. The archaeologist reached into his pocket, pulled out a few notes and handed them to her. He then touched her gently on the head with the familiarity of a grandfather before moving on.

Don gripped the phone tighter in his hand. Rossi's words echoed in his head. He watched as Señor Varane approached the door, fishing in his pockets for the key. Did he know something was wrong? Perhaps not.

Varane went into his office and closed the door behind him. Don waited for a few moments before pressing the button. He looked in the direction of the office window until he saw the flames erupt. Then he walked away quickly – not just to flee the scene, but also because he could not bear to see Señor Varane die.

2

Kodungallur, Southern India
8 June 2024

The United Nations had declared it a humanitarian disaster. What started as another rainy season in southern India developed into the most destructive rainstorm in over a thousand years. The deluge was causing widespread devastation, displacing over 200,000 people from their homes.

Food supplies to remote villages had all but stopped; only emergency services vehicles were able to get through and provide relief. Providing clean water was a priority and the government had reached out to agencies around the world for assistance.

The people of southern India were no strangers to natural disasters and were adapting to the situation as best they could, helping each other and finding solace in their gods and their families.

The rains would not relent, and villages had to be evacuated. The aid workers from around the world soon came bearing shelters, food and clean water supply and begun the hurried efforts to save lives. The violence of the monsoons would change the landscape as it had for many years now. Only this time, they were not just leaving behind destruction; they were on the verge of dramatically revealing the secrets of the past.

It had rained almost non-stop for six weeks. Not the odd heavy shower, but a solid wall of rain that seemed to have no start and no end; it had washed away crops and dragged the soil into the river near Pullut Bridge. The children, accustomed to gathering nearby in the Municipal Park to play, were now using improvised sledges to weave through the rivers of mud and dreaming up new games to enjoy despite the flooded lawns.

Arvin and his brothers had not been able to join in the new games today as they were to go with their parents to the annual Kodungallur Bharani Festival.

'Please, can we go and play in the park, Appa?' Arvin begged his father. He already knew the answer but had been urged on by his younger brother Akash to ask.

'Arvin, this festival is part of a tradition that goes back nearly 2,000 years.' His father's brow furrowed as he spoke, annoyed at being asked the same question again. 'Our traditions run deep; see, even the rain was not able to stop us from performing the necessary rituals of sacrifice – the gods will be satisfied. This only happens once a year; you get to play in the park all the time.'

Arvin hung his head at the gentle admonishment.

'Now go and play with the other children in the grounds of the temple – look how beautiful they are!'

The festival was held at the Kodungallur Kurumba Bhagavathy Temple. It sat in the middle of a beautiful ten-acre plot on the very site where Jayesh's family had erected his original magnificent shrine 2,000 years ago. It was destined to become one of the most significant temples ever constructed; a beacon that would attract visitors from around the world.

Arvin remembered the stories about the origin of the festival his father had told him back when he was small enough to fit on his lap. He now stood watching as the Raja of Kodungallur took his place on the traditional platform built around the oldest banyan tree in the courtyard even as the rains continued to thrash down. As custom dictated, he spread out the silk parasol to its full length, signifying that all were welcome in the temple to pray and study. Arvin knew that after the main sacrifice had been offered, everyone would be invited to share in the food and enjoy the celebrations, and he would be able to sneak away with his brothers.

'Sorry, Appa,' he said and withdrew quietly towards the stone well where his brothers had gathered.

The spectacle of the ceremony that followed was one of the main attractions of the whole festival. A frenzied mob of devotees rushed into the temple complex, wearing traditional red robes and carrying swords. They used red powder to symbolize blood dripping from their heads all the way to their feet. Their screams and chants electrified the atmosphere. Once the rituals were over, the feast would begin.

This seemingly bizarre custom symbolized the bloodshed that had marred the opening of the temple two centuries ago, which had long since been forgotten by the town. Back then, the screams from the temple had been genuine – tortured and anguished – and the blood that stained the temple floor had been real.

As the festivities started, no one noticed Arvin and his four brothers leave.

Akash was the youngest of his brothers, and at eight years old, he was already the most courageous of them as well. He had always loved the rains and this latest storm had brought the opportunity for new mischief and adventure. He found a large blue plastic sheet, slightly curved, about four feet in length and about half as wide. It had proved to be a near-perfect sledge the day before, providing much amusement for the brothers as they slalomed through the rain-soaked mud in youthful abandon. Akash had carried it with him the whole day and was now smiling as he would be able to use it again.

Earlier in the day, the brothers had discovered the ideal spot in their attempts to find a shortcut back home from the Municipal Park. They had walked this path down the riverside many times, past the lights of the EKD Auditorium twinkling across the water. Today, the rains had created a gentle stream running down towards the river. The water had etched a shallow trench about three feet wide into the path, which was perfect for them.

As soon as they arrived, the brothers began to take turns sliding down, squealing with delight as they were propelled towards the bottom. Then, jumping up swiftly to their feet, they'd sprint back to the top for an encore. As the eldest, Arvin knew that it was his responsibility to get them all back to the temple before they were missed. Now they were all covered in mud, wet and late. There would be hell to pay.

'Let's go. Now!' he shouted. 'I have been saying for fifteen minutes – the feast will soon be over and Appa will look for us.'

'One more run, one more? Please, Arvin. Please!' begged Akash. Arvin rolled his eyes and looked at his other three brothers.

'You go,' he called to them. 'I will bring Akash in a minute. Tell Appa we are in the line for food.' He turned back to his youngest brother. 'Go on then. One more,' he replied resignedly.

Akash beamed. 'Watch this one, it will be the fastest. I am going right from the top!' Akash dragged the blue sheet even higher up the incline. As his brother climbed, Arvin looked across at the top of the auditorium and noticed for the first time that the long finger of water that cut into the land had swelled. It must be thirty feet wide now, precariously close to the houses. They would flood if the rains did not let up. Akash was shouting at him through the rain. He strained his ears to catch his brother's words but could not make out what he was saying.

'Are. You. Coming?' Arvin bellowed back. Akash shouted something indecipherable before launching himself headfirst down the slope.

Arvin watched his brother project himself with no hint of fear down the little gully that had been created by the rain and further eroded by the boys when they had taken turns sliding down earlier. The rain water was gathering in the channel and running down like the North Indian river rapids he had read about. Faster and faster the rivulets rushed. The rains continued to thunder down, beating on the ground mercilessly. Suddenly, Arvin heard a bang loud enough to penetrate the rumble made by the storm. Akash's piercing scream reached his ears. He could not see his brother.

'Akash! Akash!' he screamed, as he clawed his way up the hill, slipping and struggling to maintain his grip. There was no reply.

As he reached the spot where he had last seen Akash, he found that a crevice had opened in the ground. Water rushed into the hole, swirling as if the earth itself was a huge bath being emptied.

'Akash!' he called again frantically whilst peering into the chamber below. It resembled the interior of an old building. He could just glimpse the bright blue of the sledge about fifteen feet down. As his eyes adjusted, he recognized the twisted body of his brother. Akash lay perfectly still. Arvin's unrestrained, panicked screams could be heard even above the sound of the roaring rain.

3

Kerala State Archaeology Department
Sreepadam Palace
12 June 2024

'I have been going over all of the original Sangam poetry that makes any mention of Muziris, especially the works of Paranar and Thayankannannar, and cross-referencing them with early Tamil literature,' Harveen said, pushing more and more sheets of paper across the desk towards Professor Prakash, the head of the Kerala State Archaeology Department. She tucked her hair behind her ear, wishing she had put it into a ponytail this morning as she usually did.

'Look, here and here, they are definitely referring to the physical features of the landscape,' she continued.

The diminutive Professor Prakash was perched behind his desk as if he had not moved since Harveen had first entered his office seven years ago. His silver hair was perfectly parted on one side and his thick, black-rimmed glasses were sitting halfway down his nose as he peered at her papers. Harveen looked around the office, careful not to disturb the professor. The older pictures hanging on the walls in perfect lines were of a younger Professor Prakash posing alone, or receiving awards or alongside renowned politicians and academics. She noted the recent additions, including a group shot in front of the Sreepadam Palace, with Harveen smiling in the front row.

'It's still quite vague,' he said.

'Yes,' said Harveen, 'but there is new AI technology that can recreate what the landscape used to look like based on this information. I reached out to the team at Oxford for it, and they sent me this.' Harveen produced two more sheets and laid them out on the desk. She kicked off her heels and walked over to Professor Prakash's side of the desk. It was a stupid idea to have got dressed up for this meeting. She was much more comfortable in her work boots and shorts.

'There are great researchers in India too, you know,' said Prakash, gently admonishing her for always returning to her alma mater for information.

'I know, Professor, but it's just more … convenient reaching out to them,' she said, flushing slightly. 'I think we should open dig sites at these three locations. I think one of them could be Muziris.' Even after seven years of searching in vain, Harveen's passion to discover the first-century Indian port was as strong as ever. She wished for just a moment that she could speak to her father about it just one more time.

Prakash fidgeted uncomfortably in his chair. 'The government has turned down our request for further funding,' he said. Harveen was shocked. The Muziris Heritage Project was the largest of its kind in India.

'I don't understand,' she said.

'It's been seven years. We have collected 50,000 items from well over a hundred sites but found no other trace of Muziris. They feel we have gone as far as we can. They will still fund the renovation of the Sreepadam Palace so it can continue to be used as a museum to exhibit our finds. You have done incredible work here, Harveen, but I am afraid without any pathbreaking leads, we will have to close down the operation in the next few months.'

'But the Sphinx ring,' she said, 'that is recent.' She was referring to the banded agate ring they had found in Anapuzha, which was identical to the ring worn by the first Roman Emperor, Octavian.

'That was over a year ago, and there was nothing else of note. I am afraid their decision is final.' Harveen was crushed. She had given up on a dream job as the Head of Research at the British Museum to take up this post. She had even turned down an opportunity to return home to Amritsar, a few years ago, to lead the restoration efforts of the Jallianwala Bagh. That role would have given her unlimited access to original letters and correspondence from the East India Company staff to create a memorial to the historic 1919 massacre that took place there.

'But this is important', she said. 'All Indians deserve to know that a part of their country was the centre of the world trade in the first century.'

'I am sorry,' he repeated. 'Without a major find, we cannot continue the digs. It was your brilliant idea to develop the museum and include other aspects of Indian history – that draws so many visitors! The new exhibition on Indian goddesses has proved to be especially popular and will continue to receive funds.'

'Yes, but spending weeks sourcing the perfect red sari to suit Goddess Parvati, or arranging a replica of a life-size lion is not really what I came here to do,' said Harveen despondently.

'There is nothing more I can do, Harveen,' said Prakash. It seemed pointless to continue arguing, so she gathered up her papers and left his office.

Harveen returned to her desk feeling slightly disillusioned. She looked out of the window at the endless rain that had kept coming for weeks now. A departmental email said that they would be evacuating the area over the next few days. There was a real chance that lives would be lost to the unprecedented downpour.

'How did it go?' asked Rohan, the senior researcher for the department.

'Oh, hey Rohan,' Harveen replied automatically, before bringing herself back to the present moment. It was always nice talking to Rohan. Although he still looked like the skinny fifteen-year-old with bright eyes who had joined the department a month after Harveen, he was now probably the best-informed researcher in southern India – and he also happened to possess infinite cheer. 'It was fine. He will need some more proof before we can open up any more dig sites,' she lied, not wanting to be the bearer of bad news.

'We got a couple of good leads today – there is a site down at Kodungallur where some boys have found a hole that opens into what look like early ruins, and there was a large discovery of ancient beads by the coast as well. We should go and check them out together!' he said cheerfully.

'You go on, Rohan. Let me know what you find. I need to come up with something really big for the next dig,' said Harveen as she pulled out her research notes and began to go over them once again. As she began to read, the last conversation with her mum began to play in her mind. Her mother had been apprehensive about this job and wanted her to do something that would bring in more money – they needed it desperately, especially with her brother's medical bills mounting. Harveen had assured her that a promotion was just around the corner and the expected pay raise would make their lives easier, but now the threat of their funding being withdrawn had appeared. The ground on which her promise had stood was now shaky.

4

Muciripattanam, Southern India (Modern-day Kodungallur) AD 7

Abhay's wife, Vasudha, was dying. When he left her side this morning, before the first rays of the sun had touched their hillside, she was mumbling incoherently, her body was hot to the touch. Even as he held her hand, she barely registered his presence. Vasudha's mother sat in the chair next to her bed, exhausted by the efforts of comforting her through the last weeks of pregnancy. She would not leave her daughter's side.

Abhay wanted to remain with his wife, but it was the peak of the harvest season. Their small plot needed to be tended to quickly as the rains threatened to come again and wash everything away. He knew that to stay now would put their entire crop at risk and the family would be left to starve. Still, he hesitated. Finally, as he turned to leave the room, Abhay saw the lunch bundles that Vasudha had made for each member of the family piled by the door. Somehow she had managed to prepare them, despite her condition. As he gathered them up, he felt a lump form in his throat.

Vasudha was strong and hard-working. They had married when he was sixteen and she twelve. His uncle had assured him that although she was not as beautiful as some of the other girls, she came from a good family and would make a loyal and devoted wife. He said a silent prayer of thanks to his long-departed uncle for his advice. Vasudha had indeed been a good companion. She had given him five sons and worked tirelessly. She had been a loving and caring wife and mother. She had determinedly remained unbowed by the grind of her life and had stood by his side through both good and bad times. Now, he felt, this pregnancy would rob him of his dear wife and give him another unwanted mouth to feed.

He had five sons and one daughter. The eldest of his sons, Nilham and Mitul, were in their fifteenth and fourteenth years and offered the best help. They were both strong, capable and willing workers. The others, Abhay had little time for, especially Avani, who was slender in frame and mostly loved to sing and paint. She was of little use in the field and even lacked the attention required to make food and mend clothes within a reasonable timeframe. The fact that in a few years she would cost him a dowry they could ill afford did nothing to endear her to Abhay.

That day in the fields was the longest Abhay could remember. He had harvested their crops before in the lashing rain and the physical tolls on his body were bearable, but he kept glancing towards the house expecting to see Vasudha's mother or sister appear to give him the bad news that he knew was coming. But the moment never came, and Abhay shepherded his children back to the house in the gathering gloom to remove their sodden clothing and prepare for bed. The traditional Nalukettu-style house they had imagined building in more prosperous years could never be completed and they were now left with only two modest structures separated by an open yard. Abhay and the family were in the slightly larger hall, whilst his wife was in the other one.

As the last of the daylight had gradually succumbed to the darkness of the moonless night, Abhay sat alone on his small bed. The rustling of the boys had turned to silence some hours ago as the exuberance of youth gave way to the fatigue brought by harvesting crops in the torrential rain. Abhay, too, was tired but sleep evaded him. He had gone to see his wife, her screams piercing through the night, but had been ushered out of the hall by her sister. She had shaken her head as she had closed the door behind him. He was filled with apprehension and missing Vasudha, worrying about the harvest, about money and how he would cope if the gods sent him another daughter.

The house finally sat in silence. He cursed the baby that would take his wife from him. As he pondered how the family would adapt, he became conscious of some noise. There was a gentle knock at his door. He waited a moment, bracing himself for the inevitable news, before opening it to his sister-in-law, who stood there beaming.

'It's a boy, Abhay, it's a healthy boy!' She glowed with the good news.

'Vasudha?' he asked anxiously.

She looked at the ground for a moment and then said, 'There was a lot of blood, but I think she may survive.'

He sighed in relief and gathered his robes before following her to see his wife and newborn son.

His wife looked exhausted but smiled at Abhay as he came into the small room. Her mother sat in the corner, cradling a small bundle in her arms. He first went over to Vasudha and squeezed her hand tightly.

'How are you?' he enquired.

'Relieved.' She managed a smile, though he could see that she was still in pain. 'Go and see your son.'

Abhay turned to his mother-in-law, who stood up and handed him the bundle of cloth enfolding his son. She looked at Abhay with great pride, delighted to have helped deliver a son to him. Thanks to her rituals and prayers, they had been blessed with six healthy boys and only one girl. Abhay took the boy carefully into his arms and the baby howled. His first sentiment at the sight of his newborn was disappointment. The child was skinny and fragile-looking, much like his daughter had been. He put his finger into the baby's palm remembering how tightly Nilham had gripped it. The baby could barely curl his slender fingers around it before he began to howl. He will be of no use in the fields, Abhay thought. Just another hungry mouth to feed. He promptly handed him over to Vasudha, who looked at the boy lovingly and clutched him to her.

'I want to call him Jayesh,' she said, 'after his grandfather.' She had made the same suggestion about their last son and he had overruled her, but seeing her smile now filled his heart with warmth. He glanced at the boy with cold indifference – he still had his face screwed into a grimace, slowly quietening down at the sound of his mother's cooing.

'As you wish,' he said as he bent down to kiss her on the forehead before walking towards his room to get some rest for another gruelling day in the fields.

5

Kodungallur
14 June 2024

Harveen had arrived very early at work; she had barely been able to sleep last night, keen to return to the ancient Sangam texts and scour them anew for any hints that could lead her to pinpoint Muziris's location. She couldn't afford for the department to shut down. After three hours of diligently poring over the sheets, she turned to look out of the window at the rain pouring outside endlessly. She was beginning to feel dejected. Soon, she would no longer be able to come into the office; they were going to start evacuating the premises.

She had barely noticed Rohan's absence until the phone on her desk rang and went on ringing. The old-fashioned Bakelite phone was somehow linked to the modern digital network. It looked like it belonged in the museum as an artefact itself.

'Archaeology Department,' Harveen mumbled absently into the handset, throwing her head back to stare at the fan whirring lethargically on the ceiling.

'Harveen?' a voice said tentatively. It was Rohan. She could barely hear him above the wind howling into the microphone.

'Hey Rohan,' she replied mechanically, curious as to where he was.

'You better come, quick. This is it,' he announced. His words tripped over each other as he spoke in a state of frenzy. 'That lead I mentioned in Kodungallur? Some boys had been messing around with a sheet or something in the rain and one of them fell into a cave-in. They sent for a doctor, but as soon as he arrived, he knew that they had stumbled upon something important. So he called his friend in Mumbai, who knew someone at the State Archaeology Department, who got my mobile from somewhere and called me up – you know how these things are usually a big waste of time, so I just went by myself, and—'

'Rohan,' Harveen interjected. 'Slow down! I don't understand – what are you saying?'

'That lead I told you about! We've found it – a complete structure, a house. I can't tell how old it is, but it must be from the first or second century, I would guess. There's even furniture and clothes inside. The main chamber is flooded because of the cave-in – where the boy fell in – but I think I've managed to plug the inflow for now. It's incredible! You have to come!'

Harveen sat bolt upright in her chair, her mind now very rooted to the spot in the present. Could it be true? A complete house? Rohan's effervescent personality made him prone to making everything sound fantastic. Even so, she had never heard him sound quite so exuberant. She really couldn't help but feel more than a little hopeful.

'Where is it?' she asked eagerly. She was already making notes on what they would need for the excavation. Could this be the find they so desperately needed to restore the government's faith in their department?

Considering they were in the midst of a natural disaster, it was impossible to put together a full dig team. Yet, Harveen managed to assemble a small group from the university to accompany her and Rohan.

As they were loading up, Harveen made a call to the local police, who had always been helpful in arranging security for them. She had the direct line for Inspector Sanj Kumar. In many ways, they were kindred spirits. Both young and outsiders in Kerala, she from Amritsar in the north and he from the bustling streets of Mumbai. Harveen had often thought there could be something between them but it had simply never worked out – work always seemed to get in the way.

'Hi Inspector, how are you? It's Harveen.'

'Ah! Our Punjabi Lara Croft! How are things?' he teased. She knew the inspector had a keen interest in local history as he had visited their museum many times.

'Oh, things are great, thanks. Listen, we have uncovered something potentially quite major. Could you help arrange for security to make sure everything remains safe like you usually do? We—'

'Harveen, we have no manpower to spare at the moment,' he began. 'Everyone's working hard to rescue and provide relief to the people in this relentless storm. No one gets even a day off.'

Harveen was disappointed. 'I understand, Inspector, but this could be huge for the town. I am told we might have uncovered a complete structure; please, can you—'

'This is by far the biggest natural disaster in living memory, Harveen,' he said. 'My officers are on the frontlines alongside the UN's relief forces of over 800 to help move the locals to safety, and it's still not enough. Whatever's been found will still be there when the storm has passed. I'm saying this as your friend: you can't go on a dig right now, Harveen. It's not safe. Do you understand?'

'But …' said Harveen, thinking about how Rohan's barricading efforts could be undone by the floodwaters anytime and the deluge would certainly destroy the ancient house. They were running out of time and this may be their only chance. It felt like her destiny was calling.

'Where is this site anyway? I think you should seriously consider postponing.'

Harveen paused for a moment before replying. 'Oh, I don't know yet; they were going to tell me today but I thought I'd have a word with you first. But yeah, okay, I guess we'll start once the rains stop. Thanks for the advice, Inspector.' As she hung up, Rohan came to her on his way to the car, carrying the last piece of equipment.

'What did he say?'

'He said good luck and that it sounds exciting; he will try and send someone in the next couple of days to guard the site. Are we ready to go?' she said enthusiastically.

Access to the site under normal circumstances would have been straightforward but given the incessant rain, the approach road had now been turned into a river of mud. The archaeology department had a large van that could hold all major equipment required for a dig, and an old Tata Safari which usually conveyed the people to the site. The van, hindered by the swampy path, was forced to turn back. They loaded as much of the equipment as they could into the Safari and pressed on.

Harveen, now accompanied by just three university researchers and Rohan, resembled a gardener amidst all the big shovels and spades in the car. They had packed – though far less conspicuously – finer tools, like a dentist might use, intended for close examinations without damaging any artefacts. The only expensive kit they had included comprised a slightly dated FM256 Magnetometer, a commercial metal detector that had proved surprisingly effective during their previous digs and a much more modern ground-penetrating radar, which would help them identify the right areas to focus the dig on. They also carried tarpaulin sheeting and poles to erect makeshift shelters to protect the site from rain and give them some cover to work under.

'This is not enough equipment, Veen,' Rohan said under his breath. 'We should come back when the weather clears. The site could be unstable. I think we should turn back.'

'It will be fine,' said Harveen with as much optimism as she could manage.

'We have nothing to support the structure with, and only basic medical supplies and safety equipment.'

'We are almost there,' she smiled. 'We can leave if it seems dangerous.'

Rohan did not reply, but he drove on slowly.

The rain angrily pelted on the roof of their car and seemed to intensify in protest as they approached the site. Rohan shouted, 'I can't see anything; we could be driving over it. I am going to get out and lead; just follow very slowly behind.'

He clambered out and made his way into the storm with the car following cautiously behind. For fifteen minutes, he braved the rain, moving one way and then another, until finally he gestured for the vehicle to stop. He was shouting at the top of his voice but the words were carried away by the storm. He pointed frantically. They could just make out a white sheet tied to a pole in the ground in that direction.

Once the car had been parked near the marker Rohan had pointed to, they began to unload the equipment. The plastic sheeting was hastily secured to the ground but it immediately billowed up from one corner, the strong storm winds ripping it off the pegs.

Rohan and Bikhu – one of the researchers from the university – cautiously went down the ladder Rohan had placed near the mouth of the cavity, into the chamber underneath. The rest of the team formed a chain to pass the equipment to them. It was a difficult process – the torrential rain made it hard to grip the equipment firmly, and they couldn't afford to have the high-tech implements get drenched. It took nearly thirty minutes for them to transfer everything. Harveen carefully climbed down using their rope ladder to take a first look at the site, whilst the rest of the team set up the small portable generator and lights. Rohan climbed back up and secured the sheeting as best he could to prevent more water from flooding the site while the rest of the team made its way down. It was tough going; the ground was getting more and more slippery.

The team found itself in a large room with stone walls. It reminded Harveen of the insides of the houses she had seen in Pompeii – certainly not akin to anything in India. There was some kind of pool in the middle of the room, perhaps designed to catch rainwater from an opening in the roof. There was colourful mosaic lining its bottom and sides. The pool was about two feet deep and was overflowing. The water came up to roughly four inches outside it. It looked like it could have been an open reception room, like what the Romans called an atrium, with doors opening into different directions. The walls may originally have been quite smooth, but now bore marks of the ravages of time.

'There was nothing in this room here when I first came. Just the fragments of a table or stand of some sort,' said Rohan as he joined Harveen. 'I tried to save it, but it crumbled as soon as I tugged at it a little.'

Harveen was speechless. A near-perfect room. Once they had found a way to drain the water out of it, who knows what they could find out about the building techniques? Why was it here? Maybe there was more to be found around here; other houses even? She tried to temper her excitement as her mind was overtaken by a torrent of questions.

'Will you guys please help me put some sandbags here?' Rohan signalled to the university researchers, referring to an ancient door concealing the room he had been so excited about. 'I don't want any more water to seep into the room and damage the artefacts before we get to them.'

On the journey to the site, Rohan had described to everyone the room that stood on the other side of the door. Even with just a flashlight, he had seen furniture, clothes, complete vases and some stone tables. There had only been a small puddle of rainwater gathered by the side of the entrance to the room, and, as luck would have it, there seemed to be a slight incline to the floor, which had prevented the water from spreading beyond and potentially ruining their find. Rohan had laid out his own coat and a few small sandbags during his first visit in an attempt to soak up some of the puddle water, before sealing the door again and calling Harveen at the museum.

As soon as the sandbags had been arranged in a small semi-circle around the door, Rohan braced himself to wrench it open once again. He glanced back at Harveen with an expectant smile. 'Wait till you see this,' he grinned while pulling the door open.

6

Muciripattanam
AD 18

Jayesh could not remember a more exciting moment in his life. When he had woken up that morning, he could never have anticipated what the day would bring.

'Up!' Nilham had said, leaning over him and prodding him with his foot. Jayesh had squinted up at his brother in the near darkness. It had taken a moment for him to realize it was morning and they needed to be in the fields before first light; his body had still been aching from the labours of the previous day.

'Up! I won't tell you again,' Nilham had said, slapping Jayesh before moving on to rouse the rest of his brothers. He had scrambled to his feet quickly, even as his body had seemed to protest. He had known that his elder brother would not tolerate any tardiness on his part. Much like their father, Nilham was quick to throw hands when his words were not obeyed.

Jayesh had grown up on the family farm. He shared the larger hall of the two in their residence, along with his brothers and sister. Their house stood near the top of the gentle hill, the side of which rolled down towards the main part of the town. It offered a natural vantage point overlooking the whole town and the sea beyond. On a clear day, Jayesh imagined he could see the other side of the world. He often wondered what fascinating places and adventures were waiting to be found just over the horizon – or was there no more world beyond it?

Jayesh's family had, for generations, cultivated pepper and other spices to trade in the town market. It was the busiest day of the week for them on which one of his elder brothers accompanied their father to the market to sell their goods, leaving the rest of them to spend the day in the fields by themselves.

'Move!' Venkat had pushed past Jayesh to gather up his clothes. The room was barely big enough for them all to sleep in, and the morning ritual of getting ready was often chaotic as they rushed around before sitting down to breakfast ahead of a long day in the fields. As Jayesh quickly dressed, a small cloth with numbers scrawled on one side fell from the folds of his top. He smiled, remembering how he had begged to keep it after being shown how numbers could be written down.

Jayesh had been educated in a small group by an uncle who taught boys of similar age for a few hours on some mornings. They mainly studied religion and sometimes basic numbers and astrology. Occasionally, they studied the history of the area and the teacher would even tell them stories. The one that Jayesh would remember well into his adult life was the story of the ship that the goddess Kali sent to Muciripattanam – made of pure gold and 100 yards long. It was laden with gold and riches so vast that it had taken a hundred men a hundred days to empty. The ship was steered by a beautiful goddess who instructed that the gold be used to build a mighty temple in honour of the god Vishnu to restore balance to the world. They had recently started working more on numbers and, as his uncle wrote them down, Jayesh was amazed and pestered him until he was allowed to take the cloth with him. He brought it home and hid it beneath his bed.

As they all had shuffled outside that morning, they had seen that their mother had already been up for some time, preparing hot breakfast and small lunch bundles for each of them to take to the fields as she did every day. She was hunched over a large pot atop an open fire. Jayesh could smell the spiced vegetables as he waited to be served. His father was already seated next to Nilham and eating.

'You are to go to the market with your father today,' Vasudha whispered to Jayesh as she gave him a bowl filled with rice and vegetables. She always made him feel so loved; she smiled at him as she delivered the news and the words filled his heart with joy. He had been asking to accompany his father to the market for as long as he could remember. He had heard snippets of conversation about the mysterious place – so tantalizingly close to the bottom of their hill and yet elusive. He was desperate to see all of the stalls for himself, but his father had repeatedly refused to take him along until Jayesh had given up asking. His mother had also been persistently trying to make his case but to no avail – until today.

Jayesh was smaller and less capable of physical labour than his brothers, and so was not as helpful in the fields. His father had little time for him. He would barely acknowledge him as they toiled in the fields together, preferring to speak to the others. They, in turn, followed their father's lead, leaving Jayesh to spend much of his time alone, or with his mother.

His sister Avani would sometimes sit with him, singing her pleasant songs and showing him how to make pretty pictures with the crushed flowers she gathered.

As he had sat eating, Jayesh had begun to doubt if he had heard correctly. He had looked at his mother, who had smiled at him, then at each of his brothers, who had all been engrossed in their food, and then finally at his father and eldest brother, sitting close together and in conversation. Perhaps his imagination had conjured up the words to fulfil his most ardent desire. Just as he had been ready to give up hope and moved to follow his brothers to the fields, his father had called out to him.

'Jayesh, load the cart.' It had been the first time in many months that his father had spoken directly to him. He had looked back at him with a big smile, but the former had already got busy loading sacks onto the cart. As Jayesh had set off to join him, Nilham had scowled. Jayesh had known then that there would be a price to pay later for his first trip to the market. Despite this, the aches in his body had simply melted away.

7

Kodungallur
14 June 2024

As soon as the door opened, a flood of water came from the next room and washed the sandbags towards them. Rohan was swept off his feet by the oncoming tide. The tallest researcher from the university immediately waded forward to help him back up. They all struggled as the water gushed ahead. The level in this second room must be five or six times higher than the room they had been in, reaching up to their waist. Harveen grabbed a torch and marched on towards the open door.

'Wait, it is not safe,' Rohan called after her, now on his feet and thoroughly drenched. She looked at him with an intense, desperate expression on her face. 'The walls could cave in with this much water; we need to get everyone out. Now!' Harveen could see the danger that she had put them in.

'Get everyone out, NOW!' she screamed. 'Go!'

As Rohan turned back, Harveen raced through the doorway. In the second room, there were at least two fissures in the roof through which jagged light elbowed past the water to pour in. The patterns of light splattered across the walls made it look like the inside of a nightclub. There were other holes in the ceiling as well, and the leaks through them were much worse. The water level slowly reduced as it drained into the first room, and now just came up to under Harveen's knees. She felt it seeping into her walking boots. She could hear Rohan shouting instructions at the team somewhere behind her, telling them how to get out.

'Take whatever you can carry safely and climb up the ladder. Stay together and get back to the Safari. No more than two trips to carry the stuff – leave behind what you can't take. I will go and get Harveen and be right with you. GO!' his voice was controlled yet urgent.

Harveen brought her attention back to the room just as a large piece of stone came crashing down from the roof, falling only inches away. In a moment, Rohan was beside her.

'You okay? Are you hurt?' he asked frantically, looking her over.

'I'm fine. Get out! I will be right behind you.'

'Nothing down here is worth dying for. Look how fast the water is coming in now!' He pointed to where the stone had fallen from and she could see a small waterfall pouring into the room. The water was nearly knee-high now and rising fast.

'You're right. Let's go.' Harveen realized it was crazy to risk their lives and followed behind him. The walls around the atrium door began to collapse and forced them both to turn back. They couldn't get out that way anymore.

'We're stuck,' Rohan said with finality in his voice. Before he had even said it, Harveen was wading across the room.

'This way!' she said. As she struggled on, a colourful vase about twelve inches in length floated in front of her. Harveen scooped it up and even in the intermittent light, she could see its remarkable craftsmanship. It looked Roman or Greek in origin and was in excellent condition. She tried to keep it aloft and away from the rising water whilst holding her torch in her other hand. Pieces of ancient clothing and broken furniture were drifting all around her and she knew that the room could not be saved in its entirety no matter what they did.

There were two large stone tables arranged side by side along the far wall, seemingly too heavy to have succumbed to the water yet. If they could get on top of those two tables, Harveen thought they might be able to buy themselves some time to figure out a way up. She moved towards them.

'Rohan! Let's get to those tables!' she shouted, pointing towards them. She saw that he also had something in his hand as he was making his way towards her. Even in the panic, she smiled inwardly; Rohan too must be grappling with the same desperation as her to preserve whatever they could of this priceless find.

Harveen reached the tables first and carefully laid the vase on top, clipping the torch on her belt so she could climb on top of them. As soon as she placed her hands on the edge of the table, she understood what had been bothering her about their position. Both tables were about three feet long and two feet wide, and were more than waist-high. They were made of stone but there was no explanation as to why they would be placed together and aligned against a wall like so. She soon realized that they were not tables but storage chests of some kind. The sides were solid, but the top was a much thinner slab, forming a lipped lid. She was able to move the lid as it overhung the front face of the chest and was clearly designed to be lifted. Gently, she set the vase bobbing in the water next to her. She noticed that the water level had risen to her waist, making her feel as if she were trapped in an ominous hourglass timer. Bracing herself to lift the lid with both hands, she was surprised to find that it was much lighter than she had expected and came away easily.

Inside were neat stacks of clothes. Harveen held it open with one hand and grabbed her torch with the other to get a better look. When she shone the light into the trove and saw what was inside, she let out a gasp, almost dropping the lid in shock. Rohan arrived beside her and exclaimed, 'My God! My God!'

There were hundreds of sheets with writing on them. They were not parchment or paper, but some type of pale cloth. Harveen and Rohan were jolted back to reality when another huge piece of stone crashed into the room behind them, bringing more mud and water into the collapsing building. Harveen recovered first. 'Rohan. We need to save these. We need something to keep them dry. I will go and find what I can. See if any of the other doors will open. If the other rooms are not as bad as this, it may buy us a few minutes.'

'There is probably no equipment left down here. I got the team to clear out everything they could with them to keep them safe. We should probably get out too.' Even as he said this, Harveen could see that he was as drawn to the written sheets as she was.

'I'm not leaving without them, Rohan. See if you can find a way out and go. I will find something to put the papers in and follow right behind you. Go. Please!' There was desperation in her every word.

Harveen made her way towards the room they had entered through. The walls here too were close to collapse. Their ladder was floating in the water and their equipment was mostly gone, as Rohan had said. There was some rope and plastic sheets floating on the surface near where the door had originally been. There were also a couple of shovels and poles. She threw the rope over her shoulder, gathered up all the plastic sheeting and headed towards the chests.

'We might be able to climb out from there.' Rohan pointed.

'Go!' said Harveen, as a clap of thunder echoed in the room. 'The whole place is collapsing around us.' Rohan moved towards a few collapsed stones and tried to climb atop them. Harveen laid out the plastic sheeting on top of one of the chests and opened the other's lid. This too was full of similar written sheets, stacked nearly to the top. She began to put them into the plastic sheeting and wrap them up.

She worked quickly and managed to get all of the sheets from both chests into two large bundles sheathed in the plastic. The ropes were too thick to tie the bundles up securely and although she had wrapped them as tightly as she could, they still needed to be held together by hand to prevent them from falling open. Harveen knew that some of the papers had got wet but if they could just get them out, they might be able to salvage something from them. Even if some sheets got damaged, this would still be an amazing find. She picked up both bundles just as Rohan returned beside her.

'There is no way to climb out from that side,' he panted.

'This way, look,' Harveen said, pointing. Where the ceiling had caved in, there was a number of large stone pieces which had tumbled down, forming a ramp of sorts and creating a potential route to help them climb to the surface. There was water and mud rushing down. 'We can make it.'

'Put the bags down. Let's get out and come back for them another time,' Rohan suggested.

'I won't leave them,' Harveen replied resolutely. 'See if you can get to the top and lower the rope. Maybe you can get the team. We can't leave these here.' Rohan looked at her in shock. The expression on her face was sure and unmoving.

'You could die …'

'Go!' she said, her intensity urging him into action.

Rohan began clambering up the steep ramp. He lost his footing several times and ended up beside Harveen. Finally, he managed to scale his way up. The water had now reached above her waist and Harveen was propping up both plastic-clad bundles between the stone wall and herself. The stone chests were now totally submerged. Harveen could feel the whole structure caving inwards as the ancient stones were finally exhaling under the weight of the flood, relieved at having given up their long-stored secrets.

'Harveen! Let's go! Leave them!' Rohan screamed from above her, peering into what was left of the room. Harveen clutched the precious packages even tighter.

'I can't,' she yelled honestly. It was her life's work – she had sacrificed so much for it. The documents could not only save the reputation of their department, but could potentially prove to the world how important Muziris had once been. 'Get to safety and try and send some help,' she urged him. To her surprise, just like that, Rohan was gone.

Harveen was left cold and drenched, looking up despairingly at the stormy sky through the gaping hole in the ceiling of the ancient ruins, feeling the water rising around her like a vice slowly sealing her fate. She clung grimly onto the two plastic bundles. A horrible thought occurred to her – she could be clutching onto worthless ramblings, dying alone. She felt her face grow warm and panic rise in her chest.

8

Vatican City
14 June 2024

Don considered how much he had paid in innocent blood to have the chance to become the head of the Santa Alleanza. As he sat in the corridor alone, he began to wonder how much further he would have to go once he was given the role.

After a twenty-year career in the Gruppo di Intervento Speciale followed by six years of service in the Santa Alleanza, Don Clemente had applied to be made the head of the secret police force of the Vatican. His boss, the legendary 'il macellaio' (the butcher) Dino Rossi, was due to retire and had arranged this meeting to formally let him know the result of his application. Clemente did not have high expectations of success as the two men had often clashed on the best approach to difficult situations. Rossi had asked him to arrive promptly at 9 a.m. and had left him waiting for nearly an hour outside his empty office.

'Ah, my dear Donatello,' Rossi said as he finally approached Don in the corridor silently, his words jolting Don out of his thoughts. 'Do come in.'

Commander Rossi had an office quite unlike anyone else in the Santa Alleanza. The office resembled what one would expect of an eccentric writer. Despite its size, the dark wall coverings and the sheer volume of period furniture gave the room a claustrophobic air. Don always had the sense of being watched from the dark recesses of Rossi's office.

A carved giltwood console table sat near the middle of the room. The table had been crafted in the eighteenth century by the renowned baroque cabinet-maker Giacomo Herman. The top was veneered with lapis lazuli with a deep blue, almost luminous, hue. The surface was held aloft by two elaborately carved gold male figures who were holding a mask between them. Don found the piece both gaudy and fascinating – its ostentatious appearance contrasted starkly with Rossi's own neat, understated demeanour. When Don had commented on the desk during his first visit, Commander Rossi had explained that he had pulled many strings to have the desk placed in his office.

Don had paid several visits to this room over the years and had started to mentally catalogue exactly how many valuable items were housed within it, including a rather elaborate drinks cabinet holding Mr Rossi's very special collection of whiskies.

Don was the nephew of a devout priest – a deeply spiritual man who was still a serving cleric loyal to the Church at the age of seventy-two. It had been expected that he would follow in his uncle's footsteps and devote his life to the service of God. But, as with the generations before him, Don was first conscripted to serve in the Italian military. He then found himself in the service of the Church – but now, his boss Rossi's view of how service should work seemed to contradict every principle his uncle had instilled in him.

Don watched as Rossi pulled a thick manila envelope from his briefcase and placed it on the table. He smiled as he extracted a battered folder from the envelope and placed this too on the table, his movements careful and precise. Neatly clipped to the front of the folder was an old picture of Don in his service uniform.

'You've had quite the career, Donatello,' the older gentleman began cordially. 'There are very few Italians who have received the Gold Medal of Military Valour, and fewer yet whose records don't reflect the prestigious medal being bestowed upon them at all.' He let the last comment hang in the air as he extracted the sheets from the folder and laid them out in front of him one by one. Across the table, Don recognized documents detailing all parts of his military career. These were all highly classified. He estimated that within the Italian military, at any given time, there would be perhaps only five men who would have access to them. There were also more recent documents bearing the distinct logo of the Santa Alleanza, which he knew to be the reports of all the projects that he had worked on over the last six years.

He watched carefully as Rossi pored over the documents with meticulous focus and an air of ceremony. Don felt very nervous. There had been several occasions on which he had not adopted the brutal methods propounded by Rossi. He knew that Rossi was a firm believer in having access to intelligence on all his key staff, and any one of these reports could contain evidence against Don's actions.

Don could feel the sweat in his armpits and running down his back. It felt as if he was under great critical scrutiny and Rossi was reading through a list of every mistake he had ever made. When Rossi looked up at him, his gaze seemed to pierce right through to his soul; every doubt, every thought, every hesitation laid bare in front of il macellaio. At the same moment, the image of Señor Varane opening the door to his own death flashed in Don's mind.

'My dear Donatello, your rise through the ranks in the military was, without a doubt, remarkable. Unit Commander of the GIS by the age of twenty-seven. Distinguished service in the Balkans, Bosnia, Iran, Afghanistan and Russia as well as numerous missions across Europe. Your team successfully performed assassinations, prisoner extractions, international counterterrorism efforts, traded secrets with foreign powers and assisted with multiple prisoner exchanges.'

'The men I had the privilege to fight alongside were brave, sir. I was but a loyal servant of the State that gave me the honour to work for the good of our beloved nation,' Don replied. They had examined his records when he had first joined the organization. Now Rossi was going over them with a fine-toothed comb. Don was familiar with his ways – he often caught people by surprise, sandwiching damning criticism between pleasantries. This kept Don on edge.

'There was considerable trust in your leadership. It seems your unit was often deployed at home as well, on projects that were too challenging for or beyond the expertise of domestic forces,' continued Rossi. Don was a true patriot. For securing the interests of his nation, he had sometimes been compelled to issue commands to carry out violent and brutal acts that had severely tested his conscience. Then, for the last six years, working for the Santa Alleanza to protect the Church and the position of the Vatican had further tested his resolve. The missions for the Vatican often involved civilians who had, in some way, become entangled in matters of concern to the Church. Dealing with them in the way Rossi wanted often caused Don moral unrest.

'I did what was required of me – I did what was right for Italy,' he responded honestly. 'And now I am honoured to serve the Vatican, the Santa Alleanza.' Rossi sat motionless for a moment before his hand instinctively moved towards a sharp blade with an exquisitely carved ivory handle, placed on his desk. Legend had it that this was the very weapon that had earned him his moniker. He turned it slowly in his hand, and then his face broke into a sinister smile. Don felt the trap shut behind him as the old man trained the smile at him.

9

Muciripattanam
AD 18

Jayesh would always remember the first time he went to the Muciripattanam marketplace. It was really nothing special – a fairly standard selection of stalls and carts spread out over the fields leading down to the sea. The local farmers had been coming here for many years to sell their wares, and it was the main trading hub for miles around. When he was eleven, Jayesh's father took him along to help unload and sell sacks of pepper from their farm, and purchase and load the vegetables and cloth they had to take back home with them.

The bumpy journey towards the market along the rock-strewn path down the hillside had started in silence; it was the first time Jayesh had spent any time alone with his father. He had yearned desperately for the kind of close relationship that his older brothers shared with him. As he watched his father steer the cart down the hill, Jayesh hoped that he would say something.

But before long, they had already arrived at the edge of the market. Jayesh had only ever looked longingly at the landscape from their home on the top of the hill all his life before then. He had been mesmerized by the sights laid out in front of him. While he had heard stories of the wonderful things that were sold there from others, he had not been able to believe his eyes when he had witnessed the scene for himself.

'Thank you for bringing me, Appa!' he had beamed. His father had glanced at him momentarily before looking back at the path in front.

'We are here for work,' he had grunted sternly in reply. The conversation had been brought to an abrupt halt and they had ridden on in silence.

Jayesh had dismounted the cart and stood frozen on the spot as the sight before him had overloaded his senses. He had never before seen nor imagined such sounds, colours and smells. There had been so many people there, moving purposefully from stall to stall. Animals he had never seen before wandered freely amongst the humans. He had taken in the wonderful aromas of foods of all kinds that had made his mouth water, along with the more familiar, intense aromas of spices. The salty winds from the sea had brushed against his face, infusing him with a freshness and energy unlike any he'd known before. The palm leaves on the roofs of the stalls had rustled in the breeze, their shade providing much-needed respite from the coastal sun to the traders so they could spend the day bargaining and bartering their goods. His father had brought him out of his trance with a gentle tap on the top of his head.

'The pepper will not unload itself, Jayesh,' he had said and glared at him. He had already unloaded half of the pepper sacks. Jayesh had looked at his father, his eyes still twinkling from his awe at the sights surrounding him.

He had enquired, 'Why here? There are many more people down there, near the food stalls; wouldn't we be better off unloading there?', pointing to the main hub of the market, closer to the seashore.

His father had looked at him with some impatience. 'We have the best pepper in Muciripattanam. It has never been a problem for us selling everything we come bearing from this very spot. They will come and find us here if they want to buy our ware,' he had retorted confidently, his decisive tone dissuading any further questioning by his youngest son.

Once all the sacks had been unloaded, Jayesh had pleaded, 'May I go and have a look around the market, Appa? Please?' Abhay had shot him a look of disappointment, his disapproving expression enough to bring tears to the young boy's eyes. It had seemed like he could never please his father.

'Go quickly, then; do not get into any trouble and come back soon. You need to load the sacks onto the customers' carts after every sale we make.' His words had been blunt and had made Jayesh want to give up on his idea and stay there with him to prevent getting a scolding, but the lure of the market was overwhelming.

'I will, I promise,' he had called as he had run into the bustling crowd. He had glanced back once to see Abhay shaking his head with displeasure.

As Jayesh had rushed around the market, approaching the sea, he had been able to sense the contrast between the sights there and those back at his family farm. Muciripattanam had been a wonderful and vibrant place. The locally grown fruits and vegetables had been aburst with colour and flavour, sweetening the town air with their aroma, punctuated by the occasional waft from the spices it had been known for.

The deep waters running along the coast were clear and blue. Jayesh had heard it said that you could walk thirty feet off the coast of the town into the sea without drowning, because there were so many fish in the water. He had stood spellbound for a moment by the pier where the small handmade boats of fishermen had been tied, while the fish had flapped around close to the surface across the water.

Jayesh had walked the aisles between the stalls wide-eyed, taking in the sights of the exotic wares. He had listened keenly as bargains were struck and goods were loaded. There had been such a wide variety of products on offer – from livestock to cloth and various tools and trinkets that had sparkled in the sunlight. He had been fascinated by how the people around him had seemed to know and understand the intrinsic value of all these items, each haggling for the best deals.

Mindful not to take too long, Jayesh had rushed from one stall to another. In his excitement, he had run into a group of much older boys. Before he could have apologized, they had pushed him hard onto the ground.

'Eh! Watch where you are going, rat!' shouted the boy that had shoved him; the others had laughed as he had fallen into the dirt. As Jayesh had tried to get up, one of the other boys had stepped forward to kick him back onto the ground. Although he had been small, he had been nimble. Having older brothers had meant that he understood all too well the value in avoiding their heavy blows. He had scampered backwards as quickly as he could on impulse, crashing into a stall and causing produce to scatter all over the ground. The older boys had laughed at him and gone on their way.

Jayesh had then been pulled up roughly by the neck of his shirt and found himself face to face with a large man. His face had been close enough for his thick black beard to bristle against Jayesh's face.

'Who are you? Where is your father? You will pay for this mess!' he had hissed, his spit landing on Jayesh's face. He had known his father's reaction would have been worse than anything this man could have done to him.

'I a–am on my own,' he had stammered.

'Bastard beggar, eh?' he had screamed from such close quarters that Jayesh could smell his breath. 'We don't want your kind here!' And he had struck Jayesh hard across the face, sending him crashing back onto the ground.

'Get out!' he had said as Jayesh had retreated, stumbling onto the main path through the market and ramming directly into a herd of cows that was being led into the area designated for cattle in the market. The cowherd had shouted at him. 'Boy! Boy! Get out of the way!'

Jayesh had run on, the market becoming a dizzy blur by now, the noise – that had seemed so beautiful at first – had now felt like it was ringing in his head; his cheek still burning from the blow. When he had finally looked up, he had found himself behind the cattle area. This side of the market had been much quieter and he had slumped down against another stall, sobbing into his hands. As he had leaned against the overflowing stall, pieces of fruit had fallen to the floor. Immediately, Jayesh had heard the sound of the stall owner rushing around to see what was going on. Jayesh had felt his presence looming over him before raising his hand up. He had had lost the will to fight back, closing his eyes and bracing himself for the slap.

10

Kodungallur
14 June 2024

For Harveen, an eternity seemed to have passed as she looked up at the sky. The storm seemed to be intensifying, ready to seal her fate. Through the pouring rain and her tears, she had seen the blurry form of a shadow looming and then flying down towards her. She could make out the shape of a man as he came close to her. It was Bikhu from the university research team.

'This is no time to be idling around, Dr Gill, if you don't mind my saying so,' he smiled as he extended his arm out to her. He had a metal cord tied around his waist and was being lowered down somehow.

'Take this,' said Harveen, placing the first plastic sheet bundle into his hands. 'Hold it tight around here. Now go!' she directed, suddenly feeling hopeful.

He seemed to float out of the chamber like a ghost, returning moments later. They hurriedly arranged themselves in an awkward embrace, with Harveen holding the second precious bundle tightly in front of her whilst clinging to Bikhu as the cord pulled them upwards. Bikhu gave her instructions to use her feet to walk on the sides of the narrow passage as the cord lifted them out.

As they cleared the roof, Harveen could see that the cord was attached to a winch on the front of their Tata Safari. The team was all there and Rohan grinned with relief and delight when he saw Bikhu and Harveen emerge from the pit.

'I knew that my abseiling lessons would come in handy one day,' Bikhu said as he unhooked the line from around his waist. His humour was somewhat lost on Harveen, who was still reeling from the rescue, going through a full spectrum of emotion from elation and relief to a sense of loss.

A crashing sound erupted behind them. They spun around to see the whole area cave in as the rain and mud finally won the battle against the ancient ruins, engulfing them entirely. Suddenly, they became acutely aware of their precarious position, unsure how stable the ground they were standing on was. They'd been very lucky to not lose anyone down there on this dangerous mission, but it was becoming clear that their luck might not hold out much longer.

'Let's get out of here before anything else collapses,' commanded Harveen, snapping back to her senses.

Harveen could not remember being quite so happy in her life before. For years, they had been searching for the fabled city of Muziris, the key Indian port used by Rome in the first century. And now here they were – they had just been standing inside a stone house with what looked like a mosaic floor and Roman vases. Perhaps this was the start of a remarkable find like Pompeii, with multiple such houses and buildings. Maybe then Harveen would go on to be able to establish Muziris as a World Heritage site. She felt delirious with excitement as they drove back from the now destroyed ancient house. She barely noticed that Rohan and the others were very quiet; she sat in the back seat clutching the two bundles of plastic-wrapped documents.

'What do you think is written in these documents, Rohan? The house looked like it belonged to an important man, right? Having a Roman-style house like that, he must have been wealthy. Did you get a look into the other rooms? What were they like?' Rohan was focused on navigating their Tata Safari through the rain, his hands tightly gripping the wheel. Harveen's mind continued to race.

'We need to get these documents stabilized immediately. Do you think that we can get a conservator in today? I will make calls as soon as we get back. Should we set up a deacidification room? It looks like it's written on some type of cloth. Maybe we get lucky and it's not so sensitive?' The lack of response from any other team member did little to stem Harveen's flow.

As they got closer to the Sreepadam Palace, where they would need to unload, Rohan finally spoke.

'We need to make sure everyone is well first and then we need to inform Professor Prakash about the find.' The name of the Director of the Kerala State Archaeology Department jolted Harveen out of her trance and she began to understand the list of priorities. Professor Prakash would be unimpressed with her prioritizing the find over the safety of her team.

As soon as they arrived, Harveen went straight to his office. She found him at his desk, peering at some documents.

'Professor?' she began tentatively.

'Harveen! How was the site? Found anything worthwhile?'

'It was an entire ancient house, Professor. From the first century, I would say. We've never seen anything like it – the architecture style was Roman, like the houses in Pompeii! We even found written records! We don't yet know what they are for certain, but there's a good number of them – Dravidian, perhaps.'

Prakash slowly removed his spectacles, taking in Harveen's dishevelled appearance and trance-like, excited state. 'What happened to you?' He sprang up from his chair and guided her to sit in the chair on the other side of his desk. 'Are you hurt? What about the rest of the team?'

'There was a … big problem, Professor … because of the floods … the house—' Harveen stopped and hung her head – she had got in trouble earlier, for not following safety protocols. The memory of her last conversation with Professor Prakash about it echoed in the back of her mind. The gravity of her reckless actions was beginning to dawn on her.

'Did you follow procedure before entering this house? Did you do your due diligence? The place was flooding and you still … Is everyone in the team okay?' he repeated.

'We did basic checks …' Harveen stammered, '… b–but we were running out of time; the house was close to collapse … the floods—'

'And you went in anyway?!' Prakash was alarmed at Harveen's carelessness. 'Is anyone hurt?'

'I think everyone is okay, but I would still recommend getting a medical opinion and having everyone checked out,' she was measured in her words, careful not to alarm the professor further, while ensuring she didn't understate the seriousness of the trauma the team had just endured. They had escaped from the jaws of death by a hair's breadth, after all.

'I will call for medical assistance right away,' said Professor Prakash. 'We can discuss the rest in more detail once we've made sure everyone is okay.' The words filled Harveen with dread. If Professor Prakash found out what had really happened at the site, there were sure to be serious repercussions – she could even lose her job.

Prakash quickly organized thorough medical examinations for all members of the team. Harveen busied herself with answering calls from concerned family members about every team member, reassuring them that they were safe and that the department had ensured everyone was conveyed home promptly; they would be home soon. She avoided crossing paths with the professor.

Harveen then swiftly arranged for her team to meet at the loading bays so they could transfer their precious finds to the department premises. Bearing sturdy archive boxes that the State Archaeology Department used to store all its important documents, Harveen and Rohan oversaw the unloading, seizing the opportunity to get a closer look at what they had salvaged from the ruins.

There were hundreds of cloth sheets made of a thin cotton-type material and cut to a uniform size. Each sheet looked like a ledger with multiple entries, all scribed by a neat hand. Harveen could not make out the language. It was certainly not the oldest Dravidian language most commonly associated with southern India. She looked at Rohan and he looked equally perplexed; he suggested it might be some variant of Tamil and that he would get a specialist the next day to have a look.

The ancient documents had sustained a lot more water damage than they had initially expected. It could have happened before they had taken them out of the stone boxes, or – more likely – in the mayhem that had followed. Much of the text was runny or blurry, and only some of the sheets were in perfect condition. Whilst they were discussing how they should proceed, Professor Prakash arrived on the scene and took Harveen aside.

Harveen had been bracing herself for this moment. She knew that Professor Prakash would be angry with her, but also felt certain that the intrinsic value of what they had discovered would surely help her win him over.

'It is an incredible find; these records are like nothing we have ever seen,' she smiled. Prakash impatiently waved his hand.

'This really cannot continue. I know that it is all very thrilling and exciting, but the safety of your team should always be your primary concern. You are responsible for them and, without them, none of this would have been possible,' Prakash did not conceal his disapproval or meet Harveen's eye. But she still pressed on hopefully.

'I know and I am really sorry, but as soon as I saw the documents, I knew that it was the big find we have been waiting for. The find that can save the department, the team's jobs – everything we have worked so hard for, all this time. We can't let them withdraw our funding, Professor—'

'I am not sure you fully understand how serious this is. It's made me reconsider whether you are the right leader for our efforts in the field. You acted carelessly and selfishly, losing sight of what's most important in that situation: ensuring nobody's safety – or life – is at risk.'

His words shocked Harveen to the core. Surely, he wouldn't do this to her. After all she had risked.

'It was like a Roman house … it was … incredible. These records we have recovered – there are hundreds of them! – I'm sure we can pinpoint Muziris's location now. The structure proves there were, in fact, links with Rome … Please, Professor, you have to understand the massive implications this could have on—'

'I think this is a good time to bring in an experienced archaeologist to lead the project and supervise these efforts. As you said, it is a major find,' he said.

'Y–you can't …' she said, struggling to find the words to express her horror. He looked at her bedraggled state for the first time during the conversation. It seemed as if the frantic events of the evening had finally caught up with her at that moment.

'You can't …' she whispered, trailing off.

'Look, Harveen, it's been a long day. Go home and get some rest; let's pick this up again in the morning.'

'Please—'

She wanted to resolve it right there, but it was clear that the conversation was over for the night.

'Tomorrow,' Prakash replied firmly. His expression was uncharacteristically hard.

By the time they all left for home, around 9 p.m., Harveen was completely exhausted. Her mind agonized over potentially losing her job and having to watch someone else head the project she had laboured so hard for. She teared up at the thought of watching someone else unveil the wonders that lay hidden within those documents. She mechanically let herself into her home and took a shower, although she did remember speaking to her mother on the phone about something before dragging herself to her bed.

She dreamt of a big stage in the Great Hall at Balliol College, Oxford, her beloved alma mater. She sat mesmerized among the rapturous audience there, as she had many years ago. The woman on the stage was presenting her astounding discovery of the ancient town of Muziris in India. She stood basking in the praise and applause from world-renowned historians and fellow archaeologists in the crowd. She scrolled through several slides containing photos of the ancient structures and surprisingly well-preserved houses they had discovered, including a great forum like those found in Rome, and even the remains of a large ship. Tears streamed down Harveen's face as she sat and watched her discoveries be presented by someone else. The sound of her alarm jolted her back to reality, piercing through the veil of her dream and awakening her to the fear of what the new day might bring. She checked the time – it was 6:30 a.m.

11

Muciripattanam
AD 18

'Hey, what's the matter with you? Are you alright?' Jayesh opened his eyes to see a tall, slender boy standing over him. His arm was extended towards Jayesh to help him up.

'I am Vikesh. Come, you can help me clear up the mess you made.'

Jayesh took his arm and stood up. He began gathering the fruit that he had knocked off the stall counter.

'Sorry,' he mumbled.

'Don't worry, it's fine. You look upset – what's wrong?'

'Nothing, I just … fell.' Jayesh was worried that his father would be angry with him for having disappeared for so long. He feared the scolding he knew was coming. Just as he was placing the last few items onto the counter, a customer arrived at the stall to ask about the prices, and he slipped away unnoticed.

By the time he returned to his father's stall, he could see that the pepper they had brought was almost gone. In fact, he found his father in the middle of a deal with an elderly man for another two sacks. He glanced up briefly, anticipating another potential customer, registered Jayesh's presence without a word, and returned swiftly to his trade.

As soon as all the pepper had been sold, his father glanced at him and said, 'What happened to you? Have you been fighting?' Jayesh looked down and noticed his clothes were muddy; his cheek was still throbbing from the slap. He knew it must have left a red mark.

'Nothing, Appa. I was so excited to see all the stalls, I didn't notice where I was stepping and fell over – I'm sorry.'

His father shook his head in disappointment.

'We need to buy vegetables and cloth. Let's go over there to Bharath's shop. He always has a good stock of vegetables. Stick close to me. You can help carry our shopping.' He gestured towards one of the larger stalls and Jayesh recognized the man standing behind the counter. He would come to their farm on occasion to deliver vegetables, and they had been instructed to always refer to him respectfully as 'Ammavan'. Bharath was a large man and unlike most of the other sellers there, he did not wear a simple white garment. Instead, he was adorned in a colourful robe and marshalled his two sons around to manage their large stall.

On the short walk over to Bharath's stall, Jayesh pestered his father with questions about the market.

'Why are similar goods not being sold in the same place, Appa? Wouldn't that be so much easier for the buyers?'

His father barely registered his question.

'Why do the same goods cost different at different stalls?

Again, silence.

'How long has the market been here, Appa?'

His father sighed and shook his head slightly.

'Do you think we could get one of those shiny necklaces from that stand over there for Amma?'

They finally arrived at Bharath's stand. His father bent down to look Jayesh in the eye and said calmly, 'Look, you are still very young and have much to learn. I have been coming to this market since my father first brought me here at your age. I observed him over the years, did as he instructed me, and now I know all I need to know about this place – all the people who come to sell and buy here, what to say to customers to make a sale and how to earn a good profit. Everyone knows me and that the quality of my pepper is far superior to anyone else's in Muciripattanam. We work hard for our earnings and that is all our business here is concerned with. Now, pay attention to how your Appa bargains and purchases the vegetables your Amma cooks and you relish. Maybe you'll learn a thing or two and become more useful to me at the market in the future. Today, just help me carry our shopping afterwards so we can load our cart and set off for home before sundown, understood?' Jayesh nodded obediently and stood quietly at his father's side.

Bharath and Abhay greeted each other with a warm embrace, like long-lost friends, and soon began a lively dialogue about the vegetables. Jayesh was struck by the ease and warmth in his father's demeanour towards Bharath and wondered what it would take for him to be treated with the same love and fondness.

He watched his father skilfully negotiate the price to almost a third cheaper than what Bharath had originally quoted. They were about to conclude their deal when Jayesh began to tug at his father's robes insistently. Abhay shot him a stern look and held up his hand. 'Shhh!' he said angrily, turning his attention back to his conversation with Bharath. But Jayesh did not relent and began the tugging again.

Abhay grabbed his son by the neckline of his shirt and forcibly dragged him to one side. Jayesh had seen this rage before; it was usually followed by a strike across the face with little preamble. 'What is it now? Why must you keep bothering me?' Abhay snarled, raising his hand to strike the boy.

'There is a young boy over there, Appa,' Jayesh frantically launched into an explanation, cowering away from his father's raised hand. He pointed over his shoulder meekly, 'He came late and his stand is not in the best spot, hidden behind all those cows, but his produce is very fresh and the prices are half of what Ammavan has brought down his price to.' There was a pause. His father glared at him and Jayesh hung his head in embarrassment.

Abhay's loosened his grip around his shirt neck. 'Where is he? Show me,' he said gruffly. Jayesh pointed in the direction of Vikesh's stall. His father marched ahead without waiting for him.

Jayesh scampered behind, struggling to keep up. Behind a huge livestock display, Vikesh's small stall stood humbly, overflowing with fresh produce. Seeing them approach, the seller looked flustered and unsure.

'Who are you? Who is your Appa?' Abhay demanded.

Although he had looked nervous, the young boy spoke with confidence. 'I am Vikesh. My Appa's name was Vinod.'

Abhay was quiet for a moment before he said sombrely, 'Oh ... I am sorry, son. I had known your father for many years. This is my son, Jayesh. He tells me that your prices are fair – how much are you selling your vegetables for?'

After some haggling, Abhay and Jayesh could be seen loading almost all of Vikesh's produce onto their cart. As they pulled away from the stall, Jayesh glanced back and saw Vikesh grinning. He waved enthusiastically towards Jayesh, who returned the gesture without realizing how much he would go on to lean on his new friend in the years to come.

As they made their way home, Jayesh had yet another question for his father. He asked in a quiet, contemplative voice, 'Appa, you paid Vikesh more than he was asking for in the end. Why?'

His father paused before answering, 'That boy has just lost his Appa, son. It would've come as such a shock to the family. He's likely the eldest and has suddenly been thrust into this new position as the primary breadwinner of his household. Such a huge weight to carry on his young shoulders and nobody to show him how. They work very hard to grow that wonderful produce that caught your eye. I bargained as I usually would and threw in a little extra as a token of my gratitude. I sensed Vikesh is a bright boy; I'm sure he'll soon know better and start charging more for his wares – then he would either have remembered us as people who took advantage of his inexperience, or as ethical customers who supported him despite it. Even after paying more than what he had asked, we still saved a lot more than we would have if we had bought from Bharath. And that is thanks to you, Jayesh. You show great promise as a trader, child. Purchasing is just as much of a skill as selling.'

The discomfort of travelling over rough terrain on the journey home was quickly forgotten as Jayesh basked in the glow of this sliver of paternal approval. For the rest of their bumpy ride, Jayesh thought of nothing else besides how he could earn even more praise from his father and get to spend more time with him.

12

Vatican City
14 June 2024

Commander Rossi put his knife down carefully. 'You have impressed me greatly over these last six years, Donatello. I have no doubt that you are my ideal successor after I retire,' he said, getting up from his seat to drift towards his liquor cabinet. Don closed his eyes with relief and let out a sigh.

He looked back at all the rather questionable and distasteful tasks he had had to perform in the name of protecting the Church. Each of them had resulted in heated conversations between him and Rossi about the latter's brutal methods. Don had been led to believe that if he could secure the most senior role at the Santa Alleanza, he would be able to bring about change, and soften their methods of going about their sworn duties. He was, after all, a devout and loyal Christian, and felt morally conflicted by the nefarious ways in which the Santa Alleanza often carried out its objectives.

'Perhaps you'd like to join me in having a small drink in celebration of your new role?' Rossi turned to look at Don as he finished his question, one of his eyebrows arched. Don absorbed the words, suddenly alert and on his guard. A chill ran down his spine as the meaning set in. In the six years he had worked for the Head of the Santa Alleanza, Rossi's drinks cabinet had only been opened to him on two occasions.

The first had been when he was tasked to kill the elderly archaeologist who had come upon the scroll about the statue of St Peter, which would surely have invited controversy upon the Vatican. After Don had retrieved the scroll and carried out the execution as instructed – taking the man's life and destroying all evidence of the document – with some assistance from Rossi's connections within the Rome police, the investigation into the fire was closed without arousing suspicion or leaving any loose ends.

Rossi had been delighted with his protégé for the way he had handled the situation, even managing a smile as they had discussed every little detail over a whisky. He had barely been able to contain his satisfaction at the precautions the younger man had taken to ensure that their actions would not be uncovered.

The second time had been when Don had successfully managed to pose as the agent of a wealthy and reclusive private antiques collector to facilitate the purchase of some extremely valuable Italian artworks. The pieces were being offered by a well-known German art dealer, who was known to source various pieces that had been looted by the Nazis during the Second World War. Once again, Rossi had been impressed by Don's ability to carefully plan and efficiently execute an operation – he had organized for funds to be released by the Vatican Bank and routed through a Swiss intermediary account discreetly so it could not be traced back to them. Thereafter, the artwork was acquired and safely transported to be deposited in the church vaults. If they were ever to be released to the public or sold by the

Vatican, would fetch many multiples on the price that had been paid for them on the black market.

On this momentous third occasion, Rossi opened his drinks cabinet, smiling as he poised to pour from a bottle. Don watched his movements like a hawk, trying to guess what he might now be asked to do. He found it remarkable how elegantly his boss's smile provided a facade of warmth, belying the cold blood that he knew ran through his veins, underneath. Don nodded slowly, understanding that he was accepting more than just a drink.

13

Muciripattanam
AD 24

Two of the most memorable things in Jayesh's life had happened on the same day. When the first event took place, he would not have believed that something even more incredible was possible.

'I am proud of what you have done here, Jayesh,' said Abhay. His father's words came as a total surprise. They had been walking through the Muciripattanam market and had just arrived at the new area where Jayesh had built a stand for his family to trade their goods.

It dominated the scene due to its central location, one end looking out over the waterside so as to make it easier to load and unload goods from boats. Jayesh had ensured that their stall was surrounded by the best food sellers on all sides, so the crowds would mill around close by for the whole day. His sister Avani had painted two large signs that adorned either side of the stand with the initial for Muciripattanam in red. She was quite skilled at creating coloured dyes and had made the bright red using the rubia plant; she had even used it to dye their market robes so they would stand out in comparison to other sellers. Each sack of their produce was also branded with the red letter.

The father and son stood side by side, marvelling at what they had achieved. Jayesh did not know what to say in response to Abhay's remark. It had taken them six years to get this far, and not once during that time had his father so ourightly acknowledged his efforts. Only his mother and sister could understand how much this moment meant to him and, as his eyes met Avani's, he could see her tearing up, smiling proudly at him.

'I have to get back to the front to welcome the customers as they arrive,' Jayesh said with a smile, leaving his father to bask in the attention at their stand. As he walked quickly to the entrance, Jayesh vowed to himself that he would expand this market even further so it drew sellers and buyers from all kinds of exotic places. Someday, he resolved, it would be the biggest market in all the lands, or he'd die trying to make it so.

It was already a wonderful sight for all those who could see it and was fast becoming a popular tourist destination. Thanks to Jayesh, in a very short period of time, the market had more than doubled in size. He had introduced a layout: designated areas for different products, dominated by a large and bustling area in the centre for all the spices; surrounding it were sections dedicated to vegetables, livestock, fish, cloth, beads, clothes, vases and trinkets. The stands were no longer mere thatched structures but more permanent and enduring; he had even hung up pictorial signs to indicate what was being sold where.

The scene was bursting with life. Vibrant colours and alluring smells created a wonderfully intoxicating atmosphere. The fresh breeze from the sea blended with the aroma of fresh spices and the sweet juices from the fruits, creating a captivating scent. Jayesh caught sight of a small boy running around and was reminded of his scared younger self being chased around the market on his first trip here. He knew in that moment that he would never back down from a fight again.

Instead of once, the market now operated thrice a week and Jayesh came on all three days, along with his great friend Vikesh, from first light. Just as Jayesh returned to his business partner's side now, another trader found his way to them.

'Good morning, Bharath. I have reserved for you a prime spot right at the front of the pepper merchants today. You will surely be able to sell all your wares for a good price there.' Jayesh knew each trader by name and thoughtfully directed them to the best area to set up their stalls so they could make the maximum profit. The older trader nodded in appreciation and headed in the direction where he had been pointed, knowing that all he had to do was seek out someone in the distinctive red robe Jayesh was wearing, and they would help him set up his stall. As Bharath's cart bumped forward, Vikesh smiled.

'Ha! The first time you told him where to set up his stall, he had laughed in your face. Now he is glad for the advice.'

Jayesh had been trying to organize the market ever since he was fourteen. It took him two years of persistent effort to persuade the majority of traders to set up in specific areas.

'They are all reaping the benefits now, which is what I wished to make them see,' he replied, before being distracted by the arrival of another merchant.

'Good morning, Surjan, let us see what you have brought along today,' Jayesh jumped off the cart he was sitting on and went over to inspect the goods.

He had an encyclopaedic knowledge of fair pricing, and inspired by the impact of his father and his first experience of buying from Vikesh, he would at times offer to buy entire stocks of certain merchants. He would usually opt to do this when he could make a handsome mark-up. He was, however, very selective about the goods he bought, offering to buy only the best of produce at the right price. As a result of this entrepreneurial acumen, Jayesh's family had the largest stall in the market and offered the widest variety of goods and produce; they earned considerable profits and were often the first ones to sell out their entire stocks.

As he concluded the deal with Surjan, he called out to Vikesh. 'Hey! We have agreed on a price for all the pepper on this cart – take it to our stall, will you? And make sure Surjan is paid.'

Vikesh nodded and got to work.

Once all the merchants had arrived and set up, Jayesh allowed himself a small break. There was still much work to be done and a short walk in the cool breeze by the sea, away from the bustle of the market would be enough to refresh him.

As he made his way to the quieter area, he caught sight of some people gathering by the coast and looking out at the sea, gesticulating frantically. Jayesh could neither hear them clearly nor see what they were pointing at, so he carried on with his business without paying them much heed, when a young man rushed over to him.

'Pirates!' he screamed. 'Pirates are coming to raid our market! Help! You have to come and help us!' Jayesh inferred he might be one of the fishermen's sons.

'They won't bother us. Don't worry,' Jayesh replied, trying to calm him down and send him on his way. The local pirates knew better than to land here on market days; there were plenty of men in Muciripattanam to outmuscle them.

No sooner had he gone when Vikesh arrived with three of his men. They looked scared too. 'Look there!' Vikesh pointed.

Jayesh frowned, turned his head and the most spectacular sight stopped him right in his tracks. At first, he could not comprehend what he was seeing. The horizon seemed to be drawing closer to them. As he began to walk towards it, what appeared to be a sailing vessel of a strange sort came into view – it was on a scale he could never have imagined.

The fishermen in Muciripattanam used boats made from carved-out tree trunks, which could hold six or seven men. They loaded them with as many fish as they could carry and return to shore safely, where they would unload before repeating the process. But the vessel Jayesh was now looking at seemed like it could carry all the boats in the land on its deck. It was at least a hundred and twenty feet from stern to bow, and at least thirty feet wide. Jayesh marvelled at how such a vessel could even be built, let alone traverse the seas.

Jayesh could see many men onboard the ship, pointing and gesturing towards the approaching shore. The stern of the ship had an elaborate carving of a woman's torso, with her head held up proudly and her arms extended towards the flanks of the vessel. The intricacy of the carving held his attention for a long while.

'It's an attack!' Vikesh said, pulling him out of his trance. 'See there?' He pointed. Jayesh spotted a flash of light on the deck of the ship. The pale-skinned sailors were putting on metal helmets and brandishing swords that glinted in the sunlight. There was no doubt about their intentions.

'What do we do?' asked Vikesh. The men around them were panic-stricken.

Jayesh was no less terrified. For the second time in his life, his instinct was to run away from the market. He had heard stories from northern travellers of pale-skinned warriors laying waste to whole towns and looting everything they found. He could sense the fear around him. The ship was only a short distance from the shore now.

Even though his heart was thudding against his chest, Jayesh closed his eyes for a moment and asked himself what his father would do. He willed himself to be strong, composed and brave for everyone's sake. Then he spoke. 'Go and get everyone you can! We have nothing to fight with, but we have more men than they do. I will try to communicate with them and see what they're after.' Jayesh said these words with all the courage he could muster – he knew everyone was looking to him for instructions. And he was not ready to lose his town's place of business without a fight.

His friend stared at him worriedly for a moment.

'Go now!' Jayesh urged.

Vikesh gave a small nod and strode purposefully in the direction of the market to warn everyone, gather all the able men and safely evacuate the elderly, women and children. Jayesh stared again at the vessel, fear paralyzing him to the spot.

They lowered a ramp from the ship into the water and, as the first two soldiers splashed into the water, Jayesh found himself striding towards them with his hands held aloft.

14

Vatican City
14 June 2024

'Before you assume your duties, I want to tell you a bit about the history of this esteemed organization we have the good fortune to work for,' Rossi said amicably as he carefully set two crystal glasses on coasters on his desk and took his seat.

'I know you have been somewhat uncomfortable with our methods and certain tasks you have been assigned to carry out. But I'm afraid that as Head of the Santa Alleanza, it will be your responsibility to issue instructions for such tasks to be carried out in the future when the interests of the Church are at stake. I believe it might help you reconcile with the nature of your duty better if you understood the background of the organization – it certainly did for me.'

Rossi paused to take a quick sip from his glass. Don was surprised that his boss had known all this while how much he was opposed to the way in which the Santa Alleanza operated. Had the man planted spies even inside his mind? Rossi seemed terrifyingly all-seeing and one step ahead; Don cleared his throat before answering firmly, 'I appreciate your concern for my moral conflict with the ways of the Santa Alleanza, but I'm well aware of the organization's history.'

The old man smiled.

'Indeed. I know how much time you spend rifling through the archives … but there is much that is hidden. Even the Secret Archives of the Vatican can't tell you the hard truths about the Santa Alleanza that we fight with our lives to protect, for the damage would be too great if they were ever revealed. Of these, you know precious little, Donatello. As the head of this great organization, you will become one of a select few who will be let in on our true history, and I have the pleasure of being your guide on this journey.'

The older gentleman exuded a quiet aura of authority. Despite being in his mid-fifties and quite small-framed, he carried himself like the soldier Don knew he had once been. His white hair was still styled in the buzzcut of his youth and there was not a trace of fat on him – just pure, lean muscle. If the stories were to be believed, even the Pontiff would hesitate to cross him.

'Do you know who founded the organization, for example?' Rossi asked.

Don had read through documents that dated back hundreds of years, but the missing detail had never caught his attention before. Somewhat red-faced, and wondering where this was going, he answered, 'I must admit I do not know the exact origins of the Santa Alleanza …'

'Perhaps that is because when it began, it was not really called the Santa Alleanza,' Rossi began proudly. 'We are far more than just the Secret Police for the Vatican. The organization traces its origins back to AD 312, when it was formed as the Scholae Palatinae by Emperor Constantine himself. Do you know anything about it? Did you happen to find any mention of it in one of your big books from the archives?'

Don felt trapped. 'My apologies, signor, I don't recall that I have,' he replied.

'They were the elite military unit that helped establish Rome as the centre of the Christian faith and enthrone the Pope as the leader of the Church. The Santa Alleanza – in all its past forms – has been the force that has engineered the mechanics of power and wealth in the Church for over 1,500 years now.' Rossi seemed to come alive as he related the history of their grand organization to Don.

'It all started with the First Council of Nicaea called by the Roman Emperor Constantine in AD 325,' he explained. 'At this meeting that took place under His Highness's guidance, a great assembly of Christian bishops debated and elected the gospel stories which would make up the Bible.'

Donatello held in a sigh, slightly annoyed at the unexpected sermon about the Church. 'Yes, signor, I suppose I have read about that. They dismissed other gospels that spoke of Jesus's humanity, but – forgive me for saying this – how is this relevant to the Santa Alleanza?' he asked.

'Ah, my dear fellow, Constantine believed that if he could establish Rome as the centre of the Christian faith and appoint his own nominated leader to serve as the head of this Church, it would be the greatest victory for the Roman empire. He would be able to collect vast riches from around the world, ostensibly for the Church, but then use the gains to further strengthen the Roman empire and fund his own conquests in foreign lands.'

Rossi took another sip from his glass before continuing. 'Constantine knew that he would need a military unit to realize his grand ambitions and thus came about the Scholae Palatinae, who were granted great powers, such as to exile or execute anyone in contradiction to the new Christian doctrine. Even more significantly, he tasked the Scholae Palatinae with establishing the stronghold of this great new Church across the Roman empire by any means necessary. It was then that our motto was born: "With the cross and the sword", and we have lived by it ever since. What we cannot achieve by conventional means outlined in our faith, we achieve by the sword.'

Don was impressed at how Rossi knew this history like the back of his hand and could recite it so promptly and eloquently on demand. If not for the undeniable hint of menace in his voice, Rossi would have made quite the history professor.

'Our mission here is not to practise the teachings of the Christian Church but rather to protect the position of the Vatican as the guard of the Christian faith, and the Pope as its head. We do this at any cost.'

Don found himself repulsed by the version of events Rossi was presenting.

'Pope Steven II and Leo III supported the Church in its mission to establish power over Rome and strengthen its financial position. The Scholae Palatinae, in the meantime, came up with a plan to transfer all administrative power from the Roman empire to the Vatican. The Papacy was thus established as the ultimate authority through a document called "The Donation of Constantine", purportedly written by Emperor Constantine himself. This document was shown to date back to AD 315, though of course, no one could verify this – it was ensured no evidence in support, or to the contrary, existed. It was translated into different languages and sent to missions around the world for bishops to take cognizance. In the 800 years that followed this fabrication, the Vatican has – through the Pope – collected great wealth and possessions for the Church. It has all been done, of course, in the name of God. This was by far the greatest triumph of the Santa Alleanza, and it compelled Pope Leo III to grant the organization independence and power to protect the Pope and the Church.

'By the time scholars around the world caught up with us, first suspecting and then unequivocally stating that our document was fake, the Vatican had already established its dominion. Even if its integrity had been compromised through irrefutable proof, it had already achieved its principal objective and there was nothing to be done.'

Don was a learned man and had, during his long career, seen the worst of mankind. Yet he could not help but feel a deep sense of unease upon being exposed to the knowledge of the sheer scale at which his Church had conducted its 800-year-long deception.

Rossi's voice brought him back to the present.

'When this truth was uncovered, the Church could have suffered catastrophic impacts – it might have lost power and authority, and been forced to repatriate its wealth and assets to the countries and kingdoms to which they belonged. However, the Santa Alleanza demonstrated that it had the ability to dictate the truth itself, whether that entailed discrediting scholars, destroying archaeological evidence, propagating contradictory information in their stead or assassinating the ones who got too close for comfort or stood in the Vatican's way. And once its influence had been established, the organization was given free rein. They could undertake missions without having to go through the Pope.

'That is where we come from, and who we represent today. You see, my dear Donatello, we may, for all intents and purposes, know the Santa Alleanza to report to the Pope and be treated as a special division of the Vatican Police, in truth, we answer to no one as long as our objectives are met. Many popes have found much of what we do to be distasteful and have rather preferred that we remain buried here under the Vatican, out of their sight, carrying on with our little endeavours, utilizing our means quite freely to make sure the Church remains sacrosanct in the eyes of Christians worldwide. And that's fine by us.'

Don interjected, 'But the times have changed, signor – we are no longer at war, we have nothing to prove—'

'We are as much at war now as we have ever been, Donatello, and you better not lose sight of that once you're at the helm of this operation. You will be judged by the yardstick of your predecessors; your ability to act swiftly and decisively in times of crisis will define your tenure. The weight of this historic, 1,700-year legacy will soon rest on your shoulders and you must be willing to go to any lengths to protect this power – by any means necessary.'

He let the implications of his words hang in the air between them. Don understood all too well the judgement Rossi was referring to. But he could not possibly have anticipated the mission Rossi had in store for him.

15

Muciripattanam
AD 24

Jayesh began to gesture as best he could for the men to stop for a moment and lower their swords; he held his empty hands up and shouted, 'Wait there, wait there! We are peaceful people. Look, I have no weapons.'

He knew as soon as the words left his mouth that they could not understand him; they continued shouting instructions to each other, clearly oblivious to his efforts to communicate. There were now eight soldiers wading towards him, swords in hand.

As Jayesh was now the leading figure at the market, he would be called upon to fend off the occasional raid from the Cheras and other local factions. Knowing this and despite his own terror, he knew that the people of Muciripattanam were relying on him to steer them out of this new crisis. He suddenly had an idea. He dashed towards the fishing boats, which were on the ready to make their first trips out to sea that morning, and began to issue instructions to the boatmen. He asked them to take all their boats closer to the large vessel and help the sailors disembark and come to shore. He decided to be the first one to go.

Vikesh arrived on the scene at the same time with a group of eight people carrying makeshift weapons. Jayesh also had instructions for him.

'Put these down, Vikesh; bring food and water for them. Set up by the temple; we must make them feel welcome. We don't need to fight them. Go!'

Vikesh nodded and set the men to work.

With fear in his heart, Jayesh got into the first boat, preparing to greet the soldiers. There was an older man standing by the vessel, shouting instructions.

'Over there,' said Jayesh. 'Towards him.' As they drew closer, Jayesh raised his empty hands again and beckoned the older man to the boat.

'We are peaceful – come and see, there is nothing in this boat; we have food and drink for you and your men.' He knew the man could not understand him, but he gesticulated as best he could.

The soldier gave some instructions, pointing to the ship. Four of the armed men got into the boat with Jayesh, and although they carried swords and shields, they showed no signs of aggression. The remaining four boarded the other boats following Jayesh's. They all rowed to the shore and as the men disembarked, one of the younger men drew his sword and pointed it towards Jayesh. The older man barked a command at him and the sword was promptly withdrawn. Jayesh inferred that the young man's name was Servius.

After the awkward moment, Jayesh quietly led their visitors to the temple, where tables had been laid out to welcome them. Vikesh had arranged for a colourful array of refreshments to be served to the foreigners. Jayesh set about trying to understand as much as he could about them and the vessel they had arrived in.

The men ate heartily, trying every dish that was brought to the table. They clearly enjoyed some more than others, and Jayesh made sure these were quickly replenished for the guests. The market crowd had gathered to witness this unusual spectacle – the exotic visitors and the wondrous ship that had brought them there. The locals were amused; there was uproarious laughter when one of the guests spat out some of the spicy vegetable dish he had unsuspectingly partaken of.

Communication with the sailors was proving very difficult until an elephant came into view. It was walking directly towards them. Elephants were fairly commonplace in the town, often used for clearing land for construction of buildings or bringing down trees to craft boats out of. Although not yet fully grown, the elephant was still much taller than any of the men. The docile creature was being led carefully by a young boy of about twelve, and its passage incited no reaction from the locals. But four of the soldiers leapt up from their chairs. The older man swiftly drew the sword at his side. Jayesh immediately stepped forward and tried to calm them down. Despite all the friendly banter, it became clear to him that this encounter was still a sensitive matter, just moments away from turning violent.

'It's okay, it's okay. It is just an elephant; very gentle animal – look,' he said as he approached the elephant and stroked its trunk softly. He invited the soldiers to join him and take a closer look. One of the soldiers approached hesitantly, extending his arm towards the huge animal. As soon as he made contact and the elephant did not react, the tension was snuffed out. The elder man spoke to one of the men, who produced a purse from a bag on his back. He opened it and brought out a handful of gold coins. The older man pointed at the elephant and then at the coins placed on the table.

'Sell it to them!' said Vikesh. 'They are ready to use their swords on us.'

Jayesh considered his advice and looked at the gold coins on the table.

He had quite the collection of gold coins back home. He used them in the northern territories, where they were commonly traded for securing goods and services. He had learnt all too well what they were worth. Some of the coins he had were sourced from the Greeks, who had tried on many occasions to invade northern India. He presumed these men were also Greek, although he had never actually seen men from these faraway lands.

He shook his head to decline. Vikesh shot him a look. Jayesh knew the true value of the elephant and the coins were not enough. The pale-skinned man produced another handful and added it to the first. Once again, he pointed at the coins and then the elephant. This time he also said something to his men. Servius poised his hand on the hilt of his sword.

No one spoke. Again, Jayesh shook his head. The coins on the table were now enough, but the man had produced them far too quickly and seemed very keen to make a deal. Although he was scared, Jayesh was wary of his eagerness. He sensed an opportunity.

'Take it away,' said Jayesh, gesturing to the boy, who obeyed. Servius stood directly in his way, his sword drawn.

'Just give it to them,' said Vikesh urgently. 'Please.'

Jayesh looked at the older man; the foreigner stared back at him. After a long moment, he reached into his bag with both hands and brought out more than double of what was already on the table. Jayesh pushed past Servius with a broad smile and instinctively embraced the older man. The deal was sealed.

Jayesh saw the size of the purse the men held and looked across at the size of their ship.

'More food, more drinks!' he commanded. As soon as the foreigners had eaten their fill, he took them to the accommodation he had had built for visiting merchants. It was enough for twenty to sleep comfortably and at the sight of it, the elder man – the captain – arranged for all his crew to disembark from the ship and come ashore, now confident that they would be met with friendship and hospitality.

On that first visit, it took Jayesh just two days to empty that heavy purse to fill the ship with his goods. The day before the ship was to set sail, Jayesh sat with the captain – a man whom he now knew was Roman, and was named Quintus – on the beach, looking out at the beautiful coastline of Muciripattanam.

They were both trying to communicate with each other. Quintus produced from his bag a rolled-up scroll, which he proceeded to spread out before them. It was a parchment which, when fully spread, was about seven feet in length and about a foot wide. At first, Jayesh could not work out what the pictures on the parchment meant, but as Quintus began to point at a few of them, he could see that there were ships drawn on the blue water and the light yellow, sand-like colour indicated land. Quintus pointed to the area of the map where they were and looked at Jayesh enquiringly.

'Muciripattanam,' Jayesh said.

'Muziri … pat … err …' Quintus fumbled.

'Mu-ciri-pat-ta-nam,' he repeated very slowly.

'Muziri … Muziris!' said Quintus victoriously and produced a small stick, dipped it into a vial he carried in a pocket, and then slowly reached over the map and carefully wrote the name down. He pointed at the new addition.

'Muziris,' he said.

'Muziris, yes,' repeated Jayesh, looking over at the market, nodding approvingly. And just like that, the name of his town had been updated to suit the Roman tongue. He quite liked the new name and, once again, began to run his eyes across the huge map in front of him. It was the first time – since he had stood on the hillside overlooking the sea as a young boy – that Jayesh began to truly consider the size of the world that lay beyond the horizon.

Quintus pointed at another location on the map. He then pointed at a picture of the sun and carefully tapped on it twenty-five times. If Jayesh was understanding correctly, it was going to take twenty-five days for the ship to sail to their next destination.

Jayesh pointed at himself, then at the ship which sat serenely on the water, ready for its next journey, indicating his wish to travel with them. Quintus raised an eyebrow in answer. For the first time since they met, Jayesh felt that he did not have the upper hand in the negotiation. Quintus continued to stare at him with the hint of a smile playing on his lips. After searching his face for a few moments, Jayesh grew impatient and repeated his gesture – pointing at himself, the ship and then the map. Quintus finally smiled warmly and pulled out his empty purse, placing it on the table between the two men with the neck wide open. He nodded at Jayesh and then the purse, inviting him to partially refill it with his share of the fare.

Jayesh was overjoyed he had struck a deal to travel to the world beyond. He couldn't wait to relate his plans to Vikesh and his family to seek their blessings. There would be a lot of preparations to make, and he couldn't wait to get started.

'Surely, you cannot be serious! Are you actually thinking about going with them?!' Vikesh was shocked. 'How can you just up and leave? The sea is a dangerous place to mess around in and, besides, look at what you have built here! Look at what we have built! Who could ever have imagined our very own Muciripattanam market could look like this? Have you even thought about how I will manage all this on my own? And what about your family? You have more than any man could wish for. Why would you want to leave it all behind? And for what?'

The excitement fluttering inside Jayesh's chest suddenly died down and disappointment filled the void.

'I thought this was such a great opportunity for us – the chance of a lifetime! Don't you see? We will be the first ones from Muciripattanam to ever travel beyond the horizon – farther than our arms could paddle us! Haven't you ever wanted to? Don't you ever wonder what else we might find? Look at their incredible vessel – what if we could learn how to make one of those for ourselves? Imagine the places we could go; the stories and exotic things we could bring back for our townspeople! I will go ahead and find out everything we need to know to realize those dreams.'

'But why must we seek such perilous thrills? You get to travel plenty by cart to other kingdoms – you even venture to the northern parts every now and again. There are plenty of wonders yet to be discovered on this side of the horizon,

I'm sure, and you can get there safely. What more do you need?' Vikesh was adamant.

'Do you not remember how we were treated when we first came here? Now we have the respect of even the Cheras, whose empire is the largest – but tomorrow, if they or the Pandyas chose to attack us, we will have no one to turn to for help. Imagine if we make Muciripattanam into a much bigger trading hub – we could learn to build ships like theirs and make weapons like the ones they have. No one will ever dare to attack us. How proud your father must feel looking down upon you from the heavens, watching you achieve all these great things; imagine if you could do even more! And your mother, she—'

Vikesh looked pained at the mention of his late father.

'I'm sorry, Vikesh, I didn't mean to stir up painful memories for you. I just wanted to make you see that doing this will not only improve business and bring prosperity to the entire town, it'll also improve the lives of our families,' said Jayesh.

'But it's not safe,' Vikesh replied. 'Even small fishing boats get into accidents every now and again. What if something happens to you?'

'I will be fine.' Jayesh concealed his own apprehensions behind a smile, reassuring but determined to have his way. 'Look at their ship – it cannot sink. It managed to carry them just fine all the way to Muciripattanam!' Although he was not without his doubts, he could not let Vikesh see it.

'But I cannot run this market on my own – it's got too big even for the both of us.'

'Vikesh, my dear friend, you have managed the market without me many times when I've had to travel. And every travel I've made has brought us more traders and goods. I think you have proven time and again that you can, in fact, take care of business matters successfully by yourself.' Jayesh struggled to keep the frustration out of his tone, although he understood how hard it must be for his friend to come to terms with the bizarre notion. 'Imagine how many more traders I could invite to buy and sell at our market – the goods they might come bearing! Look at how these pale-skinned visitors have brought along bags of golden coins and are willing to pay double the price for our pepper and spices, and even four times as much as we could ever hope to charge a native for an elephant!' Jayesh put his arm around Vikesh's shoulders. He could still see the shadow of the young boy whom he had met at the market all those years ago in his face; unsure but resilient and hardworking. He was, by nature, a cautious and deliberating businessman, and had proven to be a brilliant and capable partner at every step. Jayesh had no doubt that Muciripattanam would be well looked after in his absence. 'Just trust me,' he said finally.

Vikesh sighed in resignation. 'Alright, but you better be very cautious and vigilant.'

'I promise I will.'

Jayesh told his mother and father, and like Vikesh, they struggled to understand. His father had seen the ship for himself, and aided him in his effort to describe the vessel and the merchants aboard to his mother.

'A trip beyond the horizon on a huge vessel … pale-skinned visitors …' Her expression was confused and fraught with worry. 'What are you two saying? I don't understand – how is this possible?'

Jayesh could sympathize that it all must sound so outlandish to her; so fantastical.

'It is a chance for us to draw foreign traders to our town,' he said, summarizing his plans in a single sentence so his parents could focus on what he was trying to say. A glimmer of light flashed in his father's eyes. He swelled with pride as he considered the implications of his son's statement for a moment.

'Who could have thought it was even possible?' he said. 'Even the mighty Cheras do not trade with merchants who travel from such faraway lands on such grand vessels.'

His mother sobbed and they both spun around to look at her, 'But what if I never see you again, my son?'

Jayesh moved towards her gingerly and wrapped her in his arms. He said tenderly, 'Amma, do you remember when you and I would sit and looked at the waters together, and I would dream about what lay beyond the horizon? All my childhood dreams? I finally have a chance at making all those dreams come true! This is my destiny – it is meant to be.' He dearly wanted his mother's blessing for the journey. 'I will come to you first upon my return and tell you all the stories of what I find on the other side. I will return, I promise. And I know you will pray for my safety. I will keep you both close to my heart and remember all that you have taught me about keeping away from danger,' he said as he hugged her tight. As he released her, she looked at him and then at Abhay, relenting hesitantly with a small nod.

As Jayesh gathered up his clothes in a bag, he pushed a purse of gold coins to its bottom. Slinging it over his shoulder, as he was about to set off, his mother found him and handed him a small package. He recognized it immediately – it was the same package she had been handing him and his brothers every day for as long as he could remember, before they set off for their day in the fields. Only, this one was bigger than usual.

'What will you eat?' she asked worriedly. Jayesh held her close as he didn't want her to see the tears in his eyes. His father was waiting at the door as he left and gave him a stiff embrace – something he had never done before. As the two men separated, he gave his son a quick nod.

As Jayesh set off down the hillside he had known all his life, he heard footsteps running towards him. It was his sister, Avani. 'Wait! Jayesh, wait!' She gave him a handful of colourful flowers tied in a pretty bunch as she struggled to catch her breath.

'To remind you of home,' she said, smiling. He turned to look at the sea, towards the horizon. He could feel his heart racing with excitement at finally getting to see what lay beyond it.

'Take care of Amma and Appa, okay? I must go now. I promise I will return,' he said, turning away from a teary-eyed Avani.

As he finally climbed aboard the Roman ship, nothing could have prepared him for what awaited ahead.

16

Kodungallur
14 June 2024

The nightmare of someone else stealing credit for her wonderful finds was fresh in Harveen's mind when she came down to get breakfast that morning. She dreaded that Professor Prakash might curtail her role at the exact moment she felt ready to present her discovery.

As she was rushing around to grab a bite before heading out, her phone rang. Seeing her mother's name on the screen filled her with guilt.

'I am so sorry, Ma,' she said as soon as she picked up the phone. 'I meant to call you back yesterday, but work got so crazy.' There had been three missed calls and a message.

'I was worried, beta, when you didn't call back,' came the reply. Her mother's voice immediately flooded Harveen's mind with images of her in her sari, fussing over the stove, adding to a pile of hot puris beside it for breakfast.

'We made a huge new discovery. I got really busy transporting everything to the office, putting it away somewhere it could be kept safe, and I just lost track of time,' Harveen replied, rummaging through her cupboards for something to eat. Even after seven years of living here, her apartment still looked like a student flat.

'You're just the same as when you were a girl, always obsessing over something new. Remember when you took a fancy to sports? You were totally obsessed until you beat everyone with your stick jumping – even the boys!'

'Pole vault, Ma. And I won the state championship,' Harveen reminded her.

'Yes, and then you got hooked onto history, travelling here and there to look at old stones and bricks and whatnot. How am I ever going to find you a good husband if you can't learn to sit still and be stable, beta?'

The marriage conversation again! Harveen closed her eyes, willing herself to stay calm.

'Ma, I might be onto something with the history thing, you know? That may just have worked out if this find turns out to be what I think it is,' she said, cleverly steering her unsuspecting mother away from the subject of marriage.

'Does that mean you are close to the big discovery you won't stop going on about?' her mother asked. Harveen could picture the look of surprise on her face.

She knew that her mother wanted nothing more than for her to be successful. After all, they did need all the money they could get back home. This discovery would surely bring in more of that and also make her family take pride in her and her work. If only she could hang on to it tightly enough. She had approached her work with a manic, all-consuming energy in her bid to find Muziris. She had relentlessly pursued contacts around the world, published papers, spoken at events, been involved in all aspects of the design of the museum and personally supervised over fifty digs across southern India. Now, at this key moment, the find that she had dreamed of was in danger of being taken away from her.

'It could be,' she said as she strained her filter coffee into a cup. 'We found a complete house. It was definitely from around the first century – there was a Roman mosaic on the floor and everything ... It matched the descriptions exactly of the period that Pliny the Elder has written about in context of Muziris.'

She found two slices of bread in one of her kitchen drawers. They felt a bit hard but would have to do. She brought them over to her small dining table with her coffee.

'Muziris, eh?' her mother said, even more surprised now. 'You really think you may have found it?' Harveen had told everyone in her life all the stories she knew about the legendary port.

'Well, I can't know for certain if I keep chatting on the phone with you instead of going in to work, Ma,' she teased, desperate to get to the office to plead her case to Prakash. 'I'm just going to finish my breakfast and leave. We'll talk later, okay?'

'Veen, did you get the promotion? Your brother's operation is coming up soon ...' Her mother's voice was soft as it trailed off, but Harveen understood the gravity of the situation.

'We didn't get to discuss it because of all the excitement yesterday. I am sure it will be fine with this latest discovery,' she replied. 'I will keep you posted. Talk later, okay Ma?' They said their goodbyes, and Harveen put her phone face down on the table.

As she slung her bag over her shoulder to leave for the office, her thoughts were with her brother.

Harveen was a little surprised to see Rohan already at the office, looking busy. It appeared as if he had been there for some time; there were papers strewn all over his desk and his computer screen cast a glow on his alert face in the dimly lit room.

'Morning, Rohan, do you want some chai?' Harveen offered, turning on more lights. Although she was not much of a tea drinker herself, she knew that Rohan rarely turned down a cup, and she was eager to make it up to him for her errors from the day before. Rohan ignored her. Harveen went into the kitchen to make two cups of tea, putting one on Rohan's side of the desk.

'Come on, Rohan, I'm really sorry but you know just as well that we did need to save those artifacts and records.' He barely acknowledged that she had spoken but took a sip of the chai and grimaced.

'I forgot that you make bloody awful chai,' he said seriously. They both looked at each other and laughed.

'I really am sorry, Rohan. I shouldn't have put your lives in danger – it was not very responsible of me ...' Harveen said. 'Wait, what is this you are you working on?'

Pushing the horrendous chai away, Rohan replied, 'I couldn't get the image of the script on those sheets out of my head all of last night, which is why I came in early today and began to match it against other known ancient Indian documents from between 50 BC to around AD 50. There isn't a whole lot to go on – certainly nothing written on cloth – so mostly, I have been comparing it to engravings on buildings and tablets. I was pretty certain that it's not just a form of Old Tamil, but a mixture of multiple scripts. Some of the characters look Proto-Dravidian.' He clicked on another window on his screen. 'Also, I found this. It's a translation by Nearchos from around 326 BC. He was an admiral in Alexander's fleet. Here he says that the Indians wrote letters on well-beaten cotton cloth called *karpasika-pata*, which was made from wheat or rice pulp.' He sat back wearing a pleased smile.

'Rohan, you are amazing! I can't believe you have found out all this since last night,' exclaimed Harveen with surprise, though in truth, she was aware that this was exactly the sort of thing that made Rohan the best researcher in the whole department.

'There's more … these letters on the documents – they are out of place. I spent ages looking for them in all the Indian records I could find in the archives, and then it hit me.' He paused to let Harveen scan the document on his screen before opening another image showing a very similar set of symbols. Harveen recognized them immediately.

'Wow, they're Roman numerals?' said Harveen.

Rohan smiled. 'Yep. That's the thing. We didn't see it straightaway because they are all mixed in with Old Tamil.'

Harveen compared both documents again. There was no doubt about it. This was definitely solid evidence that Indians from over two thousand years ago were using the Roman numeral system, possibly to keep some sort of records. Now that she was able to tell the Roman numerals apart from the Old Tamil characters, it was easy to recognize their familiar form. What had confused them was that the numbers were not set out separately but blended into the main text, only sometimes being distinct. The writer had a very compact handwriting, with the letters and numbers all set closely together.

'I have been trying to work it out to get an idea of what the numbers relate to. Some of the numbers are quite large, but without knowing what the text says, it's impossible to interpret them.' Rohan scrolled through the records to show Harveen what he had found.

'This must be linked to Muziris,' said Harveen. 'They had a formidable trade relationship with Rome. There must be other houses or structures like the one we found.'

Just after 11 a.m., Professor Dev Prakash walked into the room. Harveen and Rohan were still ploughing through documents, trying to make sense of their recent discoveries.

Professor Prakash had been the director of the State Archaeology Department for over twenty years. A noted academic, he had authored several books on ancient Indian history. He was small and slight in frame, even more so than Rohan, and though he was over sixty years old, he had a full head of hair, which he always kept short and neatly combed back. He wore thick, black-framed glasses and was quite unassuming in his appearance. Not one for great formalities, he said, 'Harveen, can we talk, please? In my office?' His intonation made it sound like he was asking her for permission, when it was clear to Harveen that she did not have a say in the matter. She was being summoned.

As they arrived in his office, Professor Prakash gestured for Harveen to take a seat. Once he was seated in his own ornate chair across from her, he began, 'I have spoken to the team that was with you at the site yesterday, and I am now even more shocked and disturbed than I had been so far. You showed a total disregard for any safety protocols and seriously endangered the lives of the entire team, including yourself. Even when the building was near collapse, you insisted on staying there with Rohan. How could you have been so negligent? What if someone was seriously hurt, or worse? Can you even begin to explain your actions?'

Harveen had mentally prepared for this meeting all morning but had hardly anticipated being met with such aggression. She felt she had been put in the spot by the usually reserved professor and needed a moment to gather her thoughts. She took a deep breath before presenting her side of the story.

'As soon as I saw the written records, I knew we couldn't leave them behind, sir. We have been looking for something like this for all of the seven years that I have been here and you had just informed me before the dig that we were at risk of our funding being withdrawn entirely. That's all I was thinking about, sir, and I know it wasn't very responsible of me ...' she replied honestly.

'Can you say it was worth risking your life? And Rohan's?'

Harveen hung her head in remorse. She hadn't thought twice in the moment about what she was putting at stake, but now, sitting in front of the professor, she considered for the first time the consequences if someone had died due to her actions. 'No, sir,' she replied meekly.

'You leave me no choice. You are a brilliant and intuitive archaeologist, maybe one of the most talented that I have ever seen in my career, but you clearly cannot be trusted to be in charge in the field unsupervised. As of today, I am bringing in Dr Penny Gupta to head the team. You will be working as her assistant.'

'What, you surely can't be serious, Professor! This is my find – it's my life's work!' Harveen could not believe what she was hearing. She felt her face flush at being treated with such hostility and injustice by her superior.

'I had not finished. This is also going to reflect on your permanent record. Just remember, this is not the first time you have shown a serious lack of sound judgement in the field.'

Harveen felt sobered by the flashback of what had happened at Anapuzha. In her obsessive rush to uncover the find, two members of her team had suffered injuries, and it could have turned out a lot worse.

'I'm sorry, sir. I understand and respect your decision,' she said, defeated. 'But may I request you to please let me continue my work on this find? We might really be on to something big and I have poured so much of my blood, sweat and tears into getting here … please, Professor?'

'That will be Penny's decision, but I will recommend to her that she lets you stay involved. I must warn you, Harveen – any more incidents and it will mean the end of your work here. Do you understand?'

'Yes, sir.'

'Very well, then. You can go back to working with Rohan and the rest of the team on your finds from yesterday. It will be best if you put together a brief for Penny so she can catch up with the goings-on here. She will join us in the next few days and then she can take it from there. Until then, no more digs for you.'

17

Erythraean Sea, near Myos Hormos, Egypt
AD 24

'No! Please, don't!' screamed Jayesh, standing in front of the three Cholas bound in chains. He stood facing the Roman soldiers, but the image of his shackled fellow countrymen was etched in his mind.

'It's just food! They're starving! So what if they took some?'

An awkward standoff ensued between him and the Roman soldiers, who, having seen Jayesh in the company of Captain Quintus, were unsure of how to proceed. For a moment, they stood frozen, neither side willing to yield. Some of the crew and passengers began gathering on the deck of the ship to watch the scene unfold. They parted as Servius made his way through.

'Servius! Thank God,' said Jayesh. 'These men here just took some food, and your men are ready to kill them! Look.' He picked up a partially eaten bucellatum to show Servius what had happened. The Roman gestured for Jayesh to move out of his path with a slightly crooked smile. He sauntered over to the captives cowering before him, and the tension seemed to dissipate as he turned his attention towards the soldiers. He seemed to ask them a question, in response to which one of them pointed to the biscuit in Jayesh's hand.

Jayesh pressed on, glad to have convinced them to let his fellow countrymen go, 'Yes, yes, just food. No reason to come down hard on them, they're just—'

Servius drew his sword and in the blink of an eye, plunged it deep into the stomach of one of the captives. As the man collapsed in a heap on the deck, Servius pulled out his blade.

'No!' exclaimed Jayesh. But before he could say anything more, the other soldiers charged forward to throw the three men tied together overboard to drown. Servius walked past as if nothing had happened.

They were twenty days into their journey to Myos Hormos. Jayesh spent as much time as he could with Captain Quintus, whose quarters on the ship were luxurious in comparison to the rest of the vessel. He constantly asked questions that would enable him to learn about the ship and the Romans' trade practices. Once again, he felt like a small boy, struggling to find his way through the market and trying to understand the ropes of a new kind of trade. He pressed Quintus to tell him the value of each item in relation to the coins, and then how they compared against each other. Although their language was very strange and hence difficult to learn, Jayesh began to understand their system of defining the value of goods and pick up some simple Latin phrases and expressions. He could say 'hello', 'goodbye' and 'thank you', and ask for food and drink. His accent was a source of much amusement, but he was pleased to be making some semblance of progress.

The food was not to his liking, but remembering how his people had mocked the Romans when they had spat out their food, he vowed to eat whatever he was given – except meat. Jayesh and his family had a simple diet abundant in fish and vegetables, and he stuck with the same principle. If a food item was not to his liking, he would eat less of it and make a mental note to avoid it. When he enjoyed something, he would remember the name to be able to eat more of it.

Captain Quintus rarely left his quarters, and the rest of the ship was wholly under Servius's control.

Jayesh had been allocated a small area to sleep in alongside the Roman soldiers. He was not permitted to come and go as he pleased and was only allowed to take the food that was given to him, unless with Quintus.

There were Chola and Pandya prisoners aboard the vessel who were bound in chains and often employed to serve as slaves. When they were not performing tasks by the Romans, they were shackled together and locked up in the cargo hold.

Until today, Jayesh had only managed to exchange a few words with them to understand their plight. And now, he had witnessed three of them being killed for escaping the hold and stealing some food. As he was being escorted back to his modest quarters, he began to regret not heeding Vikesh's advice and just staying home. He resolved to always keep his guard up – he felt like he was being watched, like his life was in danger.

Two days later, a dark sliver appeared on the far horizon, and Jayesh felt relieved to finally see land again. It first appeared as little more than a slightly blurry barrier between the sky and sea, and then as the hours passed, could be seen clearly. His first journey at sea aboard a foreign ship had taught him to regard the Romans with suspicion, given how they were at complete ease with setting foot on a foreign land and taking its natives for slaves, even killing them on a whim if they felt it necessary. He was keen to put some distance between them and himself as soon as they were ashore.

Jayesh pressed Quintus to explain the route they had taken on their journey so far when they sat down that afternoon to eat together. The best that they could do without running into language barriers was to inspect the map. The water between Muciripattanam and where they were now arriving was called the Erythraean Sea, and seemed to span across a vast area. They were then going to navigate a thin finger-wide stretch of water to reach their next stop – Myos Hormos – where the ship would dock. The narrow finger of water represented on the map actually turned out to be a wide gulf easily navigable for the ship. The final destination of their journey was a place called Alexandria, which was a long journey they would cover on land.

Reaching Myos Hormos took another full day and as they approached the port, Jayesh was startled to see the sheer scale of this new world. As they entered the port area, Jayesh could see four vessels that were at least as large as their own already berthed. The port itself was on the western side of the gulf they had sailed through, and they were greeted by a largely barren and featureless landscape until they approached the town of Myos Hormos, which seemed entirely incongruent in relation to its surroundings.

Much like Muciripattanam, the water ran deep all the way into the land, which had a slight inward curve, creating a natural harbour. The local builders had built large wooden structures that extended into the sea, allowing incoming vessels to moor side by side while facing the port. The walkways would facilitate the safe passage of passengers and cargo of varying dimensions on and off the ship. Three of these four bays were presently occupied and their own vessel was carefully navigating its way alongside the fourth. Jayesh saw the dropdown walkway he had seen on the ship when it had arrived in Muciripattanam now being extended out to the wooden piers as a bridge to allow goods to be moved onto the land efficiently.

As they approached the pier, it became plain as day to Jayesh that the many men who had been held in the lower regions of the ship were, in fact, slaves of the Romans. There were about thirty of them lining up, ready to unload goods from the ship in response to the directions two Romans were yelling at them. Some of these men were darker-skinned than Jayesh, while others were paler. It was evident that the Romans were neither short of labour nor money.

No sooner had the vessel been docked than the men on the pier set about securing the walkway lowered from the ship in place and quickly scurried onboard to begin the unloading. There was no long preamble; everyone knew their jobs. As Jayesh tried to slip quietly into the crowds, he was intercepted by Servius and ushered into a large wooden building nearby.

Jayesh had never seen such a structure – it extended for quite some distance in either direction. It was about as tall as a fully grown elephant. The whole of the Muciripattanam market could easily fit inside this building. Quintus was already at the far side of this large room, sitting with four similarly dressed men around a large table.

As Jayesh arrived, Quintus pointed towards him and seemed to offer an introductory description of who he was. The three men seemed satisfied with his explanation and turned their attention back to negotiating the prices of the goods that had arrived. Even without being able to understand exactly what was being said, Jayesh suddenly felt like he was on familiar ground again. He realized that everywhere in the world, goods had value, and the man who could effectively manage supply and pricing in a way that appealed to his buyers could make something of himself. Quintus spread out a parchment and began to run his finger down its length, which told Jayesh that it was an inventory of the goods they had carried on the ship.

Jayesh was particularly interested in the goods that had been sourced from Muciripattanam. When they came in, a very lively discussion ensued and from the way that Quintus was beaming, Jayesh thought he may have made a significant profit on top of even the inflated prices he had paid Jayesh for the goods. The pepper and the elephant from 'Muziris' seemed to be received especially well by the three men and as they were all carried or led off in different directions, the four men stood up, indicating that the negotiations had been concluded.

Overjoyed at the success of his trade, Quintus animatedly invited Jayesh to have a meal with him. He also tried to explain to him that they should stock up on some refreshments and supplies before resuming their journey. Feeling somewhat safer in the company of Quintus over the others, especially now in an unknown land, Jayesh reluctantly agreed. As much as the Port of Myos Hormos was impressive in its scale, Jayesh could not help but miss home. While being in a new place evoked his curiosity, it did not incite a sense of wonder, for Myos Hormos seemed devoid of colour and character. Everyone seemed to be rushing about and the hot, still air was overbearing and uncomfortable.

They ate in what appeared to be a stone house, about double the size of his family home. It appeared to cater exclusively to travellers – all the customers looked vastly different in their mannerisms and attire, though they appeared to be sailors. The air was filled with a mix of tongues unrecognizable to Jayesh. He noticed most people pouring a red liquid down their throats, not unlike the one he saw men onboard drinking, though he had not partaken as none had been offered to him. This was his first real encounter with wine. Quintus insisted that he try it, and while initially repelled by its taste, he grew to enjoy its effects. It seemed to be the drink of choice for most men here and the natural trader instinct in Jayesh began to wonder if he could take this novel spirit back for his own people to enjoy.

Suddenly, he felt conflicted about giving the Romans the slip. Eager to return home, he only just realized that he might never have the opportunity to return to Myos Hormos again, and felt inclined to look around before they set off again. Quintus welcomed his curiosity and with a smile, said, 'Servius will show you around.' Realizing that Servius was being asked to play host, Jayesh shook his head vigorously.

'Not him, please. I want to go by myself,' he struggled to make himself understood. But watching him gesturing wildly, Quintus calmed him by placing a hand on his shoulder and saying something in a soothing tone, perhaps to offer reassurance. Servius greeted his captain before walking towards the door, clearly expecting Jayesh to take cue and follow. His deadpan expression gave way to a sneer, revealing his displeasure at having to escort the Indian around the port.

Jayesh followed him timidly, scared to incite his wrath. Every time the sunrays made the sword hanging at Servius's waist glint, the horrifying image of what he had done on the ship came back to Jayesh.

'Let's go there,' Servius pointed in the direction of another building from which people were rushing in and out. Every building in Myos Hormos seemed to have been designed in a way that would help with the efficient movement of goods. There were many buildings similar to the one Jayesh had watched the negotiations being conducted in, and gawked at the incredible range of goods passing through its gates. There were many exotic animals, spices, plants, vases, cloths, silks, scents, even large stones. Everything seemed to be in transit – on its way to either being loaded or unloaded onto vehicles and vessels of various sizes. There was a huge area where horses, camels and donkeys stood tied to large carts and carriages. It seemed that this was the preferred method by which goods were transported in this region and on just this short tour through the port, Jayesh was already brimming with ideas for the expansion of the market back in Muciripattanam.

He followed Servius down another long street flanked on both sides by warehouses, finally beginning to relax a little.

'Where are we going?' he tried to enquire.

Servius shrugged, indicating that he did not understand. 'This way,' he directed.

After walking for several minutes in silence, they came to a quiet square where three of the warehouses opened. Jayesh was fascinated at the way they had been laid out. Perhaps this was where the goods were unloaded, he thought, given the large amount of space in the open courtyard in. Servius walked into the first warehouse, which was filled with grain, and after a brief walk around it, led them back into the square. He then pointed towards the second warehouse that was being guarded by four Roman soldiers. The men approached Servius and began speaking, appearing as if they all knew each other. The conversation seemed quite convivial, until suddenly, two of the soldiers grabbed Jayesh by his arms. Caught unawares, he looked urgently at Servius, who looked back at him with a curious smile on his face. One of the other two soldiers pulled out his sword and struck Jayesh on the head with its hilt, sending him crashing to the ground.

As he regained consciousness, Jayesh felt hands running over him, tugging and pulling at his clothes. He tried to focus but felt dizzy. He put his hand to where he had been struck on his head and found it was wet. He looked at his hand and saw it was covered in blood. He heard someone shouting, and as he turned his head to look up at the figure standing over him, he saw one of the soldiers holding his purse triumphantly. He tossed it over to Servius.

Jayesh stared at him, shocked at the betrayal, and as their eyes met, he knew that his time had come. He thought of the family he had left behind and the promises he had made to them; Vikesh's warning rang in his ears. He heard Servius shout before another crashing blow landed on his head and everything turned to black.

18

Vatican City
17 June 2024

'There is another matter which I wish to press you on whilst you are here, Don,' said Rossi as he set his empty crystal glass carefully on a coaster.

'There is a kindly priest ministering to a small parish outside of Dublin in Ireland. He's been accused several times over the last few years of inappropriate conduct with young choir boys under his care. There have, of course, been reports now and again over the years, but nothing that justified us taking any … extreme measures against him.'

'Signor, my apologies, but that sounds despicable,' said Don. 'May I ask why we did not intervene?'

'Like I said, there is no real evidence of his misdemeanours and I know him to be a good man. The challenge now is that our hand has been forced; the matter has been brought to the notice of the local police by some troublesome local family.' Rossi showed no emotion, except a hint of disdain at the inconvenience the matter had caused to him.

'Is it a settlement we seek, signor?' Don enquired. While he wasn't very comfortable with the ways of his employer, he was too well-versed in them by now and understood all too well the current pressures the Church was under to fight off such threats to its reputation.

'Perhaps this time, we could try a different approach to the problem – what do you say, Donatello?' Rossi replied with misplaced levity. 'You see, the Church has stood by this Dublin friar for all these years, despite the troubling reports. However, over the last few months, things have taken a turn for the worse.'

Don was well aware that the Church had been plagued by multiple allegations of protecting its own even when the evidence against them was irrefutable. He himself had given out a fair amount of hush money and forced people to sign confidentiality agreements to dust controversial matters under the carpet effectively. Each step had been taken to prevent the lurid details of the monstrous acts these vile men had perpetrated from becoming public.

'Worse in what way, if I may ask, signor?' Don asked.

'It appears that one boy has been frequenting the police station and has made several formal complaints about the abuse the priest has been subjecting him to; his school authorities are in the loop, too. The Vatican routinely denied any wrongdoing and the priest, in his defence, divulged the details of the child's troubled past to the police to discredit him. Apparently, the child comes from a broken home and from a young age, had been in and out of the Irish care system. He had finally been sent to the home of a good Christian woman, a widow, who had taken him to church regularly.'

Don considered this for a moment.

'But signor, I don't understand. It's just some boy – if there is no evidence, the moment will pass and there's little the legal authorities can do about the man. They can't throw him in jail if they don't have anything to—'

'There have been other developments, Donatello. The priest has not been deterred by this brave young boy's actions. He has underestimated his victim, who has apparently found the opportunity to film these graphic scenes of abuse unfolding on the church premises using his mobile phone; several incidents, at that. I am told some of them are very disturbing.' Rossi let the words linger in the air for several moments. 'If these are leaked, this would be the worst time for it. The Pope himself has recently denounced such actions publicly, even going on to say that the Church would no longer tolerate this type of behaviour. While I have set some gears in motion by removing the priest from service temporarily for a period of reflection, I now need you to help me erase the video evidence.'

'Let me try to strike a deal with the aggrieved, signor; maybe they'll agree to delete it all of their own volition,' Don offered.

'And now, why would they do that, Donatello? My sources tell me that the boy has shown the videos to his foster mother, but no one else, as far as we know. His mother, being a devout Christian, attempted to confront the priest and demanded that he confess to his sins in front of the police and spare them the ordeal of testifying in court and revealing the videos. Her attempts have yielded no results so far, but time is running out for us to prevent significant damage to the reputation of the Church. What do you think of sending Vincenzo to deal with the matter?'

'Not Vincenzo, signor. Please, it's just a child and his mother, and they've already been through enough,' said Don. The mention of Vincenzo's name made a shudder run down Don's spine, anticipating the gruesome outcome of involving him.

Vincenzo was one of Rossi's most trusted assassins. Like Don, he had been a military man. While his service records listed several acts of great bravery, they also contained several other references to his brutality. He had been dishonourably discharged from the military before the Santa Alleanza took him into its fold. He had been involved in an incident where an automatic weapon had been deployed amidst civilians in Bosnia, resulting in the massacre of thirteen innocents. It was blamed on a weapon malfunction, and Rossi personally intervened to bring him to the Santa Alleanza. He had even been accused of other war crimes on his service record, but no formal investigations had been conducted into these matters.

Rossi scowled. 'This is your first lesson in becoming Head, Don. The video evidence could be catastrophic for us; it needs to be nipped in the bud before things get out of hand. If severe measures need to be taken, you cannot be afraid to take them for the protection of the Church. It is your primary duty, Donatello.'

'But … he'll kill them … that's all he knows, signor. Surely, there must be another way!' The urgency in Don's voice was reflective of his inner turmoil at the unbelievably cruel suggestion of killing a helpless, wounded victim. A child. He knew his suggestion would be ignored and Rossi's will would prevail, but he had to try.

'The evidence is irrefutable and we must stop it by any means necessary. If history has taught us anything, it is that innocents will sometimes have to be sacrificed for the greater good.'

Don's resolve to succeed Rossi was weakening. While he knew that change could only come if he was the leader of the Santa Alleanza, he wasn't certain he could stand by while an innocent boy was killed, just because he was in line to bag the position.

He sighed resignedly.

'Very well, then. Let's call him together now, shall we?' Rossi said slowly and deliberately, the triumph clear in his voice. 'I want you to monitor everything closely at every stage.' With every word that came out of Rossi's mouth while instructing Vincenzo to commit the atrocity, Don felt pained as if his soul was being wrenched out of his body.

19

Alexandria, Egypt
AD 24

Jayesh's head throbbed. He could not remember what had happened, waking up confused and sore, unaware of where he was. He struggled to see; the room was dark and all he could hear were groans of other people. He felt claustrophobic and looked up at the grille in the roof through which daylight reluctantly creeped in. As his senses began to recover, he was hit by an overwhelming smell of human faeces. The hard floor below him felt cold and damp, and he found himself sitting with his back against a stone wall. He realized his hands were chained up on either side of his head and was seized with panic. The room appeared to be rectangular, about twenty feet in length and ten feet wide, and he guessed it was just tall enough for a man to stand.

He could see several shadows lining the walls of the room; perhaps ten or twelve others were held there with him. He suddenly heard someone shouting near the grille. The handcuffs dug deeper into his wrists the more he tried to free himself from them. The clanging of his shackles had perhaps drawn the attention of his captors. The terror within him made his heart pound harder against his chest and he breathed with great difficulty. He did not want to die so far from his home.

There was more shouting from above. The voice seemed familiar – or was he imagining it? Quintus. 'Help! Help me! Somebody let me out!' Jayesh screamed. Suddenly, the grille was flung open and a ladder was lowered into the dungeon. As he tried to make towards it, he was pulled back by his chains and they cut into his flesh. He winced in pain and noticed someone was climbing down the ladder into the room. Scared for his life, he cowered as a Roman soldier approached him, now certain that Servius or one of the other men had come to finish him off. Unexpectedly, in response to the persistent shouting from above, the soldier roughly removed the manacles from around Jayesh's wrists and dragged him into the pool of light at the centre of the room, pushing his face upwards. Jayesh squinted as his eyes adjusted to the bright daylight and saw a figure obscuring the rays of the sun from hitting him directly. Before he knew it, he was being shoved up the ladder.

His limbs shook as he struggled to maintain his grip and balance, and as he approached the surface, rough hands hauled him out and flung him into the daylight. He instinctively shielded his eyes with his hands. Bracing himself for the killing blow, he tried to straighten up so he could at least try to put up a fight.

'Jayesh?' said a calm voice. He slowly removed his hand, surprised at the mention of his name and squinted. Quintus's weathered face came into view. He was looking worriedly at him. As his eyes adjusted to the light, Jayesh could hardly believe it and nearly collapsed. His fall was broken by Quintus's arms gathering him in a warm embrace. Jayesh clung to the old man and felt a flood of relief wash over him, breaking out into sobs. Perhaps he was going survive after all.

He suddenly became aware of Servius standing behind Quintus, looking at him venomously, and the fear for his life returned.

As they slowly walked towards their place of rest for the night, Jayesh tried to communicate with Quintus alone, but Servius always seemed to be in close attendance. The wound on Jayesh's head was still throbbing with pain and there was a deep cut above his eye that had not stopped bleeding. He felt weak and terrified of being left alone in the company of Servius, knowing he was in no position to defend himself.

As Jayesh sat down across the table from Quintus and Servius that evening for dinner, Servius pushed his stolen purse towards him slowly. Quintus smiled. Jayesh could not work out what was happening and had no language to try and understand. He quietly accepted the purse, looking down at it before closing his palm around it. He looked up to see Quintus still smiling at him.

After the meal, Quintus led Jayesh by the hand towards the carts and carriages standing in wait for them to begin the final leg of their journey. He saw all the cargo had been loaded and their co-passengers stood waiting to depart. Jayesh marvelled at the sheer length of the caravan – the donkey- and horse-driven coaches seemed to stretch on for miles on end. They were comprised of goods and over a hundred men not only from their ship, but from multiple others, and were distributed across thirty to forty big carts. It was difficult for Jayesh to envisage the sheer volume of goods that passed through Myos Hormos every day.

Quintus gestured for Jayesh to climb aboard his carriage before him, and followed suit, but before Servius could get in behind him, he held up his hand and told him not to. There was a brief debate between the two men, but it was clear that Quintus would have the last word. Servius reluctantly acquiesced, shooting a glare at Jayesh before leaving. As he watched him walk away, Jayesh wondered how long it would be before he could return home to his family – if ever. The possibility of not surviving this journey had suddenly become a serious consideration.

The road towards the great city of Alexandria in Egypt was mostly straight and a large part of it, Jayesh spent fearing for his life. Despite having Quintus on his side, he remained deeply distrustful of everyone around him. The horrors of Myos Hormos repeatedly flashed in his mind and he felt intimidated at the prospect of going into an even bigger city brimming with strangers who could throw him into an underground cell on a whim. Maybe this time, he would not even be found again.

In his despair, Jayesh found solace only in the memory of his family. He reminded himself of his motivations – the pride of his father at finding out that his Muciripattanam pepper had earned renown in Alexandria, the relief of his mother upon his return, the joy of his sister having her sole companion back. He felt himself ease up around Quintus and reminded himself that theirs was a strategic relationship – he had the goods and they had the money to pay for them many times over.

The wound above his eye pulsated; a constant reminder of his narrow escape from certain death.

By the time they arrived in the great city of Alexandria, Jayesh had decided his life was worth a lot more to his family and the pain of being apart from them was becoming too much to bear in exchange for a half-cooked deal with the Romans. Without learning their language, he didn't stand a chance. The market back in Muciripattanam was already thriving and he wasn't entirely convinced anymore if his ambitious plans were worth staking his life for. He prepared to return empty-handed, drowned in gloom but overcome by a longing to get back home.

20

Kodungallur
17 June 2024

'Hello, everyone! It's so good to meet you all, finally. I am Penny Gupta.' Professor Prakash's archaeology and linguistics expert had flown in from Mumbai to officially take over the project. Harveen knew that Dr Gupta was a world-renowned expert in ancient languages; she had read her research on the subject and knew that she was a very well-respected scholar and her work was often used as reference material within the department. Harveen had read her works on ancient Arabic, as well as many of the old Indian languages, including Sanskrit, Tamil and the Dravidian languages, some of it using the latest in AI. But in person, she was nothing like Harveen had expected. She appeared to be in her early thirties, fresh-faced and immaculate in her appearance. She was, perhaps, five-foot-five; wore heels and a smart shirt with light-coloured trousers. Her hair was styled in a neat bob, with not a tendril out of place. When she had first walked into the room, Harveen had instinctively looked down at her own faded jeans and dirty walking trainers encrusted with mud, and wished she had made more of an effort this morning.

'This is Harveen, and this is Rohan,' said Professor Prakash as Dr Gupta introduced herself with a firm handshake.

'Congratulations on the find – I am really excited to work with you both on it. Where can I set up my laptop?' Her voice was firm yet mellifluous; her movements precise and contained.

Rohan seemed to be in a rush to show her to the desk adjacent to his own. Dr Gupta put down her oversized bag and took in her surroundings. The inside of the building had not yet been renovated and still resembled the old post office that it had housed not very long ago. Their desks were the only modern items and looked rather out of place. Cables was strewn about in the spaces between their desks and clipped around the skirting. The ceiling fans creaked and groaned, doing little to cool the room in the morning heat. The inadequacies of the office infrastructure hadn't really bothered Harveen until now. Dr Gupta made no comment, her expression perfectly neutral.

'Okay then, shall we get started? I am going to need some good coffee – could you please tell me where I can get some? Also, I have already had a look at the documents that you had sent over and I have a few fascinating details I'd like to share about them with you; thank you for sending them to me. But before I can do that, I would like to examine the original documents as well, just to corroborate everything. How soon do you think we could arrange for that?' Dr Gupta had decided to immediately spring into action; she had whisked her laptop from her bag and was fiddling with the charging cable, while scanning the desks for somewhere to plug it in. She was the picture of professionalism and her focus and enthusiasm were contagious.

'Oh, the plug points are here, under the desk,' indicated Rohan helpfully. 'Here, let me get that for you,' he extended his hand to take the cord and kneeled under the desk to plug it in.

'Dr Gupta, we all just drink filter coffee here, I'm afraid. I'm no connoisseur myself, but I can definitely tell you where to get it,' explained Harveen, feeling a little intimidated by her while taking care to appear respectful, warm and welcoming.

'I can get you some of the Italian coffee I drink tomorrow,' said Professor Prakash. 'Could you make do with filter today or would you prefer chai?'

Harveen was a bit taken aback by Professor Prakash's unusual offer – he had never offered to bring in something like that for them or anyone else.

'I'll just have the filter today, no problem, Professor. Thanks for your offer, I might actually take you up on that. If you could point me to the kitchen, I can make us all some coffee and then let's start!' As Harveen walked her over to the kitchen, she noticed Dr Gupta's confident stride in her smart attire and high heels, and how Professor Prakash and Rohan's eyes followed her as she walked.

Dr Gupta was soon all set up with her laptop opened before her. She took an A4-sized pad out of her bag and set it precisely alongside her laptop, flipping it open to a page already filled with notes. 'What's the Wi-Fi code, please?'

'Here, let me put it in for you,' said Rohan, reaching over her laptop to type in the code. He had been a little distant from Harveen since the expedition fiasco and she found herself feeling a little jealous of the attention he was showering on Dr Gupta.

'Thanks, Rohan,' said Dr Gupta. 'So what I found was that the language that is mainly used in these documents is Old Tamil – which is surprising.'

'In what way, Dr Gupta?' asked Harveen.

'Well, the primary languages spoken in southern India during this period were variants of what are now called Dravidian languages. There were dozens, possibly even hundreds, of regional variants. Tamil was certainly spoken in this region at the time, but until your discovery, there has actually been no evidence of it written out like this,' she conveyed her admiration subtly but sincerely, genuinely impressed.

'Harveen tells me nothing of this sort – the objects and this document you speak of – has ever been found before this. Would you say that's accurate, Dr Gupta?' asked Professor Prakash.

Penny nodded. 'Yes, Professor. In fact, the document itself is very special because until now, we have found no physical evidence of Indians writing on cotton cloth. Sure, some historical documents have made references to it on occasion, particularly those by the Romans. But this is unimaginable – your team has managed to find a significant quantity of that cotton cloth, also known as the karpasika-pata, in near-perfect condition. We already know that ancient Indians would write on this paper using *massi*, which literally translates to 'crushed' – perhaps a type of ink made out of nuts and myrobalan – although I'll only be able to say for sure once the tests come back in a few days. Then we'll have a confirmation. I contacted a few fellow researchers of repute and they confirmed that no one has ever found even one sheet of this material intact, let alone with legible print and this well-preserved. What you have found is one of the most significant written records ever to be found from this period of history.'

Harveen was moved by Dr Gupta's acknowledgement, tearing up. She looked at Professor Prakash, who was smiling. She thought about how Dr Penny Gupta might be the woman from her nightmare, growing anxious at the idea of sitting in the audience while she revealed these amazing discoveries to the world. She snapped back to reality at the sound of Penny's voice.

'The language is worth special note, too. We have never come across it before – not this particular strain of it anyway,' Penny continued.

'Do you mean Tamil?' Harveen enquired, unsure of her meaning.

'Yes, but also … not quite. It seems to work just as well in translation, though, since it is similar in structure to other Old Tamil that we have come across.'

'Wait, so are you saying you know what the script says, Dr Gupta?' Harveen couldn't help but give into the excitement.

'Yes, I do. Here, let me show you.' Harveen and Rohan hunched over Dr Gupta's laptop as she opened multiple images of various documents and explained the rationale behind her conclusion that these were transaction records.

'This line here is a transaction for pepper. Here is another one – the numbers are significant. This one is for silk. This one for animals, not specifically identified. This here is for boxes of nard. What is fascinating are the volumes. This one mentions a hundred tonnes of pepper, for example, and there are many more like it. What's even more astonishing is that all the numbers are Roman numerals – I'm not sure how that could have come to be. Frankly, we have never seen anything like it. I can't wait to see the originals for myself – could we go and take a look? Where are they?'

'I could take you to the records room right away if you want, Dr Gupta?' Harveen offered.

She smiled warmly. 'Perfect, thank you. That would be great. And please call me Penny.' As Harveen led the way, she could feel her dream slipping away.

21

Alexandria
AD 24

Quintus arranged for Jayesh to return to Muciripattanam via Myos Hormos and informed him that he would have to stay in Alexandria for at least four days before his transport was ready.

Jayesh had explored a very small portion of the magnificent city, owing to his apprehensions about moving around without a trusted escort. Each time he ventured anywhere, he would spot a soldier who would remind him of Servius, and he would find himself scurrying away to hide in his modest lodgings, scared and alone.

The city of Alexandria seemed to have more people in it than the whole of India. They all lived within the great city walls and at every turn, there was a wondrous sight to behold. There were areas where all seemed to be welcome; others which seemed to be only for the Romans.

The most incredible experience – one that would also prove to be the most beneficial for Jayesh – was visiting the city library. The building was located in the Royal Quarter and, in Jayesh's view, was the most impressive edifice within the city walls. Its front was dominated by two imposing marble columns that framed the doorway. This doorway opened into a grand room enclosed by large columns and with tables spread out, where many people sat reading in silence. Some had scrolls opened out in front of them, while others at a distance were engaged in small groups, having lively discussions.

Jayesh suddenly caught sight of a brown-skinned man at one of the tables and his heart stopped. The man was very distinct-looking – nearly bald, with just a small patch of black hair above each ear, he seemed to belong to the same region as Jayesh. In the moment that their eyes met, they shared a smile and Jayesh felt flooded by a sense of relief. He wouldn't dare encroach on his privacy but when he noticed that the man was observing him as he looked around the great library, he decided to try and speak with him.

'Hello, my brother! Can you understand me?' Jayesh asked in his native language.

'Very well, brother!' the man replied enthusiastically and stood up to hug Jayesh. 'I have not heard our mother tongue in more than a year. It is so good to see a fellow Indian here in this land brimming with strangers. My name is Nannan. And yours?'

'Jayesh. I am surprised to see you too, brother – I thought I was the only Indian in Alexandria! How did you come to be here?'

'That is a long story, my brother. Come, let's talk over a meal – I will gladly tell you my story and you can tell me yours.' Nannan proceeded to roll up the scroll he was reading. 'Let me just return this first.'

The two men set off from the library – Nannan as the guide with Jayesh in tow – on a quick tour of the city. Nannan described how people of all nations seemed to be drawn to the bustling burg and many had even made their homes here. With the growing population came opportunities for business, which seemed to flourish everywhere Jayesh turned.

Nannan took them to an area where every street corner had open food stalls selling freshly made delicacies from around the world. These thermopolia, or cook-shops, had special tables with inset jars containing food ready to sell. The bigger sellers even had colourful pictorial signs indicating the type of wares on sale. Some stalls had groups of people queuing up in front of them, waiting to be served. The delicious aromas of cooked meats, fish, lentils and grilled vegetables filled the air, mingling with the bustling sounds of the thriving city.

'Let me buy you something, brother,' said Nannan. 'The food here will remind you of home.'

'That is very generous of you, I'll be very grateful. I don't eat any meat; might we find something here for me?' replied Jayesh as Nannan left him to hustle his way through the crowd. When he returned with two plates piled high with rice and lentils, Jayesh was overjoyed. Nannan directed them to a low wall in front of a house a little away from the bustle of the market, where they could sit and eat in peace. Jayesh had not realized how hungry he was until he took the plate in his hand.

'Thank you. I'm still curious, how did a fellow Indian find himself in the Library of Alexandria?' Jayesh egged him on to tell his story.

Nannan sighed and responded, 'Let's eat, my brother. I'll let you enjoy your food for now. It is a sad story, I'm afraid.'

As the men finished their meal, Nannan began, 'I grew up in North India. My mother had been employed in the service of a mighty king as his personal cook for many years and after she became too old to work, he kindly took me into his service. I worked for him as a notary, making records of our gains and ensuring that taxes were paid from the lands we controlled. Our kingdom had fought many wars until we were finally defeated by the Egyptians, who took many prisoners from among our people, including myself. I was brought to Alexandria as a slave and put to work in the Horrea. Do you know that Alexandria provides grain for the whole of the Roman empire, so they never have enough slaves to man these huge warehouses? It was only by good fortune that they discovered I was literate; I'd picked up some Egyptian and Roman and had been learning in secret. When my masters came to know, I was brought to the great library to help translate works of Sanskrit poetry. This happened three years ago.' They were silent for a few moments after that.

'The library looked magnificent! I had no idea that such a place could exist,' Jayesh said, trying to put Nannan at ease again.

'It was originally built three hundred years ago by a politician called Demetrius of Phaleon, who worked for King Ptolemy I of Egypt. It was meant to be a research centre of sorts for thinkers, an academy of learning, as well as a repository of writing. It contains either the original or a copy of every important piece of writing in the world. Works of science, mathematics, poetry, philosophy and even plays.' Nannan had to explain to Jayesh what some of these forms of writing were.

'You must really enjoy working there,' Jayesh mused.

'It is most rewarding. In that single building, there are over five hundred thousand different scrolls, all carefully indexed. There are over one hundred and fifty books in the library that catalogue where particular scrolls can be found to make it easy for visitors to navigate their way around the place. I have now become proficient enough in both Latin and Egyptian, so I can do some translation work myself.' Nannan paused before he said with the pain imminent in his voice, 'But I've begun feeling trapped here now … it's been too long, and I yearn to return home.'

Nannan noticed how Jayesh had wiped his plate clean. He laughed, welcoming the distraction, 'The food was that good, eh? It has Indian spices in it! It always takes me back …'

Jayesh's face was flushed and he laughed along with Nannan. 'It really is wonderful! Thank you, I too was transported back home for a moment and couldn't help but lap it all up greedily.' As the two men piped down, now steeped in nostalgia and homesick, an idea formed in Jayesh's mind. 'Do you know how you're getting home? Or when?' he asked.

'I have not got that far yet, brother. The wounds of my separation are still too fresh for me to begin bandaging them. Come, let us head back, tell me – what's your story?' As they walked back to the library, Jayesh began to relate the tale of his own journey. Nannan was fascinated by the idea of expanding trade to such a scale in their homeland; the very notion of having a port like Myos Hormos in Muciripattanam!

'They have arranged a transport for me that leaves from the South Gate at first light tomorrow. Why don't you come with me? I'm sure I can arrange for something for you too,' Jayesh offered.

'What will I do there, brother?' He laughed. 'I am a librarian!'

'You are my friend and you are such a learned man – there is so much you can do to help develop Muciripattanam. You will love it there! But should you still wish to return to the north, I will also be able to arrange safe passage for you. I have many friends there.'

'I do long to return to my home in the north …' Nannan admitted as they approached the library.

There was a commotion outside – two Roman soldiers were talking to the guards and bystanders. One of them spotted Jayesh and pointed at him, 'There! There he is!' The two soldiers ran towards him. Thinking Servius had come seeking revenge again, Jayesh spun around and ran. Two more soldiers were coming towards him from the other way. There was no escape.

22

The Vatican
5 July 2024

Rossi smiled condescendingly. Sofia had just confirmed that the case in Dublin had been 'handled' by Vincenzo. She had checked with local police and press as well and there were no loose ends. Don fought to keep his expression neutral as rage swelled inside him.

'You see, Don, to become an exemplary leader for the Santa Alleanza, you need to follow in the footsteps of the greats and uphold the traditions of our organization.'

Don said nothing but refused to meet Rossi's eye, repulsed by his suggestion.

'Even though you are the new head of the Santa Alleanza, I hope you can indulge me by allowing me to keep this office for a few more months?' Rossi was pacing around the ornate space as he said this; sometimes he did so whilst speaking. From his tone, it was clear that his question was rhetorical. He occasionally swirled around the rich amber whisky in the heavy crystal tumbler he held. A glass of water sat untouched on the coaster in front of Don.

'Please, signor. It is your office until you step away from your duties.' The unexpected warmth in Don's voice seemed to delight the older man.

'Excellent, excellent! You will certainly be at liberty to redecorate it as you wish once it is yours. I still remember the look on your face when you first entered this room – I expect that, perhaps, my tastes may be different from your own?'

'Forgive me for my candour, signor, but I am not as concerned with the office decor as I am with performing my duties to the best of my abilities. I would be quite happy to let it stay in the state I inherit it from you.'

'My dear boy,' responded Rossi jovially, 'it will all look so drab without my beloved possessions decorating it, you will never feel like returning to it day after day. Trust me – infusing this space with something that brings you joy will really help ground you and reconcile with the difficult decisions you will be bound to make as Head. Hang up a family photo, or some art or artefact, won't you? Just as reminders for yourself of why you do what you must do.'

'As always, signor, I will do as you advise.'

'Good,' said Rossi, 'so I trust that you also see now that taking the more decisive path in Dublin was indeed the right choice?'

No, killing off the helpless victim – an innocent child – was not the right choice, thought Don.

'I think you did what you felt was the right thing to do, signor,' he replied diplomatically.

Rossi stared directly at Don as he said, 'Right, so were you in a similar situation, you would not send one of your men to handle the situation as Vincenzo was asked to?' Rossi slowly sat down, his attention still fixed on his protégé. Don feared that he was becoming more like Rossi with each mission. Being forced to instruct Vincenzo to kill the boy and his mother had felt like the final step, but there was no denying that he had done it.

'I have ordered for assassinations in difficult circumstances before, signor, and I would not hesitate to do it again if it is the best solution to our problem.'

'Hmm … well, as I said before, each Head has free rein to operate by his own devices, but the ultimate goal is to honour our vow not only to protect this Church, but also its secrets. There is a reason you have been chosen to succeed me – I am sure that you will bring pride to the Santa Alleanza.'

Don looked down at his hands pensively. They were tied, after all, and stained in blood. He was not blameless; he had also taken lives. Breathing deeply, he felt an acceptance of his situation begin to set in – he had acted as Rossi's puppet, even if not of his volition. He was jolted back into the present by Rossi's voice.

'The Pontiff has asked me to stay on – purely in an advisory capacity – to help you through your first few months. All I'd be doing is attending a monthly meeting in his office and being available to offer you advice should you need it, Donatello. Of course, if you don't want me to be in your way, I will turn it down. Tell me, what do you think?'

Don knew what it meant to keep Rossi involved – he would be compelled to continue with his methods. But both his tone and the reference to the Holy Father were clear indications that the decision had already been made; this was just another test.

'I think you should accept it, signor. It would be my privilege to have you as my advisor,' said Don. Rossi seemed delighted with his answer and visibly relaxed.

'Your wisdom and clarity are admirable, Donatello, I knew I made the right choice. I will be merely that hand on your shoulder to help you ensure that you uphold the values of the Santa Alleanza at all times. Now, shall we move on to business?' Rossi brought out two copies of the weekly report that he received from other units of the organization. He had been sharing these with Don for several months now, so he was very familiar with them. Don also received these reports electronically each week but Rossi still insisted on working together through the printed paper copies. It was something else that annoyed Don.

The report was a compilation of all the data submitted from around the world, mostly detailing indiscretions of the Church's ministers or accusations that warranted the attention of the Head of the Santa Alleanza. It was then up to them to decide whether they should investigate any incidents further, and deploy personnel accordingly. Don had been doing this for several weeks now and so far, Rossi had largely been in agreement with him on his decisions.

They ran through each report quickly. The penultimate report appeared to Don as just another mundane summary of a historical dig; this time in India. A brief scan through it revealed that something that had been uncovered in southern India. Ancient trading records of some merchant, it seemed. The report had a red dot in the top corner, which meant that something in its contents had triggered alarm in their computer systems. This happened often and was usually easily dismissed.

'This seems innocuous enough – shall we move onto the next one, signor?' He looked up and saw that Dino Rossi's face was clouded with concern. His brow was furrowed and he seemed undecided on what to do next. After a few moments, he abruptly reached over to the phone on his desk and dialled a number.

'Sofia, it's Dino. How are you? Till when are you in the office?'

Don immediately recognized the silky voice of the Head of the Vatican Secret Archives when she replied on the speakerphone.

'I am on my way to you with Don. Can you pull up all of the records pertaining to The Brother, and especially his time in India?' Rossi continued. 'Great, thanks, Miss. We will see you shortly. Oh, and please ask Vincenzo to meet us there, too. We will need his services.'

23

Alexandria
AD 24

Without glancing back, Jayesh ran towards a small alley. If he could get there in time, maybe he could find a place to hide from the soldiers. As he turned for a moment to take stock of his situation, he collided into an old lady who had been walking hurriedly in his direction. They both crashed to the ground.

Jayesh was hauled up by one of the Roman soldiers and by the time he was on his feet, the other three were close on his heels too. One of them was shouting.

Jayesh couldn't tell what they were saying, but they appeared to be confused and were looking around anxiously. Perhaps Servius was close by. The soldier continued to shout at Jayesh as if asking a question, but he could not understand what he was saying.

'There!' another one said, pointing. The four soldiers ran in that direction, releasing Jayesh, who was relieved. He looked towards where the soldiers were running and was shocked to see Nannan darting into a building with the armed men hot on his trail.

24

Kodungallur
26 June 2024

'We have found trading records from the Port of Muziris!' said Dr Gupta triumphantly, as she came back into the office. It was exactly what Harveen was desperately hoping to hear. Muziris had been a huge trading port in southern India during the first century, referenced in many documents and generally thought to have been one of the most important trading hubs in the world at the time. But it had dropped off the radar without a trace over the course of time, somehow, until now. If they had found something that connected modern-day Kodungallur with Muziris, it would elevate the site to great historical importance. All of Harveen's ambition was being realized in this one find that was no longer her own.

The heat in the office had become oppressive, yet Dr Gupta looked exactly as she had that morning: composed and polished. Harveen and Rohan stared at her. She held their gazes intently. When she spoke, she did so in her usual precise and measured tone, but Harveen could sense the excitement in her voice. 'There are very strong references to

Muziris in the documents. I also saw some really interesting additional detail in the physical records that I can show you on the screen here.' She got busy setting up her laptop on her desk. She looked at her empty coffee mug and grunted her disapproval. 'Let me quickly get another coffee and then let's get right to it.'

She scooped up her mug and strode off towards the kitchen. There was a certain magnetism to her and Harveen could not help but notice the effect she had on Rohan and the others in the office. She returned with her coffee and opened her laptop, beckoning Rohan and Harveen to come look at her screen.

'There is no doubt in my mind that these are a combination of trading records and receipts of transactions completed in Muziris with Roman, Chinese and Egyptian merchants, as well as Indian traders.' Dr Gupta punctuated her narrative with specific instances from the various documents, translating them as she went.

'This letter "M" is on many of the documents. It has no meaning by itself and appears to be a symbol. Its recurrence in this context must symbolize the city of Muziris. If you look at this record here, it has Muziris written in full with the same stylized M.'

'This is amazing, Dr Gupta! Are these all just trading records, you think?' asked Harveen.

'For the most part, although it is clear that there are other things in here, too. I took note of a few right here, let me show you.' Dr Gupta pulled out a slim notebook from her jacket pocket and flicked through the pages.

'For example, this record shows either the purchase of a building or perhaps an order to build one. As you can see, it is quite an amount and the description shows that it is not a type of building that we expect to see in India during the period. A significant number of records indicate stone being purchased, and also, this here appears to be a reference to marble.'

'Interesting – although we did not actually find any remains in the area which used any remarkable amount of marble or stone,' said Harveen. 'Does it say where it was being sourced from?'

'Only the name of the port is mentioned: Myos Hormos,' Dr Gupta showed her the relevant bit of the document.

'That was the main port in Egypt used to ship goods from Rome to Asia! Dr Gupta, were there any maps or routes – or any other clues, really – that could help us pinpoint the locations of any of these places?'

Penny shook her head. 'I'm afraid not so far. I have only looked at a handful of the documents. The first priority was to verify the authenticity of the find and then get a basic understanding of its contents. Over the next few weeks, I will be working through the documents carefully and putting down detailed records of everything I'm able to decipher.'

'Would you venture a guess as to what period these were written in?' Rohan asked; he had been scribbling down notes while Dr Gupta had been speaking.

'There are some dates in the document itself, which is very useful. Most of the ones I have seen are from between AD 66–69, although there are some with different dates – one going as far back as AD 55. We will have a more complete range of dates once I get to the cataloguing. I've requisitioned additional resources from the university as there are just so many records to get through,' Penny responded.

'Did anything else catch your eye, Dr Gupta? Anything unusual?' asked Harveen.

Penny suddenly glanced at her watch. 'Oh, I'm so sorry, I have to rush into a meeting with Professor Prakash. We're trying to see how I can best present this amazing find. Let's pick up our discussions tomorrow. In the meantime, I would like you both to go through the records too and see if we can make some links between Muziris and any present-day sites.'

Harveen felt a surge of anger at being excluded from the presentation discussions. 'Umm … perhaps we could make the presentation together?' she offered a little nervously.

Penny seemed a little taken aback by her suggestion and looked her up and down. Harveen could feel her face begin to flush and she sheepishly tried to hide her dirty boots.

'I don't think it would be wise to change our plans at this crucial juncture – the fate of the department depends on it,' she replied curtly, adding, 'I'm sorry.' With that, she picked up her things and left the room. A heavy silence hung in the air as Harveen and Rohan processed the implications of Penny's words.

'I will not let her take credit for our work, Rohan,' Harveen said defiantly. 'I will find a way for us to get our due. We've earned it! This is our project!'

'It *was*, Harveen. Until you dragged us out into the storm and endangered the team the other day, remember? Professor Prakash has put Dr Gupta in charge now – I don't think there's much we can do about it. Maybe we should just leave it be,' Rohan retorted.

Harveen quietened down but was still seething at the injustice of it all. After a pause, she looked up at him. 'Rohan, do you think you could stay for a bit longer?' He waited for her to finish her sentence. 'I need your help. Maybe we could find another piece of the puzzle and prove that we can hold our own on the project. Maybe that will persuade Professor Prakash to let us lead the project again,' Harveen said.

Rohan sighed, then nodded slightly.

25

The Vatican
5 July 2024

'Why Vincenzo again, signor? And who is this "The Brother"?' Don asked as he and Rossi made their way to the Vatican Secret Archives.

'Ah, there is a fantastical tale that I need to bring you up to speed on, Don,' Rossi replied, briskly leading the way. 'Surely, you must know that the start of the Christian faith was not an event in time but a gradual evolution. There are many conflicting stories around it, but for all intents and purposes, we treat the Council of Nicaea as its starting point.

'But the council was convened over three hundred years after the death of Christ,' said Don.

Here, Rossi abruptly stopped to look directly at Don. 'We are not historians, Donatello, we are soldiers. Just like in the GIS, where you were given orders and you carried them out, you must now understand that your duty is to protect the truth that the Church is built on. And it is that truth which is under threat from the situation developing in India. We must be ready to act.' Then, he resumed walking.

Don felt confused and remained silent for some time before saying, 'But I don't understand, signor – what is the pressing urgency here?'

'Oh, you will soon get it,' Rossi said evasively.

They arrived at the Archives and were directed to the research desks, where several staff members were busy laying out the materials Rossi had requested. The pile was already quite substantial. Before long, the Head of the Secret Archives Sofia Gallo arrived, carrying a map.

'I have looked at the maps that we have and overlaid where this latest site is located. It's difficult to be exact, but it certainly looks like the find is in Muziris. According to our intelligence, there are over two thousand five hundred written records that have been discovered. A certain Dr Penny Gupta is the researcher-in-charge. We need more information about the contents of these documents, which they haven't yet released. It is certainly possible that they may reference The Brother or The Artefact.'

'I see. This means we must send someone to India today,' said Rossi.

'I'm sorry, I hate to interrupt but can one of you please explain to me who "The Brother" is?' Don looked at them, befuddled. Rossi exhaled and took a seat at the table, collecting himself. He gestured for the two of them to sit.

'There is a theory that Jesus Christ had a brother called Judas. Judas worked alongside Jesus for many years and became known to all as the apostle Thomas. After the crucifixion of Christ around AD 33, he went into hiding and, sometime later, is said to have travelled to southern India, gradually opening a number of churches there. There are still St Thomas Christians in India to this day. One of those churches was in or near the ancient city of Muziris – where this archaeological find was made. Thomas is also said to have written the Gospel of Thomas.'

Don knew of the apostle Thomas, of course, but not as the brother of Christ. 'Is it true?' he asked.

Rossi gave a small sigh.

'The Gospel of Thomas was explicitly rejected at the Council of Nicaea, and the Bible was upheld as the true representation of the Christian Truth – that is the thing we are entrusted to protect. But knowing you, a researcher type, I asked Sofia to prepare all the records referring to Thomas, so that you may read and digest them for yourself. There was a copy of the Gospel that appeared in Egypt in 1945, which has broadly been discredited, and you will find all there is to know about it in these documents laid out here for you. But I'll have you remember, Donatello – whatever you may decide is the truth cannot get in the way of fulfilling your duty and your commitment to protect the Church.'

'Certainly, signor,' Don concurred. 'But if I may ask, what do you plan to have Vincenzo do?'

'We need someone to be on the ground in India on this very day. Once we gather enough information about what is in those records, we will be ready to take our decisive action,' Rossi declared. He looked at Don to know if he was in agreement.

'I think I should be the one to go, signor,' said Don. He knew what 'decisive action' meant and he couldn't afford to sit by idly and watch it play out yet again. Rossi seemed surprised by his suggestion. 'If you think this could be a major issue for the Church, I believe I have a better chance at trying to negotiate with the educated researchers there and gain early access to the documents. It will give me a chance to assess the potential risk. I will take the day to familiarize myself with all this material and I will fly out tonight. Worst case, I'm well-equipped to carry out your orders and take decisive action myself.'

Rossi seemed to consider the suggestion. 'Well, I suppose you are the Head of the Santa Alleanza now. Your decision will be final in the matter, Donatello. Although I don't see why you would have an objection to sending Vincenzo ahead of you to gather information on your behalf; he will, of course, be reporting directly to you. I can't say there'd be any harm in it. Besides, that will allow you more time to become familiar with the case.'

'Certainly, signor,' Don said reluctantly, his jaw tightening.

'Excellent!' Rossi smiled. 'I will ask them to ready the plane. Perhaps we should send Paulo, too.' The mention of another of Rossi's closest associates made Don even angrier, and he was just about to express his displeasure at the decision, when the tall, blond Vincenzo entered the room.

'Ah, my dear Vincenzo, come. Let us leave Don to his reading and bring you up to speed, shall we?' Rossi said warmly, ushering Vincenzo towards one of the private rooms at the Secret Archives with a hand placed softly on the former soldier's broad, muscular back.

26

Myos Hormos
AD 24

Jayesh took a last look at the Myos Hormos coastline as his vessel sailed out to sea. He had arrived full of hope that this trip would equip him with the knowledge and means he needed to turn Muciripattanam into a great trading city. But now he was leaving with nothing.

'What are you looking so sad for?' The deep voice that pulled him out of his thoughts sounded familiar. He turned towards it.

'Nannan? Is it really you? My god, it's you!'

Jayesh couldn't believe his eyes – the mysterious librarian had appeared beside him as if by magic. He looked quite different dressed simply, wearing a cloth hat pulled low on his head. Jayesh wrapped him in a tight, warm embrace.

'I hope my invitation to Muciripattanam is still good, my brother?' Nannan smiled as he hugged Jayesh back. The last time he had seen Nannan was when he was fleeing from Roman soldiers.

'Why were they after you? How did you manage to escape? And how on earth did you make it to this ship?!'

'Ha! The Romans are great traders. I have been keeping records for a wealthy family in Alexandria. Each large transaction they had me record, I pocketed a small portion for myself to pay for my trip home, whenever the day came. It seems they found out about my little scheme and set the soldiers on me. For a foreigner to cross a Roman – a former slave, at that – means a painful death. Or, safe passage home with a new friend!' His joviality pleasantly surprised Jayesh.

'They almost got me too,' he said and told Nannan about his experience with Servius.

'You would have been killed for sure,' said Nannan. 'These Romans think nothing of killing people like you or me, brother. Your friend Servius could well have slit your throat for the coins in your purse. It'd be no skin off his back.'

'That is why I am going home,' said Jayesh. 'My friends and family warned me that coming here was dangerous, and I think they might have been right …'

'Not so fast, brother. The Romans understand trade very well – much better than most traders back home. They love Indian spices. I know how they think. We can still do business with them.'

'I won't go back ever again,' said Jayesh firmly. 'I barely managed to escape with my life this time.'

'I, for one, feel no fear coming back to these shores,' said Nannan. 'Merchants and traders are well respected here. If we come bearing things of value, they will trade with us without qualm. They love only their gods and their trade.'

At that moment, a couple of Roman soldiers appeared on the deck. They were deeply engrossed in their conversation but Jayesh and Nannan – both wanted men – took note of them and exchanged glances.

'I think it's best we continue our discussion in my quarters,' whispered Jayesh and quietly led his friend below.

27

Sreepadam Palace
5 July 2024

As the clouds and rain over Kerala began to clear and the sun came out again, it became difficult to remember just how torturous the ceaseless rainfall had been. Sreepadam Palace was finally dry. The sun beamed on its facade, aglow with splendour. It was like a new world in which Harveen was not welcome.

Dr Penny Gupta had made the desk next to Rohan's her own within the first few days after her joining. On the second day she had come in, she had brought with her a pack of large disinfectant wipes and cleaned all the surfaces of the desk, including the insides of its three small drawers. In the first of these, she had put a fresh pack of notebooks along with an unopened box of disposable ink pens. Her desk looked spic and span, the only other evidence of her occupancy being a large jar of Italian coffee that Professor Prakash had brought for her, and her own mug, both sitting on a small tray. While she was in office, her laptop and phone would be arranged neatly on her desk. She had given the entire team specific instructions on what they were meant to do and, much to Harveen's annoyance, they all seemed happy to oblige at the first request she made. Harveen had begun to wonder whether Professor Prakash had been right about her inadequacies as a leader.

'Everyone, I have something interesting to show you,' said Penny, calling the team to gather around her desk. Before Harveen had got out of her chair, Rohan was already standing next to the linguist, and the other team members were also making their way there. Harveen noticed Penny's smart suit. The one she wore today was a fetching shade of pale green, and she had paired it with a white shirt and beige high heels. Harveen marvelled at her extensive wardrobe – she barely owned anything smart in comparison.

Penny was sitting in her swivel chair and by the time Harveen got to her desk, she could hardly see the screen anymore and nobody bothered making room for her. She had to peer over to see the interesting things. A digital image of one of the sheets in the document Harveen had recovered was on display on the screen.

Dr Gupta began, 'As some of you know, most of these entries are dated between AD 66 and 69, but a number of records relate to things that happened well before that. This one is by far the oldest.' She hovered her mouse over a particular section that looked to have been damaged by water. 'It's not in perfect condition but we managed to enhance the image with our software and now I can say with some level of certainty that this record was written in AD 30. You can just about make out the date here.' Harveen and Rohan both looked at the blurred section she was pointing to, unsure about what it said and exchanging a questioning glance behind her.

'The sheet lists items like stone, some wood and costs for transportation. It does not mention from where to where.'

The initial excitement around the room had all but dissipated. 'After further enhancement, we found this.' She indicated another section which was partially blurred. 'Once we put it through a few filters, the final image becomes much clearer.' With a few clicks of her mouse, she brought the picture into better focus. The first word was still only partially visible and read 'Temp'. The second word clearly read 'Augusti'. Harveen glanced over at Rohan again, who had his eyebrows raised.

'What's remarkable about this is that it is written in Latin. This allows us to make two possible inferences, each as remarkable as the other, in my opinion. First, the writer is a native Indian who could also at least write some Latin, or that there were Latin speakers in Muziris in AD 30. We don't know which one, but either would be extraordinary. That's all I have to share with you guys today.'

Everyone began to shuffle back to their desks, lost in thought. Harveen sensed an opportunity and stayed put to have a word with Penny.

'Dr Gupta,' she started, 'we have been looking at historical documents relating to the period you defined. There is an ancient map called the Tabula Peutingeriana that covers the whole road and sea network of the Roman empire and it clearly shows a Temple of Augustus in Muziris. The map was found in the thirteenth century, I believe, although no one has yet been able to date it accurately. If what you have said is correct, we can now confirm both that the temple probably existed, while also putting down the date of its construction within a very concise time bracket. This is a truly significant discovery.'

'Excellent! That sounds wonderful, Harveen,' said Dr Gupta encouragingly. Harveen had been hiding her own discovery from the team, hoping that it would be the key to her returning to the investigation into Muziris as the project head. This felt like her moment.

'I stayed late yesterday and I believe I have come up with something. Can everyone come and have a look at it on my screen, please?' Everyone went over to Harveen's desk. She felt good being in control again, although to her annoyance, the team reverently made way for Penny to stand right beside her.

'The letter "M" for Muziris we noticed in the records that Rohan and I found – we have seen it before!' Harveen was keen to remind everyone it was her find.

'Where have we seen it?' Rohan asked, looking baffled.

'Anapuzha: the big dig that we did last year,' she replied and started showing everyone more images.

'But there was nothing remarkable there – just some Roman coins, pots, beads and stuff. We inferred there'd been a wooden building – or perhaps multiple – that had stood there at some point, but not a single major find,' Rohan reminded her.

'That's what I thought too. Until I saw this!' Harveen showed them the image of a fragment of a vase – it had originally been colourful but had faded over time. The fragment was only a few inches wide and about the same in length as well. The letter 'M' on the fragment appeared to be in the same style as the one from the sheet, but considering how small a piece it was, it could just as easily have been a random pattern.

But Rohan smiled optimistically. 'Yes, that really does look similar. We should see if we find something among the other artefacts from Anapuzha,' he said, even if he was a bit unconvinced.

'I have been doing exactly that all of last night. I have at least sixteen matches or possible matches – see for yourselves.' Harveen opened up multiple other images and showed them each one. There it was – the 'M' carved quite clearly on a piece of wood, and then again on another fragment of pottery. There were a couple of partial matches on other pieces of wood as well, but the most conclusive was the same pattern engraved into a piece of smooth stone. It was about two feet by one foot in size and appeared like a section of a building. They had initially dismissed the line as just another pattern, but looking at all the images together now, against the reference of the written records, it all seemed so obvious. The 'M' was definitely significant. Perhaps it denoted Muziris.

'Well, Harveen, you've put in a lot of hard work into this. Wonderful,' Penny acknowledged, but Harveen didn't think she was being sincere.

'I agree with Rohan. I do think there's scope for finding missing links between our recent findings and the Anapuzha site. We should certainly take another look. I can arrange for another expedition right away, actually—'

'That is a terrific idea, Harveen,' Penny interrupted. 'But I think it's better if you, with your immense knowledge and experience, direct your energy towards the artefacts you've already uncovered. No one has been as close to both digs as you to be able to spot right away if there are any other matches. It'll be really helpful if you stay. I will personally lead the dig team – I'm sure we can handle it.' She was smiling, but she could tell Harveen wasn't taking the replacement well.

'But … I'm the one who found it … I know my way around the site,' Harveen declared as she stood up, pushing her chair back aggressively, almost sliding it onto Penny's foot.

'Harveen, will you please step aside? Let's have a quick chat, shall we?' Penny said calmly after she stepped back just in time to get out of the chair's path.

Harveen followed after her as she left the room. Once they were out of earshot, Penny said, 'You are a gifted researcher, Harveen. Stick with it and stay out of trouble, or you'll lose it all – everything you've built, everything you've worked for. Professor Prakash went into a fair bit of worrying detail about what happened on your last expedition and at the Anapuzha site. I'd advise you maintain a low profile for some time and let me do my job. As soon as I feel like you're ready to return to the field, I will take you along, alright?'

Harveen was crushed and despite the calm logic, she still felt entitled to lead the project. She began, 'But is there—'

'Listen,' Penny stopped her mid-sentence, 'I have to go now. I'm supposed to meet someone who says he knows some key information about our recent discovery and it sounds very important. I don't want to be late for this meeting – he sounded very jittery. Let's talk as soon as I am back.'

'Yes, Dr Gupta,' said Harveen. As soon as Penny left, Harveen stormed back into the room where the team sat. She could see the pity in their eyes, but she was determined not to cry in front of them.

'I am sure Dr Gupta is just doing what's best for the team,' Rohan consoled her, softly.

But it wasn't helpful. 'That bloody bitch! I wish she was dead!' Harveen exploded.

If they already thought she was unfit to lead the team, what more could go wrong? After risking her life to get them this far, she was now being robbed of her moment. She ran out of the room, slamming the door behind her.

28

The Vatican
5 July 2024

'I know you are short on time, so I will be quick. Here is what we know about St Thomas.' Sofia opened a large book to a painting of Christ surrounded by his apostles.

'Thomas was one of the twelve apostles of Jesus Christ and is most commonly known as "Doubting Thomas". Little is known about his early life, but it is generally accepted that he was born in Galilee and was a humble carpenter like Jesus himself.' She flicked through several pages showing images of Thomas putting his hands into the wounds of Christ, and of Galilee.

'Right,' said Don. He knew this story.

'There is little mention of him in the Bible predating the crucifixion and, whatever there is, demonstrates his bravery and his loyalty to Christ. For example, in the Gospel of St John, when Jesus proposes to visit Lazarus in Judaea at great personal risk, it is St Thomas who says to the other apostles, "Let us also go, that we may die with him".' Sofia pointed to a page with the quote and the reference to St John 11:16.

'What is interesting is that he is referred to as Didymus, which is Greek for "twin".'

Don sat up a little, his interest piqued.

'In fact,' continued Sofia, 'there are still in existence three copies of the Gospel of St Thomas, which do not form part of the published Bible.' She spread several pictures across the table.

'Hmm …' said Don, surprised that he had never heard of this before.

'The first one is pictured here. This is a complete copy housed in the library at St Catherine's Monastery in the Sinai Peninsula. As you may know, St Catherine's is reputedly located on the very site of the burning bush Moses saw when the Lord's Angel appeared to him. The monastery contains the oldest known copies of the Bible, most of the gospels and even the Ashtiname of the Prophet Muhammad. The library is the oldest and most complete bank of ancient texts in the world and has been in use since around AD 550.' She showed Don a photograph of the historic monastery. 'We made several attempts to retrieve this copy before its existence became public knowledge.'

Don had many questions. 'But why would the Vatican want the original copy?'

'The Gospel of St Thomas starts with these words: "These are the hidden words that the living Jesus spoke and Didymus Judas Thomas wrote them down." We know the Greek meaning of Didymus, but we also know now that Thomas is Aramaic for "twin" too, so his name literally means "twin Judas twin". If there was any level of credibility accorded to this book, or if it was better known, then the very basic principles of Christianity would come into question. Which is why since the Council of Nicaea, we have been hiding this story.' Sofia's encyclopaedic knowledge of the archive and her ability to recount it in such detail without notes was impressive to Don.

'You said there were three copies?' he asked.

'We used to believe that the only other surviving copy was our own, which is in this box.' She put a small box on the table and showed Don the book inside.

'It is in excellent condition. We have protected it for seventeen hundred years. But then in December 1945, another copy was discovered near Nag Hammadi in Egypt. We made extensive efforts to discredit it. All the details of that are in here,' she said, handing him a large file. 'The last thing I want to mention is the journey St Thomas made to India. Some of this is speculative, but it begins to paint a picture and may be helpful for us to put the pieces together. It looks like St Thomas left his homeland and arrived in the Indo-Parthian kingdom between AD 40–45, perhaps at the request or with the help of a king, Rajah Gondophares. It seems that he then travelled to southern India, specifically Muziris, around AD 50. And that is exactly where these new finds have been unearthed. And that is why we sent the alert. We need to make sure that no new evidence relating to The Brother is brought to the knowledge of the masses.'

'I hear you,' said Don, gathering up all the documents so he could read them closely. 'Can I take this?' He asked, gesturing towards the copy of the Gospel of St Thomas. 'It might prove a useful bargaining tool.'

'Of course. You are the Head of the Santa Alleanza, after all.' She smiled. 'There is one other thing related to India. It may not be relevant, but I will pull up all the details about it and put them together for you, signor. This is all highly sensitive, and it is essential that we know if there are any references made to it in the records found in India.'

'Alright then, thanks Sofia.' He felt her gaze piercing into him and looked at her. She was wearing a curious expression.

'You are not at all what I expected, Donatello Clemente,' she said with a coy smile. 'I have been watching you and following your work very closely since you first started here.'

'What do you mean?' he replied. He had worked with Sofia for six years and in that time, they had spoken almost every week. As the head of the Vatican Secret Archives, Sofia was not only responsible for the written documents that were in the building, she also instructed and kept records of all the research and surveillance that they conducted all over the world. Donatello knew that the people working under her numbered in excess of fifty and, at any given time, she likely knew exactly what each Santa Alleanza agent was up to and what they were supposed to be doing. They had spent many hours together engaged in research work, but in all that time, he did not remember her ever expressing an opinion on how he did his job.

'I have worked in the Vatican for thirty years now. I joined as a researcher straight out of university. More than twenty years ago, I was recruited by the Santa Alleanza and I have served as Head of the Secret Archives for eight of them. I take my role very seriously and if we are to speak candidly, then it must be with the understanding that it remains strictly confidential.' She looked at him earnestly and as she stepped closer to him, it struck him that in her younger days, Sofia would have been an incredibly beautiful woman. She was elegant – her long, straight brown hair, striking light brown eyes and flawless smile added to her allure. The years had been very kind to her and even her wrinkles seemed to have appeared with care so as to enhance her high cheek bones. She was the picture of intelligence and sensuality.

'Of course, always. Everything in confidence,' Don said sincerely.

'You are not what I expected at all …' Sofia repeated, looking for a way to broach the subject she had in mind.

'And what did you expect I was like?' returned Don.

Sofia paused for a moment, considering her response. 'Do you know why they call Mr Rossi "Il Macellaio" in these parts?' she asked.

'I presume it is because of his brutal methods,' Don replied honestly.

'Precisely. You know, before he assumed charge, there had been only two murders performed by the Santa Alleanza since the end of the Second World War. We were mainly a surveillance service. In the most dire of situations, we'd send out some misleading information and discredit troublesome sources. Then we took to social media and sought to control the narrative in way that would attract more people to the faith. It's a very powerful medium, you know.

'But the Santa Alleanza was never actively involved in intervention ourselves. Most of the people we had were academics; the desks were often full as we carried on with our research. When I was asked to find new recruits for the Santa Alleanza, we looked in universities and research institutes for people with a deep understanding of the history of the Christian Church.'

Don was taken aback by Sofia's directness and views. 'Why are you saying all this only now? We have worked together for six years,' he said.

'Everything changed when Rossi became Head of the Santa Alleanza. He seems to take up every task as if it were a Holy Crusade. He idolizes the early leaders of this organization and has constantly tried to emulate them, including the questionable things they did.' Sofia was now leaning close enough to Don to speak in little above than a whisper. ‘Before he became the head, he had a predilection for using that ornate knife he always keeps on his desk to extract information; if nothing was revealed, he would kill them. In despicable, gruesome ways. Hence, Il Macellaio …’ She paused before speaking again, ‘But you … you contemplate your tasks very carefully. You spend a great deal of time researching and verifying the justice you are asked to mete out. I have seen the amount of time you spend in the Chapel. It is evident that you are not entirely at ease with some of the tasks you are asked to perform. And now, you are the Head.’ As she finished, Don suddenly realized that it was possible that Rossi had put Sofia up to this to find out his true intentions. He decided to be cautious about what he told her.

‘I don’t see what you mean. I think you have me all wrong, actually. ‘I am in full support of what we do,’ he lied.

‘Well, for someone who is fine with what they do, you sure thought long and hard before pressing the button on that old archaeologist in Rome – almost seemed like you wanted to spare his life …’

The shock on Don’s face was visible.

‘You know that it is my job to monitor the actions of our agents in the field?’ Sofia continued.

‘I do,’ said Don.

‘Since Rossi took over, even the confessionals in the Chapel are not safe from his prying. Everything you have ever said in there has been recorded.’

The slightest smile played on her lips while Don sat with his mouth agape, still in disbelief at what he had just learned. He felt exposed and knew that if Sofia had even breathed a word of his hesitations to Dino Rossi, it would have meant the end of his career, and possibly worse.

'Relax, Don!' she laughed. 'While it's my duty to uncover such things, it also means I get to clean up properly after you. Don't worry, no one knows, and they never will.'

She held Don's gaze for a few moments before continuing in her usual steely voice, 'What's done is done. We must now discuss your intentions for your new job and how I can help you.'

29

Northern India
AD 26

'Look out!' shouted Jayesh, but his warning had come too late. He watched in horror as his friend Aarush was killed, the enemy's sword plunged deep into his chest. Jayesh fought on. His brother Nilham fought three men on his own, blood streaming down his arm. The wound seemed to have doubled his rage and he was swinging his sword wildly.

'They are getting away!' he screamed after the last man fighting opposite him fell. The other two men were running after the cart their fellow soldiers had taken.

'Let them go,' said Jayesh, sinking into the dirt. 'It's only one cart. Quick! Come here and see if there's still something we can do to save Aarush.' His brother grunted and ran to their fallen friend's side, shaking his head grimly after a few moments of examining him.

Jayesh forced himself to get up and check on their party. Aarush was dead, three more men were wounded, including Nilham, and they had lost a quarter of their goods. He kneeled beside Aarush's body, his head bowed and tears slowly streaming down his face. His drive to build a trading empire in India was extracting a heavy toll from him.

'We have been lucky until today; I think it is best that we learn from our experience and return home now,' said Nilham. The memory of his older brother waking him with a slap when they were young suddenly returned to Jayesh. Although he too wanted to return home, the desire to prove his mettle while his brother was watching was much stronger. He wiped his face with the back of his hand and swallowed the lump in his throat to say, 'We still have goods to sell. How can Muciripattanam match the greatness of Alexandria if we allow travel and trading across India, like Ashoka did, to scare us?'

Jayesh had begun travelling extensively, not only to learn more about the intrinsic value of the goods being sold in Muciripattanam but also to find reliable sources of other goods that could be exported to Egypt and Rome.

'Help me load his body into our cart. We will perform his last rites at home.'

Since the Mauryan empire and the reign of the great Emperor Ashoka ended, India fell under the rule of local tribes, and Jayesh and his companions often had to travel into war-torn areas. They were regularly ambushed, but despite this, they had managed to build many business relationships that were sure to endure well into the future.

'They're at war!' said Nilham. 'Look around you – do you want us to become unwitting casualties? It's best we turn back now while we can!' He waved his arm in the direction of what had clearly been the site of a recent battle. 'We may not always escape an attack. They killed Aarush! Do you want them to get you too?'

'I'm not asking. I have made my decision. We keep moving,' replied Jayesh. 'Look, somebody's coming towards us.' They were being approached by a group of well-armed men.

'You are in the land of the mighty King Gondophares of Suren. State your business.' There were eight men, but they did not look like an army – each of them was dressed differently, though all of them carried swords.

'We are merchants from the South and we bring goods to trade with your mighty kingdom,' said Jayesh reverentially, despite his shaking limbs. 'We come in peace,' he said as he signalled his men to drop their weapons. They obeyed.

'Inspect their carts,' said the leader among the armed men, and two of the others began to ruffle through the carts' contents. When they were satisfied that there was no threat, the men led Jayesh and his small group to the palace.

On the journey, they described King Gondophares as a mighty ruler whose reign was spread over a huge kingdom. And yet, when they arrived at his palace, it seemed no more than a collection of huts. His inner chambers were luxuriously decorated with rugs and the soldiers that he kept close seemed well-trained and alert.

'My men tell me you are a great merchant,' Gondophares began, 'but you look like a child! Perhaps your father may care to join us?' The king himself appeared to be no older than in his early twenties. He was built broadly, with his thick hair flowing down to his shoulders. Even inside his own palace and surrounded by his soldiers, he carried a sword on his waist, the hilt embellished with jewels. His dark eyes glowed with rage, and even standing still, he looked ready to lash out at any moment.

'We are no great merchants, Your Highness,' responded Jayesh. 'We come from Muciripattanam in the south. We trade in pepper and spices and anything else of value. We are capable and ambitious and can source most goods your heart might desire.' Jayesh bowed before Gondophares, whose interest was piqued.

'Weapons. Bring me weapons to wage wars with. I have a skilled army of men, but our kingdom is so large, we suffer attacks from all sides and are always in need of more weapons. Can you bring me the finest weapons in all the land?'

'Please accept my apologies, Your Highness, we do not sell weapons,' Jayesh replied honestly. 'In a land that is filled with tribes at war, we fear for our lives. We feel it is safer for us to trade in food and livestock. If we were ever ambushed and were found to be carrying weapons, they'll kill us, My Lord. All we come bearing is some produce, Your Highness. It is the finest our land has to offer and if you like the quality, we can bring you more.'

Gondophares spent a long moment observing Jayesh. 'So my men have told me. Everyone is very impressed with your wares. Name your price, boy!' His hand drifted towards his sword.

'The first time you wish to buy from us in Muciripattanam, we charge nothing, Your Highness. But forgive me, My Lord, we do have one condition. We sell only if you allow us the honour to share a meal with you and discuss future business prospects between our lands.'

The young king roared with laughter. 'Perhaps you do not need your father to accompany you after all! Tell me, what is your name, boy? I shall certainly remember you.'

'I am Jayesh of Muciripattanam, Your Highness.'

30

Sreepadam Palace
5 July 2024

Harveen ran straight towards the grounds. She did not want anyone to see her crying. Finding a spot behind two trees where she could sit without being heard or seen, she collapsed onto the grass, looking back at the building over her shoulder, shocked at its betrayal. It looked so different now since when she had first started working there.

The Sreepadam Palace was a palatial colonial structure that sat on a picturesque plot near the northern entrance of the Sree Padmanabhan Swami Temple. The building had suffered many years of neglect until it was bought up by the State Archaeology Department of Kerala. It had not been until Harveen had joined in 2017 as Lead Researcher that work began in earnest to restore the building. Harveen smiled as she recalled each stage of the restoration process that she had supervised so closely. When there weren't enough artefacts available to dedicate a whole museum to, in the beginning, Harveen had created a temporary historical costume exhibition with outfits from every period of Indian history being recreated and displayed. It had become so popular that they had retained it to this day.

As Harveen eyes ran downwards along the side of the building, she saw the unmistakable shape of Penny leaving through the side door. She carefully looked around in all directions before rushing across the grounds towards the side gate. She did not notice Harveen behind the trees.

Harveen wondered why Penny would have to leave so surreptitiously from the side entrance. Knowing that the gate behind her would bring her onto the road not far from where Dr Gupta would exit, she instinctively made her way towards it. The street was busy and Harveen eased her way through the crowd unseen. Penny emerged a moment later, standing on the side of the street, glancing in both directions as if she was looking for someone. Harveen followed her gaze up and down the road but saw nothing of interest. This continued for a few minutes. Penny looked very out of place in her smart suit and was easy to keep track of. A silver saloon car approached rather unexpectedly, edging slowly towards her. Harveen saw her wave the car down tentatively, in response to which the driver parked the car on the opposite side of the road and waited.

The man in the driver's seat took up the whole of his side of the car; it was as if he had been squeezed into the small space by force. He was white, with a round face and black hair combed back flat over his head. His neck was barely distinguishable from his head and she could see his huge hands propped on the steering wheel. He made it look like a toy car. Dr Gupta got into the passenger side and they exchanged a couple of words before the car took off at a considerable speed.

By the time Harveen got back to the office, the team had scattered and only Rohan was still at his desk.

'I'm sorry, Rohan. I didn't mean it like that … I'm just

really hurt. This was our find, we worked hard for it,' she said a bit sheepishly.

'I know. Are you okay?' he replied compassionately.

'I think so … I just needed some air, that's all. Sorry for rushing out like that …' After a brief pause, she said, 'Listen, I have been thinking, let's see if we can find any other matches anywhere for this letter M or any more references to the Augustus Temple in India – maybe in Rome or Alexandria? Let's get the team to help us figure it out, get everyone involved. What do you say?'

'Good idea,' he said before he started tapping away at his computer.

Harveen sat at her desk to type out several emails to her network of archaeologists and historians. When she had finished, she shared condensed versions of those emails to message boards regularly visited by scholars in the field. The exercise took several hours.

Meanwhile, Rohan confirmed that the entire team was working to re-analyze the findings from Anapuzha and looking for any reference to the symbol M they had newly uncovered.

'Rohan, have you … noticed anything odd about Dr Gupta?' Harveen mustered up the courage to ask after some thought.

He considered for a moment before saying, 'No, what do you mean? Have you?'

'Oh, nothing … Um, did she mention where she was going before she left?'

'Nope,' he said.

Harveen's mind kept flitting back to the large man in the silver car and wondered what his connection to Dr Penny Gupta might be.

31

Muciripattanam
AD 32

'I can't believe you built this,' Vikesh said to Jayesh as they stood gazing at the magnificence before them.

'It's beautiful,' said Paavi, Vikesh's younger sister. 'Do they really have many buildings as beautiful as this in Alexandria?'

'So many that you can't always notice one behind the other. One day, I will take you there and you can see for yourself,' Jayesh answered. She smiled at him. He could only imagine her delight as they walked around Alexandria hand in hand.

They all stood together at the seafront of their hometown. Nannan had been the one to plant the seed in Jayesh's mind on their journey back home from Alexandria, eight years ago. He had described to him in vivid detail the impressive temples the Romans were constructing in Alexandria. On that day, Jayesh had resolved that he would build one just like them in Muciripattanam. The idea had gestated in his mind until their trade and wealth had grown by enough to make it a reality – the Temple of Augustus was finally nearing completion. It still filled Jayesh with an overwhelming sense of hope and pride. He could scarcely believe that building such a structure was even conceivable in India. Whilst he was still scared to return to Alexandria, he had managed to devise a plan to ensure they would come to him.

Jayesh had asked Nannan to negotiate with the Romans on his behalf so they could have the same builders construct an exact replica of the Temple of Augustus here. He was unconcerned with the cost. Muciripattanam had rapidly become one of the major trading ports in India, and the profits from their trade with Alexandria had far exceeded their expectations. Jayesh had observed that temples were as culturally significant for the Romans, Greeks and Jews as they were for his people. He was convinced that by building a Roman temple, he would be able to draw attention to Muciripattanam as an important trading hub, striving to match the stature of Alexandria.

'We will build temples for all religions! And there will be a big stadium … a vast port … impressive buildings and roads … We will welcome people from around the world! I've invited Amma and Appa to meet me here today so they can see for themselves what we have achieved. They will be so proud to see Muciripattanam becoming the greatest city in the world!'

'You know they call it Muziris now?' said Nannan. 'It says Muziris on the maps too.' Jayesh was reminded of how Quintus had pronounced the name of his hometown the first time the Romans had visited them, and stood smiling to himself. He had played a part in lending his town that name – something that would leave quite an impression on his father.

After almost four years of construction and Nannan's numerous trips to Alexandria via Myos Hormos to bring in skilled architects, builders and vast quantities of materials, the grand Temple of Augustus stood nearly complete. It proudly faced seaward, proclaiming its splendour to all for many miles around. The awe-inspiring structure stood on a wide, flat plot of land, positioned so that sailors coming to Muziris would notice the temple well before they even approached the shores. Jayesh had been inspired by the splendid visual impact the lighthouse in Pharos had left on him the first time he visited Alexandria and sailed into the harbour.

There had been considerable problems in acquiring the marble to construct the four main columns at the front of the temple. The Romans were undertaking huge construction projects both in Rome and Alexandria, causing the supply of the gleaming stone to become scarce. Suppliers had, as a result, dishonoured Jayesh's order on several occasions in order to prioritize the needs of the empire. Finally, he and Nannan had decided on using wood to build the columns and the roof.

Jayesh looked across at his two friends and began to describe his vision for the town now becoming known commonly as Muziris.

'My friends, the Romans and Greeks have built such incredible structures; such straight, smooth roads through the most difficult terrains and hostile climes. Vikesh, you must come with us and see Alexandria for yourself. If their architects can help us build even just a few such structures here, Muciripattanam will be nothing short of Alexandria! This temple marks the beginning of that journey.'

'I am never getting on one of those ships ...' Vikesh said with dread in his voice.

'I think you'll be able to transform Muciripattanam into Alexandria sooner than you'll ever be able to persuade Vikesh to get on a ship!' teased Nannan. The three men laughed together, the warmth of their bond becoming evident.

'I believe you may be right. His younger sister is braver than him,' Jayesh chimed in before turning to flash a mischievous smile at Paavi. She blushed and averted her gaze.

He promptly turned his attention back to his friends, 'Nevertheless, this temple will encourage the Romans to make Muziris their main trading port in India. Nannan is already on the verge of securing a lasting relationship with some of the merchants in Alexandria. Once our ties with the Romans grow stronger, we can bring in the builders and materials to build magnificent shrines to the Greek gods and for the Jews. This way, people of all faiths would feel welcome to make their homes in Muziris.'

Standing in the shadow of the impressive Temple of Augustus, the three men were looking up at the magnificent building in awe. Vikesh said, 'I never believed it could be done. You have achieved the impossible, Jayesh.'

Nannan nodded slowly in agreement.

'This is only the first step, my friend; we have a long way to go to win the hearts of good men from all over the world,' said Jayesh.

He heard footsteps and turned to see Nilham escorting his parents towards the temple.

'Excuse me, my brothers,' he said before going over to greet them.

He excitedly led them to the podium of the new temple. 'Look, Amma, how smooth the Romans can make stone!' he called her attention to the white stairway that led to the entrance. It had been built up to a height of almost twenty feet so that, to ships approaching the port town, the temple appeared to be floating in the air.

'We could make the columns only forty feet high with wood, Appa. The Romans refused to supply marble to us or it would have been much higher – like the ones they use in Alexandria.'

'It's beautiful nonetheless, son,' said his mother. 'And it seems to glow!'

'It was my idea to clad the columns in bronze so they would catch the sunlight – another thing I saw them do for their buildings in Alexandria. Aren't they magnificent, Appa?'

Abhay seemed to be preoccupied by something far more important than the spectacle that stood before him. He began, 'Son, we have some news for you, it's—'

'Look at the roof!' Jayesh interrupted him, barely hearing his father and willing him to be more impressed than he was. The crowning glory of the temple stood proudly on its apex, looking out to sea. 'It is a statue of Augustus, a former Roman emperor. I patronized a sculptor there to build it for us – it has travelled vast distances across land and sea to arrive here. He was a great ruler, his reign spread across half the world. Outside of Rome, I have no doubt that this will be the most impressive temple dedicated to him.'

'What about our gods, son? Should their temples not line our coast too?' asked Vasudha.

'Indeed,' said Jayesh. 'I have great plans to make people of all religions feel at home here, but Amma, we must attract the attentions of the Roman empire first. They are the greatest rulers in the world and we cannot turn Muziris into a major trading port without their support. Come, I have something else to show you inside.'

They entered into the portico area, where typically Roman ceremonies would be conducted, and this one was magnificently decorated. Just through the great doors, there stood before them yet another statue of Augustus. This one was propped on a pedestal and the floor around it was a beautifully detailed mosaic depicting many of Augustus's famous victories.

'Isn't it amazing? There is nothing like this anywhere in India.' Jayesh was beaming as he turned to look at his parents and brother, but none of them seemed impressed. 'What's wrong, Appa? Are you not happy with what your son has achieved?'

'Listen, son,' said Abhay, sounding slightly frustrated. 'The Cheras have been very impressed with the trade that we are doing with the Romans. They too would like to share in our profits. This is an opportunity for us to rise in society, son! Don't you see? It has taken many visits and much conversation, but at last, I have managed to find you a bride. Her name is Nandi – yes, Kokothai Marban's niece, the very same!' He said the name of the Chera king with such pride. 'All they expect in return are some concessions from us in trade, of course.' Jayesh looked at his beaming mother in shock. He had not expected this at all. His family all seemed so pleased.

'Who could have imagined that we could marry into a royal family?' said Abhay. Jayesh had never seen him look this proud.

'It will secure our business interests too,' said Nilham. 'No one will dare to invade us; we will be protected by the Cheras.'

Jayesh knew that the Cheras lorded over the greatest kingdom in the south and Muciripattanam was surrounded on all sides by Chera territory. Nevertheless, he was in shock and appalled at the liberty his parents had taken on his behalf. He had no choice but to tell them what was in his heart.

'I will marry Paavi and no one else,' he said quietly. He glanced towards where she stood and saw her turning to look in his direction, breaking out into a smile and the wind played with her hair.

'What are you saying, son!' Abhay had not expected this. His fury began to bubble to the surface. He boomed, 'You will marry who we tell you to marry, do you understand?'

Jayesh had not seen his father this angry in many years. He felt hurt and disappointed, having worked so hard merely to gain the love of his father.

'Paavi? That simpleton? Over the king's niece? Are you mad?' said Vasudha. 'And she works in the market. Remember, you now run everything there.' His desire to please his parents turned to anger as they insulted her.

'But the Romans get to choose their own wives! How can we ever hope to equal them if we still keep to our old-fashioned methods?'

'No son of mine is a Roman!' bellowed Abhay. 'You build this great monstrosity for them, bigger than any temple for your own people; you worship their ways and now you want to bring shame upon your family. The Cheras are very keen to find a way to trade with the Romans like we do. This is a great opportunity for us.'

Jayesh could not understand why his family refused to see the significance of his accomplishment. His heart breaking, he steeled himself and said calmly but resolutely, 'I will marry Paavi and no one else.'

'Are you prepared to deal with the repercussions of your obstinacy, brother?' Nilham asked him gravely. 'This is an insult to the Cheras – they could even decide to go to war against us. It may seem a trivial matter to you, but it is not. If they decide to conquer us, we would be crushed within hours.'

32

The Vatican
5 July 2024

'It's bad, signor! They 'ave recovered nearly three thousand individual documents. All sheets made of cloth with writing on them. About five per cent of them are damaged and unreadable. The rest are either partially or fully legible. You will not believe – almost 'alf of them are in near-perfect condition.' Vincenzo was saying over the phone, reporting back from India for the first time. Rossi sat at his ornate desk with his fingers interlocked, listening intently, while Don sat on the other side, taking notes in a small silver notebook. Rossi had managed to stall Don's departure to India so as to let Vincenzo do what he was best at, unhindered.

'How many people have seen these documents?' Don asked. He needed to take back some control of the project.

'A 'ole team of experts. They cannot understand the contents of the documents because they are in Old Tamil. Only Dr Penny Gupta can translate.'

'Good,' said Rossi. 'And how is our new favourite doctor?'

'Careless, signor,' said Vincenzo. 'She seemed to be very taken with Paulo; a 'int of special help directly from the Vatican seemed to delight her. She almost offered up her services before we even asked. She told us she 'as just been appointed as project 'ead, and any support from us would really 'elp 'er become a big success.'

So Paulo was there too. Don cursed inwardly at the manipulative Rossi for excluding him from all major decisions.

'That's great, Vincenzo,' said Rossi. 'What does she know?'

'She said they are trading records – definitely from Muziris. Also, something about 'ow they are all excited by the possible existence of a Roman temple of sort. Nothing concerning us so far, signor.'

Don doubted Vincenzo had the wherewithal to know if anything important enough had emerged in the findings.

'Who else is working on this?' asked Don.

'Just the people Sofia 'ad mentioned: that Prakash guy, 'arveen Gill and some junior researchers. No one new as far as we know,' he replied.

'Okay,' said Rossi. 'Keep Paulo on Gupta and inform us about anything out of the ordinary.'

'*Sí*, signor.'

The line went dead.

'I should go there today,' said Don. 'Vincenzo might not be able to tell if they're onto something potentially troublesome for us. I am well-versed with the historical records, I've spent considerable time poring over the Archives. Finding Muziris can be disastrous for us – it is at the centre of everything that we fear. It is foundational to our history. Given the kind of records they've managed to uncover, it is entirely possible that something might just emerge.'

Rossi nodded his head once in agreement. It was time for Don to take the reins.

'Thank you, signor. I will depart tonight.'

33

Muciripattanam
AD 33

'Your ambitions have killed your own brother!' Vasudha cried. 'This is all your fault!'

'Amma, what are you saying? It cannot be! He can't be dead, I saw him this morning!' Jayesh was distraught. Nilham had never lost a fight with anyone.

'He's dead! And you killed him!' Vasudha slapped Jayesh across the face. The blow landed on his heart – he could feel his mother's anguish in it, and that was the most painful thing he had ever experienced.

'Amma—' he tried to comfort her, but she pushed him away violently. Avani rushed to her side and gently guided her to sit down in a chair.

'I don't understand. We have travelled along those routes so many times; they know to expect us,' replied Jayesh. 'Whatever could have happened?'

Avani was on the floor by her Amma's feet, comforting her as she sobbed. Abhay glared at Jayesh with bloodshot eyes. Nilham was his favourite son.

'He should have been running our family business. Not you! He told you so many times it was not a good idea to venture too far from home for business. But you wouldn't relent and forced him to play along. And now he is dead! Look what you have done! If you had any sense in that head of yours, you would have accepted the hand of the king's niece in marriage and my son would still be alive!'

'Appa, please—' Jayesh began.

'No! Not another word from you! You murderer – get out of my house!'

Jayesh felt as if his heart had been wrenched out of his chest. He turned and left the house with his head down.

He saw Vikesh approach. 'Vikesh! You are alright! Oh, thank heavens, I'm so happy you're safe. My brother … Tell me what happened!'

Eight men had left Muciripattanam early that morning, including Nilham and Vikesh, carrying goods to be delivered. Only four had returned.

'It was an ambush, brother. We made the delivery as expected and collected our payment. We were halfway home when out of nowhere, an entire horde of men appeared wielding sticks and weapons. Nilham didn't shy away from the fight and was a fearsome sight, killing four or five men on his own, but they were far too many of them. I tried my best too, but …' Vikesh sat down despondently in the dirt. Nilham had been an elder brother to him too. Jayesh slumped down beside him. Nothing was making sense.

Tears streamed down Jayesh's face, his voice growing desperate for answers, 'But who attacked you? And why! Were they the king's men?'

It was true that since Jayesh had refused the king's niece's proposal, their visits had been fraught with peril, and dealings with the king's men and guards were strained and curt. But they had never suspected they would be attacked in such a gruesome way.

'I can't be sure.' Vikesh looked shaken.

'How many men were there?'

'About twenty, I would say. We were heavily outnumbered.'

Some moments passed in silence before Jayesh said, 'But … why would they leave survivors?'

'I don't know,' Vikesh answered, sighing.

Nilham had bullied and berated Jayesh for as long as he could remember, yet he was still his hero. He was everything Jayesh wanted to be – big, strong and loved by their father. But now he was dead and Jayesh needed to know why.

Nannan suddenly emerged on the hillside, rushing towards them. 'We need to go right now. Come with me at once, brothers,' he said, panting.

'Nannan, my brother Nilham, he … you must leave me to mourn him today,' Jayesh tried to reason with his friend.

'You must do as I say. I know who did this to your brother – and we have a big problem.' Nannan said as he led them to one of the warehouses.

34

Sreepadam Palace, Main Meeting Room
5 July 2024

The entire team had gathered in the main meeting room on the first floor for the presentation about the dig at Anapuzha. Professor Prakash was seated in the first row. The blinds had been drawn and the big screen was the only light source in the room. Dr Penny Gupta had sent around an email saying she had discovered the links between the dig site and the written records – this was going to be her moment. Her slideshow was ready.

'Okay, everyone,' she began, 'thank you all for coming. I won't keep you from your work for very long – I just wanted to run through the details of everything that we found at Anapuzha and share my inferences with the larger team.'

The original dig site outside Anapuzha had seen an extensive excavation led by Harveen, based on evidence that it was where an important family had once lived. They had almost immediately discovered the wooden foundations of a first-century building, after which there had been nothing more for weeks on end. They had covered a wide area of the barren landscape and found a few artefacts here and there, but nothing major had been discovered. It had been a frustrating venture, yielding nothing more than broken vases, colourful beads and riffraff. Everything they had found had been close to the surface, and there was nothing for a few feet underneath in the few spots where they decided to persist with the digging. The chances of finding anything new on this second visit had seemed remote, yet here the team was, as if in wait to be informed about some grand discovery.

'The trading records that we found showed that this symbol you see on the screen was used to denote the Port of Muziris. The symbol was seen on many of the items from Anapuzha we had uncovered before, so I led a team to see if we could find anything more there.'

Harveen marvelled at how easily Penny was stealing credit for her discovery of the said link between Muziris and the artefacts from their previous dig. Even the image on the screen had been brought to Penny's attention by her.

'We now know that stone was used to build housing in Muziris, so we focused on using the ground-penetrating radar to look for such stones. One of the advantages of the site being quite exposed is that the GPR was quite effective.'

Harveen wondered how long Penny would drag the meeting on without giving any new information.

'I decided we should use a cluster map showing the density of finds from the last dig. We started from the point where they had been most concentrated and worked our way outwards.'

Harveen glanced at Rohan to see how he was responding to Penny stealing credit for his labour too. He rolled his eyes when he saw her looking. It seemed that Penny's charms were wearing off. Dr Gupta railed on for another fifteen minutes without revealing anything new.

'Then we found this – a large flat stone. We think it might have been part of an early building,' she said, changing slides. 'As you can see, it had originally probably been rectangular in shape, though the bottom corner is missing.'

'We were very excited that it might have been part of a building and we were close, but I'm afraid there was nothing else around it – I scanned up to twenty feet in each direction.' Dr Gupta scrolled through a number of pictures of the stone. 'Tests show the stone is likely from the right era – the first century. The only distinguishing marks it bore pointed to the possibility of it having been part of a building. There were a number of shallow dents on its surface on one side, as you can see here. Other than that, it seemed unremarkable.'

With that, Penny concluded her presentation. 'Any questions?' she paused for a few seconds before saying, 'Alright then, let's get back to work.' She snapped her fingers and began to wind up her things when Harveen stood up with her laptop.

'Just a minute, Dr Gupta,' she said, smiling sweetly in the face of Penny's irritation. 'I have something incredible to show everyone.'

'Shall we not discuss it between ourselves first, Harveen?' Penny said, standing firmly in place. Harveen smiled sweetly at her.

'No need, Dr Gupta. I think it's better if everyone sees this now.'

35

Muciripattanam
AD 33

As soon as the three men entered the warehouse, Jayesh's heart stopped. In the otherwise empty building stood fifteen well-armed soldiers around a table. He recognized the man sitting in their midst and smiling at him.

'Servius!'

'Ah, my little Indian friend, we have much to discuss.' Servius looked at Jayesh with a smug grin as Nannan interpreted his words to his friend. Jayesh was reeling from the shock of recent events.

'What are you doing here?'

'He is the one, Jayesh – he killed Nilham!' Nannan exclaimed. The image of Servius executing the Cheras on their voyage to Myos Hormos flashed in Jayesh's mind. He remembered how he'd been left for dead in that putrid underground jail. Now, imagining Servius ordering the attack on his brother made Jayesh's blood boil. He spotted a stick on the floor and lunged at Servius with it. But before he could get anywhere close, one of the soldiers knocked him to the ground.

'You killed my brother! I will kill you!' Jayesh was screaming. He struggled to get on his feet and tried to attack again but two soldiers stepped in his path and grabbed hold of him.

'This is not Myos Hormos or Alexandria! I promise you will die here!' Jayesh continued to struggle and yell.

'What makes you think I don't know that? You think I would come all the way out here without protection?' Servius retorted. He had not even flinched at all the commotion and sat comfortably in his spot at the table as if in his own home. He looked rather amused at Jayesh's futile attempts to attack him.

'Why did you kill my brother, you snake?' Jayesh spat, fighting against the soldiers' grip tightening around his arms. He couldn't understand what Servius had against him to hound him so relentlessly, but it was plain that it was personal. He had come after his family; he'd killed his brother.

'You can call it an outstanding debt. You should have stayed in that hole I had thrown you into. After that little rescue operation for you, I lost my position and Quintus's trust.' For the first time ever, Servius looked enraged.

'Where is he now?' Jayesh asked, snarling with murderous intent. He had no weapon and the soldiers were on their guard.

'Oh, the old man has finally retired. Now he is somewhere in Rome playing with his grandchildren. I will pay him a visit when the time is right. For the moment, all you need to know is that I now control the trading route to India.'

Jayesh knew this was a lie; the trade to India was controlled by no one and each individual vessel was financed by traders themselves. 'Who are these men with you?'

'Well, it seems that you have many enemies in India. It was not hard to find willing soldiers within a few miles – the Chera king was happy to lend some of his men to us. They have been eyeing this port for some time, as you may know.'

Jayesh could not believe it. First his family, now his hometown? He knew the Cheras had more men than he could muster around these parts to protect Muciripattanam.

'You cold, heartless savage! What do you want of me?'

'Money, of course,' Servius said and laughed. 'You have a great thing going with Rome. Give me a fair cut and I will leave you to your business.'

'And what if I don't?'

'The Roman Senate does not take well to people who take advantage of it. The armies of the Empire are the greatest in the world. They're unstoppable. A simple word from me about your profits and your enterprise here will be finished – you will go down with it.' Servius's beady eyes gleamed; he seemed to be enjoying making Jayesh miserable.

'Rome is very pleased with what we are doing,' said Jayesh. Their relationship with the Roman merchants based in Alexandria was getting stronger with every visit.

'We'll see about that when I tell them that the Cheras and others can supply the same goods at a better price. I am happy to offer them this information.' Jayesh considered this for a moment before saying,

'And what is the price of your silence?'

'Ten per cent of all that you make from your trade with Alexandria and Rome. I want details of every transaction and I want my payment twice a year.'

'We are farmers; we don't hold such amounts of money here. We will need time to gather it. We can deliver money to you in Alexandria but it will take months,' said Jayesh. He needed time to think.

'We have a deal, then? Excellent. I knew you would see sense, you appeared to be a smart lad. I have already extracted a small portion of my payment from your brother, so you need not worry for the time being. You better start getting your records in order. I want all the details of your recent transactions along with my payment at the House of Guilds in Ostia within the next ninety days. Or else, get ready to bid goodbye to your dear port and the rest of your family. Swear on it, you little rat,' he said in a menacing voice.

Jayesh kept silent. Servius picked up his sword and held it at Jayesh's neck.

'I said swear on it,' he hissed.

'I swear,' Jayesh relented.

36

Sreepadam Palace, Main Meeting Room
5 July 2024

Penny was stoic but fuming as she reluctantly allowed Harveen to take the dais. When she opened her laptop, Harveen could sense the team's excitement in the air.

'Hello, everyone,' began Harveen. 'Sorry for taking over the meeting but I just could not bear to keep my latest findings from you any longer. We've worked so long and hard on these excavations, I think you deserve to know what has come of all of your labours. It is … spectacular.' She quickly glanced at Professor Prakash, who was leaning forward, caught up in the intrigue.

'The other day, an idea occurred to me, and I was partly sure that it would not come to anything so I had to keep it to myself. When I began to investigate, over the last twenty-four hours, the most remarkable discovery has come to light.' Harveen tapped her laptop, and the screen lit up with a picture of the stone tablet that they had discovered in Anapuzha.

'Here, you can see the stone tablet that was recovered from the dig site in Anapuzha. It is a travertine stone, a form of limestone not commonly found in India. As you all may know, we have dated it back to sometime between the first and the fifth century AD. Travertine stone from this era was mainly used by the Romans for buildings. In fact, the largest building ever made from this stone is the Colosseum in Rome.' She switched to the next slide, showing a close-up of the stone face. 'Here, you can see on the face of the stone, there are a number of indentations of various depths. They form an irregular pattern.' The next few slides showed the indentations up close with measurements and dimensions. 'It is clear that the stone has worn away over time. But we concluded that these were all holes of a uniform depth.

'I was reminded of Professor Geza Alfoldy of the University of Heidelberg in 1995 and some of his work. He analyzed an inscribed stone found at the entrance to the Colosseum. The inscription was from the fifth century, and mentioned something about the restoration of the building. It did not appear to be significant until Professor Alfoldy noticed that there were holes in three distinct lines and concluded that the stone had originally had an inscription attached to it – probably metal letters fastened with pegs inserted into the holes.' Harveen moved on to the next group of slides, showing the stone from the Colosseum and the small holes in it.

'As the letters are in a standard format – and actually Roman dedications appear in a fairly standard configuration – Professor Alfoldy was able to decipher the original message, as you can see here.' She went through the next few slides, explaining how the message had been reconstructed.

'Harveen, maybe we should discuss—' Penny tried to intervene but was silenced by the sight of the next slide, letting out a gasp despite herself. There were some surprised murmurs around the room when the original message was revealed. It was a dedication stating that Emperor Vespasian had ordered for this new stadium to be constructed using proceeds from the booty secured during the campaign in Jerusalem.

'Of course,' she continued, 'there is a bit of conjecture involved in this method, but Professor Alfoldy's findings have since been endorsed by other researchers from Germany and the University of Oxford as well.' Harveen took a dramatic pause before continuing, 'I contacted the team at Oxford, who are the most well-respected researchers in this area and sent them 3D images of the stone that we found, along with the pattern of the markings.

'As I am not an expert in Old Tamil, I had Professor Shah there help me make some educated conclusions about the lettering that might have been used in the language. We estimated where letters could have been affixed and relayed that to the team at Oxford to enter into their model.' Penny was getting increasingly uncomfortable and Harveen was thoroughly enjoying her moment. She showed a couple of slides pictorially depicting the process she had just described. 'Unfortunately, we found no success at all.'

Disappointed murmurs went around the room.

'Right, well that's that then—' Penny leapt at the opportunity to put an end to the presentation.

'Or so we thought ...' Harveen continued suspensefully. The team at Oxford put the sequence of holes into their own software, which is configured only for Old Latin used by the Romans, and they came back to us with this.' Her next click revealed the following words:

Ecclesia Sancti Thomae, fratris Iesu Christi. primo, ut ecclesia christiana, et domus tabe Muziris 71

There was complete silence in the room, most people not comprehending the meaning of the Latin words. She continued, 'The translation is as follows.' Gasps went up in unison from around the room.

Church of Saint Thomas, brother of Jesus Christ. First
Christian Church and the home of tab___(?)
Muziris AD 71

Harveen looked at Professor Prakash victoriously. He was visibly stunned by the revelation. She tried to be loud so she was audible above the buzz in the room, 'Because there is a missing piece, we cannot fully make out the last word ...'

Penny sprang up from her seat and hissed at Harveen, 'Why didn't you come to me first? Did you not think I needed to know about this before you told everyone else?'

So you could take credit for my work again? Harveen thought. But she said aloud as sweetly as she could manage, 'I'm sorry, Dr Gupta. I wasn't trying to step on your toes – it's just that the team has been working so hard with me on this for months and months before you came in. I just thought they deserved to know – don't you?'

37

Muciripattanam
AD 34

'It looks like Servius has made good on his threat,' said Nannan.

'I told you! I've been saying from the very first day that we should just give him the bit of money he wants and get him off our backs – stop dealing with the Romans altogether,' replied Vikesh, shaking his head in frustration.

'He killed my brother – you can't be serious about bargaining with a man like that? How are you supposed to trust him? Take his word? The first opportunity he found, he threw me into an underground prison to die!' Jayesh retorted angrily.

They sat looking at the document they had received that morning. Summons from the Roman Senate for Jayesh to get on the next boat sailing out of India. It was signed by Emperor Tiberius himself, and the meeting was going to be held in the presence of his closest advisors.

Jayesh, in his twenty-seven years, had travelled extensively with Nannan – but it had always been of his own volition. He felt nervous at being summoned by the emperor himself. He clearly had no choice but to go, he could not afford to find out what defying the Roman emperor might mean. He had heard many stories of their cruelty and brutal methods of meting out punishment to people who had committed far smaller wrongs than ignoring royal summons.

'We have sacrificed so much already,' pleaded Vikesh. 'You are now also my sister's husband and a part of my family in addition to being my dearest friend – please, brother, just lie low and I'm sure this will pass. Let's pay the evil man for now, get rid of this new threat and never trade with the Romans again. Think about our families, Jayesh! We already have more than any man could ever need. Forsake your grand dreams – let us live a peaceful life here. No more – I can't bear the thought of more lives being lost to this hopeless cause you're obsessed with.'

Jayesh was pained by Vikesh's words. He swallowed hard and said, 'I'm sorry, my brother, but if you want me to live, I must go.

'We cannot refuse a summons from the emperor of Rome,' Nannan agreed. 'There's no other way.'

For the first time since they had become friends, Vikesh turned his back on Jayesh and Nannan, and stormed off.

Jayesh wanted to go after him but he knew he had to decide how to deal with the situation in Rome first. 'Nannan, what of the meeting?'

Nannan looked very uncomfortable, 'I have found the man we need. He will meet us in Ostia, where we are to make the payment in person.'

'Good,' Jayesh said, feigning courage. 'As for the Senate, we have a few days until the next vessel departs. Meet me tomorrow, let's figure out what to do. I will seek my parents' blessing for the trip tonight.'

Jayesh spent the walk to his house considering how he could placate Rome, what they even knew and if his business was about to go down. The stories of Roman armies' brutal invasions were causing the panic in his mind to rise. He imagined how the next fleet of ships that landed at their market could be full of soldiers looking to plunder Muciripattanam rather than trade merchants looking for business.

'Don't worry, I will be safe and return very soon,' he assured both Paavi and Vasudha. For the first time in his life, he felt unsure. Even on his first-ever trip to Alexandria, when he had been ignorant about the world that lay beyond Muciripattanam, Jayesh had had a sense of confidence that he could overcome any obstacles in his path.

'I cannot lose you, my dear son. No more of my sons will lose their lives to this cursed business – please! Can you not send someone else in your stead, son?' Vasudha implored.

'You know I would give the world to stay here with you and Paavi, Amma. But I must go – though, on the bright side, I might get to meet the Great Emperor of Rome himself! I'll tell you both all about him once I return. Your prayers and blessings will keep me safe, Amma; they are the greatest forces of all. You must have faith.'

Since Nilham's death, Jayesh's father had not spoken to him. He was determined to make both his parents feel proud of him once again; surely, then his father would talk to him.

'Please, son! They are murderers – what if they try to …' Vasudha began sobbing. Jayesh looked to Paavi for her support.

'Amma, he will be back before we even know it. While he is away, you and I can make plans for our new temple together.' Paavi said. She was a true blessing, Jayesh knew. Despite his beloved mother's objections, ten years ago, he had insisted on marrying her. Since the blushing bride had come into their home, their lives had just felt sweeter. She had proven to be a great companion to Vasudha, and a caring daughter-in-law to Abhay. She was a doting wife and a devoted mother, and Jayesh secretly took comfort in the fact that should his trip go awry, she would be a pillar of support for their family.

'I know it's no use trying to stop him,' Vasudha said to Paavi. 'Once he gets these ideas in his head, there is no turning him – he has always been this way. But can you blame me for trying?' She looked weathered and defeated, wearing a weak smile. She gave him her blessings and he turned to leave the house, flashing a long, final glance at Paavi.

As he started walking down the hillside, he heard Paavi's steps running to catch up with him. He spun around and wrapped her in his arms. After a moment of silence, he sensed there was something on her mind. 'What is it?' he asked gently. Paavi seemed anxious. 'What's wrong, my love?'

After some hesitation, she said, 'I have been having the same dream for three nights now, Jayesh. I did not want to worry you, but I am too scared and I must warn you.'

She paused for a moment before saying, 'We have four young boys, a beautiful home, our whole lives to spend together … Don't go, Jayesh. Stay for me, for our family.' Jayesh could see tears forming in her eyes. He held her tight.

'Tell me – what did you see in this dream, Paavi?'

'The ship …' she said, her voice breaking, '… with you and Nannan on it … I dreamt that it was being struck by fire from the sky and then … it sank. It all felt so real. I knew nothing of your impending journey – this feels like an evil foreboding; a vision. What if it comes true?'

'It won't, Paavi,' he said, attempting to reassure her and himself. He laughed, 'If the emperor of Rome wishes to see me, he will have me pulled out of the depths of the ocean. Don't you worry, my love. Your fears are for nothing, everything will be well.'

As they parted, Jayesh considered for the first time that this journey might cost him his life.

38

Sreepadam Palace, Main Meeting Room
5 July 2024

The room erupted into louder murmurs as Harveen and Penny got into a rather heated exchange. Watching Penny gesture wildly, Professor Prakash stood up to defuse the situation. The room fell silent.

'Harveen, this may be our greatest find yet. I must congratulate you and the team.' The professor's genuine praise warmed Harveen's heart. It was all going to plan. 'We need to know everything about Saint Thomas's time in India,' he continued. 'The statement that he is the brother of Jesus Christ seems too far-fetched at the moment. We must keep this information under wraps until we have verified its veracity. Dr Gupta, please arrange for a team to re-investigate the Anapuzha site.'

As everyone sprang into action, Harveen noticed Penny slipping out without saying a word to anyone. Instinctively, she followed her.

She saw her going through the back door into the beautiful grounds, fumbling for her mobile phone as she walked, barely glancing back. Penny stopped at the edge of the path and Harveen quickly hid just behind the door, careful not to be seen.

'… and then she managed to decipher what was on the original stone!' she could hear Penny saying in hushed tones. 'Yes, I can bring you a copy … When?' A couple of people walked past and Harveen missed the next part of the conversation, unable to keep track over the other sounds.

'Okay, I will be there – see you then,' Penny said, finishing up the call suddenly, and turned, coming face to face with Harveen.

She appeared shocked, 'Oh, Harveen! What are you doing here?'

'Uhh … I was looking for you, actually,' Harveen replied, trying to come up with something to say. 'I wanted to apologize for not keeping you in the know about the stone. It was a crazy idea that unexpectedly paid off, and I only just received the translation from Oxford – I simply wanted to hasten our research along so we don't lose precious time. So I thought I'd just share it with everyone straightaway. They've been working so hard at this. It was the first bit of happy news we've had in some time …'

Harveen was searching Penny's face for some sign of displeasure at her eavesdropping, expecting a confrontation.

'Actually, I wanted to speak to you too – can we go back upstairs?' Penny said instead.

'Sure,' she said, intrigued.

Penny took a moment to compose herself as if the next words seemed a struggle for her to utter. 'I have been thinking that maybe you are a much better lead for this project than myself – your instincts are very good and you've already been working on this for so long now that you have a view of the whole picture. I am way out of my comfort zone at the moment – I'd much rather be behind a desk, poring over finds. My real skill is translation.'

'Dr Gupta, are you sure? I hope I didn't overstep—'

'No, no. Professor Prakash was keen to bring me in to head the project – and I must admit, I was excited by the opportunity. But it all just feels a bit unfair to you now. I can see that you are a natural at it. Your deduction about the stone was brilliant; you're clearly so invested and skilled.'

'Thank you, Dr Gupta.'

'I would really like us to work together on this,' she concluded.

Harveen gave her a satisfied smile, but then the memory of the suspicious call came back to her. She decided it was best to remain measured in her words, 'Me too,' she smiled as convincingly as she could. 'That would be great.'

As they both walked to their desks together, Penny said, 'Here, I want you to look at this AI software I developed to translate Old Tamil and other ancient languages into English – it's very accurate. If you ever need to use it, here is my password.' She scribbled it onto a piece of paper quickly. 'This is what I use to save time searching through records.'

Penny looked at her watch. 'I have a meeting right now. Once I'm back, let's go and see Professor Prakash. I'll tell him I think you should be the one leading the fieldwork and that I'll lend my expertise to what I know best. We will find a rhythm that works for both of us. Sound good?'

Harveen weighed her options. Of course she wanted her role back, but there was also no doubt in her mind that Penny was sharing their findings with an outsider. 'May I ask who you are meeting, Dr Gupta?'

'Well … I can't say just yet. It's someone who is likely to

have some pretty crucial information for us. The matter is sensitive; I'll need to go to some lengths to explain the whole thing to you. I need to rush for now – how about I tell you more when I get back?'

She held out her hand to seal their agreement but Harveen hesitated to take it. Her redemption was staring her in the eye, yet something didn't quite feel right. She swallowed the lump in her throat and shook Penny's hand.

39

Muciripattanam
AD 34

Jayesh's fear for his life were to prove true – sooner than he could possibly have predicted.

They had set sail from Muciripattanam on the first vessel they could find. On their journey to Myos Hormos, Nannan finally had the chance to prepare Jayesh for what lay ahead.

'Muciripattanam is now the most prominent trading port in India. The volume of trade with Rome is so great that on average, a large merchant ship docks in Muciripattanam every other day. Over the last two years, even China has started to use Muciripattanam as their main port of choice for trading in Indian goods. Our spices seem to be well loved in the Far Eastern lands. The Chinese have been bringing gold and beautiful silks to trade – which are a favourite with the Romans, as you already know.'

They had even constructed large wooden piers, similar to those at Myos Hormos, to enable four ships to dock at Muciripattanam simultaneously. As a result, the volume of trade had increased significantly.

'Yes,' said Jayesh, 'we will soon be earning more from the gold and silk than the pepper.

'Their new Emperor Guangwu has ambitions to not only build his own empire but to leave a lasting legacy of his dynasty's reign. I think he will help us get native speakers here like we have with the Romans.' Jayesh had already made two trips to China.

'My brother, that is the problem – the amount of money we are making off Rome. I think Servius has made good on his threat and that is why the Senate wants to see us. Look at this.' Nannan wore a worried expression. 'For every trade, the Romans pay in Roman sesterces or Alexandrian drachmas. On the first visit of a Roman merchant ship, you managed to empty Captain Quintus's purse of about a hundred Roman gold coins. Each ship now leaves Muciripattanam heavy with goods and lighter by over 100,000 coins.'

Jayesh smiled, 'And it will be even more next year!'

'Brother, you don't understand. This is not boding well for us. In the last year alone, we have taken in excess of 50 million sesterces from the Romans. We have amassed a huge fortune. I am having more trouble building safeholds to keep our gold coins than for our pepper.'

It was the first time Jayesh had considered that their growing trade could actually be a threat.

'If Servius has told them that they are overpaying for the goods they do purchase, then they would be even more enraged,' Jayesh thought out loud.

'Rome can't keep pace with the payments owed to Muciripattanam. I have been accepting written notices signed by the emperor himself, stating his promise to pay the money due. This paper debt is now over 175 million sesterces. I think we have enough money between all of us to buy every single house in Alexandria. They cannot possibly be expected to feel pleased about furthering our prosperity.

We cannot put it past them to send their armies to plunder our villages and take all their wealth back.'

With his ambitions, Jayesh had not considered the impact of having such a great hold over Rome. 'What should we do, Nannan? You know the Romans better than I.'

'I'm not sure, my brother. We don't know yet what they have been told. The numbers are substantial. I found something else, too. See.' He showed Jayesh a document written in Latin.

'It's a "receipt of goods" from Alexandria for one of our shipments. Look at this line. The Romans are now levying a tax on each merchant arriving at their ports. They are charging twenty-five per cent tax on everything we sell. This tribute is payable by the merchants. As a direct result of trade with us, I calculate that the Roman treasury collects 12 million sesterces every year! We may be a problem for them, but our goods also generate a lot of tax.'

Suddenly, there was a commotion on the deck.

'Pirates! All hands on deck!'

People were shouting from above. Jayesh and Nannan immediately clambered up. As they got to the deck, Jayesh saw six or seven skiffs closing fast on the merchant ship, each loaded with men. Fights had broken out in a corner of the deck – some of the pirates had already come onboard. In the heat of the midday sun, the skiffs were like small flies attacking a majestic lion as they swarmed around the large merchant ship. Jayesh saw two men on one of the skiffs throw a weighted rope net onto the deck, and within moments, eight pirates had clambered onboard, swords drawn.

'Look out!' Nannan shouted and Jayesh dodged one of the pirates, rushing forward to grab hold of the oars. The pirates carried an array of weapons and were easily getting past the well-fed merchants and commoners who had just set sail from Muciripattanam. There were neither warriors nor skilled fighters on the ship. The speed and ferocity of the attack had completely overwhelmed them.

As Jayesh wrestled with a pirate, Paavi's warning echoed in his head. The ship had been struck, as if by lightning. They had barely made their way out of Muciripattanam, and his and Nannan's lives were already at threat.

40

Thrissur, Kerala
6 July 2024

'A major discovery 'as been made, signor. It doesn't sound good.' The distinct monotone of Vincenzo travelled clearly to Don over the hum of the Gulfstream G650.

'Explain yourself!' Rossi barked on the line from the Vatican. The three men had hurried onto a call after an urgent message from Rossi's favoured assassin.

'The Gupta woman, signor. She called Paulo, all excited. Said something incredible 'ad been uncovered. We met 'er a second time a few hours ago.'

'Well, what was it?' Don probed. Rossi had promised that Vincenzo and Paulo were deputed to be mere observers, but he had clearly given them different instructions.

'A stone – part of a building. There is some lettering on it, an inscription that says "Church of St Thomas, brother of Jesus Christ".'

A few moments of silence ensued.

'This can't get out!' hissed Rossi, his fury evident. 'How many people know?'

'Apparently, they discussed it in a staff meeting today. The old man Prakash told everyone it was confidential, so we know 'e was there. I don't yet know who else, signor.'

'Meet Gupta again. We need to know who all were there, and the full details of what they know,' Don said. If he was to contain this, detail was key. There was a pause on the other end.

'Gupta … she is still 'ere, Signor Don … There were some … problems.' Vincenzo seemed to be choosing his words carefully. Don's stomach tightened.

'What are you saying, Vincenzo?' demanded Rossi.

'She wouldn't give us the information since the professor said not to, signor. When Paulo probed, she got very suspicious and said to leave. We 'ad to use some … force.'

'Well, can she still talk?'

'Sí, signor. For now.'

Before Don could say anything, Rossi dealt the order. He was seething at the interference but merely clenched his jaw and said nothing.

'Find out everything that happened at the meeting. Then call us straightaway,' Rossi said.

'Sí, signor,' Vincenzo said and hung up. It was only Rossi and Don on the line now.

'As soon as we have all the information, Don, we need to shut this down. This cannot get out, you understand?'

'Yes, signor,' said Don. If he had simply been allowed to handle things his way, he would have been in India right now and it would all be under control. But now his hands were tied. He had to tow the Santa Alleanza line, doing as Rossi commanded – he saw no other way.

Despite the vast resources the Vatican had at its disposal, the Pope generally travelled on commercial planes of the Italian national carrier, Alitalia. The Santa Alleanza, by contrast, had its own private plane, a Gulfstream G650 modified to their preferences.

It had only ten seats – as opposed to the original

standard of eighteen – arranged specifically to hold their meetings. There were private rooms with two separate beds and a compact kitchen area. There was also a hidden vault installed in the rear for storing both valuable documents and their arsenal of weapons. The main communal areas of the plane were luxurious, with soft beige leather seats and dark wood detailing. It had the feel of a bespoke corporate jet. The opulence of the plane repulsed Don – it was too stark a contrast to the humble surroundings of the church.

On his flight to India, Don examined the documents that Sofia had given him. The discovery of the Gospel of St Thomas in Egypt had certainly instigated the Santa Alleanza to react quite strongly. They had launched a rigorous discreditation campaign that impressed Don despite himself. This had been long before Dino Rossi's time and no blood had been spilled. Academics from all around the world had been influenced and paid off to create an overwhelming body of opinion discrediting the Gospel. This had resulted in the news of its discovery to fade without a trace. Don couldn't help but feel that was a better way to operate.

Sofia had also sent him a box called 'The Artefact'. Don did not have enough time to go through everything in detail, but before he could even start, the secure conference line rang again. He picked up immediately.

'There were eight of them, signor,' began Vincenzo without preamble. 'The main one is called Dr 'arveen Gill. She found the records and this latest conclusion too. Gupta thinks she will be made the leader. Prakash is in background for now. They are planning to dig up the original site again, signor. There are no more leads, Gupta says.'

'Who were the others?' asked Don.

'Six people, from the university 'ere– I send you their names, signor.'

'Get Dr Gill out of the way,' Rossi said firmly.

'Sí, signor,' said Vincenzo.

'Actually, I don't think so,' interjected Don. He knew he needed to somehow take control of the operation before blood was shed. 'That will not help anything. She has made her other findings public online. It's all on record now. Only a matter of time before something is leaked about the inscription. I am but an hour away from landing. Signor Rossi, I would prefer to deal with her directly.'

'What are you planning?' Rossi asked.

'I will meet with Dr Gill and find out what they know, then decide.'

'Fine,' said Rossi curtly. 'And Dr Gupta?'

'I take care of that, signor,' Vincenzo said before hanging up.

41

Muciripattanam
AD 34

More pirates spilled onto the deck from all directions. The crew was no match for them.

'Look!' shouted Jayesh. 'They are steering us that way.' The ship was turning towards shallow waters near the shore, where about twenty more men were waiting to board it.

'If they take us there, we are all sure to die!' Everyone was too panic-stricken to do anything to help the situation. 'Nannan, come with me! We need to gain control of the ship.' There were two pirates steering the vessel, both of whom had laid their weapons aside as they heaved its bulky oars.

Jayesh rushed at the first one – a large, bare-chested man with a thick beard. He grabbed Jayesh by his shirt and flung him to the ground like a ragdoll. The very next moment, Jayesh was back on his feet and attacking the other pirate. He was not as prepared and they both crashed onto the deck, arms and legs flailing about. Jayesh managed to land a couple of punches, drawing screams from the pirate. As he was about to hit him again, the bigger pirate scooped him up from behind and threw him across the deck. Both pirates were atop him, raining down blows on his body. They were only moments away from the shore now. Jayesh could hear the clanging of swords all around him.

'Stop him!' somebody was suddenly shouting and the beating ceased for a moment. Nannan was heaving one of the steering oars with all his weight. Another pirate was running towards him, along with Jayesh's attackers. The three men wrestled to pull Nannan off the oar, but he would not let go. Jayesh grabbed hold of a metal bar on the side of the ship to pull himself up, and saw that Nannan had almost managed to ground the ship away from where the other pirates stood.

'Nannan, jump!' He shouted as the pirates finally prised him off the oar. On his cue, they both jumped overboard and began to swim towards the shore.

The ship had run aground only a short distance away from where the pirates lay in wait. The merchants and sailors were frantically rushing towards land, while the pirates rushed aboard to ransack the ship from the other side. On reaching the shore, Jayesh collapsed. His body ached all over.

'Are you okay, brother?' Nannan rushed to his side. 'You are hurt.'

'It's alright. I'm fine,' he said, breaking out into laughter.

'Have you gone mad? We were nearly killed! This is the third pirate attack this week, what are you laughing about?'

'Paavi!' Jayesh said between gasps and laughter. 'She said we would be attacked. She saw it in a dream. I was so worried! But we survived, brother! Now I'm certain we will find success. Let's get back. We can take the next ship to Alexandria.'

42

Thrissur
6 July 2024

As soon as Don had checked in at the Hyatt Regency in Thrissur, he read the file Sofia had hurriedly prepared on Dr Harveen Gill. Her professional background was impressive, even without any major finds to her credit. She was reportedly single and renting a small apartment. Her social media accounts and YouTube channel were full of content about her archaeological digs.

The recent discovery of a merchant's house had garnered considerable press attention and got picked up by mainstream publications after Reuters published the original article. Dr Gill had been quoted extensively. Don had no doubt that she would continue to dig deeper and network with academicians around the world, uncovering more and more. Looking at her photos and videos, Don could see why some of them had gone viral. Even in her drab khaki shirt and shorts, and her chunky boots, Harveen was beautiful. She had long, straight black hair, dark eyes and a petite nose. When she spoke about the finds, her slightly crooked smile and the sparkle in her eyes lit up the screen. Sofia had mentioned that a YouTube video of Harveen explaining what the written records said had over 200,000 views already.

The file had her phone numbers and printouts of her numerous emails to the Vatican asking for help with her find. Don took out his burner phone and dialled.

'Hello?' her response was almost instant.

'Good evening, Dr Gill, I am so glad I got through. My name is Don Clemente, and I work as a senior researcher at the Vatican Archives. One of my colleagues forwarded your numerous emails and contact number to me. I am currently in India. We were fascinated to learn of your recent discoveries. Congratulations, signora, you must be so pleased.'

'Oh my gosh!' she replied, sounding genuinely surprised by the call. 'Thank you so much! Also, thanks for calling.'

'The Vatican cannot officially involve itself in speculative digs around the world, of course, I'm sure you understand, signora,' he said, hoping she would take the lead.

'Of course, yes,' she said. 'I am just looking for some help verifying our finds.'

'Well,' began Don reluctantly. 'You see, your finds are very close to where we too believe the apostle St Thomas to have spent much of his time in India. It is one of my personal areas of interest and that's actually what brought me here. Your discovery really fascinated me. I wonder, has there been any mention of St Thomas in the records you found?'

There was a long pause on the other end.

'Dr Gill?'

'Where in India are you? Perhaps you can come to the office?' Harveen answered. We have a mixture of intrigue and suspicion in her voice.

'I am staying at the Hyatt Regency in Thrissur.'

'The Hyatt … that's so close. Why don't you come to the museum, Mr Clemente? We have so many interesting things I'm sure you would love to see.'

Don could picture her crooked smile.

'I would really have loved to, Dr Gill. Your findings relate to much of the work I have been doing over the last few years myself, but I am afraid it cannot be. The implications of a Vatican researcher arriving at your museum just hours after such a find could be misinterpreted.'

He needed to see her alone if he was to have any chance to contain the situation.

'May I ask what type of work it is that you have been doing, Mr Clemente?' she asked.

'I've been looking into St Thomas's journey to India. We know that he came here and founded churches, but we still don't know why, or perhaps even who he really was.'

'What do you mean? Are there more than one St Thomas?'

'Well, not exactly, signora. There are some documents that offer a different view than what we think we know about him, but … I cannot say more, I'm afraid. I have already said too much. I was hoping you could help me find out more, but it seems the only way to get in touch with you is if I come to your museum, which I certainly cannot do. Perhaps it was unwise of me to have called you. My apologies. Farewell, signora—'

'Wait!' interjected Harveen. 'There is … something I might know. I can't say what as yet since we are still looking into it now – maybe if you could tell me more about what you know, we can piece the whole picture together.'

Don smiled. 'And what is it you have, Dr Gill?' he asked.

'It's an inscription … maybe from one of the churches … it appears to reference St Thomas.'

What an effortless liar, he thought. His mind once again drifted to her image from the video.

'Perhaps we can meet discreetly at my hotel. I have documents here with me that mention St Thomas – they may be helpful to you in decoding your discovery. And I could look through your work to see if perhaps I could learn a thing or two more. Perhaps … I could even verify them for you, unofficially.' Don pressed his advantage.

'Thank you so much, Mr Clemente. I don't know what to say.' There was genuine appreciation in Harveen's voice. She had taken the bait.

'No problem, signora. Shall we say 7 p.m. at the Hyatt tomorrow then? In the main reception area? I will text you my private number – you can contact me directly if you need anything.'

'7 p.m.,' she confirmed. 'Main reception. I will be there.'

'Great. Goodnight, signora. And thank you.'

Don hung up and put the phone down. He noticed his 9mm Beretta and picked it up instinctively, its familiar shape comfortable in his hand.

43

Muciripattanam
AD 34

Jayesh and Nannan travelled in angry silence by ship to Myos Hormos. Neither spoke even while on the road to the walled city of Alexandria. The last leg of their journey was by sea to the great Roman port of Ostia, and Jayesh could not wait for it to be over.

When they arrived in Ostia, Jayesh was keen to conclude their business there and move on to Rome.

'When is the meeting?' he asked.

'Later. Just so you had some time to reconsider,' Nannan said curtly.

'I will not. Let's see him now.'

'We have one more meeting before that,' said Nannan and he walked away.

Ostia was a large mercantile town. As the main port of Rome, it had been built to serve the capital's commercial shipping needs.

Jayesh had started to acclimatize to the wide, straight avenues lined with impressive stone buildings. Ostia was no exception to this architectural convention. The theatre was particularly beautiful.

The main attraction of the town, however, was just opposite the grand theatre. The Piazzale dele Corporazioni, a huge enclosed marketplace stretching for over 100 meters, with traders' offices down both sides and across the far wall. Nannan stood watching Jayesh take it all in.

'This is where we will meet the man you wanted me to seek out,' he said. It was the key reason they had come to Ostia.

'Good,' said Jayesh. 'And what is this place?'

'This place is the centre of all trade into Rome,' Nannan replied. 'Around the sides are offices set up specifically to promote trade around the world. You can find ship owners, traders and financiers who can broker, fund and organize an entire voyage.' Nannan's temper seemed to improve as they walked around. 'Look, each office has a sign above it to signify what goods can be bought and sold through it.' He pointed out each one in turn. 'That is a very famous shipbuilder who can arrange for the purchase or hire of any kind of vessel. That one there is a group of merchants who sell grain.'

Jayesh looked at each sign in wonder.

'There is the sign for the merchant who specializes in animals, and right next to it, the big elephant sign? That belongs to the office of merchants dealing in goods from the dark-skinned traders of Africa. They hold more offices here than anyone.' There were crowds of merchants bustling around the place. 'This here is the main place I visit to organize trade for Muciripattanam. There is almost no need to visit Rome,' Nannan said.

As Jayesh's eyes scanned the other offices, he noticed the largest office there had the name of Muziris prominently emblazoned above its doors with a distinctive red 'M'. As

Nannan saw what had caught his companion's attention, he declared happily, 'My brother, these are your offices!'

Jayesh stared at the sign in disbelief. His name was inscribed across the biggest trade office in Ostia. Whilst most of the other offices had black-and-white mosaic signs, the Muziris sign was emblazoned with colour.

'We have been working with traders here for several years now. I saw the opportunity to open our own offices when this site became available,' Nannan said proudly, 'so I took it. And since the office has been opened, trade and profits have both increased substantially. Remember, we are traders; not soldiers. We also have a permanent stand at the market.' He gestured towards a big stand, almost identical to the one they had back home, overflowing with their wares.

Nannan's proud presentation of their offices stung. They had been arguing for days now, yet Jayesh couldn't help but feel impressed at the sight of their own office. He patted Nannan on the back. This was one of the proudest moments of his life. 'Thank you, brother.'

'Come now, let us go for our first meeting. We are almost out of time,' Nannan said.

They had been considering commissioning a fleet of ships on their own to transport their goods without depending on the Roman merchant fleets, which cost them quite a bit of money. Nannan had arranged for a reputable Roman shipbuilder to build a great flagship for Muciripattanam's own merchant fleet. He was waiting for the builder to present his plans. He was a tall man, and looked well-built, though it was difficult to assess how old he was as his face bore the ravages of a life spent outdoors. Nannan introduced him to Jayesh as Felix.

'She will be built to the same specifications as the biggest of the merchant vessels in the Roman fleet,' Felix said proudly, spreading his drawings out on the table. '150 feet in length and 30 feet wide, she will easily be able to carry 400 tonnes of freight.' The plans were well considered, but Jayesh wanted some more specific details to be added to his first vessel.

'She must have an elaborate carving, such as the ones I have seen on Roman ships,' Jayesh said.

Felix smiled. 'Of course. We can make the ship to meet your exact demands. It is what we are known for. What would you like the figurehead to be, sir? It will make a great impression as your ship arrives on the docks.'

'Actually, I want it to be at the back of the vessel. When she sets sail onto her next destination, the figurehead is the last thing to disappear from sight for anyone standing on the shore.' Jayesh still remembered the first Roman ship he had seen and wanted nothing less for Muciripattanam's flagship. 'A lady. That's what I want on my ship,' he added.

'Of course. You will be delighted, I'm sure. We employ only the finest carpenters.' Felix went on to explain that it would take them a year to build the ship and the price they had agreed on would need to be revisited at the final stage. They haggled for some time over this until finally, the deal was struck. Nannan took out one of his cloth sheets to document the transaction.

'There is one final question, which we have not yet discussed, sir, if you may,' said Felix. 'The name. Every great ship has to have a unique name.'

Jayesh did not hesitate. 'I want to call it *Vasudha* – after my mother.' He had dreamed of this day since he had first seen a merchant ship.

The man was already waiting for them by the time their meeting with Felix concluded. He was of medium build, with a face like a rat's, and small black eyes. He wore a sleeveless woollen tunic, held tightly in place with a belt around his waist. It seemed as if he had a permanent scowl engraved into his countenance.

'This is Menes,' said Nannan gruffly. 'He comes very highly recommended.'

'You understand the job?' Jayesh asked immediately.

'Yes. Kill the merchant Servius.' He said without ceremony.

'Can it be done?'

'I have observed him. He is Captain of a ship. Whilst onboard, he has some security guards around. But at any other time, he is an ordinary merchant. He likes his wine too much and the brothels even more. The task should not be so difficult, sir.'

'He is Egyptian – he has no great love for the Romans,' explained Nannan.

'So it is agreed then. We accept your price,' Jayesh concluded.

Nannan held up a hand, asking Menes to wait.

Aside, he said in Tamil, 'Jayesh, are you quite sure you want to do this? We are traders, not killers. It is not in our culture to harbour such a deadly grudge.'

'He killed my brother, and he is damaging our business. The Romans feel no fear killing the men that get in their way. Why should we?'

'Because we are Hindus – they are not burdened by the values we are entrusted to uphold.'

'When in Rome, we do as the Romans do. Look how they have built their mighty empire. Don't you want the same for our home?'

With that, Jayesh shook the assassin's hand. He resolved he too would not let anything stand in his way.

44

Thrissur
6 July 2024

'Don, we need to shut this down. Now. We have a bloody inscription boldly talking about the brother. If it comes out, we may not be able to contain it. You must act immediately!'

Don had never heard the man quite so angry. He was sitting in his hotel room in Thrissur, 6,000 miles away from Rossi, and yet the older man's presence filled the room.

'I am meeting her tomorrow. She is bringing along all her documentation. We need to know if there is anything more, we can only decide how best to deal with it then. I assure you, signor, it will all be under control soon.'

Don tried to placate him.

'Don, you are the Head because you are a military man. I am not sure you fully understand the gravity of the situation. I thought we had an understanding; a tradition to honour,' Rossi's agitation was clear.

'Everyone knows that St Thomas went to India, signor. The Gospel of St Thomas has been around for 1,500 years. When a copy was discovered in 1945, it hardly caused a ripple in the mainstream. Why do you think this will gather any more attention?' asked Don. He knew anything that cast a shadow on the divinity of Jesus Christ was significant, but to him, Rossi's reaction seemed a bit extreme.

'Donatello, it is the damn internet! In 1945, all we had to do was to have noted academicians and religious leaders writing to the press condemning the Gospel of St Thomas as a fake written at a much later date. We simply drowned out all other voices. We ensured there was more noise against it than in support of it. You have seen the records. Do you think in this era of Facebook and blogs and the like, you can contain this once it gets out? That was just a book – this is a sign. A possibility that they can find not just the actual first church St Thomas established, but perhaps even more damning evidence to disprove our fabrications. What if they find his remains? The Christians will all want to flock there and see it for themselves. It will draw pilgrims and spark all kinds of debates questioning the status quo. Questioning whether Our Lord Jesus Christ was the Son of God at all, or just an ordinary man.' Rossi showed uncharacteristic patience in trying to explain to Don what was troubling him. But the menace lurked just beneath the surface.

'Signor, pardon me but even if they could prove that there was a church and it was established by St Thomas, the brother of Jesus Christ, surely the Vatican would still remain the ultimate authority of the Christian Church?'

'That is not our only concern, Don. There will still be other major issues for us to contend with,' Rossi bristled. 'You must know the Vatican generates its income through three primary means. There's the Peter's Pence, or Holy See revenue, or the donations from Christians from all around the world. This alone amounts to millions of Euros. There are still millions of people around the world who donate a portion of their income to the Church. It's an ongoing legacy since the Donation of Constantine.' His voice came alive when talking about the great deceptions of his predecessors.

'If there was another Church established elsewhere in the world with a purported relationship with someone closer to Christ than St Peter – like Christ's own brother, or even twin brother, perhaps – it would confuse those who donate to Peter's Pence. No doubt, any new buildings or investment required to re-establish such a church would cause Christian donors from around the world to come forward. With some rather creative uses of this fund in the recent years, we cannot afford for it to run further into a deficit.'

Donatello was well aware that members of the Church had bought luxurious properties around the world with funds donated to Peter's Pence. The Pope himself had spoken about the misappropriation of these funds.

'Secondly, there are the 10 million or so visitors to the Vatican each year. Many of them are here to see the beautiful architecture, but we must logically assume that many are here on religious pilgrimages, to visit the first Church of Christianity. We have long sought to protect this position and we must not weaken in our resolve at this critical time. Any new church would certainly attract a proportion of our current visitors. We will lose on a large portion of our income if visitors don't come to the Vatican and buy souvenirs and make donations. We collect nearly half a billion Euros each year from tourism.

'Finally, and most importantly, is the Vatican Bank, Don! The Bank of the Christian faith, and the Pope himself, is a private bank and based in our own little country here – free from the rigours of regulation which restrict and govern the activities of the others. We act in favour of many Christians and our other key supporters around the world. We have more than 8 billion Euros under management and it only grows with each passing year. Not being the "first bank" could prove disastrous.' Rossi let his words hang in the air for a while. 'If you do not act now, Don, I say this with the utmost seriousness, you will regret the immeasurable damage you will cause to the Church. It would be a sheer negligence of your duty.'

'What would you propose I do, signor?' asked Don, flustered.

'St Thomas was known to be a prolific writer. We have no idea what the Indians know but they seem to have found the site of his church. You must find a way to gain firsthand insight into all their operations. We must stop this woman.'

'I will do what must be done,' said Don reassuringly.

'Get Vincenzo to help you.' Rossi had made his stance on the matter clear.

Don resisted the urge to scream at him. 'I believe I will know more if she tells me of her own volition, rather than if I coerce her. I understand my duty, signor. I would ask you to please trust your own judgement.'

There was a long pause on the line. Then Rossi spoke again.

'Very well, Don. I am always right here should you wish to speak to me. I expect you to take care of the matter quickly and tie up any loose ends.

'Yes, signor,' said Don calmly. He felt it in the pit of his stomach – he had just kicked the cobra's basket.

45

Rome
AD 34

'Servius will kill you if he survives,' Nannan persisted with his argument as he and Jayesh approached Rome. They had been debating this point for the entire duration of the journey along the Tiber River, continuing well after their horse-drawn carriage began trundling towards the city.

'What are these buildings?' said Jayesh, trying to change the subject again.

'They are tombs,' Nannan explained absently. 'In Roman tradition, they do not cremate their dead. They bury them. It gives them somewhere to go and remember those that have passed. Burials are allowed only outside the city walls and wealthy families secure the largest plots by the roadsides to build ever more elaborate structures to commemorate their loved ones.'

'Most of them are bigger than the houses of the living in Muciripattanam!' Jayesh marvelled. They rode along in silence for a while, contemplating what was to be their fate at the hands of the Romans.

'The Senate – what if they are unjust to us? They could be preparing to invade Muciripattanam in the meantime! We must plan our course of action,' said Jayesh suddenly, as they arrived in the city. He had begun feeling anxious again.

'Our hearing is not until tomorrow. I have arranged for you to see the city today. Let us enjoy our time here – there is much to enjoy. We have plenty of time to prepare.'

'No. This is no time for a tour, Nannan. I would rather go to a quiet place and prepare for the hearing tomorrow.' Jayesh was getting jittery.

'Let me at least show you the Senate building,' Nannan said, steering their carriage towards it.

As they made their way through the city, the buildings got bigger and bigger. Each was unique, beautiful and impressive, with mighty columns made of stone at the front, stretching up to a height of forty to fifty feet. As they approached the centre of Rome, the huge buildings which had appeared, from a distance, to be jostling for position on the skyline, revealed themselves to be seated comfortably, surrounded by roads and courtyards.

They first arrived in the main forum of Rome, where some crowds had gathered. Just like in Alexandria, there were people from various cultures clustered in one place, rushing about, engaged in their business. The difference in Rome was that there appeared to be much more of a well-defined division between the rich and powerful, and ordinary citizens. There was also a very visible military presence. There were a handful of buildings whose entrances were guarded by Roman soldiers, their hands resting on the hilts of their gladius swords, always ready to strike. Every entrant would be vetted before they could enter these buildings, and most were turned away.

Nannan pointed to one such building. 'That's the Curia Julia, where we will meet with the advisors to the emperor tomorrow,' he said.

Jayesh looked at the building – a most spectacular edifice, no matter where in the world it may have been located. In the Roman Forum, however, it seemed almost nondescript.

It was slightly elevated from the forum's level with a dozen steps in the front leading up to a wide veranda. Soldiers stood tall in the colonnaded porch. There were ten marble columns in all, four to the left of the huge entrance doors and six to the right. It looked slightly unbalanced as the porch extended past the building to its right side, like a solid awning. Above the red roof of the porch were three large windows cut into the gleaming white marble walls. The building was topped with a pitched roof. The Curia was home to several statues of various gods. The Goddess of Wisdom, Minerva, stood proudly in the small portico at the front, and a large fifteen-foot-high gleaming statue made of gold, of the Goddess of Power, Victoria, stood commandingly on the crest of the rooftop with her outstretched wings. She held a wreath aloft in one hand and an ornate spectre in the other. Her elevated vantage point seemed to challenge the onlooker to question her might.

A skirmish broke out in front of the steps leading to the Curia Julia, distracting Jayesh and Nannan. There were two men arguing with the Roman soldiers at the entrance. Just when it looked like the situation was calming down, one of the Roman soldiers drew his sword and struck down the smaller of the two men. He crumpled to the stone floor and Jayesh could see the blood slowly spread in a pool around the body.

'We'd better leave,' he said, grabbing Nannan's wrist, suddenly reminded of how his fate and that of their entire enterprise were hinged on the meeting the following day. Clearly, if displeased, the Romans would not hesitate to ensure their error of judgement proved fatal.

'Yes, brother, I think you are right,' said Nannan, the colour draining from his face. 'Let's hurry, shall we?' He led them out of the forum.

They continued their debate as they retired to the privacy of their lodgings. Jayesh was fearful of what the Romans had planned for the meeting. He had made his own plans prior to his journey but hadn't realized that the huge levels of debt Rome had accumulated would endanger them so. He had kept his concerns – and his plans – from everyone, including his trusted friends Nannan and Vikesh, for fear of alarming them. He had reviewed every possibility in his head over and over, and rehearsed his responses. Even after the arduous journey here, his worries kept him from falling asleep. When he finally managed to slip into slumber, many hours later, it was fitful and haunted by vivid nightmares. He pictured him and his closest friends being led into the great arena of the Circus Maximus to be slaughtered in front of a baying crowd.

46

Hyatt Regency, Thrissur
7 July 2024

Don would have preferred the privacy of his room to meet Harveen, but he knew that the hotel lobby presented a much less threatening space and help him gain her trust. Having stayed up through the night reading the materials sent to him by Sofia, he could only get a few hours' rest before it was time for the meeting. All he had to do was find out everything she knew. His instructions were clear: Contain the situation at all costs.

Large double-height windows dominated the facade of the Hyatt Regency Hotel. These opened into an expansive lobby with a grand reception desk to the left. As is often the case with luxury hotels, here too the lobby area was meant not only welcome guests but to fill them with awe. Huge, artfully arranged metal orbs sat on a granite plinth taking centre stage in the space, rising from the ground only to be met by a lavish lighting display cascading from the ceiling above. Discreet seating areas were carefully arranged around the periphery. Don found a quiet corner table with a panoramic view of the entrance lobby and waited for Harveen to arrive.

Before long, Harveen's taxi pulled up at the entrance. Don calmly took notice of his target, recognizing her immediately from her social media. She did not see him watching her walk through the gates. Tall and fit, she wore a colourful dress and sandals, her hair tied in a loose ponytail and carrying a black satchel. She had dressed to impress the Vatican.

'Dr Gill?' Don stood and enquired as she approached. 'Good afternoon.'

'Yes, hi. Good afternoon. Mr Clemente?'

He nodded his acknowledgement and gracefully kissed her on both cheeks in the customary Italian manner, gallantly presenting to her the chair opposite his own.

'Please, I insist you call me Don, signora. Have you come alone?' Don asked the question in as nervous a manner as he could manage, trying to mask any hint of a different secret agenda. He was enjoying playing the part of a studious and angsty Vatican researcher – it took all his effort not to smile.

'Yes, of course, just as I had promised,' Harveen replied. As she settled herself into her chair, Don rummaged around in his pocket and produced a crumpled business card he had got made on the previous day using the printer on their private jet. The Vatican logo seemed to impress Harveen, and she smiled brightly at him. He, in turn, stared at her a little too long, leaving them both feeling slightly awkward.

Don cleared his throat and regained his composure. 'As you may appreciate, the Vatican does not ordinarily share information from its Archives other than in very special circumstances. I think yours to be just such a case. I'm sure you understand that we must exercise the utmost caution in handling any information we encounter. We do not ordinarily verify archaeological documents field researchers unearth every now and again. But because the nature of the finds is so sensitive, it felt important to bend our rules. Perhaps, if we could come to some sort of arrangement …' Don tried to sound persuasive but cryptic.

'I am not sure I fully understand what you expect of me, Don,' said Harveen. 'If it is confidentiality you seek, I assure you, I will cooperate in every way.'

Don smiled. This was proving easier than he had envisaged.

Feigning relief, he said, 'Oh, I'm so glad to hear it, Dr Gill. We cannot afford for anyone else to find out that the Vatican is validating or confirming your deductions. Researchers will flock to us from all parts of the world and that is simply not the kind of scrutiny we want to attract to ourselves. The only thing the Vatican will need from you is to keep this conversation and anything I show you totally confidential.'

For the first time, Harveen hesitated as she considered what he could possibly show her.

'Of course, Don. Rest assured, my team and I understand the weight of the responsibility your cooperation puts on us and you can completely trust all of us here. Not a peep travels beyond the gates of the museum's research department.'

'Ah, Dr Gill. Unfortunately, this is too sensitive a matter to entrust more than one person with. We have seen a few instances when people have become rather excited by some of the information in our archives, and blurted it out in front of the wrong people. I feel comfortable sharing this information only with you, as I have decided to trust you based on your great work and instincts. I'm sure you'll find it most illuminating. In return, I would expect you to share anything you find out about St Thomas with me first – we don't want spurious information to spill into the public domain as that can cause great harm to all those involved. I can't go into too much detail, I'm sure you will understand.' Don chose his words carefully and let them sit in the space between them. A long pause followed.

'I'm not sure that I feel fully comfortable agreeing to something like that, Don. The team works very closely with one another; hiding facts and knowledge from the research department would be detrimental to our work and I'm not sure it's the right thing to do.'

Don could sense Harveen wrestling against the excitement of getting a peek into the Vatican Archives. He opened his aluminium briefcase case ceremoniously and carefully retrieved a small wooden box from it and put it on the table between them. The Vatican logo was visible on the lid. He noticed Harveen sitting still, bewitched.

'You see, it's not merely a matter of my trust. The Secret Archives are heavily safeguarded and contain confidential information related to all facets of Christian history. I assure you, signora, you have no idea of what lies in store.' He opened the small box and turned it to face Harveen. He watched carefully as her expression changed. Her eyes widened and sparkled.

'Is this …'

'Yes,' he said. 'Signora, this is the best-preserved of the three copies in existence and it has not been displaced from the Archives for 1,500 years.' Harveen's hands shook as she looked at the original copy of the Gospel of St Thomas. As she leaned forward, he gently closed the lid. I fear that, perhaps, I have already extended far beyond my remit by showing you this, but I am hoping we can have a very special working relationship based on mutual trust.' He left the box on the table. Harveen, unable to help herself, kept looking at it.

'Don … I am sorry, I'm sure we can work something out. I assure you I will do everything in my power to keep this between us. Thank you for showing such faith in me. Here, let me show you what we know so far as a reciprocation of my faith in you. These are some of documents we found in a recent excavation. And here is something that no one else has seen. We have found the location of the first church built by St Thomas.'

'Oh my, really? That's so interesting!' Don said, feigning surprise. 'Would you mind telling me everything from the beginning? I can't wait to know the whole story – this is incredible!' He took out a small pad and pen, ready to make a note of every detail.

Harveen recited the story of their journey from the discovery of the merchant's house through to the present moment. As she related the events, Don couldn't help but feel captivated by her. She had an easy smile and a natural enthusiasm for her work. He watched as she reached into her bag and produced a number of sheets of paper.

'The originals are made of cotton paper and can't leave our preservation rooms. They are very delicate.' Don took the documents carefully. In truth, he had no interest in seeing them, but this was an important step in establishing the trust he would need.

'They are absolutely amazing – congratulations,' he gushed with as much enthusiasm as possible. 'Have you found any records that specifically relate to St Thomas?'

'Not as yet, but there are over 2,000 records – we have only just begun to translate them.'

'May I ask how you managed to pinpoint the location of the first church you mentioned using these?'

'Oh – no, we found … a stone. It had an inscription on it … We worked with some researchers to work out what it may have said. It appears to be a sign, based on our understanding so far, marking the Church of St Thomas. It calls him "the brother of Jesus Christ". But we don't know anything to verify that as yet …' She showed him the images of the stone and the inscription, and explained how they had managed to deduce the original inscription.

'Incredible!' he said, taking note of the name of the researchers who had helped. He saw an opportunity to discredit their translation by altering what the missing original letters may have read.

'Anything to do with St Thomas is of great interest to the Vatican – we don't know enough about him and cannot devote resources to finding out more about his time in India without drawing attention to ourselves. If you and I have an understanding, I'd be happy to extend our support to you in complete confidentiality to further your research.

'We do have our own agenda, of course. The Vatican is always keen to make sure that any significant religious releases are based on fact. There are so many headlines deriving only from speculation. Can we agree that I will help you and that you will show me anything else that you find first, just so we can have our experts assist you with authentication?'

He could see that she was coming around to the idea. 'Maybe with the resources of the Vatican at your disposal, we could find his Church together …' Don could sense what her answer would be. He pressed on, 'So, we have a deal, signora?' He held out his hand.

Harveen stood up and shook his hand without a word.

47

Rome
AD 34

'Are you alright, brother?' Nannan asked.

Jayesh had not slept a wink the previous night. His plan seemed weak and ineffective to him now. 'Of course. I'm sure it will be fine,' he lied.

They had arrived very early at the Curia Julia to await their audience with the Senate. There was still a light morning frost and their clothes were not enough to protect them from the chill. They had been notified to appear at the Senate in the morning, but no specific time was mentioned in the summons. The pair had decided to arrive as early as possible so as to avoid the jury's displeasure. As they walked into the Forum now, they were surprised to see it was already beginning to fill with people in the grey daylight. It seemed as if the centre of Rome was never quiet.

As they approached the steps leading to the Curia Julia, two Roman soldiers halted them in their tracks.

Jayesh was relieved when Nannan stepped forward. 'I am the Counsellor to the great Jayesh of the city of Muziris, who has travelled from India at the direct invitation of the great Roman Emperor Tiberius Caesar Augustus for a meeting with his Consilium Principis.'

Jayesh marvelled at Nannan's ability to speak Latin as though it was his native tongue. Even after ten years of use, he still did not feel the same comfort with the language, often having to pause to recall the appropriate words. He hoped his effort at honing it may help him today. He could not afford to make any mistakes.

The Roman soldiers looked somewhat dubiously at the dark-skinned visitors and did not immediately allow them to pass. Instead, they relayed Nannan's message to one of their colleagues, who rushed inside the building to verify the details presented. When he returned, he addressed them both. 'Follow me.'

They were led into the building through the grand double doors made of bronze. On the inside, the Curia Julia was not at all what Jayesh had envisaged. It was a rather austere and plain structure, about eighty feet long and fifty feet wide. There were three broad steps lining either side, clearly designed to serve as seating. Jayesh estimated that every step could accommodate up to sixty or seventy people. If the room was full, it could hold up to 400 people. The walls were lined with simple white marble, almost up to the ceiling. The floor caught his eye – it was decorated with a colourful mosaic and, at the far end of the hall, was the statue of a goddess stood atop an atlas holding a wreath. The statue presided over an ornate seat, which Jayesh presumed to be the throne for the emperor.

There were only about twenty men in the building at the time, seated on the stone benches at the far end of the hall, close to the statue. There was a table at the front with a few seats around it. The soldiers motioned Jayesh and Nannan to sit and wait there. Each of the Roman men was dressed in an identical fashion. They wore togas, a large woollen garment which looked rather cumbersome. The material was draped over them, with no obvious shape or fixings, such that it hung loosely from their arms and shoulders. It reminded Jayesh of the colourful sarees that the women back home wore, only these togas were plain white, much thicker and somewhat ungainly.

As they sat waiting, Jayesh felt as if they were about to be sentenced for their naivety. He noticed that the armed guards did not leave the room.

A man walked up to them and introduced himself confidently. 'We are the Consilium Principis – the Emperor Tiberius Caesar Augustus's most trusted advisors. Together, we constitute the Senate and advise the emperor on the matters of concern to him related to the mighty Roman empire.'

The man was about fifty years of age and seemed to have led a very comfortable life. His face was round and rather featureless, except for his large prominent nose that had a visible kink about halfway down. He was much shorter than Jayesh and Nannan, and as he lumbered towards them with an unwieldy gait, each stride seemed to take monumental effort. His toga struggled to disguise his corpulence and in the few steps it took for him to arrive to address his visitors, he was already panting.

'Please remain seated, we have much to discuss with you.' For the next two hours, the members of the Consilium Principis interrogated Jayesh and Nannan over a wide range of subjects. They were mainly concerned about the level of trade and resulting profits being earned by Muciripattanam from the empire on an annual basis. They held detailed records of all the trade dealings and often punctuated their comments with readings of sections of certain trading documents in detail. Jayesh suspected these had been provided by Servius.

Everyone in Rome appeared to be a skilled orator. They took as much pride in the flamboyance with which they delivered their comment or posed their question as they did in their actual contents. Every time a question was asked, Nannan would look to Jayesh for counsel before answering, but the latter was paralyzed by fear such that he was of little help. Nannan did his best to answer despite this, while Jayesh was haunted by images of the underground prison where he had been left to die alone on his first overseas journey.

'We are troubled by the growing debt owed to you by Rome,' began one of the Senators. 'Given our current financial position, Rome would struggle to settle the balance, if you were to demand it. What would your people do then? How would you enforce such a debt?' He looked at his fellow Senators, who seemed equally amused at the ridiculous nature of Jayesh and Nannan's situation. They all mocked and heckled the two men and their ability to force Rome to pay. Jayesh sensed they had been trapped.

'Are you aware of the size of our legions?' the Senator continued. 'The mere mention of the Roman Army is enough for most countries to offer us better trading terms.' The atmosphere was becoming increasingly hostile. 'I am given to understand that other traders in India offer better prices for nard, pepper and other spices as well.' The influence of Servius was clear as day.

'And animals!' interjected another Senator. 'Their prices for the animals are far better than those from Muziris.' There were howls of derision at the comment.

The ruthless questioning over all the types of goods that were purchased from Muziris continued. Whilst Jayesh remained quiet, Nannan gave succinct answers to every question.

Finally, the interrogation ended. The corpulent Senator summarized the proceedings for everyone's benefit.

'The Port of Muziris holds a large debt over Rome and this is seen to be from your flagrant profiteering from Roman merchants that frequented your waters. The emperor of Rome, who commands the greatest armies in the world, is concerned about the situation and has asked his trusted Senate to broker a solution by any means possible.'

Jayesh could see a glimmer of hope. Although there seemed to be no supportive face in the crowd, they had at least not been directly threatened with military action as he had feared.

'There is an outstanding debt of 175 million sesterces, expected to exceed 200 million by the end of the coming season. Only the wealthiest of men are permitted to hold the office of a Senator in Rome, who have to their name a wealth of upwards of 1 million sesterces, including property.' He was displaying considerable skill with his closing summary to incite reactions from the crowd – the mention of precise amounts drew screams of outrage and indignation from the other members of the Consilium Principis. The Senator finally finished his speech with a flourish, which was met with some applause from his colleagues.

'So, gentlemen, you can see that we find ourselves in a very difficult situation that must be resolved. We have invited you here today to perhaps reach a mutual understanding on how we can proceed in a way that may suit all parties.'

There was a tense energy in the room. Nannan looked nervously at Jayesh. Although the Senators had stated that they were looking for an amicable solution, the threat of violence was clear and ominous.

48

Sreepadam Palace, Main Meeting Room
9 July 2024

'But Professor, Dr Gupta said that she wanted me to run this project,' insisted Harveen. She found herself standing with her hands planted on the meeting room table. They had been having the same conversation for ten minutes and making no progress. The heat of the midday sun lingered in the room, making the atmosphere even more stifling. Harveen could feel the sweat running down her back, sticking her khaki shirt to her body. But Professor Prakash seemed impervious to the heat; his perfectly ironed shirt was somehow unblemished.

'Has anyone been in contact with Dr Gupta?' Professor Prakash asked everyone in the room. Penny had not come into work or been in contact with anyone for three days. 'This is most unlike her.' He looked at Harveen closely.

'No, Professor,' said Rohan. Harveen was annoyed that he had not backed her up to run the project again.

'Me neither. Not since we spoke after the meeting the other day,' repeated Harveen for a second time that afternoon.

'Sorry, could you please repeat to me exactly what she said to you after that meeting?' Professor Prakash leaned forward slightly, his expression sceptical.

'Well,' Harveen replied, choosing her words carefully, 'she mentioned that the deciphering of the lettering was clever on my part and that she believed I had good instincts for fieldwork. She also said that she was happier working behind a desk in office anyway, especially with languages, which is her true forte. She hoped I'd be happy to work together under the new arrangement.'

Prakash and Rohan exchanged glances.

'I'm afraid it didn't seem to me like you two had a very close working relationship, Harveen,' Prakash said.

'But this is true!' Harveen said, a touch of anger in her voice.

'And did she say where she was going?'

Harveen was cautious to not betray Penny's secret. 'No, she didn't,' she lied.

Prakash took a long moment to consider her words. 'Okay, well, keep trying her number. I will call Inspector Kumar and ask him to look into the matter immediately.' He made a small note in his book. 'You can handle things until we hear from Dr Gupta, alright? Now, where were we?'

'Thank you, Professor. You will not be disappointed, I promise. So we have reopened the site at Anapuzha as the "St Thomas Church site",' Harveen said quickly, relieved how things had panned out for the time being. 'We now have a full team of twenty-two. We've split them in two – one faction is looking over everything we found originally, and there is another team on site. All artefacts with any connection to the Christian church found in the last ten years are now going to be manually re-examined.'

'Find anything new?' asked Prakash hopefully.

'Nothing of note as yet, sir,' Rohan said.

'I am sending a team to St Thomas's Church in Palayoor. Maybe they will find something there,' Harveen interjected. 'Palayoor is well known as the first church founded by St Thomas in or around AD 52; the second and third sites being Muziris and Parur, respectively. This, we believed to be true at least until we found the stone. We know that the existing building in Palayoor stands on the exact site as the original. It was substantially rebuilt around 1610, but there are items at the museum there that were found on the original site.'

'Good work, Harveen,' Prakash said, nodding.

'St Thomas founded at least seven churches. One of these was in Kodungallur, which could be where the stone came from. The others were in Palayoor, Kottakkavu, Kokkamangalam, Niranam, Nilackal and Kollam. There's word of another church in Thiruvithamcode as well. It seems that St Thomas spent around twenty years in this part of India until around AD 70 or 71, when he travelled northwards, potentially being martyred near Madras around AD 72.' Harveen knew this information by heart, but it seemed to be of little use to them at the moment.

'Excellent!'

'Rohan and I have turned our attention to the records found in the house and narrowed our search to any references to temples or churches.'

Harveen opened a folder and took out some documents to show both of them. She had been working all hours using the software Penny had directed her to.

'The written records span across a date range from AD 50–72, and between AD 50–70. The references to churches or temples are minimal – there are only about forty entries in total. These records refer to donations of singular items, but also to commissioning the construction of entire churches. I have a few examples to show you here.' She pointed to various images. 'Each record contains details of the name of the church or temple, the date, what was bought and the amount paid.

'What is fascinating is that from AD 70 onwards, the number of records related to spends on temples or churches goes from four or five per cent of the documents to around eighty to ninety per cent. The sums of money in modern terms are huge – equivalent to millions of dollars – donated to religious projects, mainly Hindu temples.' Harveen showed them more records in a similar format. 'Here you can see money donated to build a temple. It would be around half a million dollars in today's terms. What is also interesting is that no location is mentioned, and sometimes, there is not even a name. If you look at earlier records, however, the scribe was meticulous in recording dates, monetary amounts and locations.

'By looking at the graphology of the writing, we concluded that the records were all authored by the same person. But there had been a change in policy, it would seem. Here is another large donation – this time for a building and several statues. This next one to buy land and build another building. There is another here – the largest sum we have found so far, well over 10 million dollars today – this time to erect the temple itself, and then to provide a yearly donation to protect the buildings in its complex, and even provide food for the poor for a significant period of time. The record is quite badly damaged, so we cannot say for sure how long the donation was meant to provide for ... possibly ten years or so? There are many more documents that show such donations to at least fifty different projects.'

'What do you think happened around AD 70?' asked Prakash.

'Well, that is exactly what we are trying to figure out. It's really difficult to pinpoint. Perhaps the Port of Muziris became so wealthy, their leaders began to make major donations to secure their legacy, and omitted to record locations. It's definitely something we need to look into.'

'I see. Well, I wish you best of luck. Thank you both – this is truly impressive work in a very short span of time,' said Prakash.

Harveen smiled. She wondered about Penny. Since her mysterious meeting, no one had heard from her. Harveen fished out her phone and called her number again.

49

Roman Senate
AD 34

Despite being in the firm clutches of terror, Jayesh got to his feet. As he looked around, there was not a single supportive face in the room. He glanced at Nannan, who shook his head slightly.

'The great Indian trader has lost his tongue!'

As Jayesh looked up to see where the taunt had come from, the Senators began to laugh.

'It is my great honour to address the Consilium Principis. Please forgive me if I am not eloquent in the way I express my thoughts – Latin is not my native language. I have been trying to learn it as a show of respect and deference for the Empire and Great Emperor of Rome on behalf of the people of Muziris.'

Jayesh gave a deferential nod to the Senators. The seating arrangement gave them a superior position, allowing them to gaze down at him as he spoke. He felt like a small boy again, staring up at them and struggling to explain himself. There was more heckling as he started to speak. Watching him fumble for words, the shouts from the Senators became louder.

'The issues you have raised are also of concern to us, and we have given thought to how we may resolve them as well. I know that you are the wisest and most learned men in Rome and you have a great deal of information about the trade you engage in with India and beyond. But, my lords, there are factors which may not have yet travelled to you across the seas.'

The shouting from the benches continued. Jayesh feared his message would not be heard.

'If you would please be so kind as to let me speak for just a few moments, I would like to tell you about these issues so we may arrive at a suitable resolution, my lords.'

'Liar! Cheat!' the audience cried.

'The people of Muziris are but simple farmers. They do not seek great riches or to embark on great travels,' he pleaded. 'They have farmed the same plots of land for many generations, and I have no doubt that their children will do the same. Like the Romans, Indians devote their time and wealth to their temples and in Muziris too, we have built a temple dedicated to our Hindu gods.' The use of wealth to build a temple was met with a faint murmur of approval from a couple of the Senators.

'As soon as we gathered some wealth, the people of Muziris all agreed we must do something to honour our benefactors in Rome. The most fitting tribute we could present was to build a temple in honour of the Great Emperor Augustus. We did this as a show of our loyalty to your grand empire, and also to provide a place for visitors from your holy land to hold religious ceremonies, offer their prayers and sacrifices. We sought the services of the best architects from Rome to design the temple and it is built in the same style as you would expect here, in your own magnificent capital. It is the most magnificent building in all of Muziris, far superior to even our own humble temple. We would be honoured to welcome you to come and see it for yourselves.' There were more approving murmurs and even some applause.

'There was another reason behind building a mighty temple in honour of Emperor Augustus,' Jayesh continued. 'In recent times, we have seen a surge in visitors from the Kingdom of China. They claim to be a far more powerful kingdom than Rome, and their Emperor Guangwu of Han has expressed a desire to trade with Muziris. They too have a love for Indian spices, and our sworn loyalty to your grand empire irks them.' The mention of the emperor of China drew howls of condemnation from the Senators, whose attitude towards Jayesh was visibly softening.

'Our Temple of Augustus is built atop a pedestal so it may be seen by any ship that draws to within a thousand feet of our shores. This is to remind those from China that we are loyal to none other than Emperor Tiberius Caesar Augustus!' Jayesh raised his voice while naming the emperor, which was met with cheers and more applause.

'I have here a drawing of this majestic temple as seen from the sea to offer as a gift to the Senate. It is where we have poured a great portion of our trading profits from Rome.' Jayesh produced a scroll that was bound in two places and unravelled it across the table. It was a beautiful drawing of the Temple of Augustus, towering over the shoreline of Muciripattanam. The Senators descended from their seats to view the drawing closely. It gave Jayesh and Nannan a valuable opportunity to speak to them at closer quarters and build a rapport. As they returned to their seats, exchanging praise for the drawing amongst themselves, Jayesh spoke again.

'There are growing problems with Muziris continuing to supply to Rome. The Chinese regularly remain on the lookout to ambush our vessels and loot our goods for themselves. Indian pirates too pose obstructions to our trade, knowing how we sell the best of our goods to Rome. Just in the last month, we have lost over a hundred thousand sesterces in this way as well as over fifty tonnes of pepper. Gentlemen, as you may expect, this is our greatest challenge for now. Even merchants from Alexandria seek to bribe and threaten us, inserting themselves into the trade relationship as dishonest middlemen and charging Rome a premium.' Even if Servius had survived the attempt on his life, Jayesh wanted to make sure he was known as the villain he truly was.

'We will invade China!' one Senator declared boldly.

'The pirates would not dare to attack a Roman ship,' shouted another.

'My lords, I propose that we establish a Roman fort in Muziris, right next to the Temple of Augustus, so that we may protect our alliance. We will use our trade profits not only to pay in full for the costs to build the fort, but also to provide food and salaries to the soldiers stationed there. This will also enable Rome and the emperor's most trusted Senate to get direct reports on Muziris and its dealings. This funding can be taken directly against the outstanding debts owed to Muziris.' Jayesh held his arms out in a show of openness. The Senators all nodded their approval; some even descended from their seats to shake his hand. Amidst all the conviviality, Jayesh sought to press another small advantage.

'There was earlier a mention of the prices for spices, pepper and animals from Muziris by one of you esteemed gentlemen. I wish to make a small point, if you will indulge me for a moment longer.' The crowd was now appreciably in the palm of his hand. 'We know that there are huge markups on the prices of goods sold in Rome from what your merchants pay in Muziris. For pepper, this can be as much as eighty times higher. Nard is the same and animals only slightly less, yet we sell at the same prices as always. Even when we are offered a higher price by others, we still remain loyal. The twenty-five per cent tax that Rome applies to these goods should provide us both a good incentive to increase trade and maintain prices so that the Senate can collect more.' Jayesh's encyclopaedic knowledge of the prices of their goods once again became key to them continuing to prosper.

The debate resumed once again and yet, now many of the senators were openly on Jayesh's side, arguing that the prices remain as they were. Some even suggested that Muziris be allowed to increase their prices. They finally agreed to maintain status quo and to allow Jayesh to handle Rome's debts to Muziris in the manner he had proposed. In a little over four hours, Jayesh and Nannan found themselves leaving the Senate in elation, once again weaving their way through the hubbub of the Roman Forum.

Nannan turned to his friend with a broad smile.

'I think that of all the miracles you have managed to make happen, this maybe the greatest one yet. We went in fearing for our wealth, the well-being of our port and even our lives. And now we are walking out with a win-win deal – a Roman army for Muciripattanam to protect our goods, and perhaps even the opportunity to increase our prices! When did you plan all this?'

'Honestly, I did not plan it as well as you think. I had thought about it, but without knowing what they were going to say, it was difficult to judge,' Jayesh replied.

'Only one other thing comes to mind, Jayesh. You have known for so long the extent of the incredible markup the Romans have been enjoying on our goods and yet you did not raise our prices. I have never known you to miss an opportunity ... Why didn't you take it?'

'It is no charity, my friend,' Jayesh began, remembering well the lesson his father had taught him on his very first trip to the market. 'The Romans have merchants and soldiers in every part of the world. Sooner or later, they would have found out exactly how much more profit we were making. But this way, they will remember that we had nothing to hide, offered them a fair deal, and our trade relationship with them will last much longer.' The memory of his first meeting with Vikesh flashed in his mind – relationships were the most important piece of the puzzle, as he had learned that day.

'What we have done today, Nannan, is simply bought ourselves more time. Make no mistake – the Romans will eventually tire of letting us take so much from them. We must invest as quickly as we can and attract the Greeks and Jews to trade with us as well. There is great wealth in these nations and if we can provide a safe place for their people to worship and study, then before long, I'm sure Muciripattanam will also rise to become the greatest empire of them all.

50

Dr Penny Gupta's Apartment, Kochi
16 July 2024

'She has not yet returned, I am sorry, madam.

'Did she say anything about where she was going?'

'No, madam.'

Harveen was at Penny's apartment building, hoping to find some trace of her there. But the security guard was not being helpful. The apartment was in a newly built block and lavish – something unlikely for an archaeologist to be able to afford. It was the type of place that she had only ever seen in magazines, with a grand front entrance for the residents.

'Can I have a look in her apartment? Do you have a security key? Maybe she's unconscious or in need of medical help! Please!' The look on the man's face remained unaffected.

'Madam, I will have to ask you to leave the building now.'

'Look, I am her sister. I am worried – she hasn't called in a few days. I just want to make sure that she is okay.' She was getting more and more anxious about Penny's disappearance.

'Sorry, madam. There's nothing I can do. Only the resident can let you enter. Please leave now,' the guard said and began to usher Harveen towards the door.

'Okay, okay, you don't need to push me.'

She figured there must be another way in for the staff and walked down the alley beside the building. About halfway down it was a small side door into the building; it was propped open, and two men in white uniform were sitting on the step outside, smoking.

'I'm late for a meeting! Shhh!' Harveen said sweetly, winking at them and scurrying past them as they exchanged a confused look.

Once inside, Harveen looked around for Penny's apartment. Her flat number was twenty-four. The building was so well laid-out, it only took a few minutes for her to find the door on the second floor. Harveen tried the handle – it was locked. She knocked.

'Dr Gupta?' she called out. 'This is Harveen. Can you open the door, please? Are you in there? No one has heard anything from you. Everyone is really worried.'

No answer. Harveen knocked again, louder this time. 'Dr Gupta?'

Still nothing. She went back towards the staff exit.

The staff area was unkempt compared to the rest of the building. There was a small staff room and a bigger area with three cleaning trolleys and a couple of doors, one of which led into the alley. Harveen searched the cleaning carts until she found what she was looking for – a keycard.

She rushed back up to apartment number twenty-four.

51

Dr Penny Gupta's Apartment
16 July 2024

Don carefully searched through Penny's apartment. It had been easy to gain entry via the metal fire escape at the back of the building, and even easier to open the apartment door, despite the keycard lock.

Her apartment was immaculate. Her wardrobe housed clothes folded into neat stacks, suits hung up and shoes precisely aligned against the wall – nothing more.

Don figured her laptop might still be in the office but found a good number of written notes to go through until he could get his hands on it. After about half an hour of rummaging through the rest of the apartment, he took out his phone and dialled.

'Sofia, there is nothing at Gupta's apartment. Can you check all her outgoing calls to make sure she hasn't contacted anyone else?'

'Already done. Looks like we are in the clear for now.'

'I'll call you back,' he said, hearing footsteps in the corridor outside, followed by a familiar voice.

'Dr Gupta?' The voice just outside the door called out. 'This is Harveen. Can you open the door, please? Are you in there? No one has heard anything from you. Everyone is really worried.'

Don put his phone into his pocket and picked up his 9mm Beretta, its silencer already attached.

Hearing a louder knock, Don positioned himself by the side of the door in the ideal position to shoot if the door opened. Tense but alert, he waited. He couldn't be seen around here.

He heard Harveen scurry away from the door and breathed a sigh of relief. He did not want to kill her, but would not hesitate if necessary. It had been a close call. He quickly rearranged the few things he'd moved so the room looked exactly like he had found it, and was poised to leave when he heard the footsteps again.

He rushed back into position, his finger on the trigger. The door card was inserted into the slot. The door unlocked with a click, and he saw the handle move downward.

52

Taxila, Royal Palace of Rajah Gondophares
AD 46

'I'm warning you, my friend, the Romans will kill you if they find out you keep this man with you. He barely escaped them with his life this time. Next time he may not be so lucky – why endanger yourself by getting involved?' Rajah Gondophares asked.

'They do not concern themselves with what we do here, Your Majesty,' replied Jayesh, with more hope than belief.

'Jayesh, I understand you have every right to be so sure of yourself. You truly are a magician – you managed to bring the mighty empires of Rome and Egypt under your heel and now you have the emperor of China at your beck and call. Don't push your luck any further. Leave it well alone and enjoy what you have. I will simply not allow otherwise,' the king declared. 'Now, can we return to our discussion about the price for this latest shipment of pepper?'

Jayesh had nurtured relationships with many important and powerful leaders over the years. Rajah Gondophares was one such man. Their decade-long relationship was built on mutual respect and admiration, and they both genuinely enjoyed each other's company.

'I have watched you turn feuding tribes into one of the greatest kingdoms in the world, Your Majesty,' replied Jayesh. Under the aegis of Gondophares, the Indo-Parthian Kingdom had become the biggest in the North after claiming territory back from the Egyptians and Romans. Thanks to his military prowess, the Rajah had built an empire that spanned across hundreds of miles – from Minnagara in the south, along the Indus River, to Kabul in the north. 'Surely, nothing scares you.'

'With loans from you, my friend, I will never forget what you have done for me.'

When the rajah had been engaged in the process of building up his armies and financing the wars to protect his kingdom's borders, Jayesh forwent payments for his goods and even gave him loans to fund his growing military. The king had long since gathered great wealth and repaid his friend in full. 'Allow me to repay your kindness with my own. Take my advice and do not start a war with Rome. You will be crushed and all your life's work would have been for naught. Do not let that dampen your spirit now! Come, let us enjoy the feast.'

As the two men made their way towards the dining hall, Jayesh marvelled at the new changes made to the palace complex. It had once merely been a collection of impressive huts, this massive, awe-inspiring stone edifice sitting prominently at the centre of a large-walled courtyard. The interior was resplendent with gold furniture and silks adorning the walls. Its opulence was beyond anything he had witnessed even in Alexandria or Rome.

'The feast is, as usual, beyond compare, Your Majesty,' said Jayesh as the two friends sat and enjoyed the grand meal laid out before them. He had been relaying news to the Rajah of his progress in developing his trade relations with Alexandria and Rome. He also mentioned initiating trade with China, where he saw immense potential.

'Oh, I've heard a thing or two about your plans, dear friend. People often tell me stories of this trader in the south who does business with everyone in the world. Your legend grows by the day!'

'You flatter me, Your Majesty. The Judaists are the only group I cannot seem to appeal to. They hold considerable influence in Alexandria and Rome, but try as I might, I cannot tempt them to come to Muciripattanam. If I could succeed, I might surely build a kingdom as great as Ashoka's,' said Jayesh. He took another sip of his spiced milk and sighed contentedly. The hot, spicy blend of milk, cardamom, cinnamon and ginger infused him with new vigour after his long journey. 'They are very religious, much like our own people. They have never set foot on our land until now – I must beg you to let me take this man with me back to Muziris, Your Majesty. He could help me understand them better and perhaps build a great church so they come to us.'

'Jayesh, in all our years of doing business together, I have never refused you. Until today, when I must.' The king rose to his feet and declared, 'The danger is too great for you. Now you must stop persisting. You have no idea the perils he has endured to arrive at our shores and it is best you stay away.'

'Tell me, Your Majesty. I want to know.'

'Two weeks ago, he was dragged into my court to appear before me. He claims to be the blood brother of the Messiah of the Jews – the one they call Jesus Christ. He said he has fled from his homeland to save his life. He has travelled with a small group of his followers. He told a most fantastical story of how he had been hidden away almost since his birth to escape the Roman King Herod's slaughter of thousands of children. It was he and his brother the king was after.'

Jayesh could scarcely believe it. He had never heard anything about Jesus Christ having a brother. 'Where are you holding him?' he asked.

'He is in my temple at Jandial and he is not to leave it. Why do you ask?'

'If you could be so kind as to let me meet him, Your Majesty. Surely, you could afford me that much.'

'Fine. Finish your drink and let us go see him together. He comes in peace as an emissary of his faith. You may speak with him, but no more.'

'Your wish is my command, Your Majesty,' Jayesh said and bowed his head. But in his mind, he was already hatching a plan to leave with the man for Muciripattanam – with the king's permission or without.

53

Dr Penny Gupta's Apartment
16 July 2024

Harveen put the keycard in the door and heard the lock click open. She pushed the handle down and paused for a moment. Did she really want to break into Penny's apartment? What if she got caught? Suddenly, her phone rang. She let go of the door handle and looked at her phone. It was Rohan. It was unusual for him to call in the evening. She was worried.

'Rohan, are you okay?'

'Harveen – I think I've found it. I know where it is. I know where the Church of St Thomas is,' he said, panting at the other end.

'What? How? Where is it?' Harveen could not believe what she was hearing.

'I can't tell you over the phone – it's better if I show you. It's a combination of things. I am at the office, but I can come to you right away if you like.'

'Uh …' Harveen looked around and decided to cut her losses and get out. 'I'm coming to you. It'll take me forty minutes to reach.'

'Of course, no problem. We can even do this in the morning …'

'I'm on my way,' she said decisively and hung up. As she walked back down the corridor towards the exit, she put the keycard into her pocket.

The drive to Sreepadam Palace seemed far too long – she was getting restless to see what Rohan had found.

Night had fallen and the air felt heavy with a sense of foreboding as she walked into the office at that hour. The main office was well-lit in contrast and Rohan looked up at her with a smile as she came in. The familiar smell of his chai filled the room and calmed Harveen's nerves. It looked as if he had not left his desk since the last time she had seen him.

'Hey you,' she said. 'I couldn't stop thinking about what you said and just had to come down immediately. Tell me all about it,' she slumped into the chair across from Rohan, getting comfortable.

'Oh! Well … can I get you a drink or something?' he replied, gesturing towards his mug.

Harveen shook her head vigorously and excitedly leaned forward.

'Okay then, let's start. I was looking through all the records we had found. Most of them detail huge donations made to several temples. They are all quite similar, as we'd already realized – either towards funding for temple construction or donations of items like gold statues.'

'Yes,' said Harveen, 'it seems like whoever they were, spent the last few years giving most of their money away to temples. In today's terms, they would probably be running the largest ever charitable operation.'

'Yep. There was one record that stood out to me. I kept going back to it. It is one of the last records that we found in that house, going by the dates, written in AD 73. Unfortunately, it has been damaged quite badly and this is all we have left.' Rohan clicked his mouse a couple of times and turned his screen towards Harveen. 'It says this huge sum of money is to go to Shiva – or more likely, to a temple dedicated to him.'

'Yes, I did see that one. But there are no records of temples like that anywhere in Muziris. As with most of the later records, the name of the temple is here, but there are no details of its location. It could be anywhere in India.'

'Exactly, but a couple of things about this one stand out. The sum of money is huge. Even compared to the other donations, it's at least ten times more than the biggest one, if the record is accurate. Look at the line that follows: "to protect the people, to provide food for those in need and to ensure that the temple and the well of stones within the temple grounds are never disturbed." It also says how long the dedication is to last. I enhanced the image and it looks like it says one hundred years – not ten, as we'd originally thought.'

Harveen had studied this document many times herself.

'That's all great, but even if it does say that, we still have no evidence of where this temple was. We haven't found anything useful so far.'

'Well, I called to tell you that I found the missing link. Did I ever tell you about my first job for the State Archaeology Department, Veen?'

Harveen was a little confused at the change of direction. 'Umm … you mean how you were running errands for the people who worked here when you were twelve?'

'No, not that. I mean the very first specific job,' he replied.

Harveen was scratching her chin, trying to jog her memory.

'So you don't remember then. Well, there was a dig at a temple site – the Kurumba Bhagavathy Temple. I used to go there from time to time to see what they'd found. They always had fresh chai and snacks in the morning, and I couldn't resist. I had gone a few times in the morning to offer help and they always kindly shared their breakfast with us volunteers. That day, it was not only food that I got; I also managed to get a job fetching and carrying for the State Archaeology Department,' Rohan said this proudly. It had been his first step towards securing his current role.

'They had started the dig after an unusual item had been found in the grounds of the temple: an ivory pomegranate.' As he finished his sentence, he opened a picture of the small ivory artefact on his screen. 'This is the one. It was missing a couple of the five original prongs at the top. As the dig progressed, they found one more, which was completely intact, and the fragments of a water jug with what appeared to be Christian markings on it.' A few clicks brought up a number of fragments being arranged together to clearly show a section of a bowl or a jug with some faded markings.

Rohan smiled at Harveen, as if he had made his point.

'Sorry, Rohan, I don't get it,' she said.

'The pomegranate was a symbol used by early Israelite priests. They were worn only by the most important officials – there is a reference to Aaron, the elder brother of Moses who served as the High Priest of the Tabernacle during the Exodus, wearing a robe with ornate pomegranates. The symbol is found throughout the history of Christianity.' Rohan clicked again and a picture of two complete ivory pomegranates appeared on his screen, with a scale to the side showing that each pin was about an inch long.

'It was an odd find, so they spent weeks looking for any related clues or objects, but in the end, no big conclusions could be drawn. So, they inferred that the pomegranate pins had likely been brought to the site by a visitor. It was all duly catalogued and stowed away. Every day for six weeks, I had my lunch at the temple and sat by the Samadhi of Vysoori. Look, here is a picture – does it remind you of anything?' He showed her a picture of a round well made of stones.

'That looks like … a well!' It was beginning to dawn on Harveen.

'Yes,' said Rohan, 'it sits in the grounds of the temple and is supposed to have the powers to cure all manner of illnesses and diseases. It has been there for centuries. The temple was even supposed to have originally been dedicated to Lord Shiva. Why would Muziris provide for a hundred years of protection for a temple and specifically mention the "Well of Stones"? I think this was originally the Church of St Thomas.' He watched as Harveen's expression changed with realization.

'Rohan, you are a genius!' she gushed. 'Of course! That site has been there forever! What better way to protect it than to build a temple on the spot and endow it with a huge fortune to ensure its protection?'

'Wait, that's not all. There are even legends of a hidden chamber to the east of the sanctum there. The wall there is made of granite, and apparently, no one has ever attempted to enter it. It is said to contain great riches donated by ancient kings, and a secret passage, though no one knows why it is there,' Rohan further revealed, adding that it would be impossible to persuade the priests to let them look inside.

'We must take this to Professor Prakash. Maybe he could find a way to get us permission to carry out archaeological investigation at the site. Do you think you could help me locate other materials from that dig you mentioned? Maybe we could build a stronger case. I will meet with Professor Prakash first thing tomorrow morning. Let me search for any other references to an early Christian church around this area until then.'

Rohan stretched and sighed contentedly, standing up to gather his things. 'You do that and I'll head home. I have a good feeling about this, Veen.'

Long after Rohan had gone home, Harveen was still searching in vain through the myriad documents. What am I doing? She leaned back in her chair and thought about the one contact she had who could grant her access to the Vatican Secret Archives. She would certainly find something of use in there. Despite scrolling to his number a few times, she had not been able to bring herself to call. But they needed a strong case. Coincidences and a good feeling simply weren't going to help convince Professor Prakash.

She pressed 'call'.

'Hello, Don? It's Harveen.'

'Oh, hello Dr Gill, how are you? It is quite late – are you alright? Can I help you with anything?' Don sounded like he wasn't expecting her call.

'Oh, please don't worry, I'm fine. I just – can I ask you something?'

'Yes, of course, signora.'

'I think we may have found something. I think we know the location of the Church of St Thomas ... but I can't be sure without more information and I was hoping you could help me verify our findings.'

'That's marvellous, signora! Of course, please tell me all about it.'

54

Jandial, Indo-Parthian Kingdom
Temple of Rajah Gondophares
AD 46

'I will not use my armies against Rome, I told you!' said Rajah Gondophares as they arrived in the sprawling temple complex.

'It will not come to that, Your Majesty,' Jayesh said confidently.

'They have already sent out their men to look for him. We have denied he is here. Now, be reasonable, Jayesh.'

The front of the building was dominated by two large columns, over one hundred and twenty feet in width. It resembled a vast Greek temple, and its grandeur would not have seemed out of place in Alexandria. Jayesh marvelled at the interiors. There was an open area with a staircase leading to an upper floor, and cool stone flooring. Although the temple was a Zoroastrian one, the building had no worshippers in attendance today. There stood a lone, pale-skinned man who Jayesh presumed to be the one he sought. He was seated at a stone table with a book open in front of him.

As they approached, he stood up and bowed before the king, nodding to acknowledge Jayesh and introducing himself.

'I am Thomas, also known as Judas, the twin brother of Lord Jesus Christ. Are you the great trader His Majesty has spoken of so highly? Jayesh, if I recall correctly?'

Jayesh was taken aback by the stranger's forthcoming mannerism and fluent Latin. He was tall and slim, his long, dark hair extending to his shoulders. He had a full beard and brown eyes that sparkled with kindness and wisdom.

'I am Jayesh of Muziris, Your Excellency. I can scarcely believe it – if you would be so kind, how did you come to be at our shores, my lord? Our land is blessed!' replied Jayesh reverently in the same tongue. He bowed before the man and took a seat beside the rajah who had already made himself comfortable at the table.

Judas pushed towards them the book laid out in front of him. 'I have written down the teachings of my brother so men may learn from it. This book is an emissary in its own right, striving to spread the word of God as given to man by his true disciple and son, Lord Jesus Christ. Alas, the Romans – they have killed him. They nailed my brother to a cross so he may meet a most painful end … But his words – they cannot take the power of his words away. For many months after my brother's crucifixion, I had been in hiding. His disciples fear for their lives and some of us got together and decided to flee our homeland to escape the threat of death so the word of God may live on. The Romans … they slaughter anyone who preached my brother's teachings.

'My whole life, I have had to keep my true identity hidden. I have had to live in the opposite way my brother chose, so no one would catch wind of our resemblance and, by extension, our relation. He wore his hair long and kept a full beard, so I cut my hair short and shaved my face. I shadowed him as the Apostle Thomas. He was truly blessed by God. An honest disciple, no doubt. But I knew my path led elsewhere. When I came out of hiding, my hair and my beard had grown as you see them now, and my brother's ardent followers sought respite in the belief that Jesus himself had been resurrected when they saw me. They spoke of miracles and looked to me for guidance.'

Silence filled the air as Thomas paused to compose himself. When he spoke, his voice was weighed down by emotion, 'We were not just brothers in name – we were born of the same womb, on the same day. Yet my courage failed me. I could not bear the thought of shouldering the same burden my brother had – I was no saviour; I could not bear to live out the rest of my days as an impostor. At the first opportunity, I gathered my closest allies and we set out on our journey to these lands with no goal in mind. At least at first.'

'But why come here?' asked Jayesh.

'When my brother and I were born, we were visited by three wise men, two of whom were the scholars Melchior of Persia and Balthazar of Babylonia. They told our parents about the great responsibility Jesus would have to bear for God's race, and how they must prepare him for them. The third man was a king from India called Caspar, who bestowed great gifts upon us and vowed that his family, the House of Suren, would always provide us with food and shelter if we should ever be in need of it. Now, with nowhere to go, seeking sanctuary from persecution, we set out in search of the kingdom of Suren and, finally, set foot on your great lands,' Thomas concluded.

The rajah spoke, 'The Royal House of Suren was one of five ruling families of the Parthian kingdom. The Gondophares family are direct descendants of the House of Suren and as the king of the mighty Indo-Parthian Kingdom, I seek to honour the vows of my ancestors. Lord Judas is safe here.'

Thomas bowed his head in reverence of the king. He explained, 'And for that, I am forever in your debt, Your Majesty. Before my brother was taken, he said to me, "You know who you are, and you know what you must do." I did not understand then what he had meant but ever since I have arrived here and no longer felt fear for my life, I have found the time to realize that I am destined to be a messenger. I must spread the word of God and bring my brother's teachings to your blessed lands. When His Majesty King Gondophares mentioned you, a merchant who had ambitions of building a great church for the Judaists, I felt that we were destined to meet and persisted in my requests despite His Majesty's refusal.'

'Your Majesty, you must let me take him to Muziris – it is meant to be! He is the man I seek,' Jayesh whispered to the king frantically.

'It's not safe, Jayesh – they will come looking for him. We cannot take his word for who he says he is – do you really believe him?' Gondophares replied.

'Your Majesty, they know to seek him here, which is why they keep coming. You must trust me to keep him safe. He shall remain hidden until they stop looking. No one will know to come searching for him amongst us traders in Muciripattanam. You and your kingdom will remain safe.'

'You don't understand, Jayesh – he is a cursed man. We have had nothing but trouble since he arrived and now he refuses to remain hidden! He must be killed or our lands will be ravaged by the cruel Romans in search of him!'

'But we need him, Your Majesty! You have no use for him here but Muciripattanam does. He is the missing piece in

Muziris's destiny – to become an empire as great as Alexandria or Rome! I have never hesitated to extend a helping hand to you in any of your endeavours, Your Majesty, and look at your mighty kingdom! Must you deny me this small mercy now?' Jayesh pleaded.

The king relented, nodding slowly. Jayesh could sense his apprehensions.

55

Sreepadam Palace, Office of Professor Prakash
17 July 2024

'Under no circumstances will I authorize the excavation of the Kodungallur Kurumba Bhagavathy Temple,' Professor Prakash was adamant. Harveen and Rohan had been sitting in his office for nearly twenty minutes, arguing their case from various angles, knowing that the professor would be reluctant to nod his assent to their idea at the outset.

'But Professor,' pleaded Harveen, 'the evidence is compelling that this may be the location of the original Church of St Thomas. We know about the long-standing legends of treasures concealed behind a granite wall on the eastern side – who knows what we might find?'

'Yes, Professor, the records from Muziris indicate that there a significant bequest had been made to a temple of Lord Shiva for its protection and that of a stone well,' chipped in Rohan hopefully.

'I have looked at the record you are referencing, Rohan. There is no mention of a temple of any sort. How many temples dedicated to Lord Shiva do you estimate there were around southern India in the first century? And how is this different from the large number of significant donations these people have made to other temples over the two-year period in question?' His logic was sound.

'Because it is unusual, Professor. This one is promised to the temple for a hundred years,' argued Harveen.

'I cannot say I agree. You are basing this on your digitally enhanced photo of the document – the record itself is incomplete and it could even just have said ten years, originally. And if that happens to be true, there are several other donations like it and we have no reason to dedicate resource to this goose chase.'

Harveen and Rohan felt defeated.

'Well, it appears we are at an impasse. Where is Dr Gupta when you need her?' Prakash said.

The mention of the missing Penny Gupta made Harveen flinch. 'Any word from her yet, sir?' she asked.

'Nothing ...'

Harveen's thoughts went back to nearly breaking into Penny's apartment.

'But Professor, what about the secret room beyond the granite wall? And the well? Surely, that can't be a mere coincidence—' Rohan interrupted Harveen's thoughts.

'Rohan, there are hidden chambers like that in temples all across India. They are protected fiercely by the priests. I am sure that many of them contain articles of significant religious, historical and intrinsic value, but our job here is not to desecrate holy temples. We are here to better understand the history. What is special about the well? They are quite commonplace in temple grounds too.'

'Just that this is the only well that is specifically mentioned in any of the donations from Muziris, it must be special in some way.'

Prakash seemed unmoved.

'But we found something else, Professor. Christian symbols on artefacts recovered from the site – I have photos of them here,' Harveen continued, opening a folder and laying the images of the ivory pomegranates across the table for Prakash to see.

'Pomegranates, as we know, are a powerful Christian symbol and featured on the robes of the highest of priests. These were also found within those temple grounds.'

Professor Prakash paused, taking up the pictures in turn. 'Hmm … I remember this dig, actually. We concluded at the time that they may have been brought to the site by a visiting priest; we even discussed St Thomas, if I recall correctly.'

'But Professor, this also means that there have been historical digs in the grounds of that temple before, so this wouldn't be a first!' blurted Rohan.

'In the grounds, yes, but no one was allowed to dig around within the temple itself.'

'Professor, I agree with you completely. It would be sensible for us to start in the temple grounds as before. The new ground-penetrating radar (GPR) we have will be really helpful in guiding us to any potentially interesting finds. We can then reassess the situation when we have more information. We might even have newer information to corroborate our findings,' Harveen said and smiled, knowing she had made her case sound convincing enough.

'You are both very persistent, indeed,' Prakash said, smiling. 'Fine. Let me make some calls and get us approvals and you can carry out discreet investigations on the grounds. Until our permits are in, you are to conduct no digs anywhere else and go nowhere within the confines of the temple building. Are we clear?' He glanced at Harveen and Rohan in turn, then pointedly back at Harveen. They both nodded their agreement.

'Absolutely, sir,' said Harveen, beaming with delight.

The door to the office opened and Inspector Sanjay Kumar walked in. The usually jovial inspector had a grim look on his face and was accompanied by two other officers. All three men were in full khaki. Harveen noticed that both deputies had sidearms on their belts. They nodded at everyone in turn before Sanjay turned to Prakash. 'Professor Prakash, I'm afraid I have very bad news,' he began. 'Dr Penny Gupta was found dead this morning. Due to the circumstances of her death, I will need to question everyone who worked with her. Would you mind coming along, please?'

Harveen couldn't believe what she was hearing. 'Dead? What do you mean? And what of "the circumstances of her death"? What happened to her?' she asked.

'Harveen, I'm sorry but I cannot say anything yet. Professor Prakash, if you could please follow me.' One of the deputies opened the door and Prakash stood up to leave.

Before leaving, Sanjay told Harveen and Rohan, 'We will need to question you both as well. Please wait here.'

Harveen's hand instinctively slipped into her pocket. The door key to Penny's apartment was still there.

56

Muciripattanam
AD 52

'The Romans have ordered us to not open the church and to hand you over to them, Your Excellency,' Jayesh said.

It had taken them more than five years to build the first Christian church in India. Jayesh had secured a beautiful, expansive plot for the project, just outside the main Muciripattanam town. But just weeks before the magnificent church was due to open, the Roman fort had issued its decree.

'But we have been building this for so long, why do they stop us now?' St Thomas asked.

'As your reputation builds, they fear that you may develop a following like your brother's and they will not tolerate a potential threat to their empire. They would sooner kill you than allow it.

'What can we do?'

The plot was over twenty acres and offered room for expansion to the church for when its congregation grew. Jayesh and St Thomas had shared their vision for a church like the ones in Jerusalem – a marble-and-stone structure that could accommodate thousands of people. In its grounds, they planned to build a beautiful library to house the greatest religious texts from around the world. The plot had been flat and clear, with only a few banyan and peepal trees in the grounds.

The first structure they had erected was a wooden building over two storeys high, with a steep pitched roof, built near the centre of the plot.

'My Lord, I have told them that we will stop today and turn this compound into a great Indian temple,' Jayesh told St Thomas, who was crestfallen. He added, 'But fear not, Your Excellency. For now, we will create an underground chamber where you can conduct your church sermons whilst we work out a deal with the Romans. They will not be able to stop you in your noble endeavour.'

Thomas had been holding services outdoors and these gatherings were getting more and more crowded. Jayesh did his part to ensure that they were well-attended and provided a plentiful feast to those who came. He invited all the important families in the region, including the wealthy Cheras to the northeast, who had built some of the most lavish temples in India, as also the Nedumpally Brahmin family from the north. The Cheras treated the new religion as a novelty, while the Brahmins seemed to be enthralled by St Thomas's eloquent sermons and returned frequently of their own volition. They even wanted to build other churches in southern India for him.

'Roman soldiers came to see me this morning, my lord,' Jayesh said. 'They expect you at their fort before sundown.'

'And so I will go, for I do not fear death, my son. But we have much work to do here,' St Thomas replied.

'No, my lord. I shall tell them you have disappeared – that you left before I arrived. My men will arrange to hide you away. I have a good relationship with the Romans here and know them well. I am sure they will ask Rome for guidance and not resort to any extreme measures on their own. It will be many days before they do anything,' Jayesh said. Rajah Gondophares's words echoed in his mind.

57

Kurumba Bhagavathy Temple, Kodungallur
19 July 2024

'It's my fault that she is dead,' Harveen said, her voice shaking. She had been able to think of little else since Inspector Kumar had told them about Penny. Fortunately, he did not seem to know she had visited Penny's apartment but had told her there would be a follow-up interrogation soon.

'What – what are you talking about?' Rohan said while parking the jeep in the temple grounds.

'Dr Gupta told me she was meeting with someone,' Harveen revealed quietly. She looked into the distance pensively, marvelling at how vast the grounds were. The temple sat on a plot of over ten acres, partially covered with trees and vegetation. She felt it was time she confided in someone about what was going on. The situation had grown to unthinkable proportions. 'Do you think … I mean … I feared it may have had something to do with our recent discoveries.'

'What do you mean, Veen? Who did she meet?'

'I don't know! I just saw her slip into a silver car with a man. She told me later when I walked in on her speaking to somebody over the phone that she had a meeting to go to …

maybe it was with the same man? I really don't know what to make of any of it.'

'Did you tell Inspector Kumar about all this?'

'Not yet. I promised Penny that I would keep it a secret. She asked me to … I don't know if it's connected … maybe I'm just linking the two things …'

'If it does have to do with the person she was meeting and with our discoveries … do you think that means we are in any danger?'

Harveen realized she was causing Rohan some worry and distress. She immediately dismissed his fears, 'No, no. Of course not, Rohan. Forget I said anything. She was always so immaculate in her appearances, I'm sure she came off as someone wealthy and attracted undue attention. Perhaps it was just a mugging after all; Inspector Kumar is yet to say anything solid on the matter, let's not speculate. I'm sure we'll be fine.' Her instinct was nagging at her. She wondered if she should tell Inspector Kumar about the big man behind the wheel of the silver car. What if Penny had fallen prey to foulplay?

'Let's focus on what we're here for. I'd say we start with the GPR close to the temple building, and work our way outwards,' she said, changing the subject. They had permission to use the site only for a few days and had to work quickly.

'Agreed,' said Rohan. 'Let's start near the eastern side, where we think the secret room is supposed to be located.'

'Yeah, maybe if we can prove that there is something of note there, we may be allowed to make a small dig?'

'The priest will certainly not let you open the chamber even if we find it. Let's check around the Samadhi of Vysoori too.'

Harveen was excited to go have a look at the stone well they had been talking about.

The Kodungallur Kurumba Bhagavathy Temple was one of the oldest temples in India and the legends and myths surrounding it had grown complicated and intertwined over the centuries. There were red-tiled roofs atop all the buildings sprawled across the site's distinctive red soil. The banyan and peepal trees provided some much-needed respite from the scorching sun.

'Let's start on that side of the temple,' Harveen suggested.

'Yes,' said Rohan. 'Can you give me a hand with this?' They unloaded the ground-penetrating radar together and charted their route along the perimeter of the temple buildings, and then around the well.

'This new machine is pretty accurate up to a depth of about twenty to thirty feet. It can detect large stones, cavities, metals, unusual objects – anything. It's not great with certain types of materials, but this soft ground should not present any issues,' Rohan explained to Harveen as he set up the GPR. Harveen was pitching their tent by the side of the stone well.

'Um, Rohan, did Sanjay say anything else to you about Dr Gupta? I tried to ask him about any details, but he simply wouldn't tell me,' she said.

'No, he didn't. He just asked me where I had been on certain days and if I could think of anyone who would want to hurt her.'

On and off, Penny kept coming up in their conversations throughout the day. They were both troubled by the news of her sudden death.

After a full day in the scorching heat, they had still not made a single discovery of note. They were finally getting ready to pack up and head back to the palace.

'I don't think we are going to find anything here,' Rohan was despondent. 'I think we should just go and join the team in Palayoor. It has been famous as the site of the first Christian church for a long time now. Maybe there is more to be found there like the stone we chanced upon and I'm sure they could use the extra resources.'

Harveen was likewise very disappointed. She had felt so sure that this was the place.

'Let's try and dig through the top of the well. Maybe there is something just under the surface? There is no one around – we will work quickly, and it will be easy to replace a few stones.'

Rohan stared at her with surprise. 'Harveen, we can't just start digging up a heritage site. You heard what the professor said – nothing without his prior authorization.'

She sighed, still determined to leave the site with something. 'Okay, fine. How about we try and look under the temple buildings and the well? If we can make a shallow dent in the ground at an angle, we should be able to get a better read. It'll just be another hour or so.'

Rohan recognized the look on her face. He knew she had made up her mind and would do it by herself anyway if he said no.

'Sure,' he said, 'let's give it a try.'

For the next two hours, they carefully went around the temple complex, about four feet from the edge of the building, using the GPR to scan underneath the building. A couple of the images around the Samadhi of Vysoori seemed to show a shadow of some kind underneath the well.

'Look at this, Rohan, couldn't this be something?' Harveen pointed at the shadow.

Rohan examined the readings but seemed unconvinced. 'Hmm … I am not too sure, let's take some more readings. The shadow could just be indicative of a different type of stone near the bottom of the well.'

They continued to take readings around the well, but none turned out clearer than the ones obtained initially.

'We need to dig to get a better look,' Harveen persisted.

'You know the professor will not allow it. Let's just go back and speak to him first. None of this is going anywhere – we have time; why are you in such a rush?'

But Harveen was not listening. Her eyes had a faraway look in them. 'I have an idea. But maybe you should opt out for the next couple of days. Go to the other site, like you said. They could use your help.'

Rohan shuddered. 'What are you planning? Please, Veen, don't get into any more trouble.'

She turned to smile at him. 'I will be fine, you can trust me.'

With that, she started scrolling through the contacts on her phone. Rohan shook his head and busied himself with packing up their equipment.

Please pick up. Please. The line connected. 'Hi, it's Harveen. I need a favour.'

58

Santa Alleanza Conference Line
19 July 2024

'Signor, that Gill woman 'ad brought a team of builders to the temple site today. They are not officials – the owner of the company is 'er relative, I think,' Vincenzo reported. Don gritted his teeth in annoyance. She had told him there was nothing at the site.

'The private contractor they work for builds residential projects. She was supervising them alone. They dug a number of boreholes under the well. It took them hours, signor,' Vincenzo sounded bored.

'Boreholes?' asked Rossi. 'Whatever for?'

'Small cameras and such for looking under the buildings, signor,' Don explained.

'That's right, signor,' said Vincenzo. 'They seemed very excited about it after around four hours. She was shouting about some chamber very loud and excited.'

'A chamber? What kind of chamber? What did they find?' Rossi sounded panicked.

'Nothing as yet, signor. It seems the old man has not given his permission.'

'I will find out what they saw in there,' Don interjected. His dealings had been futile so far – Harveen could clearly not be trusted. 'If the woman poses a problem, I will deal with her too.'

'Excellent, Don, you do that,' said Rossi.

Don could picture his satisfied grin.

59

Muciripattanam
AD 71

'It is a summons.' The general handed Jayesh a scroll. 'You are to leave for Rome immediately. The new Emperor Vespasian has sent for you personally.'

'Me? But why?' asked Jayesh. They shared a cordial relationship and he felt he could ask the general for his honest opinion.

'I have never seen such a message. Not directly from the emperor, at any rate. I was sent instructions too. If you are not on the first ship to Rome, I am to convey you myself. By any means necessary.'

Jayesh was gripped with fear. He leaned against the wall of the impressive fort. It was one of his crowning achievements. No one had dared to invade Muciripattanam since the Roman battalion had been stationed there, just as he had anticipated. Pirates avoided the port entirely. However, he was not oblivious to the havoc the Romans were capable of wreaking.

'What did you say to them? What do they know?' Jayesh demanded of the general.

'The Port of Mucirípattanam has become our most important trade ally in this region. I know that you come up in discussions often, but a personal invite is rarely good news, my friend. I am sorry.'

Jayesh reluctantly accepted the scroll. His first thought was whether he should turn St Thomas over to them to save his business and his life. He decided to seek the counsel of his trusted friends, Nannan and Vikesh.

'I bet it has to do with the Chinese trade,' said Nannan. 'They are a major trading ally for us and the translators who help us in our negotiations are mandated to send reports about these dealings to Rome.'

Jayesh had been to China twice to meet with their new leader, and had been impressed with the scale of the empire and its ambitions to prosper.

'Remember how they reacted the last time you mentioned China?'

The Senate had been furious at the mere mention.

'No, I think it's the amount of money we charge Rome for our goods,' said Vikesh. 'Why can't we just let them trade with the Cheras and the Pandyas and have this be their problem? Haven't we had enough already? You act like their king is your king; their gods your god!'

'We will not be told how to trade!' Jayesh said. He had set up routes all across India and the east. Goods were coming into Mucirípattanam from as far north as the Himalayas, and recent times had seen a great rise in the imports from China as well. The growing metropolis of Mucirípattanam was proving to be quite the magnet for commerce and the demand from Rome was insatiable.

The once sleepy port town was now becoming known as a place where fortunes could be made and attracted immigrants from all parts of India and beyond. Roman ships laden with gold would arrive daily and depart loaded heavily with spices and silk. They would dock in Muciripattanam for many days, and as they waited for the optimal sailing conditions to appear, business flourished. Jayesh had built food and drink joints not unlike the ones he had seen in Alexandria, and these were always well-stocked with Roman wine and foods from all nations.

'This is our lifetime's work,' said Jayesh. 'Do you even remember the small market where we met as young boys, Vikesh? Look at it now! It is the envy of the world. Goods that we had never even imagined could exist are now traded in our market. We simply cannot step back now.'

'It's not all progress,' said Vikesh. 'You copy Rome even when they go against our culture. Alcohol flows freely, and flesh is traded in these streets, too – this was never the case when we started.'

The Roman fort had generated a demand for brothels like in the Roman empire, and although Jayesh would have no part of it, others stepped in to meet the demand. Local women were considered 'exotic' by traders and soldiers who ventured into these parts, and the owners of the brothels earned far more profits from them than the slave girls who were brought aboard the ships from Europe. Vikesh had been staunchly opposed to this grim new trend.

'What about the business?' said Jayesh. 'Is it nothing? The wealth the Romans bring with them?'

'You are becoming one of them.'

'And you refuse to expand your mind.'

Nannan intervened to dispel the growing tension between the two men. 'Rome is in turmoil. Each new merchant brings news of a new emperor. The throne has changed hands four times this year alone. Each new reign has been more unstable than the last. I think we should stay put and bide our time.'

'I agree,' said Vikesh.

'We cannot do that. The general is under instructions to take me by force if I am not onboard the next ship,' Jayesh replied. 'I have no choice but to go. My brothers, come with me. You are my greatest strength and I would not know how to conduct myself there without you.'

'I am never going on those ships,' Vikesh said.

Jayesh and Nannan could not hold back their laughter. They slapped Vikesh's back but he did not look amused. They composed themselves and Nannan said, 'Jayesh is right, we must go, we don't have a choice. A summons from Rome cannot be ignored. There is a Roman fort on our shores, they can take up arms against us and force us to do their bidding. That will certainly only cause more damage. It's best we go peacefully.'

They persisted and finally convinced Vikesh to make the journey with them. They could use all the help they could get.

Before they set off on their journey, Jayesh went to take his mother's blessings and his wife and children's leave as per tradition. They shared a meal together and Paavi told him about the latest adventures of his sons.

Before they parted, Paavi asked to speak with him in private. They walked some distance down the hill before she began to cry. 'The dreams, Jayesh. They haunt me. After so many years, they have come back. And again, you mention this voyage … I can't bear to go through it all again. I nearly lost you once.' Jayesh held her in a tight embrace, hoping she could not tell his heart had dropped to his stomach.

'Is it the one about the ship?' he asked her gently. She nodded through her tears.

He held her by the shoulders and looked into her eyes. 'I promise I will be careful, alright? If I could avoid making this journey, I would drop it in a heartbeat, my love. But I must go.' He kissed her forehead and soothed her. 'I have Amma's blessing and St Thomas will grant me his blessings too. With so many powerful gods watching over me, nothing can hurt me. I promise.'

Paavi smiled and nodded again, trying to compose herself for her husband's sake. An evil sense of foreboding chilled Jayesh to the bone.

60

Sreepadam Palace, Conference Room
20 July 2024

'You don't mind if I record this meeting, do you? We're supposed to, for our records, as this is a murder case,' said Inspector Kumar.

'Of course, Sanjay,' Harveen said weakly. He flashed her a look that reminded her that this was not an informal meeting before turning on the recorder. Even though they were sitting in one of the small meeting rooms at Sreepadam Palace, it felt like they were in a police interrogation room. In addition to Inspector Kumar, there was another armed policeman present. Kumar listed all three of their names and the date as they began recording, and then eased into his questions for Harveen. She was intimidated by the setting and scared of saying the wrong thing.

'I have been given to understand that you had some sort of a disagreement during a recent meeting involving Dr Gupta on the fifth of July,' Kumar said, referring to his notes.

'I don't remember us having a disagreement … must have just been a difference of opinion on professional matters, at worst,' she replied.

The inspector frowned and checked his notes again. '"I wish she was dead." Is that something you might have said?' he asked.

The memory flashed in Harveen's mind at the mention of her exact words. She felt the room closing in on her. 'No, wait. This is a misunderstanding – I didn't mean anything by it, I just—' Her hands began to shake.

'Are you saying you didn't say that?' Kumar was looking at his notebook. 'Several people have reported that you did and quoted you exactly in those words.'

'Well, yes, I did say it. But I didn't mean it literally …'

'Uh … why did you say it then? Could you give me some context as to what happened that day?'

'She was taking over my projects and I was afraid of losing my job. I was actively being sidelined, and I didn't think it was fair.'

'So you felt jealous of her?' Kumar seemed to be leading her towards a certain response. She felt trapped.

'Absolutely not. I was just upset and worried about what that might mean for my career. I'm passionate about my work so I blurted something out, but we worked through our issues and it's all sorted now. I am running the project again.'

Inspector Kumar examined her face curiously, frowning. 'Walk me through how that happened – how is it that you regained your position as the lead of the project? I've been told she'd specifically been invited to join your team because things were spiralling out of control under your leadership. How did this change of heart come about?'

'I'm not sure, actually … I presented some of my work the other day and Dr Gupta said that she had felt very impressed and thought it was best I lead the team since I was so heavily involved. She said she preferred working behind the desk.

She just put me in charge and—'

'Then mysteriously disappeared?' An awkward silence followed.

'You can't be serious … Sanjay? You know me – you know I couldn't possibly have had anything to do with this. I don't even know what happened to her!'

'I know you are very passionate about your job. Another thing I know based on recent events is that you are passionate enough to risk the lives of your team members to get what you want. You just admitted you were very upset at Dr Gupta being put in charge of a project you thought was yours to lead. You even said in front of a room full of people that you wished she was dead. Lo and behold, within days, she wound up dead.'

'I wasn't really mad – I was just frustrated! I even went to find her straight afterwards to apologize.'

'Yes, you say that, but no one else seems to have witnessed this second meeting where she put you in charge. Then she just … conveniently disappeared.'

'Sanjay—'

'The evidence against you is strong, Harveen. I need you to understand the gravity of your situation.'

Harveen sat in silence. Was he really going to arrest her?

'Have you, by any chance, ever been to Dr Gupta's apartment?'

The change of direction came as a surprise to Harveen. She had thrown away the keycard. Surely, there was no evidence that she had been there.

'Harveen?' he pressed.

She knew she could not lie to him. 'Yes. I was really worried when we didn't hear from her for a few days. I went to see if she was there. I knocked on her door and called her phone but when she didn't answer, I left. I came back to the office, in fact.'

'And did you pretend to be her sister?'

Harveen was flushed. 'The guard wouldn't let me in … I couldn't think of anything else to say so he would.'

'So you lied to get into her apartment?'

'No, I never went in. I did enter the building, but not into her apartment – I got a call from Rohan just as I knocked, so I rushed back here. You can check with him if you want.' Kumar made a note in his book.

'I have a question for you too, Sanjay. You have said nothing about how Dr Gupta died. When you spoke to Professor Prakash, you said that she had been found dead. How do you know it is a murder now?' she asked.

'Well, there were some very unusual things about the body when it was found. Her valuables, including a watch and rings, were all still on her, which ruled out a mugging. There were also extensive signs of what can only be described as torture. I have never seen anything like it.'

Harveen was shocked. Torture? Who would torture Penny? And what were they after? Could she be in danger too? She knew she had to mention the man Dr Gupta had met.

'Sanjay, I must tell you something. There was a man …' she began slowly. 'He came to meet her in a car … I don't know who he was but I saw her with him.'

'Wait, when was this and where?' Kumar flipped open his notebook and started scribbling as Harveen spoke.

'I don't remember the date exactly, but it was the same day as my outburst – I was in the grounds and I saw her sneak out of the building by the side entrance. I followed her from a distance and saw a silver car slow down on the opposite side of the road from her. There was a large man behind the wheel and she slipped in beside him before they drove away.'

'Can you describe the man a bit more? Did you get a good look at him?'

'Yes, he was really big and he wasn't Indian – he was white, in fact, with dark hair combed back. I remember noticing his hands were huge.'

'How tall would he have been?'

'I don't know. He never got out of the car.'

'What kind of car was it?'

'I don't know … it was silver and it looked new … sorry, I am not very good with cars, so that's all I can tell you.'

'And why didn't you mention this before?'

'Well,' said Harveen, 'I didn't think it was significant until now. I had no idea who the man was or what her relationship with him had been … Oh, wait! Just before we argued, she told me that she was rushing into a meeting of some sort … She didn't say who it was with but maybe that was him?'

'Harveen, I'm sorry but that doesn't help me at all. I have interviewed everyone in the department and no one has mentioned any erratic behaviour on Dr Gupta's part. I could take your word for it but I barely have anything to work with here. You haven't offered any reasonable explanations for your own behaviour or mentioned this mystery man until just now, when you felt threatened by my line of questioning. I have enough cause to officially name you as a suspect.'

'Sanjay, please. I'm sorry, I should've told you,' she pleaded. 'You know I couldn't possibly have – you know me.'

'Do I?' he said. His stare was cold. There was a long pause before he said, 'Interview terminated, 3:22 p.m.'

'The man … you have to find him—'

'We will look into it,' he said. 'I would like you to come down to the station in the next couple of days to make a formal statement. We would also like permission to search your house.'

Harveen nodded weakly.

61

Muciripattanam
AD 71

'I have been summoned to Rome. It may be about you and the church. You may have to think about running away and hiding, Your Excellency. I am afraid I can no longer protect you,' Jayesh said.

'So be it,' said St Thomas, 'but I will not run again.'

'The forces of Rome have already displaced over a million Jews. They are serious about quelling a potential uprising here. Muziris could get caught up in the turmoil too. And I … I may never return,' Jayesh was beginning to feel very worried about the summons now. What if he was killed in Rome, what would become of his family and the people who relied on him?

'They cannot stop us now. We have already built seven churches!' St Thomas said.

'If they can destroy the whole of Jerusalem without hesitation, Your Excellency, they will not hesitate to crush Muziris and its surrounding areas, I am certain.'

'Impossible! The Temple of Jerusalem is one of the best-protected buildings in the world. There is an entire mighty fort dedicated to its protection, built by King Herod himself. Can the reports even be true?'

Jayesh had heard reports from various sources and had no reason to doubt their veracity.

'I am afraid so, my lord. Every last wall has been knocked down … people have been slaughtered mercilessly and the entire temple has been razed to the ground. Over a hundred thousand have been taken as slaves back to Rome. The Roman forces have left the city in flames.'

St Thomas could not believe his ears. He began to tremble and struggled to stay on his feet, slowly lowering himself onto a seat with Jayesh's support. Jayesh could see tears welling in his eyes as memories of his homeland mixed with images of the Great Temple of Jerusalem burning to the ground. Finally, he shut his eyes as if in prayer for those who had fallen, getting up gingerly to walk towards the altar. He returned to Jayesh a few moments later.

'Tell me, Jayesh – is there nothing we can do? We cannot sit by and let this happen!' St Thomas said. 'We must rebuild the Tabernacle here.'

'The Tabernacle, Your Excellency?' Jayesh said.

'The Temple of Jerusalem was the centre of Judaism not because of the buildings, but because it was home to the Tabernacle over a thousand years ago. The original temple was built by King Solomon to replace the Tabernacle in the Sinai Desert,' St Thomas explained. 'Moses is the most important prophet of the Judaist religion. He received the Ten Commandments directly from God, which became the laws of the religion. He also received instruction on how to preserve them for the ages. They were to be placed in a box called the "Ark of the Covenant" and stored in a sacred room, which came to be called the Tabernacle. It was little more than a tent to begin with, but it is characterized by the specific items that it needs to contain to qualify, such as the Ark and the Menorah. King Solomon built a temple to house this room.' He went on to list other items that were kept inside the Tabernacle as well.

'King Solomon's temple was destroyed and it was another 500 years before the next one was built. But even then the history of the Tabernacle is rife with war and controversy. Only since King Herod fortified the Temple of Jerusalem has it been afforded a settled existence. Now, if what you say is true, the Tabernacle is lost once again. Is there no way to ascertain what happened to the priests and the precious items stored within the temple complex?'

'If the reports are to be believed, my lord, then nothing remains in its place. The Romans have an eye for items of value, so they may well have plundered the gold and jewels, but I fear there is no way to know if they have preserved the items that hold religious significance ...' He deliberated for a moment before asking, 'What would it take to recreate the Tabernacle here, Your Excellency?'

St Thomas considered his answer for a moment.

'We will need the items that would qualify a room as a Tabernacle, most importantly.'

'But the items that you mentioned – the Menorah, the gold lamp stand, the veil and the woven curtains ... Surely, they could be recreated even if the Romans have destroyed the ones in Jerusalem?'

'It may be possible,' said Thomas, 'but it would still not be able to acquire the significance that Jerusalem had. For this reason, it is most important that the Tabernacle be rebuilt there.'

'But until it is, my lord, could we not try? I shall take note of the items inside the Tabernacle and try to find out what happened to them once I get to Rome. We can create a Tabernacle of our own here, in the underground room we have constructed, so that the items remain safe. We can start work on this straightaway, in fact. We donate statues to our temples, and I would like to extend the same courtesy to your people, if you will accept it. If they become your followers, then this building can serve as your church. But should they wish to have a dedicated place of worship as Jews, I would be more than willing to arrange for another structure to be built which would be all their own.'

St Thomas considered the prospect of having Muziris serve as a focal point for the growing Christian community.

'I will immediately set about ascertaining my people's wishes,' he replied.

'That would be most useful, my lord,' Jayesh said, 'Now, you must pray for my safety so I may return from Rome bearing favourable news. I will instruct my men to begin the construction of the new Tabernacle upon your assent. Allow me take your leave now, Your Excellency.'

'May you find success and fortunate news, my son.'

62

Sreepadam Palace
20 July 2024

Harveen sat at her desk alone, holding the phone to her ear. Everyone else had already left the office hours ago. Inspector Kumar's words were swimming in her head as the line connected. 'Hello … Mr Sharma?' she said tentatively.

Mr Sharma sighed at the other end. 'What is it now? Another problem?' Harveen's landlord had been reluctant to rent the small unit in his house to an unmarried girl, at first. It had taken some persuasion from her as well as a call from Professor Prakash for him to finally relent. He was a conservative man and did not approve of Harveen's unusual hours as it involved him having to let her in. They shared a common entrance and they were often pulled into small talk and awkward conversation as a result of this.

'Yes – well, no,' Harveen struggled to find the right words. 'You remember I mentioned a Dr Gupta from work?'

'The woman who took your job?' he asked.

'Right. Well, I just thought it was best you hear it from me before you find out any other way. She went missing a few days ago and, well … a few days ago … they found her – her body …'

'Her body? What – what do you mean?' He sounded impatient.

'Well, she's dead,' said Harveen. 'And the police says it was likely a murder …'

'A murder?! Harveen, what on earth – what are you telling me this for? You better not be mixed up in this or I swear—'

'Mr Sharma, I promise I have nothing to do with it,' said Harveen. She did not want to lose her home owing to a massive misunderstanding – she was innocent. Her job was already under threat after she had decided that no matter what, she would sneak a look inside the chamber underneath the temple. 'It's just that, as a matter of routine, the police have to search the office and the houses of all the staff here, so—'

'What!' interrupted Mr Sharma. She could picture his round face turning red as he got angrier. 'The police want to search my house?!'

'We will need to cooperate with them, Mr Sharma, it is a sensitive matter. They are on their way right now. I am sure they will only be a few minutes and will only need to look through my apartment. I assure you, they will find nothing – please, just keep calm, everything's going to be fine.'

'This is preposterous! I think we need to discuss whether you can continue to stay here. I can't have the police showing up here. What will the neighbours think! Are you going to be here soon?' he finally asked.

'No, I have to work,' she lied, dreading the worst. 'We can speak when I come back later.'

'Fine,' he said and hung up.

Harveen sighed and held her head in her hands at her desk. After allowing herself a moment, she turned her attention back to the written records from the merchant house they had uncovered, open on her screen. She was putting them through the software that Dr Gupta had given her access to. She struggled to focus on the translations; her mind kept circling back to Penny's murder and how she had come to be a suspect. She thought about the implications of this, worrying about where she would live if Mr Sharma kicked her out, how she would pay rent, what would happen to her family, how they might be affected by the news, if she should tell them at all …

Just as she was skimming through the translated records, her mind refusing to keep still, one particular item jolted her back to the present. She stared at her screen, wide-eyed, unsure of what to do next. She wanted to call Rohan, but wondered if she should consult Professor Prakash first, as he would know what she should do next. She sat deliberating for what felt like a long time before picking up her phone and dialling a number.

'Harveen? Hi! It's so good to hear from you.' The man on the other end sounded like he had been waiting for her call.

'Hello, Don? I am sorry – did I disturb you?'

'No, it's fine. I was just completing some paperwork at my hotel. What can I do for you?'

'It's just … I have found something just too incredible to believe and before I tell anyone at the office about it, I need to be sure. I was wondering if you could help me …'

'Of course. Is it about St Thomas?'

'No, something even bigger.'

63

Myos Hormos
AD 71

Vikesh had been seasick throughout the journey to Myos Hormos. He had wanted to turn back since the day they had first set sail from Muciripattanam. Nannan too seemed to have lost his enthusiasm somewhere along the way.

'Rome is under significant financial strain. Their new emperor has spent his life so far leading legions to victories around the world. His only solution will be military,' Nannan said.

'But then why would they summon us to Rome?' Jayesh was scared for his life too, though he was clinging on to the hope that he could still persuade the Senate that Rome would only benefit from the growth of Muciripattanam into a formidable ally.

'I don't know! So we are at their mercy and agree to everything they say? To kill us? I have seen them bring in foreigners just to parade them through the streets and execute them publicly for the crowd's entertainment.'

'Let them have what they want ...' Vikesh said weakly. 'But if either of you survive, look after my sister.'

The first time Jayesh and Nannan had visited Rome, the empire had been under the rule of Emperor Tiberius of the Julio-Claudian dynasty. Jayesh vividly remembered that visit and how they had been enthralled by the glory of the capital city. Each step had been an assault on the senses – a new vista opening at every turn, full of little details for them to absorb; it had almost felt overwhelming. This visit was cloaked in uncertainties: debts, the church of St Thomas, the expanding trade with China – they had a lot to explain.

The forum buzzed with news about the new emperor and the changes he was bringing about. His son, Titus, had led a victorious campaign against Judaea recently, which had resulted in people all over Rome engaging in animated discussions about his conquest. He had returned with immeasurable treasures to fill the coffers of Rome with. There was to be a great parade to celebrate the victory and people were excited at this prospect. The procession would wind through the streets of Rome, with the final spectacle being the public execution of the captured Jewish leaders. The mere mention of these executions terrified Jayesh. Romans had a reputation for being entertained by the spilling of blood, and he feared that perhaps he too had been summoned to add to the thrill of the populace.

Nannan arrived at their lodgings with more news about the impending meeting. He seemed a little disoriented.

'Our meeting will not be at the Senate tomorrow.'

'You mean they have called it off?' asked Jayesh hopefully.

'No … we have been summoned directly to Emperor Vespasian's palace.'

The news came as a total shock, and the other two men stared at Nannan, unsure of what to think.

'Is that … normal?' Vikesh finally asked.

'As far as public memory can be trusted, it has never happened before.'

'Could it possibly be good news?' Jayesh asked.

'I doubt it,' Nannan replied. 'I don't know if you have noticed, but there are soldiers stationed right outside our lodgings. They are to watch us tonight and then escort us to the palace tomorrow. I fear we are not being invited to meet with the emperor, for he will not be there tomorrow. It is the day of the executions.'

64

Hyatt Regency, Thrissur
20 July 2024

'What is it, Harveen? You must tell me everything,' Don replied. She sounded excited.

'I looked at one of the records in the sheets we retrieved from the house of the Indian merchant. It was in the same format as the others, but with sections removed,' Harveen spoke quickly. 'I need to verify if my conclusions can possibly be true.'

'Would you like to go through it together?'

Harveen paused for a second before she started talking again.

'One of our team members died. Dr Gupta … The police think the circumstances are suspicious … they think she's been murdered …' her voice shook as she conveyed the news to Don.

'Oh my, that's terrible, signora – I'm so sorry. Are you alright?'

'I'm fine. We are all just in a state of shock right now. Anyway, she … gave me access to a software which I'm using to translate the records. It may not be perfect, but here is what I've got: "Ark from the Temple of Jerusalem. 400 m sesterces. Titus. J Muziris."'

Don was stunned. He was glad she couldn't see him clenching his jaw in nervousness. He was quiet for a long time before he spoke, 'Was there anything else in this document?'

'We are lucky to have found it in perfect condition in every way, other than the sections that have been carefully removed. There was certainly more information on the document before. I also checked the sheets directly before and after it – both of those are perfect too. This record was tampered with after it was written; the original record would have had more information which has since been erased – though I'm not sure when.'

'And what is it you have concluded that you wish to corroborate, signora?'

'It's the record of a sale – the Ark of the Covenant by the Emperor Titus, to someone called J. Muziris, for what would today amount to over 1 billion US dollars. But this would mean that the Ark was brought to Muziris. That would mean it must be somewhere in India … somewhere here.'

The moment Don had feared would come. Despite all his patience and efforts, he was finally in the position where he had no choice but to kill Harveen and retrieve the records before anyone else could find them.

'I need to know if it's true. I need to know where to look,' she continued. 'It's just too shocking to believe.'

'It's not here,' he replied quietly.

'What?' she said. 'What do you mean? How could you possibly know that?'

'Who else have you told about this record?' Don asked in a gruff voice.

'Uh, no one … I wanted to first make sure if it is true …'

Don cleared his throat before saying, 'I have something related to this in the Vatican. But I will share the documents with you only on one condition.'

'What's that?'

'You must swear to keep the matter absolutely confidential. If word about the Ark gets out, every treasure hunter and religious nut in the world will come flocking to India in search of it. But it's not in India … it never made it here.'

'Sure, I mean, I swear – but what documents?' she asked.

'First-hand accounts – I have them with me. I can show you. They're in my suite, 501. I can't move them out of there, so you'll have to come there to see them. But first, delete any digital records, scans or emails mentioning these records. I need you to bring the original to me so I can examine it for myself.' He needed to get that document in his hands before dealing with Harveen.

'I have it with me here. I'll bring it along.'

'Great. See you,' he said. The situation could still be controlled.

Harveen's answer was immediate. 'Sure, see you there.'

Don slammed his phone on his bed and paced around, trying to compose himself. He went to one of the cupboards and dragged out the box that Sofia had left on the plane for him. He opened the lid and grabbed the first folder. It was simply labelled 'The Artefact'.

65

Palace of Vespasian, Rome
AD 71

The soldiers pushed and prodded Jayesh, Nannan and Vikesh on their way to the palace of Emperor Vespasian. Vikesh had still not recovered from his illness and lost balance, causing the men to drag him for part of the way.

They spoke amongst themselves in their native language. The tension was palpable.

'We need to understand their demands,' said Jayesh, remaining hopeful of striking a deal. He needed to keep their spirits up, taking confident strides despite the rough treatment. He feared that if the Romans saw how afraid they were, it would be disastrous for them.

The interior of the palace took them by surprise. It was quite modest, unlike most important structures in the city. Jayesh had been expecting opulence and blatant show of power, but instead, the impressive facade opened into a chamber with simple white marble flooring and basic furniture. The reception area was large and dominated by a statue of Vespasian – the only sign of his esteemed position. They were led into an expansive courtyard. The open quadrangle contained ornate fountains emanating cool sprays in their vicinity, encircled by exotic plants. It was surrounded by the palace's covered colonnades. Despite the intense afternoon heat, the courtyard was cool and comfortable. But for the Roman soldiers, it would have been a relaxing space to enjoy the beauty of the central garden.

Three men were already waiting to receive them when they arrived. Vikesh, who spoke no Latin, slumped into a chair whilst Jayesh and Nannan were presented before the Emperor Vespasian. Titus, the emperor's son, was also present, along with a third man who was not introduced to them. He appeared to be a scribe or advisor, sitting quietly, waiting to record the proceedings. Once the formalities were dispensed with and wine glasses filled, Vespasian began.

'It is good to finally meet the great Eastern trader, Jayesh of Muziris, who does so much business with Rome.' Jayesh kept his head bowed in reverence, bending lower at the compliment but keeping his guard up in wait of what was to come.

'The honour is all ours, Your Majesty. In nearly fifty years of trading with Rome, no Indian has yet had the blessed privilege of meeting the Great Roman Emperor himself, let alone enter his home, my dominus.' Jayesh gave a deferential nod to both the emperor and his son. 'We have also been given to understand that felicitations are in order for the great victory of your son, Titus, in his conquest of Judaea.'

Vespasian seemed genuinely pleased at Jayesh's reverential manner. With the required pleasantries now concluded, the emperor moved directly to the question of why he had asked them to come to Rome.

'In the first year of my reign, my focus has been to restore the prosperity of the Roman empire. The Senate under the previous emperors has not treated our finance with the urgency it warranted. Provinces have got away with not paying their fair share of taxes and yet others have been allowed to profit by unfair means due to our lack of vigilance. I have decided to put an end to this. An important step in this direction would be to ascertain Rome's allies and her enemies. We learnt of the divided loyalties of Judaea and the outcomes of inciting our displeasure are for the world to see. Both my son and I have been steadfast soldiers, committed to protect the motherland. We have ascended to the throne from the legions. Some might say that this is the reason we have a rather simple view on what constitutes an effective solution to many of the empire's problems.'

Vespasian had the disposition of a candid and straightforward man. Jayesh had no doubt he would make good on any threat he issued.

'Muziris has always been loyal to the Roman throne, Your Majesty. We have even built a temple in the honour of Emperor Augustus and been rewarded for our allegiances with a Roman fort to protect the Great Empire's interests in the region.'

'Yes. I believe I have heard of this temple. It is said to be beautiful. Our soldiers report how well they are taken care of, but they also speak of the great fortunes that are made in Muziris. The best of Roman wine flows in the bars in copious quantities such that any man may drink his fill; the streets are abundant in Roman gold such that any man may fill his purse.' Jayesh looked closely at Vespasian as he spoke. His hair was thinning and the furrows of age were visible on his face. But his torso and arms looked as if they belonged to a much younger man, scorched by years of exposure to the sun and hardened by a life spent fighting wars. Titus too was cast in his father's image; he sat carving fruit on his plate with a sharp knife drawn from his belt. Jayesh knew the next few moments would be critical for the future of Mucirippattanam's relationship with Rome.

'Indeed, Your Majesty, the prosperity of Muziris is owed to Rome. As in the markets of Rome and Alexandria, the most successful merchants love to demonstrate their success and wealth. They do this in Muziris too. It is not to the taste of our local people. We think that building a city even half as grand as Rome may not only help us increase our trade prospects but also the taxes that Rome can collect. We still live in humble wooden huts; the people of Muziris cannot even begin to imagine the grandeur of the marble and stone buildings you have here.' Jayesh was surprised when Emperor Vespasian suddenly began to laugh.

'You weave and twist the language of Rome like a seasoned Senator! There is certainly a career for you in politics, but be warned – that too can be a deadly game to play. For a man who lives in a mere wooden hut, you are owed a debt of over a billion sesterces that grows by the day. If you lived here in Rome, you may be the richest man within the city walls, residing in a palace like Nero himself.'

Vespasian casually swept Jayesh's argument aside.

'Would Your Majesty be so kind as to tell us what he would desire we do?'

'You will waive the debt. All of it. From today, I decree that the taxation on goods from Muziris be increased to one-third from a quarter. The royal scribe, Mucianus, here shall pen the terms on which you may trade with Rome and you shall assent to it before you are permitted to leave.'

The scribe immediately began to jot down the terms on a large sheet of papyrus. Jayesh and Nannan sat in stunned silence. Their work of a lifetime was wiped out by a single sentence.

'You're quiet, trader. Perhaps you would prefer a different approach?' Vespasian made a small gesture with his hand, prompting the soldiers to come forward and point a sword at Jayesh's throat. 'Speak! Which shall it be?'

66

Hyatt Regency, Thrissur
24 July 2024

Harveen arrived twenty-five minutes later at the Hyatt Regency reception. Even thought she was in a white T-shirt, khaki shorts and work boots, Don thought she looked striking. They sat at the same table as when they had first met.

'Can I order you a drink? Coffee perhaps?' said Don kindly.

'I just need to know if this can be real,' she replied, and pulled a document folder from her satchel. She pushed it towards him and waited for him to handle it in the appropriate way so he could examine the ancient receipt for himself, just as he had asked to do. There was a translation on the opposite page. Seeing the actual document before him took Don's breath away.

'So, is it real?' she asked again.

He looked up into Harveen's eyes. 'Yes, signora. I am confident that the document is real. The Vatican has been aware of this deal being struck for over 2,000 years, though it is also known that the Ark of the Covenant is not here in India. What we didn't know was that there is a document that contains the record of the sale. This is unbelievable, for sure.'

Harveen reached for the translation, 'It says here that he bought the Ark. We also have another record stating that funds were dedicated to protect the church for a hundred years for some reason. How can you be so sure it never arrived here?'

Don admired her spirit and intelligence, feeling a little sorry that he would have to kill her. Perhaps she could still be of some use to them if she defected to their side.

'The Vatican Apostolic Archive, previously known as the Vatican Secret Archives, spans over fifty kilometres of library space and houses over 250,000 separate documents – some dating as far back as the 34 BC. That's the section of the Vatican in which I work. The most important and sensitive information is held there, including everything we know about the final resting place of the Ark of the Covenant.'

'Care to enlighten me?' Harveen smiled.

'Well, there are actual documents related to the deal that trace what happened – they prove that it is not in fact in India. Eyewitness accounts. They are in my room. I cannot bring them down here, but you are, of course, welcome to come see them.' Seeing the conflicted look on her face, he hastened to add, 'My room is right by the lift. You can sit by the door if you wish, but I assure you, you will want to see these documents.' Finally, she gave a slight nod and Don led the way to the elevators.

The moment that would seal Harveen's fate was finally upon them. Don noticed her determined look and knew she would not give up until she had all the answers. He was surprised that she had agreed to come to his room at all. Now, he had the advantage.

Once they arrived in Don's suite, he led the way to the small sitting area where there was a small round table and two chairs. His boxes were laid out on the floor next to one of them. He gestured for Harveen to take a seat as he got comfortable in his. She stood nervously between the chair and the door, clutching at the strap of her satchel.

'We know exactly where the Ark of the Covenant is and how it got there. Let me show you.' He opened one of the boxes by the curtains and placed some papers on their table. 'These are photographs of the pages of a journal General Tiberius Julius Alexander had kept.'

Harveen quickly sat down and leaned over the table between them, completely absorbed in the ancient text. Don smiled to himself as he got up and walked across the room to make them both some coffee.

'So, what about him?' she asked when he returned.

'Well, as you may already know, Tiberius was a general in Vespasian's army. He fought many campaigns for him. After the fall of Nero, the throne changed hands three times in under a year. During this time, Vespasian carefully garnered support so he would be named the next emperor. When he set off for Rome, Tiberius was left in Judaea with Vespasian's son Titus in AD 70 to bag the final victory in Jerusalem. The journal of Tiberius tells us how he came to have the Ark and perhaps even why it was sold to Muziris.'

Harveen tucked her hair behind her ear as she tried to take stock of all the information Don was supplying. He watched her closely.

'Vespasian knew the importance of a swift and legendary victory on foreign soil in strengthening his position in Rome and restoring the finances of the empire. Their reserves had run dry under Nero and the huge, increasing debt to Muziris was only making matters worse. The journal of Tiberius details how, in truth, the Jewish Revolt had pretty much already been crushed by his father over the preceding four years and all that remained for him to do was to destroy and loot the walled city of Jerusalem.

'I know about this,' she said. 'There is no evidence that the Ark was there when Jerusalem fell.'

'In a little over five months, Titus, under the guidance of General Tiberius, brought Jerusalem to its knees. The mighty Roman army had slaughtered over 300,000 Jews and captured another 100,000 as slaves, who were then taken back to Rome. They looted every treasure, religious artefact and jewel they could find. They systematically destroyed the walls of Jerusalem and were on the verge of entering the Holy Temple complex at last, when something happened.' He pointed the relevant sections of the document to her as he spoke. 'See here, the journal tells us that Tiberius, a Jew himself, was very reluctant to loot the temple. Even though they knew about the incredible treasures that were there, they were scared of the curse that would befall them should they remove the holy Ark of the Covenant.'

He waited for her to finish reading the translation corresponding to the section he had pointed to. In it, Tiberius had explained that he tried to persuade Titus not to loot the temple. He had comprehensive knowledge of the kind of curses that had befallen people who had tried to steal the treasures before. He told Titus about Alexander the Great, who had come to loot the temple 400 years prior. After defeating the Jewish armies, Alexander's men began to drop dead as they tried to enter the temple with their weapons. The king himself left the temple a sick man and died a few months later. The Ptolemies ruled over Judaea after that, and they too would not enter the temple for fear of being cursed.

When Antiochus decided that he would take over the Temple of Jerusalem, he attempted to safeguard himself by erecting a statue of Zeus in front of the building and offering sacrifices at the altar. The priests suddenly turned and started killing the Greek officials one by one. The Jews stood their ground and fought on, defeating the Greek armies.'

'Forgive me, Don, for interrupting. All this is fascinating, but it still tells us nothing about whether the Ark was there or not,' Harveen said a little impatiently.

'It tells us enough. It tells us what we need to know – the Ark is a very dangerous object. Its history is steeped in blood. For over 1,500 years, our experts have been dedicating their energies to figuring out what would even be the right thing to do if it were ever to be found again.' He looked at Harveen gravely.

'But … I thought you said you knew where it was.'

Yes, I am coming to that. He handed her another document. 'The original is here and the translation is below.'

> Every last treasure in the Temple was taken and safely stowed. The riches are far beyond what the legends have boasted – enough to rebuild Rome a hundred times over. The Tabernacle was intact and contained the greatest treasures of the Jewish faith. The Menorah made of gold, the Gold Lamp stand and the Golden Altar of Incense. The Tabernacle is the Jews' Holy of Holies. No one other than the highest priests and priestesses are allowed to pass into that room, and yet we took to it with soldiers. The priests would not allow our soldiers to pass at first, protecting the most sacred items with their bodies, unafraid of sacrificing their lives. We had

> to remove them by force – some were even killed inside the Temple.
>
> But the greatest treasure of all was concealed behind a veil at the head of the Temple on an elaborate plinth. It is known as the Ark of the Covenant and contains the Jews' most important religious artefact. The box is covered in gold and the top is adorned with two elaborate golden sculptures. The priests had formed a chain around it and our soldiers had to slaughter them to get to it, splattering their blood all over the Ark. The High Priestess of the Temple pronounced that the Ark cannot be removed from Jerusalem and a curse shall fall upon anyone who attempts it.

Don could see the look of astonishment on Harveen's face as she went through the contents. 'Who is this "High Priestess of the Temple"?' she suddenly looked at him and asked.

'We believe, judging from other accounts, that she is the great-granddaughter of King Herod. Her name was Berenice.'

'And Titus was married to Berenice …'

'Very good, you know your history, signora! Yes – they went back to Rome together.' Don took some more books from his box and opened them on the table. 'Since the very first day of their journey back to Rome, they were beset with problems. Here we have an account of the fall of the Temple written by a Jewish priest. Most of it is lost, but this fragment here suggests that as the Romans set about loading the Ark into the large cart which contained much of their treasures, it slipped. A soldier reached out to grab it, instinctively, but as he touched it, he let out a chilling yell of agony, falling dead where he had stood.'

The book had copies of all the pages; however, as the original was in tatters, many of the words were lost. 'The originals are far too delicate, but you can see here what I mean. It mentions how the journey to Rome was due to take two months, but we know that it took them more than a year to return. As they left Jerusalem, huge storms erupted in their path without warning, worsening with each passing day. Instead of Rome, they had to change course towards Caesarea Maritima, a busy port with a vast deep-sea harbour that could accommodate large vessels. Perhaps they planned to set sail from there, but when they did so, the weather would not turn in their favour until the seasons changed, forcing them to stay on in Egypt. Then, they sailed to Berytus and then on to Zeugma. They paraded their riches though Antioch and Memphis, until they finally arrived in Alexandria, ready for their return to Rome. But once again, the skies turned black and the storms began to rage. This is the last entry from Tiberius.' He turned the book towards Harveen.

> For three days, we attempted to sail from Alexandria and for three days, the storms lashed at us. Finally, on the fourth day, Titus was persuaded to leave the Ark of the Covenant and the Priestess behind, at the Palace of Alexandria, and within moments, the sky turned blue and we were able to set sail for home.

'So the Ark ended up in Alexandria?'

'We cannot quite be sure. We have the exact details of its final journey – this document you have found helps complete the picture. We knew that it was sold to a great

Indian merchant, and even the name of the vessel aboard which it had sailed to India. Now we know the merchant's name and the vessel's destination. But we don't think they ever completed their journey.'

67

Palace of Vespasian
AD 71

Jayesh shot a glance at his friends. Vikesh and Nannan both seemed scared for their lives.

Suddenly, Titus – who had not spoken until that point – took a draw of his wine and set his chalice down next to his knife before turning to address his father.

'Muziris has been a long-standing and loyal partner to Rome, Father. They are also a reliable source of goods from China.'

Vespasian gave his son a cold stare. 'Rome's debts must be waived. That is my final word on the matter,' he stated before standing from his seat and marching back into the main palace. There was an uneasy silence for several moments until Titus spoke again.

'I have received reports that you are a supporter of the Jews and wish to welcome them to Muziris?' Jayesh and Nannan exchanged a suspicious glance.

'Your Majesty, Muziris wishes to welcome people of all faiths and creeds. Jews are no exception. I wish to clarify that it is in no way reflective of our loyalties towards Rome,' replied Jayesh cautiously. Titus seemed pleased by this answer and the smallest hint of a smile crossed his face. He waved his arm, prompting the soldiers to retreat. Jayesh finally had the opportunity to steady his breath.

'You don't need to tread so lightly around the subject, merchant. The Jews are well-regarded in Rome and hold many importance offices here. The war we fought and won was to discourage their rebellion. But it has, unfortunately, left the Jews with nowhere to go.'

'My lord, they are welcome to come to Muziris,' said Jayesh, not quite believing his good fortune. The conversation had taken its own course and put him in exactly the position he had wished – offering a solution to Rome's pressing issues.

'And how do you propose to earn their trust so they may come?' Titus picked up his knife by its hilt and a fruit to cut open with it.

'I look to you for your wisdom and guidance, Your Majesty.'

'Build them a temple like the one in Jerusalem.'

'Forgive me, Your Majesty, but we were told it is destroyed and along with it, everything it held is gone too,' Nannan interjected.

'The temple is no more, it's true,' said Titus, 'but what was inside has been saved. You shall see those prized spoils of our glorious campaign during my victory parade through Rome. Perhaps you might be interested in one of the most precious items? The Ark of the Covenant – perhaps you have heard of it?' He seemed to be toying with Jayesh.

'Your Majesty, I would not know how to place a value on a holy object of such significance—'

'My father has already named its price. In return for waiving Rome's debts, you could walk away with something you want, and of course, your life.'

Jayesh considered Titus's proposal for a moment. 'Your Majesty, what of the Jews? How are they to get to Muziris when they have nothing left?'

'Rome will pay for their passage,' said Titus decisively.

'Perhaps, Your Majesty, the funds could come from Muziris?'

Titus smiled, impressed at Jayesh's shrewdness. 'What do you propose, merchant?'

'Half, Your Majesty,' said Jayesh boldly. 'We sign over half of the total debt for the Ark of the Covenant. Muziris will pay for anyone who wants to travel and settle in Muziris and we will continue to fund the Roman fort in full.'

'Congratulations, merchant. You have a deal. Come back in a year's time – let us see how your plan works out for both of us.'

Once the document was penned and signed, they were allowed to leave Vespasian's palace. Jayesh was quick to celebrate their success.

'I cannot believe this, my brothers! We struck an agreement with the Roman empire to acquire the greatest icon of the Temple of Jerusalem … It is a great day!'

'It doesn't feel right, brother … let's leave this well alone,' said Vikesh.

'Why not? This is exactly what we wanted! Don't you see? Muziris will become the greatest city in the world – home to people of all religions and faiths, welcoming men from all over the world! Isn't this what we envisioned during my first visit to Alexandria all those years ago, Nannan? Tell him!'

'I must say I agree with Vikesh on this, my brother. It feels too easy; I can't help but be suspicious. He had a sword to your throat … he could have made you sign any deal he wanted there and then. Why did he let us negotiate with his son? Why did he let us get away with waiving only half? We still have a fortune,' Nannan asked.

'Don't you see, Nannan? We have an advantage over them. They need us! We generate taxes, we offer a solution for all the Jews they have displaced in their war. Before another uprising, we can help the people migrate to a thriving new land which is not only safer but at a safe distance from the empire. With the Ark of the Covenant in our hands, the Jews will come flocking to St Thomas's church in hordes! They will want to live where it resides and lend their expertise and labour to help Muziris grow into the world's greatest metropolis!'

Nannan and Vikesh looked at Jayesh like he was a madman, but he remained undeterred.

The Ark was in Alexandria and they intended to take it back with them on this same trip. Titus had directed them to meet with someone at the palace in Alexandria who could help them arrange for their journey to Myos Hormos.

Jayesh felt that fate had conspired to ensure all three of them were on this journey together. They spent their voyage to Alexandria arguing about what to do next. Vikesh and Nannan had their reservations, but Jayesh was persistent. He had resolved to take the Ark back to Muciripattanam. Nothing could stop him from making his hometown the greatest city in the world.

68

Hyatt Regency, Thrissur
24 July 2024

'Until your discovery, we believed this document to be the only surviving reference to the sale of the Ark of the Covenant.' Don produced a folder and took out a number of sheets. 'These are images of a scroll written by Mucianus, who was, for many years, a close advisor to Vespasian.' He handed them to Harveen. 'The account is mostly unremarkable. It describes in detail the huge sums of money wasted by Emperor Nero. There is also a detailed description of the Domus Aurea, his Golden Palace.

'It goes on to explain the various ways in which he and Vespasian worked together to stabilize the finances of Rome. They closed down Nero's palace, raised taxes and sold off all the major imperial estates in Egypt. Towards the end is the part that you will find most interesting – details of what was taken during the campaign in Jerusalem.' Don leaned over and showed her the relevant section. For a moment, he was close enough to smell her perfume.

'It was much more than they expected,' Harveen read the translation. 'Enough for them to build a great stadium for the people.'

'Yet there was still one major problem. One debt that was very large. Pliny refers to it as well, but here we have something else – look at this.'

'They arranged to meet him?' Harveen was in disbelief at the scroll's contents. It noted that the biggest debt owed by Rome was to a king from Muziris, and that he was to be brought to Rome where they planned to offer the great treasure from Jerusalem to him in return for waiving the debt. 'How does no one know about this?' she asked.

Don ignored her statement and went on, 'Until your find, we did not know the name of this ruler, even though we do have detailed records of the Ark's final journey aboard the *Vasudha*, a great trade ship. Three journals full of them, carefully preserved.'

'Really?' said Harveen, leaning forward, her eyes sparkling with excitement. Her smile was magnetic and Don couldn't help but feel drawn to her. Sharing their mutual love for history appeared to be having an intoxicating effect on him, as if they were siloed off from the world, in the comfort of his luxurious suite. He composed himself.

'You won't believe what the journals say. The Ark of the Covenant was sold to a great Indian king who planned to take it back to his homeland for unspecified reasons. He was to set sail from Myos Hormos, one of the main ports in Egypt at the time, to Asia. The most complete record we have of the journey is a scroll dated around AD 80. It is an eyewitness account, accompanied by an elaborate sketch of the great ship being torn in half after it was struck by lightning just as it left the port. In two other sketches, sailors can be seen trying to swim back to the port as the rains lash down on them, while the great ship is consumed by the ocean in the background.' He showed her the copies of the document contained in a large folder with the Vatican logo at the top.

'This is incredible,' she said. When she looked up, their eyes met and sent Don's heart racing. He cleared his throat and immediately turned his attention to the papers in front of him.

'Yes, but I think the most interesting document we have was written by a Roman merchant, who was actually on the road journey with the Ark from Alexandria to Myos Hormos.' Don handed her another set of copies. 'As you can see, the document is damaged in places, but the bits we do have clearly show that the Ark was sold to an Indian merchant so it could be conveyed to the subcontinent. The Roman merchant was supposed to be on that ship with it but was not allowed to make the journey as some important emissary had been deputed in his place to escort the Ark on the final leg of its journey. We now believe this to be J. Muziris himself.

'His account says nothing of importance about the journey, but mentions that the Roman merchant was keen to catch a glimpse of the Ark. As it was being unloaded, the skin or leather covering it came loose and revealed two golden sculptures of angels sitting perched atop the lid. No sooner had these been revealed than the clear sky turned black, and rain such as he had never seen before began to pour, accompanied by fierce, jagged fingers of lightning that scorched the ground as thunder filled the air.

'The box had then quickly been repackaged with care and conveyed to the vessel. The dark clouds had remained in the sky for some time afterwards and a great storm followed, causing the ship to sink before it could make its way out of the Myos Hormos harbour.' He showed Harveen the section of the document that described the sinking of the ship. It was in remarkable condition.

The final document was a series of sketches depicting the scene pictorially. An uncovered Ark of the Covenant being carried by four slaves resembling pallbearers. The wooden poles they were holding passed through golden rings along the edge of the Ark. There were drawings showing the prized object being loaded onto the ship after some sort of ceremony, following which the ship departed. In the subsequent scenes, the skies split and a divine figure appeared to be reaching through the clouds, aiming a bolt of lightning like a spear at the ship, and it sinking along with all the men onboard. In the last two scenes, this godlike figure was rescuing the Ark from the sinking ship and lifting it towards the sky, presumably for safekeeping.

'I have seen these images in person. You would be amazed at how rich the colours still appear – the conservators have done a splendid job preserving it. Perhaps … you too could come see it one day …' Don ventured.

'So it sank with the ship then?' Harveen completely ignored his suggestion and slumped in her chair with her arms crossed. Don stretched and finished his strong coffee in one final sip. He dragged a large journal out of the box to place it between them. The only thing left in there now was his Beretta with its silencer attached. The document Harveen had discovered was now in his possession. She would soon meet her end. He carefully concealed the gun in his lap under the table.

'Yes. This journal documents all the expeditions that the Vatican has commissioned over the years to recover the *Vasudha* from around AD 1000 right up to a series of dives in the 1960s. There were some small successes – we found Indian coins, some remains of a ship, even bones, but nothing that provided conclusive proof of the location of the ship or its cargo.'

'Do you think there is a chance Muziris or the Romans might have recovered the Ark? Maybe they came aboard another ship?'

'Not a chance. We don't even know where exactly it was being taken.' As he spoke, he slowly lifted the Beretta sideways, pointing it at Harveen centre mass, still under the table.

'I think I do …' said Harveen. 'We have located a secret chamber in the grounds of a temple here. It would certainly be the right size for the Ark, based on these descriptions of it.' Don was beginning to see that Harveen's evidence pointed to a possible location for the Ark of the Covenant. He needed to figure out how his team could get to the site first so as to reclaim the Ark, if it was really here. He dropped the gun smoothly back into the box as he began to speak. He would need her help to get access to this site.

'But I told you how the Ark is known to be an extremely dangerous object. It's not safe to handle it without knowing exactly how to. No one knows the powers it holds. If there is even the slightest possibility of it being in India, you must let the team from Vatican accompany you to any dig. You absolutely cannot breathe a word of this to anyone, especially not social media or the press. It will cause much mayhem – we are purely speculating, and there is a pretty good chance we're way off. The best experts from the Vatican would be willing to come down for a finding of this magnitude – I just have to say the word. The Vatican already knows Professor Prakash and will want to deal with him on the matter … but you know, I could put in a good word for you …'

Harveen's eyes widened. Don was thinking on his feet, preying on her demons – her ambitions to lead, win accolades for her life's work, validation. 'Well that is only to be expected. You surely understand how significant this is, signora. You're smart enough. The Vatican cannot possibly relinquish control of such a crucial find to a foreign government, and no one will stand in their way when they decide to step in.'

'They can't do that!' She was shocked and visibly destabilized by the mere mention of the Vatican's involvement, perhaps realizing for the first time the forces she was interfering with. But he saw her righteousness waver and knew his arrow hit just the target it was hoping to.

'Look, at best, I can buy you a few days so you can round up your team and get things in order. I'm duty-bound to keep the Vatican informed. Don't worry, signora, I'm sure they'd love to work with you just as I have. You can lead them effectively as a local expert. But in the meantime, I must ask you to leave this document with me … they will want to look at it, you see.' He watched as Harveen seemed to be wrapping her head around all that had just happened and what appeared to loom on the horizon for her career.

'Okay. As long as you allow my team and I to have the final say on how we deal with matters if we do discover something – because after all, it is because of me that we got this far – we have a deal. We get to decide our methodology, what we say to the media, how and when we make announcements – everything. I won't object to involving the Vatican, but I need to know that my team and I will get the credit for our contributions. I've been burnt before … I cannot risk being burnt again.'

'Signora, these documents I have shared with you have not been shown to anyone outside the Vatican for nearly 2,000 years. I have risked not only my job, but also my faith and the stability of the Church, by letting you in on all these resources. I have placed immense trust in you too. What can I, a lone researcher, do to stop you from leaving and posting about it all on your social media? I think we've come this far and now we have no choice but to work together.'

He held out his hand and Harveen shook it. They both smiled at each other. Don felt his heart flutter and quickly withdrew his hand.

'So … is the offer to let me see the originals still on?' she said with a tentative smile.

'Of course, signora,' Don said.

As he closed the door behind Harveen, Don Clemente made two calls. The first was to Rossi.

'Signor, the Gill girl has found a document showing the sale of the Ark to an Indian merchant. I have it in my possession now. The threat is handled. She's the only one who knows anything about it.'

'That's fantastic, Donatello. You prove my decision to put you in charge right every time. I believe if you are finally in agreement with the methods of our organization, you have dealt appropriately with the girl?' Rossi asked.

'We need her to nip the problem in the bud rather than finding temporary solutions, signor. She has a potential location for where the Ark may be hidden. We have been searching in vain for it for 2,000 years! We cannot miss this opportunity. The chamber Vincenzo mentioned – she thinks it might be there.'

'Ah, so the girl lives. I assume you have a plan of some sort. Enlighten me, will you?'

'She has agreed to allow a team of researchers from the Vatican to be involved in the expedition. An extraction team is being readied right now – Sofia is arranging for the charter. Even if something is found, our team will be right there to handle the situation as it suits us best, and no one will suspect a thing.'

'Good thinking, Donatello. But for such an important matter, I think we need to consult with the Pontiff himself. Fly back now and we will see him together. I hope your little Miss Gill won't betray you while you're away ...'

'I already have a plan to take care of her, signor. You must trust me.'

As soon as they hung up, Don called Vincenzo to put him in charge of getting rid of Harveen.

69

Royal Palace, Alexandria
AD 71

Finally gaining admittance into the Palace of Alexandria filled Jayesh with excitement. The palace was beautiful, although its magnificence was no match for the High Priestess Berenice, the guardian of the Ark of the Covenant. She was flanked by a dozen guards, who were not in Roman garbs; they had an oddly ceremonial look about them, like royal guards, with their shining armours and gold swords.

The priestess had a magnetic aura, holding Jayesh's stare boldly with her alluring eyes as she entered the room. His immediate, overwhelming thought was that she was the most beautiful woman he had ever seen. Her skin was pale and smooth like marble, her long hair dark and flowing, and her beautiful, large brown eyes sparkled. She was simply dressed, but her clothes had a luxurious quality – the red cloth wrapped around her torso was embroidered with gold and stopped just a few inches short of her waist, where her red-and-gold, loose-fitting bottoms began. These were tied at the ankles, and on her feet were sandals intricately decorated with colourful jewels. She appeared to be gliding when she walked, and her regal grace caused her to exude an air of power and undeniable authority.

'This is not some trinket for men to buy and sell. It holds incredible power and has been guarded closely for centuries because we do not – and cannot – understand it.' Jayesh could see the anger in her eyes as she examined the contents of the scroll he had presented to her. It was sent by Titus. 'He swore that he would come back for it; that he would safeguard it – how dare he insult us and our God like this?!'

Her anger sent a shudder down Jayesh's spine, but he attempted to console her despite it. 'High Priestess, I may be a mere merchant, but I beg that you give us the opportunity to safekeep the sacred Ark. I understand what this means to you and your people … Muziris is building a great Tabernacle to house it in accordance to all the rules outlined in your holy scriptures. Surrounding it will be a church as great as the temple you lost to the Roman campaign in Jerusalem.'

'And how will you ensure that the Ark will be safe there? The glorious Temple of Jerusalem was guarded by one of the largest Roman-built forts in the world.'

'And they turned on you, High Priestess. A man's loyalties to his motherland are rarely transformed by the constraints of his profession. But Muziris is a land for people from all lands and all faiths. We will put a priest you trust in charge, if that would put your concerns to rest.'

'You do not understand … The Ark of the Covenant must be returned to Jerusalem. It cannot be moved. You will surely perish if you attempt to displace it!'

Jayesh was taken aback at the suggestion that the Ark could cost them their lives. He looked at Vikesh and Nannan, both of whom looked fearful too.

'Please, Jayesh. Leave it be. Surely, it is not worth risking our lives, brother?' begged Vikesh in Tamil.

'There must be a way, High Priestess … is there some way we could carry it without angering the forces that guard it?' Jayesh persisted.

'The only correct way to carry it is using these wooden poles and ensuring it always remains covered. It must not be unveiled outside of the Tabernacle. But these are all concerns for later … if it even makes it there.'

'Surely there is some myth to the legend, madam?'

Berenice was indignant at the suggestion. 'You think these are tall tales, do you? I was in the temple when the Romans were on their rampage. I watched as their battering rams smashed the walls into rubble. I stayed with the other priests, waiting for the greedy Romans to have their fill and leave with the loot. We never did believe that they would take the Ark – its history is too well known.

'It was the riches they were after, and the temple was brimming with them. It took them ten days and hundreds of soldiers to carry it all away and load onto their boats. We thought that would be enough for them … but it seems nothing ever is. Fort Antonia, which was meant to protect the Temple of Jerusalem, was built specially by my great-grandfather, King Herod. He knew the power of the objects contained within the Tabernacle. And so did Rome.' Berenice's eyes betrayed her pain.

'What is this power, exactly, High Priestess? What can it do?' Jayesh could not keep his curiosity to himself.

She flashed a glare at him before saying, 'It rains great death and destruction upon those who seek to use it to fulfil their own selfish objectives.'

'Jayesh, you must believe the priestess!' Vikesh tugged at his friend's elbow with urgency, picking up on the sense of foreboding in Berenice's tone. 'I have a bad feeling about this.'

'You should listen to your friend,' said Berenice, sensing Vikesh's fear. 'For four generations, my family has protected these treasures, and in that time, we have seen the great devastation the Ark can bring. These are not mere stories. The Temple housed many a scroll detailing events throughout the Ark's bloody history. When the Philistines defeated the Israelites in the Battle of Eben-Ezer, they slaughtered the priests inside the Tabernacle, splattering their blood across the Ark. From that moment on, death has loomed over them like a shadow. The curse lifted only when they returned the Ark to my safekeeping. Blood has been spilled to acquire it for years and years – the wrath of God will fall upon you and every life you touch, should you persist in your attempts to take it.'

Jayesh clenched his jaw and fixed his gaze on Berenice and her guards. He looked again at the religious markings on their robes and pulled out his winning card. 'No matter. We are taking the Ark of the Covenant only in order to put it under the apostle St Thomas's care, whom we have sheltered for five long years now. It is his wish that a Tabernacle houses the holy Ark of the Covenant in Muziris.'

'The apostle … he is in Muziris?' she was surprised. 'It cannot be!'

'But it is, High Priestess. Before travelling to Rome, I met with him and enlisted builders to repurpose a vast underground chamber beneath his church in Muziris to become the new Tabernacle. St Thomas is personally overseeing that everything aligns with the scriptural rules and no detail, however minor, is ignored. The last I heard from him, there is to be an ornate wooden plinth for the Ark to rest on in the centre of the room, behind a veil draped across four marble pillars. This will be the new inner sanctum, and only St Thomas and his appointed priests will be allowed inside. The outer room is to contain a gold lamp stand and a Menorah, which would hold seven oil lamps. The priests' robes and the veils will have the sacred symbols of your faith on them, all carved from ivory, like pomegranates and such.'

'You are very knowledgeable – I would never have guessed it. But that alone cannot ensure your safety.'

'Titus boasted that he had taken everything else in the Tabernacle and he planned to parade his spoils through the streets of Rome in his triumphal procession. I am an honourable man, High Priestess. True to my word. If he may be more amenable to sell the other holy objects to me once his victory arch is built, I will ensure the Ark is installed in its new Tabernacle in no time at all.'

At that moment, two guards rushed in and requested private audience with Berenice. Jayesh's worst fears had come true. Titus had changed his mind.

When she returned, Jayesh could see a fire raging behind her eyes.

'An honourable man? Tell me: have you murdered a Roman merchant named Servius? The assassin you had sent has confessed and identified you! These soldiers demand that we hand you over so they may bring you to justice.'

70

Sreepadam Palace, Office of Professor Prakash
21 July 2024

'You need to come down to the police station and make your statement in the Dr Penny Gupta murder case today.' Harveen listened to the voice message again whilst waiting for Professor Prakash outside his office. She needed to find out what he knew about the murder. Could it be that the mysterious Don from the Vatican Archives – who had magically appeared out of thin air – had something to do with it? As she was considering this, the professor approached with Rohan in tow.

As the three of them entered his office, Harveen began to detail the recent events in an attempt to present her case for the excavation and her sudden decision to collaborate with the Vatican. She started with the chamber underneath the well in the temple grounds, showing them the video footage she had managed to capture.

'So, as you can see, there is a complete room beneath the well. It's circular and a little smaller than the circumference of the well itself.' She had run through the video on her laptop twice and was now showing a diagram of the site to Prakash. 'As the well is considered to be undisturbed since it was originally constructed, we must conclude that the room below was designed and put in place by the original builder of the well – somewhere around 1,500 to 2,000 years ago.'

'Wait, how did you get this footage?' he interrupted her to ask.

'Well,' she said, 'we saw the clear signs of a chamber beneath the well and were going to come and seek your permission to investigate further, but before that could happen, something extraordinary came to light.' Harveen had been rehearsing this conversation since her meeting with Don. 'I carefully went through all of the records that we had found in the ancient house and have been translating them using Penny's software. I came across this record here.' She pulled out a copy of the document she had given to Don.

'And here is the translation.' She watched as they both read about the purchase of the Ark of the Covenant by J. Muziris.

'This is incredible! Why didn't you show this to me right when you found it?' Prakash replied, wide-eyed at the revelation.

'I wanted to make sure it was even plausible. So, I had a friend of my uncle dig a couple of small boreholes into the chamber to record this footage and see exactly what it held. It turns out, it is the right size to hold the Ark.'

'I thought we agreed there were to be absolutely no digs in the temple grounds?' Prakash said indignantly.

'Of course, that's why we used boreholes the size of my little finger to just get some footage and confirm our theory. I even ensured they were filled in right after, so it's as if we were never even there,' she dodged his anger deftly.

His interest was piqued. The evidence was hard to refute.

This could be groundbreaking for them. 'Could you figure out what was in the room?'

'Unfortunately, the light from the borehole camera is limited and can only shine on what we point it at. The picture it brings back is not that wide either, so we were restricted in what we have seen so far, as you saw. All we can say conclusively is that the inside of the room is also made of stone, similar to the well. This would indicate that it was designed as a chamber. The original well was dug up to a certain depth, then a roof was put in to create the room.'

'Hmm … but could the well have been just that? A well? We know there is water at the site. Maybe at a later date, for ease, they only filled in the top part, leaving the space that you have seen the way it was?'

'It's possible,' said Harveen. 'Rohan and I discussed that possibility. From what we could see, there is no evidence that the inside of this structure was ever a well. Even if it was once in use, it was for a very limited time.'

Rohan added, 'The other factor here is a different record which says the site is to be protected for a hundred years. If the record indeed relates to this site, then why would they ask to specifically protect this well and not just the temple, unless there was something else there to keep safe?'

'If the record is related to this site at all, as you said,' Professor Prakash added thoughtfully.

Harveen interjected, 'The stone we discovered at the Anapuzha site – where we currently suspect the original St Thomas Church had stood – bore an inscription that said the first Christian church was in Muziris, built or opened in AD 71. We are fairly confident that the area around modern-day Kodungallur is Muziris. And that site is yet to yield any more evidence to support that the church had, in fact, stood there.

One of the other early St Thomas churches survives to this day in Palayoor, so it is reasonable to assume that the first or most important church here in Muziris should also have survived, especially if it was built using similar techniques and materials.'

'But this temple has a well of stone. Around the Kodungallur Bhagavathy Temple, we have found ancient ivory pomegranates like those that would have been worn by a Christian high priest.' She could see that Professor Prakash was listening enraptured. 'We believe there is a good chance that this was the original site of the first St Thomas Christian church and for some reason, it was converted into a Shiva temple. We also believe that the well is protected for a specific reason and the room below holds the secret as to why – maybe St Thomas himself is buried there, for all we know.'

'What do you want to do?'

Harveen looked at Rohan. They had already discussed their ideas. 'We believe using a small diagonal tunnel could help prove our findings.' She took out her notepad and showed Professor Prakash the diagram she had drawn. 'It will be away from the temple complex and the entrance will be covered with one of our tents. It will get us to the very bottom of the well, into the chamber, and be just wide enough for us to crawl through. If there is nothing in the chamber, we can easily refill the tunnel again and leave the site as we had found it. But if there is something there, we will need to come back to the drawing board.'

'Yes, that seems like a good idea. Give me a few days, let me think it over, look through these materials again and get you the permissions you need.'

'No!' blurted Harveen. She was worried about the Vatican swooping in and taking over in the meantime. 'This is so sensitive, we cannot rely on it remaining contained. I have already received word from researchers at the Vatican about the stone we discovered. And they are insisting on us involving them in everything we do from hereon. It is a matter related to their faith, after all. We need to move quickly on this before more news leaks and we find ourselves in an awkward position, explaining things to the Vatican—'

'Wait, what is this talk of the Vatican? Why didn't you tell me?'

'Oh, it's … nothing. Just junior researchers reaching out to me on social media – it was not official correspondence or anything,' she dismissed his concerns.

'Professor, I agree with Harveen on this. We need to inspect that well – something could be buried there. The size is just right and there has to be a reason why Muziris sought to protect it for a hundred years. The dates match the historical record too,' Rohan said.

'I think you are right, Harveen. I have had a message from a researcher at the Vatican too; his number is here on my desk somewhere. I have not had a chance to return his call as yet.' Harveen's heart was racing. 'Perhaps I'll delay it for a couple of days. You can start preparing the plans for your dig. Involve no one but Rohan. There will be mass hysteria if anyone finds out we may have uncovered the final resting place of the Ark of the Covenant. It was Titus, wasn't it? Who plundered it? When was that?'

'His reign was from AD 79–81,' she said, 'but he looted the Temple of Jerusalem in AD 70. The dates match.' As they took their leave, she wondered if she had made a terrible mistake.

Was Don about to go behind her back and steal her greatest discovery yet?

71

The Vatican, Office of Sofia Gallo
25 July 2024

The possibility of the secret chamber in Kerala could be the location of the Ark kept running through Don's mind. He hoped his plan to get rid of Harveen had worked.

As soon as he arrived in the Vatican, he went directly to Sofia. She had urged him to see her before his meeting with Rossi and the Holy Father. Her office in the Vatican was like what he imagined the inside of her mind was like: serene, neat and organized.

She greeted him as if they were old acquaintances meeting at some elegant coffee shop at the edge of the town square – with a kiss on either cheek. She was wearing a simple maroon dress and matching high heels. The only jewellery she wore was a string of pearls around her neck, but she still managed to exude an air of affluence.

Don and Sofia sat on opposite seats around her meeting table. She had some rather sensitive documents to show him. They were laid out precisely alongside her notes. 'These may provide the distraction you will need if the news from India leaks out,' she said in perfect English with an Italian accent.

Don looked carefully through the sheets for several minutes before asking, 'Who else has seen this?'

'Just you and me,' she replied. 'I told you I would help you.' She looked at him sincerely. There was a signature at the bottom of the last page of the eight-page document that helped date it. AD 4. Sofia had also prepared a translation. Don read it and could barely disguise that he was impressed. 'This is fantastic, Sofia. I'm sure it will work. How did you even find it?' He was taken by her brilliance.

'Purely by chance. It has been in the Vatican Archives for 1,500 years. It appears that this document was concealed between the pages of one of the many volumes the Vatican had acquired from the Library of the Serapeum before it was destroyed in AD 391.

'The Library of the Serapeum?' Don enquired.

'The Library of Alexandria was on a gradual decline after the Romans came to power and was probably destroyed somewhere between AD 250–300. The Library of Serapeum seems to have saved a small number of their most important texts, most of which were then transferred to the Vatican in AD 391, before the Pope of Alexandria ordered for the building to be destroyed,' Sofia showcased her encyclopaedic knowledge of the Archives' contents.

'The interest in this document would draw the focus away from anything to do with St Thomas. I am sure if Harveen were to see this, she would abandon her pursuit of St Thomas's Church or even that of the Ark. We may be able to avert the whole issue.' Don was encouraged by the possibility that he may not have to follow Rossi's methods. Besides, if he could prove that Harveen was still key to his plans to ensure the safety of the Vatican, she may not need to die.

'Exactly. We need to get this to her immediately.'

Don was relieved that he and Sofia were on the same page about how to move forward.

'We have some time – I expect she is probably being held in jail right now. I had Vincenzo plant the knife that killed Dr Penny Gupta at her house and inform the police.'

'What quick thinking, Don! Impressive. Perhaps you do not need me anymore,' she replied with a coy smile.

'I can't have you cleaning up after all my operations.'

'Let me check with local sources if she has been picked up.'

'Thank you, Sofia. I will explain our plan to Rossi in our meeting with the Pope and then I will go straight back to India with this,' Don carefully put back the document and the translation into their protective folder. 'Can you find out where the meeting is going to take place? I should head there now.' Sofia smiled and picked up her phone. In the meantime, Don considered the translated document again and imagined the interest it would generate when the media found out about it. The smile on his face faded when he saw the look of alarm on Sofia's face.

'What is it?'

'Rossi has spoken with Vincenzo and Paulo directly – they are planning to inspect the chamber themselves and clean up any evidence, including witnesses. He had no intention of meeting with you today!'

'What do you mean, Sofia? He can't do that! Where is he? That coward, I'll go to his office right now and—'

'He is not there and there are people waiting to detain you at his office. He claims he is working under the instructions of the Papal Office.'

They both knew he was lying. Don felt his world crumbling around him.

'Where is he now – do you know?' he asked, furious.

'Yes, he is at home in Bergamo.'

'Okay, leave Rossi to me. Can you get a message to Vincenzo? Tell him Rossi has gone rogue and that he is to call me directly if he wants to keep his job. We need to speak to him as soon as possible.' Don could feel the blood rushing to his head. He got a little dizzy.

Sofia placed her hand on his arm. She said slowly, 'You know Vincenzo is loyal to that scheming bastard, Don. He will never listen to you. Rossi has his loyal followers planted everywhere in this building. Don't make decisions in haste; precious lives are on the line. You need to think carefully about the implications of your next actions.'

Don closed his eyes tight and tried his best to calm down. 'When you said you would do anything to help me, did you mean it?'

She looked him in the eye. 'I did.'

'You understand what will happen if he finds out you helped me?'

'Of course. What do you need me to do?'

Don marvelled at her composure.

'Speak to Vincenzo anyway ... See what you can do to stop him till I get a hold of the situation. What have we got to lose? Call me the minute you learn anything. We need eyes and ears in India to relay any information to us about whatever happens as soon as it does. I will try and reach Harveen – she has no idea how much danger she is in ... and it's all my fault. I need to fix this. If anyone asks you, tell them I'm headed to Rossi's office.'

'Got it. Keep me posted.'

'Wait, Sofia. One more thing – you mentioned earlier that there were other agents like us who were not in agreement with Rossi's methods. Do you think they would help us?'

'There are a few. What do you have in mind?'

72

Port of Myos Hormos
AD 71

'Servius was a thief and a liar! He even tried to kill me, but fate intervened. He deserved the fate that befell him, High Priestess! You must believe me,' said Jayesh. Vikesh and Nannan winced at the outburst. 'Please grant us safe passage so we may convey the Ark of the Covenant back to Thomas the Apostle.'

Berenice looked at him. 'Alright. My instinct tells me I can trust you. Now listen carefully – all palaces in Alexandria have secret exits; this one has multiple passages. Take my guards with you – they will show you the safest way out and give you what protection they can, and they also know how best to handle the Ark. Keep it safe. I will speak to the emperor's men and delay them as much as I can.'

'I am truly grateful, High Priestess.' Turning to his friends, Jayesh said, 'Let's go!'

'Yes, you must leave immediately,' said Berenice as she glided out the way they had entered, while her guards picked up the Ark of the Covenant and led the three men towards another door.

They came out onto a covered side street through a small tunnel. When the door was closed behind them, it looked unremarkable, like any other house entrance. They rushed back to their carts and loaded their precious cargo discreetly. Looking around to make sure they were not being watched or followed, they set off quickly. There was a narrow window of time available for them to take advantage of the favourable trade winds to sail back to Muciripattanam, and it was essential for them to set sail before Servius's men caught up to them.

The usually calm and dry weather they associated with Myos Hormos took a rather unexpected turn. Their carts were lashed by rare dust storm, blowing sand and shingle at the travellers, although they managed to join a convoy of about sixty large carts heading to the port. But the storm had got so violent by the time they approached Myos Hormos, many abandoned the journey altogether, seeking shelter in Alexandria and awaiting a less treacherous time to resume travel.

'We should turn back, Jayesh. I have never seen such a cruel storm in these parts – it's unheard of!' said Nannan.

'No! We have no choice, Nannan,' said Jayesh. 'Servius's men will kill us if we get caught.'

'Look! They already have!' Vikesh shouted, pointing in the distance behind them at a group of men on horseback braving through the storm. Berenice's distinctive-looking guards were farther away, chasing after them.

As they managed to scramble into the Port of Myos Hormos, the storm worsened. Livid black clouds appeared in the skies above and seemed to turn day into night as the distinct smell of approaching rain hung in the air. The soldiers on horseback were nearly upon them when the driver of their cart stopped at the top of the pier. 'Well, we are at the end of our journey, my friends. Good luck for your voyage,' the driver was saying as the three men jumped off his cart. Jayesh hurried to load his goods onto his ship.

Some commotion in the distance caught Jayesh's eye – Berenice's guards had finally managed to stall the progress of Servius's men in their devious mission. They displayed their prowess in battle with their fierce attacks, despite being seriously outnumbered.

He moved quickly and, taking advantage of the distraction, rushed to find the captain of their flagship, *Vasudha*. The captain was an experienced and hardy sailor they had recruited in Myos Hormos. Jayesh insisted they set sail right away, but he simply shook his head, ignoring his franticness.

'Please! It is a matter of life and death!' Jayesh begged; however, the seasoned sailor knew they could not travel in the severe weather.

'It is sure to be a big storm. No one is sailing out today – you can only pray we are able to try tomorrow.'

'Listen, I will double your fee when we arrive in Muziris. Look there!' He pointed at the raging battle at the end of the pier. It was clear that Servius's men were winning as another of Berenice's guards fell. 'They're after our lives. Please, you must understand!' The captain considered the situation for a second and nodded before barking some commands. His men began to load the Ark onto the ship. 'We have a lot of cargo to load, sir,' he said.

'Leave it all behind except that,' Jayesh said. They tried to move the Ark in the exact manner Berenice had instructed. Its heavy animal-skin covers were needed to shield the Ark completely. But as the men rushed to load it onto the

Vasudha, the covers came loose, giving everyone on the scene the slightest glimpse of the lid adorned with two breathtakingly beautiful golden sculptures.

As they were undocking from the port, three of Servius's soldiers jumped aboard the ship and a huge bolt of lightning struck the ground near the pier at nearly the same time. It illuminated the evening sky with jagged trails of fire and the sheer violence of the strike froze everyone in place. The ensuing clap of thunder pierced their eardrums, reverberating around the dock and causing the surrounding buildings to tremble. Nannan was the first to be heard above the cacophony. 'Jayesh, they are on board! Look!'

Vikesh sprang into action. 'Get it into the hold!' he shouted to Nannan, pointing towards the Ark. 'Come here and help me,' he said to some of the sailors standing rooted to their spots, picking up a stick and rushing towards the soldiers. 'Jayesh, get us out of here!'

Jayesh rushed to the captain at the front of the ship as the sky suddenly turned the deepest black. It became impossible to see anything; the malevolence of the sky was blinding and unyielding. Nannan disappeared into the hold with the Ark, even as dark waves pounded angrily against the hull of the ship, rocking it dangerously.

'It isn't safe to sail, sir! We will all die! We must turn back!' the captain shouted.

'There are three soldiers on this ship. There are at least ten more on the dock – we will die if we go back too. The storm will yield – keep moving!' Jayesh commanded. He looked back at the stern of the ship where Vikesh and a few of their sailors were bravely fighting the soldiers. Jayesh rushed towards the action.

The *Vasudha* edged out of the port, groaning under the weight of the gathering storm. Another flash of lightning lit up the port for a few seconds, followed by torrents of rain descending in sheets, sawing away at the wooden ship. It grew even darker. The ship's helm seemed to cut the darkness as she edged into the depths of the ocean. The captain was screaming instructions to make himself heard above the caterwaul of the wind and rain. 'We need to be in front of the storm!' He was pointing into the distance.

Jayesh glanced back for a moment, unable to distinguish between the darkness of the skies and the immense murky depth of the seas. He saw the outline of another large wave rising and crashing onto the deck, tossing the sailors about like rag dolls. He could also see the stern of the ship, just about visible in the few remaining twinkling lights from the port and the shadows of the men fighting. Terror gripped him, but he focused on finding Vikesh to fight alongside him.

Two bolts of lightning struck the ship near the stern, lighting up the faces of the men who stood there. He could clearly see Vikesh's terror-stricken face as he cowered before the raised sword of one of Servius's men, its blade gleaming in the light.

'No!' screamed Jayesh, pumping his legs to get him there quicker. It seemed as if the fingers of lightning were wrapping around the deck in a lethal grip for those few moments.

Then the flames erupted. A deafening roar echoed above the terrifying shrieks of the storm as the wood ripped apart. As the lightning vanished, the night was set aglow by the raging fire consuming the stern of the ship. The flames soon subsided and the ship seemed to break in half as the stern sheared off and fell into the ocean with a tremendous splash.

The boom of the thunder drowned out the bloodcurdling screams of the men on board.

Jayesh couldn't move. He could hardly believe he had just witnessed his best friend's death. His heart shattered into a million pieces. He had a sinking feeling that they were all going to die. As if reading his mind, he heard someone yell, 'We're going to die! The ship is sinking!'

All he could think of was Paavi and her warning before everything faded to black.

73

Kurumba Bhagavathy Temple, Kodungallur
23 July 2024

Discovering the Ark was bound to be a career-defining find, and Harveen shuddered at the thought of the Vatican taking it away from her. In just two days, Professor Prakash had arranged for all the permits they needed to begin digging through the grounds of the Kurumba Bhagavathy Temple. She and Rohan were to be present on the site at all times to supervise the proceedings, and they were the only two people allowed into the chamber underneath the well.

They had faced no obstacles so far – the red soil was soft, yielding with little to no resistance. A tent had been erected to mask their excavation as per plan; this also served as a covered storage area for their equipment.

They reached the stone wall concealing the cavity at the bottom of the well and carefully started removing the stones one by one so they were easier to replace at the end of the dig. The tunnel walls needed to be reinforced to allow the team to climb through; a little more than half a metre in diameter. The process of setting up this narrow passage was slow and careful, taking an entire day more than anticipated to complete. As soon as it was completed, Harveen could not wait to descend. She envisaged finding the Ark of the Covenant and all the glory it would bring her. It would be the moment when this would become one of the most important archaeological sites in the world and she would be the one to thank for it.

'Come, let's go,' she said excitedly to Rohan. They carefully lowered the portable light before Harveen climbed down the tunnel, aided by a rope.

She found herself in a circular room with stone walls. Rohan was at her side before long.

The room, bathed in torch light, revealed a circular chamber of a similar circumference as the well above. An earthy damp smell filled their nostrils, creating a claustrophobic atmosphere. The cavity was about six feet in height and both the walls and roof had been fashioned out of the same type of stone. The floor was hard compacted soil, appearing darker than the red soil of the temple grounds. At first glance, the room seemed empty and there was no sign that it had been used for anything ever before.

'Seems like there's nothing here,' Rohan said, looking closely at the floor. Harveen examined the walls with her torch.

'Look, Rohan, there are torches on the wall,' she replied, pointing with her flashlight. On opposite sides of the well, just above head height were two torches in circular holders. 'I think this was never a well …' she said slowly.

Rohan grinned at her. She said, 'Let's have a look under the ground here, see if there is something.' She pulled out the hand tools she carried in her small bag. They would be sufficient to peel back a few layers of soil. The two of them worked for several minutes, digging holes and quietly hoping something interesting would reveal itself. But they found no evidence that anything had ever been buried there.

'Maybe we were wrong …' she said. Rohan looked despondent. They looked around for several minutes, feeling their way around the walls and the floor, checking to see if any of the stones were loose. It seemed they had no choice but to give up.

'You go up, Rohan. I will fill in these holes and bring up the lights.' Harveen felt dejected. Rohan nodded and made his way up to the surface. She set about filling in the holes they had dug and thereafter, dusted off her clothes. As she grabbed onto the rope to make her way up, her flashlight hit a section of the wall which looked out of place.

A couple of the stones seemed much smaller than the rest. She pulled out her small trowel to chip away at the edges of the three stones. It didn't take long to prise the first one out. The second stone was slightly larger, and time had ensured it was firmly stuck. It took a while longer to work it loose. As soon as it gave way, Harveen noticed that it had been covering the mouth of a small cavity.

Electrified, she grabbed at the last remaining stone, noticing a faint marking on its surface when she brushed the dust off its surface. A small 'M' revealed itself. She shone her torch into the small hole and could scarcely believe what she saw. It was a little wooden box. With trembling hands, she pulled it out, adrenaline coursing through her veins and her breath quick. It was a plain box with a simple pattern carved into its lid – a thing of beauty owing to its evident antiquity. The carving was the same as the one on the stone. An 'M' for Muziris. She quickly put the box in her bag and replaced the three stones.

As she returned to the surface, she saw that Rohan was busy packing away their equipment. He rushed over to her.

'Veen, are you okay? You look like you've seen a ghost. What took you so long?'

'I guess I have,' she said, showing him the box. 'This was hidden inside a small cavity in the wall. It was covered by some stones.'

Rohan mirrored her shock. He reached out to touch it but stopped short. His hand was shaking. 'O-open it?' he asked nervously.

Harveen set it down on a table in the tent and carefully prised open the lid. Inside was a single sheet of cotton paper with writing on it. It was faded but clear.

'We need to get back to the office and translate this right now,' she said.

74

Muciripattanam
AD 71

'Vikesh? Vikesh!'

'Jayesh? Can you hear me?' A familiar but faraway voice responded.

'Vikesh?' Jayesh called again. Maybe he could still save him. He felt a cold towel pressed to the side of his head as he slowly came to.

'No, brother. He is not here … it's me.'

Jayesh slowly opened his eyes. The world was spinning. He struggled to focus on Nannan's kind face hovering above him. He could hear the rain pounding on the deck above them. Light poured into the room through the open hatch in the roof.

'Nannan? Is that you?'

'Yes, brother.' Nannan bent down to wrap him in a gentle embrace and sighed with relief. 'I knew you would come back.'

'What happened? Where are we?'

'The ship – do you remember?'

Jayesh was thinking hard, but his mind was awash with random images. A huge storm, lightning, monsters climbing out of the sea, Vikesh fighting soldiers, the ship sinking, Paavi drowning … He could not make sense of what was real and what he had seen in his nightmares. 'We sank … I saw the ship break in half.'

'You have been unconscious for three days. We did not sink. Amidst the storm, a part of the main sail's rigging came loose, and it hit you just as you were making your way to Vikesh. I thought you died. You need to get more rest, brother.'

'Three days?'

Jayesh looked around and saw that he was on a single cot in the cargo area of the *Vasudha*. The outline of the Ark of the Covenant was visible on the other side of the hold, covered with cloth. There was a table beside him with water and blood-stained rags, and another cot.

'We brought you here. There was a lot of blood. No one else thought you would survive.'

Jayesh felt his head – the bumps of his scars were painful to the touch and made him wince. 'You've been here with me all this time?' he asked, looking at the other cot.

Nannan nodded.

'And … Vikesh?'

'Brother, please get some rest first. Then we can talk about all that.' Nannan gently lowered Jayesh back onto the bed.

'No, I need to know.' But in his heart, he already knew.

Nannan shook his head sadly, his eyes welling up. Jayesh felt the pain of losing his friend all over again, like it had only just happened. His mind flashed memories of Paavi's warnings against the trip and Vikesh begging him not to persist at every turn. He wished that he too had died on the stern.

'It is not your fault, brother,' Nannan said, seeming to read his mind.

'We both know it is. He never wanted to come. I forced him …'

They shared a long moment of silence.

'He fought bravely till the end. He did believe in the cause, you know. For all his reluctance.'

Just then, a huge wave crashed against the ship and flooded the hold. Jayesh suddenly remembered, 'But the ship – it was struck by lightning and broke in half …'

'We lost about a third of the crew. Likely, everyone who was at the stern at the time was killed instantly.' Nannan wore a resigned, grief-stricken look on his face.

'What do you mean, "likely"? Don't we know for sure?'

'There is little room for doubt, brother. The lightning cut the ship near in half, the stern was in flames as it sunk. It is a wonder we have remained afloat. In the total darkness during the storm, we had no way of finding out or saving anyone who may still have been alive. Besides, so many men were injured on what was left of the ship, we needed to move quickly to make sure they were safe. The captain insisted we get out of the storm and continued moving ahead. I was still in the hold, hiding the Ark when he steered us out. They thought you were dead too. By the time I could come up and take stock of what was going on, we were already well on our way … The captain had decided not to turn back to check for survivors.'

'So you just left him there?' Jayesh asked incredulously. In truth, he believed that Vikesh may have been dead before he hit the water; he had seen him fighting a losing battle against a soldier.

'We would all have perished. I am sure of it,' Nannan said.

'So I've killed him … Just like I did to my brother. He kept warning me … but I wouldn't listen.'

The ship lurched, bringing them both back into the present. The light from the hatch disappeared as dark rain clouds blackened the sky.

'Where are we now?' asked Jayesh urgently.

'We continued on our original course but the storm has not yet passed.'

'And the ship?'

'It is torn in two. God has blessed us, brother, there's no reason why we should be afloat right now, considering the vessel's condition. The piece that fell into the waters was the top half of the stern; the hull is still intact. A little water is getting through, but as long as we keep moving, it looks like she will be able to hold out for the entire course of our journey.'

Jayesh said a silent prayer and considered their position. He winced as he tried to get up. 'I need to see it,' he said. 'Can you help me up?'

Nannan came forward but another jolt caused Jayesh to fall back onto the cot.

'Are you sure? You need to rest, brother,' Nannan asked, concerned for his friend.

'I just need to see it.' He was resolute, managing to get on his feet with great effort. As they clambered up to the deck of the ship, it was just as Nannan had described. It seemed impossible for the ship to not have sunk – its whole rear was missing. Jayesh slumped onto the deck.

'What have I done, Nannan? I killed my best friend and Servius's men are still after us … they won't spare our lives when they find us. Everything is ruined! How will I face Paavi? She warned me … she told me not to—'

'Brother, this is no time to feel sorry for yourself. You are the strongest man I know. We still have half a crew and terrible weather to endure, we cannot afford to lose you. We need you well and strong so we can all get home safely.'

'I can't … Not just yet …'

Nannan helped him to his feet. 'You can, brother. You have to try. For all of our sake.'

It usually took between eighteen and twenty-five days to get from the Port of Myos Hormos to the Port of Muziris. This was dependent on weather conditions – in particular, the winds. Nannan had encountered all kinds of weather during his journeys along this route over the years. An adverse wind could add many days of travel and an unsettled sea could make the passage very uncomfortable, but even he had never seen anything like the weather they were seeing now. The rains and winds seemed to intensify by the day, throwing the huge merchant ship around the sea as if she were no more than a bobbing cork on its surface. The sky continued to turn black periodically, making it impossible for them to distinguish night from day.

But the harsher the going, the tougher Jayesh's resolve became.

The ebony sky hid the Pole Star and the sun, leaving them at the mercy of the sea with no way to determine if they were moving in the right direction. The captain used his wisdom from years of experience and the direction of the winds to determine their course, correcting it when the sky became visible. The *Vasudha* did not have a galley of rowers on board and was entirely reliant on her three vast sails to propel her. At times, the wind seemed vindictive, trying to rip her masts off. The large steering oars at the front were all she had left now, which enabled her to change direction when necessary.

It took them forty-two days to reach Muciripattanam. Four more men had died, each weighing heavily on Jayesh. The weather did not improve for more than a day at a time and the journey had seemed increasingly torturous, severely testing the resolve of every man on board. If not for their captain, they would all surely have perished. Nannan was certain that the great treasure was the source of their ill fortune, just as the priestess had warned them.

'It's bad luck, Jayesh. It would be best for us to cast it into the sea,' he suggested. This time, Jayesh did not hesitate to agree. They hauled it onto the deck together, but as they prepared to throw the Ark into the sea, something began to gnaw at Jayesh.

'It is the greatest treasure of their religion … we cannot simply cast it into the sea,' he said.

'But look at the destruction it has caused!' pleaded Nannan.

'If this was a pillar built by the mighty Ashoka, embossed with the teachings of the Buddha, would you ask me to toss it in this way?'

Nannan hesitated.

'We cannot. We made a promise to the priestess and we must keep to our word. St Thomas will surely know what we should do with it and it is merely our job to ensure it reaches him.'

'But at what cost, brother? What of us and the rest of our crew?'

'Nannan, this one item will make us more money than we have ever spent. It will be a beacon for visitors.' Jayesh could still make Muciripattanam great. He would repay his mistakes by bringing greater prosperity to his hometown.

'And what of Vikesh?' Nannan shook his head. Jayesh

reflected on the death of his dearest friend and the price that he had paid for ambitions not his own. If they succeeded in restoring the Ark to a Tabernacle in Muciripattanam, the glory of their hometown would be unmatched. He considered how this may be their only chance at honouring Vikesh's memory.

'We can't give up now, or he would have died in vain.' Jayesh was pensively looking out at the sea. 'Take it back down to the hold,' he commanded.

When they finally approached Muciripattanam, their food supplies had been all but exhausted. The fresh water had to be replenished using rainwater many days ago and several of the remaining crew had developed a fever. But their elation at reaching their destination was quickly replaced by despair when they set eyes on the shoreline that awaited them. The storm they had brought along had caused the piers to be consumed by the tumultuous sea and leaving no place for their ship to dock. Jayesh could only gape in horror at the havoc the winds were wreaking on the marketplace he had built with his own hands. The wooden structures were defenceless in the face of the battering gales.

The captain bellowed to him, 'There is nowhere to moor the ship, sir!' Everyone on the ship was filled with anguish, desperate to leave the ship as soon as possible.

'Run her aground!' Jayesh commanded, sensing everyone's discomfort. 'Get us as close as you can!' He was sure that if anyone spotted them, small boats would be brought out to assist their approach – everyone recognized the grand *Vasudha* and the people of Muciripattanam were hardened to the frequent rainstorms along the coast, though nothing like this had befallen them ever before.

The wind enabled the ship to gather some speed as they

headed towards the coastline, presenting a ghostly sight against the thunder and lightning in the backdrop. As the mighty *Vasudha* ran aground with a loud crash, she could be heard screeching above the howl of the wind as her hull scraped along the seabed. She finally came to a halt. In the same moment, the relief of arriving at their destination washed over the men onboard and in harmonious fashion, the rains and winds finally began to let up.

The gods had finally abandoned their campaign against the new guardians of the Ark of the Covenant.

Jayesh sighed at the sight of his people appearing on the shoreline, a few minutes later, shouting instructions to each other to rescue them. He prayed that their misfortune was finally at an end and grew impatient to convey the Ark safely to the church of St Thomas. 'Nannan, we must secure the Ark first. Let's take it to St Thomas quickly and he can tell us what we are to do with it. I won't feel safe until we see this through.'

Nannan nodded. Jayesh sent his men to arrange for a cart large enough to hold the Ark. He told them to bring along all their soldiers, although their army was merely one in name. They had been trained by the Roman soldiers stationed at the fort, but were mainly ceremonial, employed from day to day only in overseeing the safe transit of goods as the town's merchants travelled across the country. For this reason, Jayesh felt they would be best equipped to help him transport the Ark swiftly and safely. 'I will take it to the church myself. You make sure that everyone is looked after and take stock of the damages in the market and warehouses,' he instructed Nannan.

Perhaps because Jayesh had already been anticipating the worst, the Ark's journey to St Thomas was a breeze in comparison to what had unfolded at sea. The rain had almost stopped and the winds were starting to settle. The presence of the soldiers also provided some comfort.

St Thomas was not there to greet them when they arrived, prompting Jayesh to immediately send for him. The construction of the underground room had been completed while they were away and lined with wood as per the saint's instructions. An ornate plinth had been commissioned for a replica of the Ark to sit on; never could anyone have imagined that they would come into possession of the original Ark itself. A wide stairway inside the church led to the lower level. The veil to conceal the Ark was ready but they still awaited the four marble pillars that were yet to arrive from Alexandria to be positioned around the plinth. The architect, Anand, was proud to show Jayesh what they had achieved, and rightly so.

Now that the Ark was inside the church, the fatigue of the journey finally caught up with Jayesh. He savoured a moment spent sitting in the tranquil silence of the church, allowing his muscles to relax. He could not bear the thought of risking his family's safety and decided to stay put until the Ark was placed on the plinth in the new Tabernacle. He tried to find comfort in the hope that when Paavi saw the Ark and its potential to put Muciripattanam on the world map as a metropolis in its own right, she would surely find the strength to bear Vikesh's loss. His sacrifice would not be in vain – everyone would see.

75

Sreepadam Palace
26 July 2024

Harveen was relieved there was no one in the office when she and Rohan arrived. She sat down at her desk and gently set the box in front of her. It looked old and fragile, and the 'M' inscribed on its lid reassured her that it had lain undisturbed for nearly 2,000 years. It was slightly damp. The lid gave way with gentle pressure. Inside was a single sheet of the cotton paper. It was in remarkable condition – slightly discoloured but legible. Harveen was trembling with excitement as she unfolded it and put it on the scanner. She watched the little disc on her screen spin as the document was processed by the software Penny had given her access to.

A few moments later, the deciphered text stared back at her and Rohan.

> Beyond here I have entombed the most holy symbol of Judaism, the Ark of the Covenant. It has power beyond human understanding and has killed many men on its journey to Muciripattanam. With it lies the body of Judas Christ, the brother of Jesus Christ, whose own faith and belief was not enough to contain the Ark's destructive

power. With what means I have remaining, I have sought to protect the Ark's resting place so that their God may once again reclaim it and grant me forgiveness for my actions, although I believe my fate is already sealed. If any man should find the Ark and seek to use it for his personal gain as I did, then I would implore you to abandon your mission and let it rest here for eternity. My pursuit of this cursed object has cost me my family, my friends and my fortune. I have in these final years of my life come to realize what is important, and have banished forevermore the desires to further my wealth or power. Judas Christ has told me that the Ark is a harbinger of death and destruction for all who have sought to use it selfishly. It can only be laid to rest in its original home in the Temple of Jerusalem.

Jayesh of Muciripattanam

'My god!' said Rohan.

Harveen was struggling to process the information. She had been sure that the Ark had not made it back to India. The records that she had seen were very persuasive. 'Do you think it is still there?' she asked.

'I don't know. It can't be. We looked everywhere – the room is too small.'

'But look,' said Harveen, 'It says "beyond here" – maybe he means the wall?'

Harveen's phone rang. It was Inspector Kumar.

'I better take this,' she said, walking away from her desk. 'Hello?'

'Harveen, this is Inspector Kumar.'

'Hi Sanjay, sorry, I haven't been in touch, it's been very crazy here—'

'Veen! You need to come to me right now. In fact, tell me where you are and I will come get you. You will be safer that way.'

'What? No, I can't right now! I'm in the middle of some very important work. Can I please just drop by tomorrow?'

'Harveen, they are going to arrest you. I should not even be calling you about this. We have received direct orders from the State Director General of Police – there are officers searching your house and they're also on their way to the Sreepadam Palace.'

'Are you serious? But why?' Her head was spinning.

'We got an anonymous call. Someone saw you hiding the murder weapon, they say. A knife. They even gave a location and the police are on their way to it. If it turns out to be a match, the DGP is talking about a death penalty case considering the state of Dr Gupta's body when we found it. She was tortured using a knife before being murdered.'

'I swear I don't know anything about a knife. What knife?' Harveen struggled to stay on her feet.

'Tell me where you are and I'll come get you. If they take you into custody, I won't be able to help you.'

'But it wasn't me! I didn't kill her!'

'I don't think you did, but we never released information about how Dr Gupta was killed. A knife was used and we never found the weapon. There's no time to get into it all, Harveen, but it's not looking good …'

'Thanks for letting me know, Sanjay. I'll come right away. Tell me where to meet you.'

'I am at the station – you need to come and turn yourself in. That can buy us some time to figure out what happened. How long will you be?'

'I am leaving now. I will be there in twenty.' She hung up. Harveen was shaking, filled by a sense of foreboding that things were hurtling towards a devastating end. She remembered reading something in the news about some men who were sentenced to death a couple of months ago for murdering a well-known politician in front of his family. All their appeals had been denied. What the DGP deemed justice was bound to be delivered quickly. She did not understand what to make of the knife or how they had connected her to it despite her having had nothing to do with the murder.

She wrestled with thoughts of what might happen if she was not able to see beyond the walls of the well. And how she was running out of time to ward off the threat of the Vatican taking over. Maybe it had something to do with the big man who she had seen Penny with – maybe this is what they were meeting to discuss. Perhaps he was after the artefacts too; maybe he already knew what to look for and was one of those treasure hunters who sold religious finds.

As she walked back into the office, Rohan looked up at her, concerned. 'Are you okay? Who was it?'

'I just … can't believe it,' she managed to say. 'It was Professor Prakash. He said to go straight back to the well with the GPR and find out what is beyond the wall … Something about turning our phones off and not speaking to anyone, and reporting directly to him what we find.'

Rohan looked surprised.

'So I guess we should go?' she said before he could ask her any questions. 'Come on, get the radar. We need to rush.'

As they were leaving, her phone rang again. It was Don from the Vatican. Harveen declined the call, turned off her phone and put it in her pocket. Regardless of what happened afterwards, Harveen wanted to ensure she was the first to see what 'Jayesh of Muciripattanam' had hidden behind the wall.

As they rushed downstairs to collect the GPR, Harveen heard police sirens at the front of the building. The fright on Harveen's face was clear as day to Rohan and he stopped. 'Veen, what on earth is going on?'

'I'll explain it all to you in the car, I promise. Quick, get this loaded into the jeep.' They ran with the equipment into the parking at the rear of the palace. As they got to the door, Harveen saw the big man she had seen with Penny in the car. Instinctively, she pushed Rohan back inside.

'Whoa! What happened? What is it?' he asked, startled.

'I think I just saw Dr Gupta's killer. Where is your car?'

'What – what do you mean?'

'Rohan, tell me where your car is! I will explain everything later. We need to leave right now!'

'It's – it's in the staff parking right by the side exit.'

'Take this, I am right behind you. Do you have the keys?'

Rohan tapped his pocket and nodded.

'Go!'

As he sprang into action, Harveen turned on her phone and made a final call.

'Sanjay?' she said as he picked up. 'The silver car I told you about. It's in the parking behind the Palace right now. The man I saw is here too. The police have arrived. You must tell them to find him. He's very distinct-looking and will be easy to spot. Just tell them what I told you the other day. If he's not in his car, he could be inside the building. I don't know what he's doing here.'

'But where are you?' Sanjay said, concerned.

'I am on my way to the station – like I said! I just need to do one thing first. Please ask your men to hurry.'

She hung up, turned off her phone and ran to meet Rohan. As she reached the top of the stairs, two policemen entered the stairwell and spotted her.

'There!' One of them shouted and they both sprinted up the stairs. Harveen bolted back into the office and shut the door behind her, looking around frantically for another way out. She headed for the fire exit through the kitchen. As she burst through the door, she saw there were policemen below, waiting. Seeing her, they too started sprinting up the emergency exit stairs.

Harveen was stuck in the office. There were only two other exits: through the preservation rooms, or the museum. There would still be a few visitors hanging around the latter and the access to the main front door was sure to be guarded.

The police team were being led by Inspector S. R. Ashwin, who reported directly to the DGP. He was a veteran, having been at the job for twenty years, and was well known for his efficiency. He was unmistakable with his handlebar moustache and highly decorated uniform, towering well over six feet and marching through the Sreepadam Palace building waiting for news from his young officers.

'Sir, we have seen her – she is here. She's wearing green shorts, a khaki shirt and black boots. We cut her off at the staff entrance and the fire escape, and our men have all other exits covered too. The building is a bit of a maze – it may take some time to track her down.'

'Clear all these offices one by one and spread out in two-man teams,' Ashwin commanded as they walked through the offices into the museum. 'Why are there civilians still here? I told you to clear out the building.'

'Yes, sir, right away. We couldn't clear the museum as there was a school party here – we didn't want to raise alarm among the children, sir. Everyone is being checked at the door. They are all being escorted out shortly.'

'Huh, we'll see about that,' said Ashwin, marching into the museum. 'You two there, we have to clear the museum, could you please exit through there?' he said to a European couple who were looking at a display of coins. They shuffled towards the door.

'Hallo! Hallo, please!' he called in his thick Malayalam accent, 'The museum is closing early today. Please make your way out by the main exit at the front, same way you came in. Please cooperate for the routine security checks – nothing to worry about. Move quickly, please!' He began to usher the remaining people towards the door. A small child tried to protest, but her mother pulled her by the arm and rushed her along. An older Indian man was standing close to one of the exhibits, scribbling down notes in a little book. He gave a small salute to the policeman as he made his way towards the exit while a lady in a red sari bent to touch the DGP's feet for blessings before following the man.

'You see,' he said to his young assistant. 'If you stand tall and give clear instructions, you will always be respected. Now, where else could she be?'

'There is another corridor down there, where Professor Prakash's office is. There is also a boardroom and a couple of storage rooms there.'

'Show me,' said Ashwin, walking on ahead. A moment later, Ashwin turned to check if his assistant was in tow and found him staring at one of the displays.

The little sign below it said 'Parvati – the Hindu Goddess of Power'. The statue of the goddess that stood next to the lion wore a khaki shirt and at her feet lay a pair of dusty black boots. His assistant pointed at them and said, 'Sir, Goddess Parvati wears a red sari ...'

Ashwin charged towards the exit.

76

Bergamo, Italy
27 July 2024
5:04 a.m.

Don had secretly been to Rossi's house on two previous occasions to monitor his movements. Experience had taught him to be wary. Thus, he had a good understanding of the level of security at his home. Rossi's private life had turned out to be the exact opposite of his flamboyant professional career, which had been a surprising discovery for Don. He lived in a small farmhouse in Bergamo with his wife, their two daughters having flown the coop sometime ago. His wife, Alessia, had her own life, clearly accustomed to her husband's frequent travels and long absences while he was at the Vatican. She tended her lovely garden and walked their two dogs twice daily. She seemed to have a busy social life, spending most of her time with her group of close friends.

When Rossi was at home, Don noticed they shared a warm and cordial relationship, taking supper together and enjoying each other's company for brief periods during the day but also that they would promptly return to their respective independent routines. Both their daughters had moved out long ago and only the younger one lived close enough to make an occasional visit. She worked at a luxury departmental store in Milan. Her elder sister had moved to New York with her husband a few years ago.

Don had initially assumed that someone in Rossi's position would have installed a sophisticated security system at their home. Instead, he had found that there was only a basic keypad-activated alarm adjacent to the front door, like some of the retired farmers' houses in the neighbourhood. He had managed to find out the code on a previous visit. Monitoring the household's movements was also relatively easy, thanks to the several dilapidated buildings right opposite their residence, one of which offered excellent vantage points with a clear view of all the front-facing windows.

Don had already reconciled with what he needed to do to stop Rossi from interfering further with the India operation. As soon as he noticed Rossi's wife was leaving, he saw him enter the living room and settle in front of the fire with a bottle of whisky and a book. He watched patiently until Rossi drank half the bottle. He estimated that his wife would not return home until the following morning, judging by the overnight bag she had been carrying. At 4:30 p.m. exactly, the cloned phone in Don's pocket began to buzz. It was configured to transmit any calls made or received by either Paulo or Vincenzo. Sofia had warned him against installing the spyware on Rossi's phone as he took care to have it checked daily when he was in the Vatican and was likely to take notice. She was able to remotely install the surveillance software on all other Vatican-issued devices, though.

Don glanced at the phone and saw that it was an outbound call from Paulo. He guessed it might again be to his mother, whom he called frequently. He pressed the button and raised the handset to his ear. As he looked through the telescope again towards Rossi, he saw him pick up his mobile from the table next to him, sitting beside the whisky and answer the call. 'Rossi,' he greeted in his standard way.

'They have started to dig at the temple,' wheezed Paulo.

A second's silence. 'Follow them carefully. Do nothing until you actually see that they have found something.' Rossi's tone was neutral, but Don could see the change in his expression as he became alert and sat upright in his chair. The news must have instantly cleared the haze from the whisky.

'And if they do?'

'Bring it all back. Anything to do with St Thomas or the Ark. I need this to be a clean job. No witnesses.'

'The assistant, Rohan, is with her too. The police are already looking for her. They will stop her if they can, no, signor?' Paulo spoke in a dull, bored monotone.

Rossi clenched his jaw. 'We can't rely on the police, Paulo. If you see anything of interest at the site, kill the girl and her assistant, and bring it straight back. Make sure you leave no trail. Make it look like an accident; like the roof caved in or something. Seal them both in the chamber and clean up after yourself. Close up the passage to the site. There should be no evidence for the police to trace it back to anyone else but those two. I will have a team ready to go to handle the fallout, should something arise. Nothing about the St Thomas or the Ark can be allowed to leak.'

'Yes, signor.'

They hung up. Don sat in silence, watching Rossi calmly return to his book. It was too late for him to protect Harveen or any of the other researchers in India. He shut his eyes in resignation – this was his biggest failing yet. He waited until

Rossi was sound asleep in his bed before moving from his position.

Gaining entry into the house presented no issues – the antique wooden door at the rear was unlocked and the alarm system did not get triggered when he opened it. He had memorized the layout of the house and quietly made his way upstairs to Rossi's bedroom.

He paused at the door. If only the old man had been as watchful at home as he was at work, he could have saved his own life. But as things were, he was going to die in his bed. Don eased the door open, thankful that it did not make a noise. Rossi lay on the right side of the large wooden-framed sleigh bed, tucked comfortably in his sheets. The left side was undisturbed. Don eased around to that side, his gun raised and aimed at centre mass. In case Rossi sprang up, he was ready to shoot him dead with two 9mm Parabellums from his Beretta M9 immediately.

Rossi was fast asleep. Even as Don approached him, the older man did not stir. He pulled the sheets back sharply and took one step back, keeping the gun levelled at Rossi. In the dim light, Don suddenly realized that he had been tricked – under the sheets were a mannequin head and a line of pillows giving the impression of a man's body.

'Drop the gun where you are, Don. And do it with two fingers only. My wife rather likes these sheets, and she would be quite upset if they had your brains splattered all over them.' The familiar condescending tone of Rossi's voice cut through the air. He stood behind Don, who held the gun away from his body as he had been instructed, and turned his head slowly. Rossi was pointing his own gun at Don with the slightest hint of a grin on his face. Don held his Beretta in a very loose grip with just two fingers and dropped it carefully and deliberately onto the bed. He then turned to face Rossi.

'My dear Donatello, ever the misguided child. In what world did you think you would get the better of me – especially in my own house?'

Rossi stepped out of a concealed doorway in a corner of the room which Don had never seen before. He was dressed in loose-fitting chinos and a dark-coloured shirt. He had clearly been expecting him.

'But … how did you know?'

'Sit down, Donatello,' commanded Rossi and pointed his gun in the direction of the ornate armchair behind Don. He sat down. Rossi seated himself in the one right opposite him, on the other side of the window, his gun still aimed at Don's head. They were about six feet apart.

'From the moment they realized you were not coming to my office, my men have been onto you. I believe you did not notice Rocco and Tony? They have been hot on your trail since you left the Vatican – they are outside right now as we speak, in fact, ready to dispose of your body when I'm done with you. I also sent Luca and Daniella to Pescara as a … sort of an insurance policy, you could say.'

The mention of his coastal hometown where Don had grown up brought back many memories, but they were dominated by those of his uncle – a devout priest, a spiritual man who remained a serving cleric, loyal to the Church at the age of seventy-two; his last remaining family.

'He has been a loyal servant of the church his whole life. Leave him out of this, Rossi.'

'That, Donatello, is up to you. The leaders of the Santa Alleanza have always been afforded honourable deaths. Should you agree to remain on this path, I will spare his life and ensure you get a hero's send-off.' Rossi produced an ornate knife from his side pocket. 'Emperor Constantine's own son was a traitor and his throat was slit in a hot bath.' He smiled and looked towards his ensuite bathroom. 'Alternatively, you could take a coward's route and I can kill you where you are sitting. The choice is entirely yours.'

'Choice, you say? I don't trust you. I know you and your methods … You'd leave no loose ends.' He was well aware that Rossi often used family members as leverage and made good on his threats regardless of what his hostages might say or do.

'I see. Do you have another solution in mind?'

Don was disgusted – Rossi seemed to be enjoying this, caressing his knife in anticipation. 'Let me speak to my uncle. I want to know if he is alive and unhurt right now. He's all I've got. At least let me say goodbye. Call Luca right now.'

'Alright, alright. Calm down, will you, Donatello? I will also need you to make a confession that says that you came here tonight to murder me. Tie up all loose ends, as you said.'

'Fine. I will make a statement.' Don hung his head.

'Excellent,' said Rossi, taking out his phone.

Don stood up tentatively as his former boss dialled. He put the phone on speaker as it started to ring.

'Hello,' came the familiar voice of Luca, one of Rossi's assassins.

'He wants to speak to his old man,' Rossi said.

'Uh … The hostage has a message for you, signor.'

Rossi's brows furrowed a little. 'By all means, put him on.'

Following a small scuffle on the other end, a voice came on. Don watched Rossi like a hawk.

'Dino? *Chi e questa gente? Cosa vogliono da me?* (Who are these people? What do they want from me?)' a female voice asked Rossi. She sounded terrified.

'Alessia?' Rossi recognized his wife's voice. His expression morphed from triumphant to outraged.

'Thank you, Luca,' said Don, 'You've done well. I will ring you in five minutes. And if you don't hear from me, make sure you kill her.' With that, he snatched the phone from Rossi's hand and terminated the call. Rossi clutched his knife tightly.

'So, here is my confession,' began Don, 'If you don't ring Vincenzo now and call off your little operation in India, I will have your wife killed. However, if you do as I say and tell him to take instructions only from me from now on, her life will be spared.'

'How could have you done this?' Rossi was incredulous. For the first time since they had met, he had lost his air of superiority.

'They are not all loyal to you, Rossi. The Santa Alleanza are servants of the church. Over the last couple of years, some of them have opened their hearts to me and expressed their discontent. I had hoped that you would quietly retire and things would never come to a head like this. When Sophia alerted me to even more unhappy agents, I made sure to call them before I left her office. Luca and Daniella were sent here to pick up your wife when she left the house, not to Pescara. Rocco and Tony were not following me – we all came here together as allies. They are waiting to dispose of your body. So go ahead and make the call; save your wife. I would guess you have about … three minutes.'

Rossi's shoulders dropped. 'Every leader of the Santa Alleanza has had to make sacrifices, Donatello, some more than others. You too will learn this, I suspect,' he began. Don saw him glance down at his gun. 'Today—'

Before Rossi could say another word, Don crashed into him with his full weight, knocking the armchair to the floor as well. The gun spun across to the other end of the room, but Rossi still had his knife. Don grabbed his wrist and smashed it on the hardwood floor repeatedly until he finally let the knife drop. Don quickly pushed it away.

As Rossi jostled and tried to push Don off him, he gripped the older man's throat with his gloved hands and squeezed hard. Rossi stared directly into Don's eyes, his shock writ large across his face. He thrashed and kicked as Don's grip got tighter. Suddenly, Rossi's hand flew to punch Don hard in the side of his torso. He saw the knife sticking out of his side and Rossi trying to pull it out.

Don pushed his whole weight down on Rossi's neck, and slowly watched the colour drain from his twisted face; the thrashing came to a stop and his body fell limp. A fleeting smile appeared on his face as he took his last breath, an acceptance of his demise apparent. Or was it a twisted sense of triumph at the realization that Don was, in fact, capable of making truly difficult decisions? Was it relief he felt at the heavy burden of running the Santa Alleanza finally lifting from his shoulders?

Once he was sure Rossi was dead, Don rolled off him and examined the wound in his side. It was deep and extremely painful. He made a quick call to Rocco and Tony to come and clean up the house and take care of Rossi's body. He also asked them to bring a first-aid kit so he could bandage his wound.

Don called Sophia on his way to the plane that was waiting for him on a small airstrip in Bergamo, in the lap of the alpine region of northern Italy. He was heading back to India, but unfortunately, he was a little too late.

'It is done,' he told her. 'Rocco and Tony are cleaning up the house now and will bring the body back straightaway. His wife is cooperative and will be conveyed back to the house safely once things are in place.'

'Did he speak to Vincenzo?' Sofia was worried.

'No. He was prepared to die for it. I am on my way to India right now. It might be too late to save their lives, but I still need to deal with Vincenzo and Paulo. Hopefully, we can at least recover the artefacts without any further issues.'

'I will make the arrangements for his funeral. Death in service. Leave it to me. Will keep trying Vincenzo. Call me when you land.'

As the flight took off, Don wondered whether Dino Rossi, the man they called 'il macellaio', could have imagined that his life's work could have ended this way. He had served his country with distinction throughout his career before joining the Vatican, even going on to head the Santa Alleanza. He had strived to emulate his predecessors, each of whom had vowed to protect the prominence and wealth of the Vatican by any means necessary. In this intent, perhaps Rossi had surpassed those who had held the post before him.

Don sat alone with his thoughts for quite some time before pulling a thick manila envelope out of his briefcase. There was a battered folder inside, which he placed on the table in front of him. Sofia had given him this envelope weeks ago and he had scrutinized its contents many times. He looked at the old black-and-white photo of a young man in his service uniform. He noticed the innocent and hopeful look on the soldier's face; the twinkle in his eyes that he had first seen six years ago.

Don glanced at the photo of the young Rossi one last time before falling asleep.

The pilot woke Don some hours later.

'We are in India, sir. Cochin International. There is a car ready for you.'

'Thank you,' he replied, stretching out.

As he walked to his rental car, Don sent a message to Sofia.

'Any word from Vincenzo?'

The reply came almost instantly. 'Nothing.'

77

Kurumba Bhagavathy Temple
27 July 2024
7:09 p.m.

Harveen jumped into the passenger seat of Rohan's Maruti Brezza.

'Drive!' she said, crouching low. As Rohan was driving out of Sreepadam Palace, he suddenly noticed what Harveen was wearing.

'Is that a—'

'Yes.'

'I don't understand ...'

'It's ... complicated,' she said, adjusting the elaborate red sari she had thrown on. She was itching to tell him the truth about what had happened over the last couple of days.

'It's that guy that I saw with Dr Gupta in the silver car – I think the police are after him. Maybe they want to ask him about what happened to her. There are policemen everywhere. I didn't want him to recognize me ... just in case.'

'Recognize you? Veen, are you sure you're okay? I'm so glad you're safe.' Rohan appeared deeply concerned. Harveen looked back at him. She was scared, but there was no way she could tell him the truth about the police. At least not yet.

'I think so. Don't worry, I've called Inspector Kumar and told him about that man. I had given him all the details before, when he interrogated me.'

'He interrogated me too. I think he spoke to everyone in the department.'

'To tell you the truth, Ro, what happened to Dr Gupta and then with this find ... I'm just a bit shaken up. Actually, I think I'll just focus on what we are planning to do tonight.' She changed the subject.

When they arrived at the Kodungallur Kurumba Bhagavathy Temple, Rohan drove straight into the grounds. Harveen had called earlier and explained there was a problem with their equipment and that everyone should be cleared out of the temple premises as it was potentially dangerous. She was glad to see that the temple was deserted. They reversed the car up to the Samadhi of Vysoori, the small stone structure that sat on its own to the left of the main temple building.

As they both got out of the car, the night shrouded them in an ominous darkness, blocking out the chatter of birds or even a breath of wind. Harveen could hear the beating of her own heart as they approached the samadhi.

The tent they had set up during their earlier dig remained exactly as they had left it. Harveen struggled to climb down the hole wearing a sari but somehow managed to do so with Rohan's help. Once again, they set up their portable lights in the chamber and worked in complete silence. Harveen was struggling to process the magnitude and repercussions of what they might find on the other side of the wall if her conclusions were correct. The mix of emotions she was experiencing was difficult to describe: excitement, responsibility, apprehension, fear and hope – all churned together and making it difficult for her to concentrate. What did this evening have in store, she wondered.

The circular room was exactly as Harveen remembered it. They were surrounded by a ring of stones about six feet in height. The roof was constructed entirely of stone and the only escape was through the narrow tunnel they had excavated, leading out into the grounds of the temple. Despite the stone surroundings, the air was heavy and damp, giving an earthy tang they could taste. Even with all their lights on, the room felt like a claustrophobic cell around them. Harveen cast her flashlight around the walls, hoping they might reveal some clue to the secrets they guarded. As before, for almost 2,000 years, they remained resolutely silent now, providing no indication of what they had been entrusted to protect.

'Let's get the GPR,' she whispered. Each word seemed to hang heavily in the musty air. She welcomed the brief escape that fetching the radar from the car would offer from this oppressive room, just to allow her to gather her thoughts. It looked like Rohan had the same yearning; he was quick to ascend the tunnel and return to the daylight outside.

They unloaded the device from the car. While it was powerful and fairly portable, it had not been designed to pass through as small a passageway as the entry tunnel. After struggling for some time, they finally managed to have it in place. To get an accurate reading quickly, they would need to remove at least one of the stones at a time. The entire process was rather time-consuming as they would replace each stone before taking the next scan in another spot.

Rohan would switch the device on, moved it into position and with a quick questioning glance at Harveen, make sure they were good to go. She would nod and he would press the grey button to generate a reading. The GPR was fairly accurate up to thirty feet, regardless of terrain, producing 3D images.

They both stared at the screen. It appeared as if it was solid ground all the way. Harveen pointed at a shadow to one side of the image.

'Could that be something, you think?'

He shook his head in response. 'It's too small and it's not a cavity … Maybe just a rock formation or something.' His voice was flat and Harveen knew he was probably right. Her desperation to find what they were seeking was overwhelming.

'Let's go again.' She was still hopeful.

Rohan shuffled the device through fifteen or twenty degrees and repeated the process. Waiting for the little blank screen to light up was agonizing. Negative again. They both looked crestfallen. After Harveen had risked everything to do this, they had found nothing. She knew that her career was as good as over, what with the police hot on their trail and her being named as a suspect in the murder of Dr Gupta.

'Again,' she said, letting her desperation show. 'Try this way.'

Rohan nodded and moved the GPR device before pressing the button. He was gazing at her closely as she stared at the device. The dim glow lit up her face and she looked as if she was slightly puzzled. Rohan checked the screen too.

'Another negative reading – just solid ground all around us like the last two. Sorry, Veen,' he said.

'But what about that, Rohan?' She leaned forward slightly and pointed.

'What are you looking at? There's nothing there!'

'At the very edge of the screen. Is that a line? Move it around and go again.' She felt a tiny tinge of anticipation this time.

'That's just the edge,' Rohan sighed. 'Veen, it's an old machine … looks the same to me as the last reading we took.'

Reluctantly, he moved the GPR round by another twenty degrees and pressed the button again. Harveen held her breath. The green light from the image illuminated their faces once again.

Her eyes widened in astonishment. She looked at Rohan and saw that his face mirrored hers. On the screen was a clear straight line extending off into the distance and being crossed at ninety degrees by another line. It was right in front of them, whatever it was; no more than two feet away. Just beyond the wall they were both now staring at was a very large room. The stone structure was not lined precisely alongside the room; it looked like it was towards the corner. The GPR did not penetrate far enough to show them the full dimensions of anything lying beyond, but this room was almost certainly more than thirty feet long and at least ten feet wide.

'What in the …' Rohan could not help but gape in shock.

Harveen had expected to feel ecstatic on making the discovery of a lifetime. But instead, she felt the cold grip of terror tighten around her throat. The Ark of the Covenant was not only the greatest undiscovered historical artefact there had ever been, it was also widely associated with death and destruction. The person who had buried it in this crypt nearly 2,000 years ago had left a clear warning that it should not be dug up again. Yet here they were …

78

Kurumba Bhagavathy Temple
27 July 2024
8:03 p.m.

'Do you really think it's possible? Is it actually here?' Rohan was incredulous.

Harveen had gone quiet. Drawing a deep breath, she nodded slowly. At last, she said, 'We must be absolutely sure, though. Let's get our digging equipment down here. I can't explain why but I feel like this is our only chance. Once we have confirmed that the Ark is here, we can seal it up and go to Professor Prakash tomorrow to work out what would be the best thing to do.' She feigned confidence, while on the inside, her conviction was wavering at the wisdom of what they were about to do. The danger of getting arrested or the Vatican swooping in to steal their find weighed heavy on her mind. This may be her only chance.

Rohan too looked unsure.

'I know it could just be an empty room. But the only way to find out is to do what we need to, to be sure. Come on.' Harveen led the way back up the tunnel.

Fifteen minutes later, they had brought their pickaxes and shovels down. When they had dug up the approach tunnel, they had found that the pickaxes were sufficient to work their way through these ancient walls. They worked in tandem, striking away at the wall until the stones broke and dislodged, and then gently pulling them apart. They gathered the stones they had removed into a pile on the other side of the small room.

The wall behind the stones gave way quite easily and before long, they were pulling out fragments of wood and mud. Using their shovels, they built up quite a pile of rubble.

It had been at least twenty minutes since either of them had spoken. It was evident they were both nervous and trying to process the scale of what they were potentially about to find. Harveen gave the wall another strike with her shovel and it went straight through. She extracted it carefully and looked at Rohan. 'This is it. There's the chamber. Are you ready?'

Harveen could see from Rohan's face that he was very nervous.

'I don't know, I don't know … Should we really be doing this?' he appeared a bit panicked. 'We may be digging up the crypt where the body of Saint Thomas the Apostle lies along with the Ark of the Covenant. They've been here for 2,000 years! It's nerve-wracking and I can't think clearly. You decide.'

'I am scared too.'

'I'm all my family's got. It terrifies me to think I could bring ill fortune upon them or even just myself … what will they do if I'm not around? I'm not sure if it's worth it, to be honest, Veen …'

Harveen suddenly realized she was risking both their lives as she'd done once before. They made it out alive then, but this time, she didn't feel so sure. Her bravado slowly started diminishing.

'Hey, how about you go up to the car, use whatever little phone signal you get to send a message to Professor Prakash? Tell him that we have found this chamber and that I am going to take a look inside. Alone. If something happens to me, at least he will know where we are and what happened. He'll be on call to send for help, if you need it. I will take a quick look and be with you in five minutes exactly, okay?'

He considered it for a moment before he said, 'Okay'.

'See if you can take the GPR with you. Just leave the pickaxe and shovel here so I can reseal the entry. Just go up and prepare for our quick exit. Let me see what is in there.'

Rohan didn't argue and once he had safely climbed up to ground level, Harveen found herself all alone in the small chamber. On one side of her was a tunnel that led to safety, and on the other was a small hole beyond which lay a potentially glorious future for her. She stood momentarily paralyzed.

With every passing moment, the small antechamber seemed to shrink around her. As soon as she touched the opening in the wall, Harveen thought she heard a scream from the chamber beyond. She froze in place and listened carefully. There was nothing but silence.

Her excitement and fear ran circles around each other as she continued to work at the opening until finally, summoning all her courage and strength, it was wide enough for her to climb through. She stood still, permitting herself a brief respite to compose herself. A bead of sweat rolled down her spine like a cold, crooked finger.

The smell that wafted in from the room was entirely different from the air of the antechamber she was in – it was more pungent and metallic. The haunting silence of the revealed space made her senses heighten. Every little sound seemed amplified.

Harveen shone her torch into the vast room beyond the aperture. The light danced around, landing first on the object in the middle – a dark box on some type of plinth. From where she stood, it was impossible to make out any more. The hole she had made seemed to be near a corner of the room. She estimated that the room was over forty feet in length and about half as wide – larger than it had seemed in the GPR readings. In the torchlight, the walls nearest to her appeared to be made of wood carved with an intricate pattern. The walls seemed to be in remarkable condition considering how old they were, but she reminded herself to be cautious. She shone the torch across the floor. Suddenly, she let out a scream.

About ten feet ahead of her lay a human skeleton; the remains of what looked like a red robe were still draped over its body. Once she recovered from her initial shock, she knew she had to leave. It felt ominous to be staring into this chamber of death; the Void itself. She took a step backwards tentatively, bumping into a yielding surface. She spun around to find a pair of piercing blue eyes staring back at her. A tall, blond man. The trace of a cold smile on his face had swiftly rearranged itself into concern. She felt a shudder go down her spine.

79

Kurumba Bhagavathy Temple
27 July 2024
8:59 p.m.

'Wha—' Harveen stumbled backwards in shock, struggling to string a coherent sentence. The man was tall and muscular, with a pale complexion and cropped blond hair. He looked almost ghost-like in the small room.

'Oh, did I startle you, Signora Gill? I'm-a very sorry,' he began in his deep voice and thick Italian accent. 'Signor Donatello Clemente has sent me. I 'ave been here just a moment. Before I could even find a way to get your attention without alarming you, you 'ad seen me. Forgive me, signora. Where are my manners? My name is Vincenzo.' His voice was gentle, bearing no trace of a threat. 'He told me that you had agreed to his offer of letting the Vatican 'elp you?'

Harveen was confused but began to ease up despite herself. 'Y-yes … but what are you doing here? How did you find me? I don't understand—' She remembered her agreement with Don, but didn't remember telling him she would be here tonight. How on earth could he have found out?

'I'm afraid I do not know all the details, signora. I lead the field team at the Vatican. I was told to meet you here and assist you in whatever way I can. Signor Clemente had been trying to reach you on your mobile, but he said he could not.'

Harveen felt a little guilty for not returning Don's calls over the last few days.

Vincenzo continued, 'He was worried about you. He called your Professor … Prakash, if I recall correct? He agreed with 'im that I would be coming to 'elp you on behalf of the Vatican tonight. It is he who told me that you might be here tonight. So well, 'ere I am, at your service, signora. I even brought a colleague, but I asked 'im to wait outside.'

She couldn't distinguish between the dread from chancing upon the chamber and the suspicious circumstances of Vincenzo's sudden appearance, but decided to trust Professor Prakash's judgement. He must have had sound reason to trust the young man from the Vatican so much that he gave away their plans and location so precisely.

'Now, signora, please carry on with what you were doing. Don't let me distract you, sì? I'm just 'ere to 'elp.'

Vincenzo looked at the hole in the wall.

'My assistant – Rohan … he is here too. Could you go get him? He just went up a moment ago.' Harveen suddenly wished she had not sent him away.

'Ah, sì, sì, Ro'an. We met him on our way down. He seemed scared to come down with us. Might be best not to force him back here, signora, sì?' His tone made it clear he was not here to take instructions from her. 'May I ask, signora – what made you scream?'

Harveen felt very uncomfortable. She should have felt safer with this strong man from the Vatican with her. Considering he was a scholar himself, he may even have more knowledge about the Ark and how best to handle it. But something in Vincenzo's cold stare scared her. If only she could call Don to verify this man's backstory. But if he were here right now like he had wanted, he would surely have taken over.

'*Dottoresa* (Doctor)?' Vincenzo pushed.

'I just saw a box on a plinth in the middle of the room. I can't make out what it is from here. There is also at least one skeleton on the floor just there, in front of us. I just … did not expect it so I got scared …' she said, revealing no more than what would meet his eye in the torchlight. His expression remained unchanged.

'Shall we take a closer look, signora?' he asked calmly.

Harveen hesitated for a moment, but her own desire to see what lay in the chamber was insatiable.

'Yes, of course. I should go in first. Why don't you stay here for now? We don't know what we could find in there.'

He extended his hand to help Harveen through the hole. As she climbed through and entered the chamber beyond, her red sari posed a minor obstruction. As soon as her bare feet landed on the soft ground on the other side, she was struck by the damp, foetid stench of the chamber. She instinctively put her hand over her nose and mouth. Her stomach churned but she focused her mind to stop herself from vomiting. She grabbed a wall for support with her other hand to brace herself, closing her eyes and breathing slowly. In a few moments, the nausea subsided and Harveen looked back to see Vincenzo peering at her through the hole. She felt uncomfortably tense under his piercing gaze once more.

Harveen returned her attention to the room. The beam of her torch barely seem to make a difference, as if the room was absorbing the light.

'Signora, 'ere, take this,' said Vincenzo from behind her. He had managed to light one of the ancient torches and the light was a lot better. Harveen took it, considering for a moment how it could also be used as a weapon. She could still only make out darkness beyond the plinth. The floor seemed like it had originally been made of wood and the damp ground underneath had rotted away over the years. With every step, it disintegrated into the soil. She carefully walked in a straight line towards the plinth. To her horror, she could see multiple skeletons lying about the room. She passed eight or nine of them, all wearing tattered red robes. She saw the silver blade of a sword wrapped in the bony fingers of one and noticed that the others were armed too. It appeared that they had all been soldiers who had perished and come to be entombed in this room for some reason.

Harveen felt her side where copies of the note of warning written by Jayesh of Muziris sat snug in the pocket of her shorts. A line from the ancient document flashed in her memory: 'I would implore you to let it rest here for eternity.'

Harveen was now stood in front of the plinth. It too was made of wood and was about three feet high. On top of it sat a box, about four feet long and less than three feet high, partially covered with leather which had decayed and tattered over time. Through the gaps, she could see that the box underneath was made entirely of gold. On top of the lid were two beautifully crafted cherubim facing each other, their wings stretched out such that they touched in the middle. Along both flanks of the box were wooden poles extending beyond it by several feet on either side. She could see that the poles passed through gold rings attached to the side of the box.

That's when she knew she was looking at the Ark of the Covenant.

She fell to her knees instinctively, her head bowed. At first, she could not bring herself to look at the Ark. She drew up her sari over her head in reverence and remained looking at the ground for several minutes. It was the greatest archaeological discovery in history, and yet …

She couldn't bring herself to displace it from where it sat. She felt the urge to leave it here and seal up the chamber.

That's when Vincenzo's deep voice shook her out of her trance.

'Signora? Are you alright, signora? What do you see?'

Harveen looked up slowly. The Ark looked out of place in its surroundings and at first, she could not quite work out why it looked wrong. Then it struck her. The room, the leather covers, the floor and everything around her had been subjected to batterings of time as one would expect. But the Ark – it looked brand new. The gold flanks of the box gleamed in the torchlight as if they had recently been polished.

It appeared to pulsate as it rested on the plinth. Harveen was likely imagining this, her mind projecting all the misery she knew the relic had inflicted in the past onto the object before her, imbuing it with an evil life-force of some kind. There was no doubt that the Ark had its own dark gravity, seeming to create a vacuum around itself. The plinth below displayed a meshed array of spider webs within the original latticed patterns. As she waved the flame from her torch to get rid of them, a small creature scuttled out from under it and away into the darkness. She followed the rodent's path. It led her to the grotesque remains of a skeleton lying next to the Ark, a hand still resting on the bottom of the relic, and the body slumped across the plinth. Under its other arm was a book.

The clothing on this one were not the same as the others. It seemed to originally have been clad in white robes and these seemed to be in much better condition too. The original embroidery was still visible in parts. Harveen crouched down to take a closer look at the book in its bony grasp. Only a little larger than a normal paperback, it had a dark cover. She had recently held an almost identical book in her hand.

The Gospel of St Thomas!

This meant that these were possibly his remains.

'Well done, Signora Gill. Well done!' The words came from Vincenzo, who was now towering over her, adding his own flashlight beam to her torch's flickering glow, his eyes firmly focused on the book.

'I … I don't know what this is …' Harveen lied. If he had arrived to snatch the Ark away from her, perhaps she could get away with just the book. She turned to him, 'You think maybe I could—' She broke off suddenly.

Vincenzo was pointing a small gun directly at her.

80

Muciripattanam
AD 71

The first screams that escaped the underground room pierced through the silence, jolting Jayesh from his tormented thoughts. He had been sitting on a pew a few yards from the new stairway, which led into what was to become the new Tabernacle. The yells of horror had erupted from the bowels of that very chamber.

Jayesh rushed to see what had happened. Just as he reached the bottom of the stairs, he saw that one of his soldiers was trying to pry open the Ark, his face frozen in a twisted, sickening grimace, as he fell backwards. In a moment, his red robes fell in a heap on the floor. Two more of his soldiers' bodies were lying motionless at one end of the room. One looked like he had been trying to run away when he fell, and was lying at the far end of the room. Anand, the architect, too seemed to have perished. He was lying on the ground, clutching the covers which had concealed the Ark.

Jayesh looked up to see the Ark of the Covenant completely exposed. It stood proudly on the beautiful wooden plinth and, in that moment, he believed it was the most beautiful thing he had ever seen. The Ark itself was made entirely of gold and even in the dim light, it shone as if it had its own luminescence. It was about four feet in length and less than three feet high, much smaller than Jayesh had imagined. The side facing him had eight square panels in two groups of four, which formed an ornate moulding. Rounded gold legs on each corner extended about two inches from the bottom of the chest. What he could not take his eyes off was the lid. There were two gold sculptures of two winged creatures facing each other, stretching their wings that were touching in the middle. The vacant space between the touching wings created the impression of a seat.

Jayesh was entranced. It was only when Thomas arrived and shook him that he realized what was happening.

'What have you done? What have you done?!' repeated St Thomas frantically, yanking his arm. 'Why have you brought this here? This was not the way!'

Jayesh was still in shock. Another soldier came down the stairs.

'No!' Thomas shouted at the soldier. 'Don't enter! Wait there.'

'I think … they tried to open it …' Jayesh was still hypnotized by the sight of the Ark and struggled to take his eyes off it.

'Stop anyone else from coming in here,' shouted St Thomas. 'Go! Now!'

It took all of Jayesh's concentration to avert his eyes from the Ark and rush back up the stairs. As St Thomas approached it, Jayesh paused for a moment and watched him pulled the covers back over the chest. He then took a book out from under his arm and held it in one hand whilst kneeling beside the Ark, his head bowed. He stretched out his other arm towards the relic as two more soldiers approached the stairs.

'Stop!' screamed Jayesh, finally free from his trance. 'No one is to go down these stairs! You stand guard here.' As he said these words, Jayesh heard a long, haunting scream from the chamber below.

The next day, only Jayesh was courageous enough to descend the stairs into the belly of the large underground room. One that would have housed the Tabernacle and the most magnificent collection of Christian artefacts collected from all around the world. This would have been his crowning achievement, his lifelong ambition to immortalize the Muciripattanam name realized. He was certain that the collection would have attracted millions of Judaists, in particular, possibly even becoming a haven for them after their homeland had been destroyed.

He had spent the previous night haunted by the warnings of Berenice, the advice of his departed friend Vikesh, the dreams Paavi had seen and Thomas's final death scream. He realized his own faults too late. His own ambition had been blinding and somewhere along the way, his mission had changed from building Muciripattanam into a great trading hub to protecting the Ark at all costs. He was now left to pay the price of his avarice.

He was nervous as he walked down the stairs once again. His men confirmed that no one had entered the chamber since the previous day. There was no longer a need to post guards at the entrance – there was nothing left to protect. The news and terror of the previous days' events had travelled far and wide, and no man dared to go near the buildings anymore.

The intricately carved wooden platform in the centre of the room had been constructed specially to display the Ark of the Covenant: the sacred chest containing the original stone tablets that Moses had brought down from Mount Sinai, created by their God himself with the Ten Commandments engraved into them. The latticed side panels were designed to allow light to pass through the plinth so as to create the illusion that the Ark was levitating. There was space around this platform for worshippers to gather and pay obeisance.

But now, the chamber was a tomb strewn with the bodies of his men. Their blood which had doused the ground the previous day had not yet dried and Jayesh could feel his feet sticking to the floor, as if desperate to avenge their deaths by taking him as their victim. The distinct metallic smell had intensified in the heat of the morning.

The Ark stood proudly on the platform, partially covered with the leather sheets that St Thomas had managed to throw over it. Its dark maleficence was still tangible, even from underneath the heavy covers. Jayesh felt the weight of grief and responsibility churning within him, along with the unsavoury disappointment that was eating away at him.

The walls were lined with beautifully carved wooden panels, but all the other great plans Jayesh had for the grand chamber had now shattered, never to be fulfilled. He had forced himself to come down here today to pay his due respects to the dead and allow himself to feel the full weight of his guilt. He could not bring himself to believe that Thomas, the brother of Jesus Christ, had also perished by the hand of his own God. But then he noticed that his body lay closest to the Ark. His face was twisted in a frightening grimace, capturing his last moments spent in excruciating pain before the merciful release of death. His arm still outstretched in a final gesture begging for mercy.

Jayesh had come down here this day to order his men to retrieve the bodies so their final rites could be performed, but not one man would obey. They were terrified at the prospect of going into the chamber, lest the curse befall them. Jayesh had no choice but to abandon his mission. As he ascended the steps, dejected, he realized that the curse of the Ark had not spared him, either – his dreams and his friends, he had lost it all. He was now destined to spend his remaining life trying to make amends.

81

Kurumba Bhagavathy Temple
27 July 2024
9:06 p.m.

'Fantastico!' said Vincenzo, almost to himself. He looked at Harveen, his admiration for her intelligence evident in his tone. He was standing about four feet away from her and his gun was held nonchalantly at waist height, pointed directly at her. 'The Vatican 'ave known about the Apostle Thomas for a very long time. We 'ave done good job blurring that part of 'istory ...' His eyes kept drifting towards the Ark of the Covenant. 'But ... è impossibile. This shouldn't be here ... It sank off the Myos Hormos coast! How did it get 'ere? Oh no, no ... this is a big problem for us.'

Harveen stared at Vincenzo. He clearly knew how to handle a gun and even without it, there was no way she could hope to win in a fight against him. 'Rohan will come looking for me anytime now. You can't just get away with killing me down here,' she said desperately, trying hard to keep the tremor out of her voice whilst hoping she was wrong and Rohan didn't intend to come. She hoped he was already making his way home. There seemed to be no escape for her.

At that moment, another man came into the chamber. He was slightly shorter than Vincenzo but much burlier. His neck seemed indistinguishable from the rest of his head. His physique almost bulged through his jacket – he was well-built and powerful, resembling a bodybuilder more than a researcher. His dark hair was slicked back neatly, and his small, beady eyes scanned the room. Harveen recognized him immediately as the driver of the silver car. It was all connected after all!

'Signora, meet Paulo. 'e 'as been with me since I was in Rome. Paulo, this is Dr 'arveen Gill, whom I told you about.'

Harveen couldn't hold back and blurted, 'You killed her! You killed Dr Gupta!'

Vincenzo looked at Paulo, confused.

'I saw you. You picked her up that day in your silver car. I've told the police about you. They know your plate and even have your description. They will find you. You will not get away with it!'

'*Idiota*!' Vincenzo lashed out at Paulo. 'And what did you do to the other one?'

A smile spread across Paulo's face. Harveen realized they were talking about Rohan.

'Ah, her little friend. Oh, that was easy … he was standing by his car when I found him. I grabbed hold of him but before I could finish him off, the little rat managed to scream for help – I thought she may have heard it.'

Harveen remembered now – she did hear the scream when she working her way through the opening. She had been stupid not to realize it was Rohan. She could have saved him! She should have rushed to his aid when she heard him scream. He had come tonight only because she had persuaded him, and now because of her impetuous desire to uncover the Ark, his worst fears had come to pass. Her heart sank to her stomach and sobs tugged at her throat. She needed to buy herself time to think up a way of getting out of here alive.

'What are you planning to do with me?' she asked him, trying to delay her inevitable end for a bit longer.

'Take a guess!' Vincenzo sneered, 'We will kill you, signora. Don't you want to be buried next to your precious findings? The ones you 'ave spent so many months searching?' He was enjoying the moment. A sadistic grin spread across his face. 'Surely, you know no one can know about this, sì? *Dio mio* (My God)! Can you imagine if the world found out that Our Lord and Saviour Jesus Christ had a brother? *Che pazzo* (How crazy that would be)! No, no. We're going to take the Ark of the Covenant back to Vatican. We will, of course, destroy this little tunnel of yours. Then we will speak with your Archaeology Department and settle the matter once and for all. *Capiche* (Do you understand)?'

'Look, I know your boss – Don. Let me speak with him, please. He knows me and wanted to be part of this. Let me at least talk to him once!'

Vincenzo started laughing. 'Ha! Whatever for, signora? What do you want? To teach the Vatican about the Ark of the Covenant?' He exchanged a few words in Italian with Paulo after which the bigger man left. 'Well, this 'as been most enjoyable, Signora, but I'm afraid we 'ave work to do … Let us say our goodbyes while Paulo sets up the explosives. My men are coming to clear out the chamber, don't worry. Your friend and you will get to lie 'ere together in death. You will like that, sì?' He was clearly enjoying watching Harveen in a helpless state.

But a vague plan was taking seed in her mind. 'Please,' she begged, getting to her knees. 'If you are going to kill me, at least let me look inside the Ark to know what's inside.' She glanced up at him.

If the legends were true, the very act of removing the covers may be enough to kill them both and hopefully, the other big thug as well. If she was going down, she was going to take them both with her. Paulo was out of sight, but Harveen could hear him moving around in the antechamber through which they had entered. He was probably close enough.

Vincenzo smiled. 'Is that all, *mio caro* (my darling)? Why not? Come, 'ave a look. Consider it your dying wish granted.' He gestured towards the Ark with his gun. Harveen stood up carefully and took a tentative step in that direction. She carefully reached for the first cover, making sure not to come in contact with the surface of the Ark itself, and slid it off. As she did so, another cover dropped away, revealing the entire lid and the two sides closest to them. Even in the gloomy light, the Ark gleamed and pulsed as if with some unknowable energy. She had been bracing herself this moment, but nothing happened. She stole a glance at Vincenzo; he too seemed unmoved.

Harveen lifted her hand towards the Ark, hoping Vincenzo was not as well read on its deadly history as she had become over the last few weeks. She was confident he would want to impress his boss, Don, and this may be the only opportunity for her. She paused inches away from the Ark's lid.

'Maybe ... you should open it?' she suggested to Vincenzo. 'It's been here for 2,000 years ... you work at the Vatican – don't you want to know?'

For the first time, his calm demeanour slipped. 'Step away!' he sneered. 'I'll open it myself! Get back!' Harveen slinked back into the darkness, gently setting her torch down, and continued to step further away softly, once she was sure he wasn't looking. With her hands, she shielded her eyes from what may be revealed from within the Ark.

Vincenzo slipped his gun into his pocket, approached the relic, pointing his flashlight steadily at it. He was about to open the Ark of the Covenant.

82

Muciripattanam
AD 71

'My love, it's your brother … h-he died … and it is all my fault.' Jayesh had been dreading this moment since he had set foot in Muziris. He was sitting alone with Paavi outside their house on the hillside. He hadn't had the courage to step inside yet. This was the same place where he had stood as a boy, wondering what lay beyond the horizon. He wished that he could reach back into time and tell his younger self to abandon those dreams as they would only lead to misery. 'You had warned me … you had told me about your dreams … your visions. They all came true, Paavi. We were struck by lightning and the rear of our ship burnt off and fell into the seas. We would all have died together if not for the front part of the ship enduring and managing to stay afloat somehow. It was your prayers …' He held Paavi tight as she sobbed and shook. Her tears were tearing him apart. He had overcome the biggest challenges by leaning on one constant – the happiness of his wife and children.

'Are you sure he is dead? What if he survived?' she asked through her tears, searching his face hopefully.

'I'm sure he is dead,' he decided to spare her the details of

Servius's soldiers that had hunted them down. Her heart was broken again.

'Did you find his body? You brought him home, didn't you, Jayesh?'

'No ...'

For the first time, the look in her eyes turned from sadness to anger.

'No? You just left my brother there?'

'His body fell into the stormy sea – there was no way for anyone to retrieve it, Paavi. You must understand I'd have done anything to bring him back.'

'You left him?' she screamed. 'I warned you and you didn't listen and you just let him die! I wish you had died with him!' She threw her balled-up fists at his chest as she spoke, but he gathered her into a tight hug. He felt her tears drench him.

'Everything I have done is just ... wrong. I wanted to make my family proud. I wanted to make my father proud. I wanted to build a mighty kingdom to show everyone what I could do. How could I have been so blind? I never stopped to consider what I would do if things didn't work out ... and now my best friend in the world is dead ...'

'You've killed him! How could you have left his body and only saved yourself!'

'I will make it up to you – to every one of you. Where is father? Is he on his bed? I must go and apologize to him. I know we have not spoken in many months but I will fall at his feet and then—'

Paavi's face hardened.

'What's wrong, Paavi? Why do you look at me so? What happened?'

'Appa passed away while you were in Rome, Jayesh. He

caught a fever and it would not leave him. He was delirious in his final moments and asked for you. He wanted to tell you not to live your life as he had – consumed by ambition and obstinacy.'

Tears streamed down Jayesh's face. He felt like a cursed man – the Ark had not spared him after all. From his best friend to his men and now his father too. He had wrought destruction upon his entire world, blinded by his greed.

83

Kurumba Bhagavathy Temple
27 July 2024
10:23 p.m.

A sudden scream pierced the air and sent a chill down Harveen's spine. She peeked through her fingers at the scene and saw Vincenzo's hand somehow affixed to the Ark, as he yelled in agony, trying hard to detach it. With a monumental effort, he managed to wrench his hand away and landed on the floor some distance away from the Ark. He crouched on his knees, still screaming, holding his hand up near his face. Harveen knew this was her only chance.

She rushed towards him, kicking him hard under his chin. The blow landed perfectly, and she heard a crunch as his teeth snapped together, sending him sprawling across the floor. At the same moment, she saw a flashlight beam through the opening, some twenty feet away. A gunshot added to the cacophony of pained screams, filling the chamber. Vincenzo continued to writhe on the damp ground. His torch was on the floor by the Ark, the dim glow slowly dying out and drowning the chamber in darkness. Paulo was shouting from outside, listening occasionally for Vincenzo's voice to try and make sense of the situation. But there was no answer. Vincenzo's pained cries seemed to be weakening.

Harveen lunged at the opportunity. She hastily pulled out the wooden pole lodged into the rings on one side of the Ark and sprinted towards the opening, aiming her weapon at Paulo. She was about ten feet away when Paulo's flashlight shone directly at her, illuminating the skeleton of the Muziris soldier in her path. She dodged it, just as Paulo fired at her again. Her right arm was jolted backward, followed by a burning sensation. The bullet had found its mark. She raged on towards the large Italian, who was now only five feet away, his frame silhouetted quite clearly.

Reminded of her pole vaulting days at school, Harveen kept the pole level and aimed at the Paulo's chest. She gripped it as tightly as she could to ram it into him with the maximum force possible. Just as she was about to strike, the torchlight lit up her target's features.

The look of shock on Paulo's face would stay with her for years to come. He was prepared to take the kill-shot from close range. But he was not prepared to be met by the pole first, as Harveen came charging towards him like a primordial warrior. He didn't register what was happening until the very last moment and though he tried to dodge out of its path, the pole still managed to catch him just below his chin. There was a wet thud as it struck him in the neck. Paulo's hands flew to where he'd been hit as he crumpled to the floor. A shot left his gun but the bullet harmlessly hit the ceiling. Harveen's adrenaline-fuelled assault had worked. Her legs burned as she crashed to the ground.

She willed herself up again, leaning into the opening, still holding the pole, shaking. She could see Paulo lying on his back, holding his neck. Blood gurgled out of his mouth and his legs thrashed about like an insect stuck on its back. She knew she needed to strike him again but could not bring herself to do it. This was the man who had killed Penny Gupta – and now Rohan. She dropped the pole and climbed through the opening. She retrieved Paulo's gun and shone his flashlight back through the gap to check if Vincenzo lay where she had left him and found him on the floor, his screaming ceased. He lay perfectly still. She turned the flashlight towards Paulo. His head was now lying in a small pool of blood. The impact from the pole had caused his throat to collapse in on one side and turned a deep purple. Blood was still trickling from his mouth. His eyes were rolling around unfocused in their sockets. Suddenly, she felt a pang of remorse. Had she just killed a man? She had risked everything to open this chamber and added two more men to the tally of corpses strewn about it. What other havoc was yet to unfold?

Gathering herself, she noticed the line of explosives set up around the entrance to the chamber and at the exit to the tunnel that led up to the surface. They were attached to a timer that had a digital display reading '03:00'. Beside it were some green and red buttons. As Harveen crouched down to take a closer look, a huge blow landed on the side of her head, knocking her to the ground. As she clutched her head on reflex, she looked back to see that Paulo was unsteadily holding a second large rock above his head. He was ready to hurl it at her. Harveen braced herself for the killing blow.

84

Muciripattanam
AD 71

'The power of the Ark is devastating. We must do what we can to protect everyone else from it. Destroy the church so no pilgrims or treasure hunters come seeking the cursed object. Most other people who know of its location are now dead,' Jayesh said morosely.

'I have already instructed men to seal the entry to the staircase leading into the room,' said Nannan, referring to the grisly tomb which was to be the new Tabernacle. 'Destroying the buildings aboveground won't be hard. They're sealing the entrance with granite so no one can enter, even if they find it by chance.'

And just like that, they pronounced the death sentence of the magnificent church which had taken more than five years to build.

'The Ark must, one day, be returned to its rightful home in Jerusalem. The Temple of Jerusalem must be rebuilt around it so that the power of the Ark may be respected and guarded in its rightful place – just as their God intended,' Jayesh declared.

'But how do we do that?' asked Nannan.

'Nannan, it would take a more learned and wise man than myself to accomplish this task, in fact to even envisage such a feat. We must hide the Ark's current resting place. The risk of people with nefarious intentions seeking it for its power is too great. The Romans know we have it, as do the Egyptians and possibly some of Servius's surviving soldiers.'

Jayesh decided they would build a well deep into the ground adjacent to the underground room that housed the Ark. The stone well took several weeks to excavate. Whilst his men laboured, Jayesh had ample time to consider the best way to warn anyone who came seeking the Ark in the future. He wrote out a note carefully by hand, using a clear script, and provided as candid an account of his encounter with the sacred object as he could muster. As soon as the well was completed, Jayesh placed his note in a cavity in its wall, and sealed it, some twenty feet below ground level. The note was enclosed in a wooden box bearing the 'M' monogram on its lid. Once he had placed it in the small alcove, he etched one of the sealing stones with the same distinctive 'M' so it was easy to catch notice of. Once satisfied, he had his men seal the cavity as well as they could and fill the rest of it up so it was inaccessible.

Jayesh's next task was to ensure that the site remained protected so as to avoid any fear of the well's desecration. He created a perimeter of over ten acres and allotted the entire plot to the building of a temple to Lord Shiva, the destroyer of evil. He ordered for a magnificent shrine to be built and endowed the temple with significant wealth so that it could welcome all kinds of visitors to eat and pray at the temple for at least a hundred years. He believed that if the shrine was sacred to the people of Muciripattanam, protecting the well in its grounds from intervention would be a lot easier for long after he was gone.

As he stood back, envisioning his plans coming to life, Jayesh said a heartfelt prayer beseeching that if ever the room that held the Ark of the Covenant was opened again, the ones who came upon it would look favourably on his actions and its wrath would not befall anyone else.

85

Kurumba Bhagavathy Temple
27 July 2024
10:29 p.m.

It felt as if the next few moments went by in slow motion. Harveen looked at Paulo, ready to strike, when suddenly, she heard a thud beside him. She found Don standing there, holding a small black gun. Don looked around the chamber. He seemed to be assessing the situation. Catching sight of Harveen, he pointed his gun directly at her. As their eyes met, she finally understood. He had been behind everything: from Penny's murder to this. She saw Paulo grinning at her. Suddenly, half of Paulo's face disintegrated, the hot, wet splash of his blood hitting her face. He stared at her for a moment with one lifeless eye before toppling forward. Behind him stood Don, a small wisp of smoke emanating from his gun.

'Harveen, are you okay? You're bleeding!' he said, rushing to her aid. She flinched and felt around for something – anything – to defend herself with. Her head was spinning. She had just seen him aiming his gun at her.

'I'm sorry,' his voice echoed in her ears, 'this was not my doing. I rushed here as soon as I could. I found out about the Vatican's plans – wait, where's the other guy?' He looked around, his gun at the ready in his hand as his eyes scanned the scene.

'He's ... dead,' she managed between sharp breaths.

'Where is he? He is a trained assassin; he won't go down so easy. We need to be sure.' Harveen noticed that he was wearing military fatigues. She gestured towards the chamber and in an instant, he jumped through the gap and disappeared out of sight.

She crawled towards the explosives, deciding she would set them off and find her way back to the surface. If she managed to get away, she could explain everything to the police – Inspector Kumar must still be expecting her. She looked at the green button on the timer. It was the right choice, wasn't it? she wondered. But what about the Ark of the Covenant or the last remains of the brother of Jesus Christ? The sharp pain from the bullet wound in her arm was becoming unbearable. She reached out for the only lit torch she could see and pointed it towards the chamber.

Don was crouched beside Vincenzo when the light shone on him. He looked up at Harveen. 'He's dead alright. But ... how did this happen?' He noticed the frightened look on her face and raised his arms to indicate that he was harmless. 'Signora, you have to trust me. I have no intention of harming you. I swear this was not me. Here, you can take my gun. I just need to understand what happened.' With that, Don used his left hand to hold the gun by its barrel and slid it across the chamber. It stopped just a couple of feet short of the opening. 'Please,' he said, 'Tell me what happened.'

He walking slowly towards her across the chamber, his arms still aloft in surrender.

Harveen wasted no time in stepping back into the chamber and picking up the gun. It felt cold to the touch.

'Stop! Don't come anywhere near me! Stay there!' she was surprised at the firmness in her own voice, pointing the gun at Don with one hand and the torch in the other.

Don stopped in his tracks, ten feet away from her.

'Signora, I don't mean to hurt you. I just need to know how this man died. His hand is charred but he has no other wounds – I have to know.'

'The Ark … it … it seems to be cursed. The legends … they're true. He tried to open it and as soon as he touched it … he started screaming in pain and then he just … fell dead.'

Don shut his eyes. 'I was afraid something like this might happen. There are many accounts of the power of the Ark, but there was no way we could be sure they were true—'

'They killed Rohan – you! You killed Rohan!' She was gripping her wounded arm as she looked at Don with disgust.

'Your assistant? He's not dead, signora. I found him by the car – he had a deep wound on his head and had lost some blood, so he'd fallen unconscious. I bandaged it up for the time being – there was a first-aid kit in your car, thankfully. His pulse is weak, but I think he'll be fine – we do need to get him to a hospital quickly, though. And you, too.'

'Wait, he's alive? Really?'

'Yes, but he needs a doctor. As do you. We need to move quickly. Can you take care of that while I clean up this mess? We'll worry about handling it later, once your friend is out of danger. Now go, go, go.'

'But … these bodies? What about the Ark?'

'Signora, you must leave. Let me figure this out. I have a team of people waiting for my instructions. We'll handle the situation – you need to get your friend help or you'll lose him. I promise that when you come back, the artefacts will still be here. We will clean up everything else, no one is going to touch the Ark.'

Harveen looked across at the Ark. It seemed to be drawing her in. She still had the gun and Don was defenceless. He had betrayed her before – was this her opportunity for vengeance? Could he really be trusted to watch over her career's most precious discovery? She could kill Don and walk away with the prize that would win her glory and clear her name.

Suddenly, the image of Rohan flashed in her mind. 'You won't move anything? You promise?' she asked.

'Just go. Now. There's no time to argue – he is in a really bad way. Go now!' he urged her. He seemed sincere and she considered how he could have killed her just as easily when he had arrived. The wound in her arm jolted her into action. She nodded at him and rushed out of the tunnel, over to Rohan's car. His body lay slumped in the passenger seat. He wasn't moving at all, or showing any signs of life. There was blood all over his face.

Harveen jumped into the driver's seat, and touched him softly. 'Rohan … hey, Ro, can you hear me?' There was no reply. She held her breath as she felt for a pulse – it was very weak, but steady. She sighed with relief, the lump in her throat dissolving into tears. She checked if his wound was appropriately dressed – it was, just as Don had said.

She found the first-aid kit at Rohan's feet and used a bandage to stem the flow of blood from her own head. She felt woozy as the adrenaline subsided, and her right arm began to throb. A heavy weakness overcame her, forcing her to examine the injury before she could drive them to the hospital. Blood was running down her arm in little streams and her sari was soaked. The bullet had skated close enough to cause a deep injury and she strained her eyes as she looked for a cloth in the first-aid kit. She used her teeth to tie it around her arm tightly. She breathed and waited for her head to stop spinning and then slammed down the pedal.

She managed to drive them all the way to the emergency department of the Kodungallur Government Hospital, halting abruptly in front of the entrance as she finally lost consciousness, her head hitting the wheel. The last thing she heard was distant shouting: 'Excuse me, madam! You can't park here! Excuse me, hello?'

86

Muciripattanam
AD 74

Muciripattanam sat on the southwest shoreline of mainland India. It was remarkable for two reasons: firstly, being in the wettest part of the country made its soil very fertile for growing spices, especially pepper. Secondly, it was once able to enjoy the status of being the greatest trading port in Asia. For over fifty years, it had been the main trading hub for the empires of Rome, Egypt and China to conduct their business with India.

The great warehouses that had been built along the beautiful coastline contained all manner of goods from around the country, gathered there by the great traders of Muciripattanam, who sold them to the men who came aboard merchant ships that would dock in the port area. Goods were stamped with the distinctive red 'M' of Muciripattanam, and loaded up onto the huge vessels, ready to sail. Majestic elephants, fierce tigers and playful monkeys would sail alongside nard, ivory, beads, scent, spices, jewellery, silks and, of course, pepper, to the faraway lands.

It had been a bustling and vibrant place at the time, a popular destination for visiting merchants. The hospitality of the locals was almost as legendary as the goods available to purchase. Nowhere else in the world did the sweet Roman wine flow so freely, the fresh fruits and vegetables be so colourful and bursting with flavour, and the spicy food and rice quite so delicious. From the crowds of merchants emanated a mix of many tongues, as they enjoyed the wonders of the peaceful coastline or made pilgrimages to the many temples of various faiths housed in the wondrous town.

The Roman influence was visible everywhere in Muciripattanam – a fort that stood right next to the great Temple of Augustus; Roman soldiers in the crowd, and the marketplace flowing with wares their merchants sought. But unlike Rome, Muciripattanam had been a secular haven for people from all religions to gather and be treated with respect. Even a Jewish community had burgeoned around St Thomas and his new church in the later years of the town's glory.

But the great storms of AD 71 decimated the work of fifty years in just a little over two days. Out of nowhere, on a calm and sunny afternoon, the tranquil blue skies suddenly turned black. A storm crashed onto the shoreline, moving at a frightening pace as if enraged. It was fierce enough to rip up entire buildings and hurl them to the ground within moments. The piers where several ships could dock were swept away by the sea as if they were mere twigs; the great warehouses ripped apart and cast aside. The arrival of the great ship *Vasudha* into the crumbling port amidst the horror had barely been noticed as she crashed onto the shore.

Once the storm had passed, the people of Muciripattanam had still not lost heart. They were sure their town would be rebuilt as a bigger and even more impressive destination. Their great leader had, after all, overcome any obstacle that was placed in his path. The town's traders were the greatest in all of India and had immense wealth.

But where was Jayesh?

Some even believed that he had not survived the wrath of the mighty storm on that fateful day. And thus, the Port of Muziris was never rebuilt. In just a few years, it was transformed into the inconspicuous village of its early days – a mere shadow of its former glory remained. The Romans took their interests and purses elsewhere, to other ports along the same coastline that sold the goods they were after. Their fort in Muciripattanam was swiftly abandoned as the town's fortunes dwindled. The great Temple of Augustus was stripped bare of its valuable materials and repurposed into other edifices elsewhere. The wealthy traders came no more and the glorious 'Muziris' was wiped from the memory of the world as swiftly as it had appeared.

87

Kodungallur Government Hospital
29 July 2024

Harveen slowly came to. It took her several moments to understand where she was. Her vision was blurry and her head was spinning. The unmistakable smell of phenyl flooded her nostrils as her sleepy brain slowly started back up – she was in a hospital. She had made it, after all. She was alone – in a private room. The monitor beside her bed was blank and apart from a splitting headache, she did not feel pain anywhere else in her body. The room was small, with bright sunlight streaking through the gaps between the dark green curtains covering the small window on one wall. The bed was against another wall, a single chair on one side. On its other side was a small table.

It was hot inside. Harveen slowly moved her arms and legs. They felt stiff, but she didn't feel any pain except in the upper part of her right arm, which still throbbed. She raised her hand to feel some sort of dressing or bandage on her forehead. Then she slowly traced it with her finger – it ran from above her right eyebrow to about an inch past her hairline. There was another bandage around her right arm. Two plastic bags hung from a pole next to her bed, dripping fluid into an IV connected to her left arm. One contained red liquid, while the other, a clear liquid.

She noticed a small vase sitting on the table beside her bed. It had fresh flowers in it. Placed next to it were her iPhone and watch. She was just about to reach for her phone when the door opened gently. A doctor stepped in. He seemed very young, his complexion fresh and his thick black hair spiked up. Following right behind him was her boss, Professor Prakash.

'Hello!' the doctor chirped as he came over to examine her. Professor Prakash quietly drifted to the corner of the room, looking sombre.

'I am Dr Iyer. Good to see that you are awake,' he continued. 'How are you feeling?'

'Groggy,' Harveen answered honestly.

'Quite understandable. You had quite the wound on your head, Miss Gill.' He was looking over her charts and then came closer to examine her head. 'Quite the bump, indeed. Hmm ...' He then took her arm and checked her vitals. 'The wound in your arm was quite deep, but fortunately, it has not caused any lasting damage.'

'Wait, Rohan – oh my god, where is Rohan? Is he okay?' Harveen suddenly blurted out, the recent events slowly coming back to her. Her eyes darted questioningly from the doctor to Professor Prakash. 'Please ... is he alright?'

'He will be, I believe,' Prakash responded quietly. 'He was quite badly injured in your little adventure and we're lucky he's still with us.' His tone was severe and he made no effort to mask his disappointment in her. Yet his news made Harveen smile and she sighed deeply with relief. She allowed the doctor to resume his examinations and waited for him to pronounce his findings.

'You have a concussion. You received quite a blow to your head – we had to put in eleven stitches to seal up the gash and although it will heal, I am afraid the scar might remain visible.' As he spoke, he scribbled a few notes on the clipboard that hung at the foot of her bed. 'You lost quite a lot of blood, so we're transfusing some, as you may have noticed. The nurse will be here shortly with more painkillers. All you have to do is rest. I will come back in the morning. If there are no complications, we should be able to discharge you tomorrow itself. Is there anyone you would like us to call? I am afraid you were unconscious when you came in and we couldn't find any emergency contacts or identification on you, so we have not been able to contact your family.'

'I informed her family – they should be here soon. Thank you, doctor.' Professor Prakash informed him curtly and dismissed him. The doctor looked at him for a moment, grunted his acknowledgement and quietly left the room.

Harveen and Prakash looked at each other in tense silence. He finally spoke, 'I'm relieved that you are okay. I was very worried when I first saw you here – the injuries looked severe. But obviously, I am very disappointed in the way you handled the situation. You said nothing to me about how closely you were working with the team from the Vatican all this time. Have you no regard for protocol, Harveen?'

She felt confused. Her headache was making it hard to concentrate. 'I'm sorry, Professor, but I don't understand—'

'Yet again, you foolishly ventured into an unstable location on a treasure hunt without my permission. You knew that the site was dangerous and even so, you put both yourself and Rohan in grave danger. I know that you were very excited by the prospect of what could have been inside the temple, but you should have shown better judgement. We spoke about it in clear terms. If it wasn't for the team from the Vatican, you would have both been killed for sure.'

Harveen hung her head in shame, knowing he was well within his rights to phrase his disappointment in the harsh terms of his choosing.

'I'm sorry, Professor. May I ask … what happened to the Ark?' she asked, fearing the worst.

'What a shame that it was not there. I just came from the site. It is clear that the plinth there was built to hold it but Mr Clemente showed me the documents which state in no uncertain terms that it sank along with the ship that was to carry it to India.'

'Wait, you've been to the site? You saw the room? But … the dead …' Harveen's mind was struggling to keep up.

'Yes, fascinating. They look like they could easily be from the first century. We even found the Gospel of St Thomas!' The scholar in him couldn't conceal his excitement. 'You have made the biggest finds in a century, I must say, Harveen. Mr Clemente explained that they agreed to the terms you negotiated, so we would be able to keep everything we found on the site, as long as we allow his team to work with us. It all belongs to our museum. That deserves many congratulations. I'm proud, Harveen.'

She smiled and asked, 'And Mr Clemente … is he still there?'

At that moment, Inspector Kumar entered the room.

'I thought I had made it clear that no one was to speak with her until I arrived,' he said without preamble.

'Right. I am sorry, Inspector,' Prakash replied. 'I'll wait outside.'

Once they were alone, Kumar turned to Harveen and said, 'I hope you're feeling better, Harveen. We have a lot to discuss. Shall we?'

He pulled out his notebook from his pocket.

88

Muciripattanam
AD 74

There were two hillsides on the outer edges of Muciripattanam. On the larger one, to the east, was the plot of land that belonged to Jayesh. His family had owned it for five generations and although it was less fertile than the land in the valleys below, it was the origin of one of the largest trading empires known to the world. Once an unassuming house, Jayesh's family farm had now grown to comprise a collection of large buildings – the centre of Jayesh's business empire. He had been married at the age of seventeen and blessed with four sons, all of whom worked with him. He was rarely ever found at home, spending long stretches travelling around the world. Even when he was home, his days were spent hosting visitors who came seeking his advice or to discuss business prospects. From first light until long past dark, the town's business dominated the household.

After the great storm of AD 71, Jayesh had all but stopped leaving the family home, other than to pay a visit to the Shiva temple he was building. His long years of labouring over the great port were catching up to him. His youth seemed to have been washed away by the storm, leaving behind the hollow shell of an old man. He met no visitors, living as an introspective recluse even amidst his family. He had donated considerable portions of his wealth to building churches all around town, although he visited only one. His ambition and drive had been snuffed out and he seemed to perpetually be carrying a leaden weight on his slender shoulders.

For many months after he first abandoned it all, his dear friend Nannan visited him daily to update him on the town's goings-on, only to be met with vacant stares. All Jayesh seemed to care about was his new temple and making massive donations to temples all across India. They were both wary of travellers and traders from Rome or Egypt in search of the great treasure which they had buried away and whose secret location they would take to their graves. This was the only subject Jayesh was interested in talking about, fleshing out the many details of their plan over and over again.

When Nannan told him about Roman merchants taking their business to other neighbouring ports and Muciripattanam's business dwindling by the week, Jayesh seemed indifferent. It had long ceased to be the most important trading port in the world – it was not even worthy of that title on their own coastline.

Nannan finally arrived one day with the news that he had been dreading. They sat outside, enjoying the pleasant breeze of the early evening. The sun was gently descending below the horizon, painting an orange streak in its wake over the sea.

'I wish to return home – to the land of my birth. I long to see the mountains of Himachal and bathe in the Ganges once more, before my time comes.' Nannan had often spoken of his desire to return home, but there was always one more unfinished task to hold him back.

'I always knew this day would come – since the moment

you joined me on that ship from Alexandria,' Jayesh was overcome with nostalgia. 'And yet, it feel as if it has come too soon. What will I do without you?'

'I will surely return to see how you are, brother,' Nannan reassured him, 'and to make sure you have not turned my beautiful Roman house into another Hindu temple.' They shared a laugh.

'It shall remain exactly as you leave it.' Jayesh hugged him warmly.

They recalled their great adventures together and how they missed Vikesh dearly. Finally, Jayesh bid Nannan farewell, wishing the best for him. As he watched his friend depart, he felt certain he would never see him again.

It had taken a little over three years but finally, it was time. Jayesh opened the new temple dedicated to Shiva, appearing before the townsfolk after years. Many people could not immediately recognize the old man stood before them, walking with the aid of a stick.

The main temple building was a magnificent, red-roofed structure with a large veranda at the front, supported by carved pillars. The primary chamber contained a seven-foot-high statue of the goddess Kali. The small chamber to the west had a section covered by granite, and the people forewarned that a curse would befall anyone who attempted to open it. The temple stood in beautiful grounds populated with banyan and peepul trees.

A large crowd had gathered to witness the opening of the grand temple and waited patiently for the old man to address them. Standing on a platform built around the largest banyan tree in the temple courtyard, Jayesh delivered a heartfelt speech, declaring that he would be devoting his entire wealth to the protection of the people of Muciripattanam, and towards the upkeep of the new temple complex. He spoke with great passion and at length about how all religions must be respected and how he had witnessed the power of the gods. He claimed that the new well he had built had the ability to cure illness and shower blessings upon its worshippers – it must be protected forever.

To honour the memory of those who had fallen, he had performers reenact the massacre from three years ago in dramatic presentation. They dressed in the bright red robes of Muciripattanam, rushing into the temple to save the endangered lives of their companions. One by one, they enacted falling to their deaths. The crowd was moved to tears. For just a moment, the shadow of the younger Jayesh appeared in his face. His eyes sparkled and his voice rang clear and true as he spoke of the almighty power of this temple, and the grave misfortune that would befall any man who dare desecrate it, which would spread to the whole town. A great and terrible curse, akin to the wrath of all the gods combined.

His speech would remain engraved within the memory of Muciripattanam, and the dramatic act would be performed for over 2,000 years in an annual ceremony to honour the temple – an enduring reminder of the curse that was concealed within the secret chamber.

After the temple was opened to visitors, Jayesh retired to his home. His end loomed near; he could feel it in his bones. Once again, he took in the sublime view of the Muciripattanam skyline – Muziris, as the world outside called it. Once again, his eyes were drawn to the great sea that lay beyond the shore and he felt his tears well up. He no longer wondered at what lay in the great beyond as he once had. Now the tears that came were not for the hunger of adventure, but from profound regret and a deep, aching sense of loss.

Jayesh walked the short distance from his home to his family's shrine. Carefully inscribed and carved stones had been lovingly erected in memory of each departed family member in a quiet area, overlooking the magnificent sea. The stones were neither grand nor elaborate; unassuming and enduring just as the people in whose memory they had been placed. Each of his family members had been cremated in accordance to Vedic rites and their ashes were scattered in the sea below.

It was a tradition borrowed from the burial tombs he had seen in his youth outside the walls of Rome, so he had a place to feel their presence in peace. He took turns standing and paying his respects before each stone. Taking the time to recall their antics and characteristics should perhaps have made him sad, but a gentle smile played on his lips despite himself as he remembered Vikesh – so full of hope and excitement as he sold his produce at the market. He remembered Nilham marching in front of him as they set foot on new lands, fearless and mighty as a lion. A cool breeze caressed his face, bringing him back to the present. It felt as if he had lived many lifetimes in just one life.

His time had finally come.

89

Kodungallur Government Hospital
29 July 2024

'I didn't kill her! I didn't kill Dr Gupta. It was the man I described. I found out his name is Paulo.'

'I know. The Head of the Vatican Police explained everything to me. Why didn't you tell me that you were working together with them?'

'Working together? What did they say?' Harveen asked, surprised.

'You don't need to keep lying – he has told me everything.'

'Who has? Don?'

'Yes. I think it is totally wrong that you were used as bait to lure out this man, Paulo, out into the open. You could have been killed – I would never have allowed it.' He seemed angry on her behalf.

'I – I didn't have a choice, Sanjay … I did not really know what was happening, I was just focused on the … greater good …' Harveen was careful not to say the wrong thing. 'Is Don here?'

'Yes. He is waiting outside. He wanted to speak with you, of course, and make sure you are okay.'

'And what of the murder investigation?'

'Well, it appears you were on the money. There are a number of warrants out for this man, Paulo, all around the world, apparently. It was not just the Vatican that was after him. Clemente has testified that he confessed to the murder of Penny Gupta, planting the murder weapon at your apartment and making the anonymous call to the police implicating you. He was killed while he was trying to make his escape. The DNA was a match for the murder weapon that was used to kill Penny. The knife I mentioned.'

Harveen couldn't help but feel impressed at the Vatican's slick operation.

'I should have told you everything long ago,' she said, slipping into the role carved out for her.

'Well, I can't argue with that,' he replied. He looked at her and for the first time, she could see there was the hint of a smile on his face.

Harveen smiled back. She did not want to say too much until after her conversation with Don. She touched the bandage around her head and flinched, trying to give the inspector a hint. 'I think that it would be good for you to rest. We can discuss all this later, when you're feeling better,' he said, taking her cue.

'Right, I think that would be best,' she said meekly. Kumar left the room quietly.

Harveen sat in silence, gazing at the ceiling for several minutes. Her only companion was the dull pounding in her head. The door opened again and Don Clemente walked in, wearing a perfectly tailored dark blue suit and carrying a small silver briefcase.

'Good afternoon, Dr Gill,' he said. 'I was so pleased to hear you are recovering well, signora.'

'What did you say to everyone? I don't understand … and what of the Ark? Where is it?' Harveen was full of questions for him.

'The Ark of the Covenant has a complicated history, signora, one riddled with relentless bloodshed and death. Due to its infamous legacy, we decided it was best it be taken back to the Vatican for further investigation. There is no way we can leave it here. You, of all people, must understand that. It is you, after all, who told us the legends were true.' Don seemed earnest, but Harveen had seen him lie effortlessly before and struggled to take his word.

'But you'd promised that we could keep all the artefacts here.'

'I have left behind everything else. Everything I could. Believe me, the Vatican would not want a copy of the Gospel of St Thomas to be left here. I did not even get a chance to have someone look at it. There could be plenty of problematic writings for the Church within its pages. The room looks untouched; nothing has been destroyed. I have kept my word. Except for the remains of St Thomas and the Ark, everything else is for you to lay your claim on. There are some … fantastic finds in there; the room itself looks like it can be restored. The plinth, too.'

Harveen knew he was right. But the Ark? It was the biggest prize for any archaeologist, without the shadow of doubt.

'I want to see it,' she demanded almost involuntarily.

Don smiled. 'I do not know if I can allow that … What happened to Vincenzo is really troubling. We are performing an autopsy; I'm sure we will know more only after that.'

Harveen considered things for a moment. 'So you sent

them to kill Dr Gupta, and then you sent them to kill me too?' The image of him pointing the gun at her flashed in her mind.

'I tried to let you know that the operation they were conducting was not authorized. It is the main reason I am here. It will never happen again, I promise, signora.'

'But the murders?'

'Both men have paid the biggest price for their actions, would you not agree? What more can we possibly do?'

'Well, the police will be the judge of that.'

'The investigation has been closed. The police here were happy to concede jurisdiction to the Vatican Police for Paulo. As far as they know, he was an international-level criminal. A thief of important religious artefacts, who died as we tried to arrest him.'

'What about me? They said that I was involved?'

'Well, you, signora, are the heroine of the story.' He smiled. 'You insisted on going to the well at night to draw him out – they are very impressed at your act of selfless bravery.'

'Why did you say that?'

At this, Don paused. 'I don't know,' he began. 'I trust that you will do the right thing, signora. I actually came to make an offer to you, if you are interested.'

Harveen's headache was hindering her from processing all the information. Two men had died. The man in front of her had killed one of them while she watched, just last night. She was alone in a hospital room with a real murderer. She felt a sense of panic rise within her but tried to maintain as calm a mien as possible.

'They will find some evidence. Two men died in that room. There will be some trace.'

'Now, now, signora. Don't you underestimate how efficient our teams are. We know what we are doing.'

'I don't … anyway. You said you had an offer for me?'

'There are many things that have troubled me about the way the Vatican has handled these situations in the past and we are putting measures in place to ensure they do not happen again. I hope that you will trust me on this. The thing is, signora, we cannot afford for anything relating to the Ark to ever be publicized. I know it is a big ask – but the chaos that would unleash would be uncontrollable. There would be anarchy.'

Harveen remembered J. Muziris's warning.

He continued, 'The story of St Thomas being in India is well documented and poses less issues for us. I have been very impressed with how you handled everything. I believe I may have a solution that suits both of us.'

Harveen watched as Don opened his briefcase and carefully extracted a slim package from it.

'If you agree to forget all about the Ark, I will express my sincere gratitude to you in the best way I can. Consider it a compensation in some way for the injury inflicted on yourself and your colleague. I would like to offer you a clue to another amazing historical find. One that perhaps could steer public attention away from the current situation effectively while establishing you as the truly remarkable archaeologist you are. I am truly sorry, Signora Gill, for everything that happened. I just hope that you can find it in your heart to forgive the actions of my men and my office. I also need you to destroy the copies of the note from J. Muziris.'

Harveen was struggling to wrap her head around all that was unfolding. Her head was spinning. The man in front of her had originally told her he was a researcher, then appeared in the underground chamber like some type of special services agent, and was now standing here in a suit having persuaded the police to drop a murder charge against her, asking her to give up her greatest finds.

'Who even are you? You're no researcher,' she said. Her eyes were drawn to the slim package in his hand.

'Well, I'm afraid I cannot say, signora. I can only offer you this unique opportunity,' he said, holding the package out to her. Harveen sensed she had some leverage for the moment.

'And no one will come after either me or my team ever again?'

'You have my word,' came his stoic response instantly. Several moments passed in silence as Don patiently waited for Harveen to consider her reply.

'Your word has not been worth much so far.'

'I did just save you from getting arrested, signora. I could easily have left you with the murder charge. I could have killed you in the chamber. I've had plenty opportunity to stab you in the back, but I haven't done it. I can't explain why I didn't do it, yet the fact is that I didn't.' The look he gave her was disarming. He had tricked her before; this felt different.

'Tell me about this other artefact …' Despite herself, Harveen was beginning to feel a hint of the same excitement she always experienced at the prospect of a new archaeological adventure.

'Well, it's something that has been in the Vatican Archive for over 1,500 years. It perhaps arrived with other records that were originally salvaged from the Great Library of Alexandria. There are eight pages in total and they were found hidden within the pages of another book. The text is in Egyptian, but the author and date are at the bottom of the last page. I have a translation here. I have no doubt that you will find it rather fascinating, signora.' He pulled a folded sheet out of his pocket. 'What is particularly interesting is that it is written on your Indian cotton paper and our historians here believe the date to be quite accurate.'

Harveen's mind was racing with possibilities again.

Don offered the sheet to her and she squinted at the text, struggling to focus despite her headache as best she could. The writing was elegant, precise and the Egyptian was clearly legible. She looked at the bottom of the page. There was indeed a signature and a date. The translation written neatly underneath left her confused.

'Charmion, AD 4, it says here.' She pondered, 'Cleopatra's handmaid?' She was the only Charmion she could recall.

'Have a look at the translation.' He smiled. 'She was also her closest advisor.' Harveen quickly scanned through the document. As she read on, she couldn't help but be stunned by the contents. It was well known that the famous Egyptian queen had killed herself at least thirty years before the date mentioned in the letter. She stared in disbelief at the document … Could she still have been alive in AD 4?

'What else can you share with me? How do I contact you again? How do I know this is real?'

He smiled. 'So we have a deal?'

Harveen was already thinking about the implications of being made privy to this information. 'Not yet. I want to see the Ark. If you agree to that, we have a deal.'

'Sorry, signora, I'm afraid—'

'Just me. Promise. I only need to know what you intend to do with it. Just once.'

He looked at her for a long moment. 'I can try. But no promises.'

Harveen considered this. The document could uncover something truly sensational.

'Okay. Deal,' she said and held out her hand, which Don shook firmly. He felt his palm warm in her grasp. As Harveen tried to let go, he held on for a moment longer.

'For my own selfish purposes, I hope this document does what I intend for it to do. Draw attention away from St Thomas. Well, I must take your leave now, signora. It has been a pleasure. Goodbye.' He bowed slightly.

'Wait, when will I see you again?'

'All in good time, Dr Gill,' he replied. 'A deal's a deal after all.'

He closed the door behind him as he left the room.

Acknowledgements

When I naively set out to write my first novel in 2020, I thought it would be a solo effort, sitting in front of my keyboard, fuelled by tea and cake. As it turned out, I was only right about the tea and cake.

This book would not have been possible without the help of so many people who came along with me on this journey.

My wonderful wife Kalpa, who patiently listened to all my ideas for potential books set during the Second World War, the rise of the Mughal Empire and the earliest days of the East India Company, before settling on the fascinating first-century Port of Muziris. Without her constant encouragement (and tea), this project would have run aground long before it ever saw the light of day. She has been my sounding board, my beta reader, my cheerleader and a shoulder to cry on.

My lovely agent Jane Compton, who believed when others did not, who still puts up with my late-night rants, and still comes up with crazy ideas for promoting the book – you are amazing.

The impossibly positive Holly Domney, who helped to turn the early rambling manuscript into something that looked like a historical thriller. For constantly making life awful for all of my characters and not giving them a moment's rest.

Teesta Guha Sarkar and Udyotna Kumar, my editors at Pan Macmillan India, for picking up all of my many mistakes, for giving depth to the characters and believing in this project from the first day.

The team at Pan Macmillan India: Rajdeep Mukherjee, Vijay Sharma, Saburi Sumran, Pooja Sharma, Divyanshi Dash, Isha Banerji – you made my dreams come true.

To the legendary Keith Bishop for your support, ideas, contacts and good humour. Steve, Clive and Phil, your support and commercial ideas have been invaluable (not so much your humour!).

Mo, who takes tough love to a new level: your savagery made me a better writer. Never lose that intensity.

My early readers like Ellie and Tory: your insights were so helpful. Your positive words came at the right time.

Paul Waters, your advice and guidance, especially on matters regarding the church, were invaluable.

The writing community that has given me encouragement. Each kind word, each inclusion into a group or chat, each like on a post is the fuel that keeps me going through the late nights.

Vaseem Khan, who grabbed me at my first author event and introduced me to a bunch of people.

Amish Tripathi, who is an inspiration as a writer and historian, and has been so generous with his time and support.

Amita and Jessica, who cast themselves into the film adaptation of the novel the first time I met them; Jericho Writers, who helped me understand this business a little; and Abir Mukherjee, who always has (what at least he thinks is) a witty comment.

Great thanks also to the organizers of some of the best literary festivals who have taken a chance on a debut author.

The Beaconsfield Literary Festival, Chiltern Kills, the Jaipur Literature Festival and the DESIblitz Literature Festival.

Finally, my gratitude to you, dear readers. If you have made it this far, I thank you for taking the time. I hope that this first effort has provided some entertainment and distraction from daily life. When I set out, I was looking to find a few people who might take to the intrepid Harveen Gill and want to follow her journey. I look forward to sharing her next adventure with you.

Hamish